The Alien Intimacies

By

Jim Cleveland

This book is a work of fiction. Places, events, and situations in this story are purely fictional. Any resemblance to actual persons, living or dead, is coincidental.

ISBN: 1-4107-3399-8 (e-book)
ISBN: 1-4107-3398-X (Paperback)

Library of Congress Control Number: 2003092672

This book is printed on acid free paper.

Printed in the United States of America
Bloomington, IN

1stBooks - rev. 6/18/03

TABLE OF CONTENTS

PROLOGUE v

ONE: A Recent Arrival -1999 AD 1

TWO: A Woman Out of the Sky 14

THREE: An Intimate Integration 36

FOUR: Into Separate Realities 56

FIVE: A Few More Imaginative Interludes 79

SIX: The Serpents of Eden 105

SEVEN: Behold the Prehistoric Life! 131

EIGHT: Naked in the Storm 151

NINE: Oaks, Acorns, Infusions 167

TEN: To Struggle in Love 192

ELEVEN: Separate Ways 209

EPILOGUE: Flowers and Seeds 220

Update on the Planetary Rebellion 224

PROLOGUE

The Place: Urantia, planet no. 606 in the local universe of Nebadon of the superuniverse of Orvonton, approximately 811,000 years ago. Later to be known locally as Earth.

Anvil's eyes opened from the lightest of sleeps at the roar of the big cat. He gazed coldly into the night.

The beast wanted to return to the sanctuary stolen by the bedraggled band of surviving colonists. Anvil leaned forward, straining his eyes to see, rustling his furry cape, guarding the cave's entrance in the moonlight. His shaft was at hand, also the bow and quiver of steel arrows they had fashioned before their retreat from the gardens. He looked back into the darkness of the cave; all were asleep it seemed. The embers of the fire glowed faintly.

The predators and victims screeched and screamed all through the night here, an ever-repeating orgy of killing and dying that they had been plunged into. Such a twist of fate to be cast back into this wilderness of a planet, a doomsday misfortune of getting entangled in the blasphemous affairs of their planetary prince.

The cat might boldly venture forward tonight, all the better for him to put an end to this deadly game. It smelled them certainly, their sweat and their excrement, and the rotted carcass just down the embankment would also help lure the beast. Anvil would be ready.

He turned at the rustle behind him. Tara's bright eyes emerged from the cave's shadows into the moonlight and she eased herself beside him with gentle eyes and a look of affection that Anvil truly shared.

He greeted her only with a finger to the lips. Quietly, she edged even closer to snuggle into his furs. She looked into his eyes affectionately and kissed him on the cheek of his bearded and scarred face. Her small tender body felt good within the strength of his arms and he longed for her to remain here, but he knew they must pull away. He kissed her softly on the lips, gently pushed her away and turned again to peruse the landscape at the mouth of the cave. The cats moved silently, and were deadly.

"Will you get him tonight?" she asked in a whisper.

"It is a 'she,'" said Anvil. "The females do much of the hunting. They are killers, like much else on this truly God-forsaken place."

"What happened, Anvil?" she asked, pleadingly. "You have not told us all of it, have you? What really happened in Dalamatia? Did Lucifer really defy the other Celestials, the Ancients of Days? Is that why the primitives attacked the city? How could they have been so bold? I thought the

Dalamatians were here to help the evolving tribes. I thought they were all supposed to have the God spark inside them and it would be developed?"

"You are full of questions, my gentle beauty. Now, whisper more quietly. For I must listen for our predator and prey." He looked away, then back at her with the benevolence of an elder brother.

"I did not want to worry our beleaguered brothers and sisters with these horrors, Tara. They are gardeners; they can't grasp it all. I can hardly grasp it myself. It's too enormous. I had just as soon not talk about it. It does not matter any more."

"Anvil, you must see that I am here with you in this calamity. We share each other's fates and it is fair that I know the situation. Do not speak of enormities, other than the enormity of our plight. You must be honest with me. I want to understand where those monsters who destroyed the gardens and orchards came from. They are out of time here. The evolving tribes could not have done this. Dalamatia would hardly seek to destroy its own outposts with these beasts. And certainly we have proven loyal to the One God. It could not be the Celestials who would bring us misfortune. Yet, we are in despair. There is no force that does not now stand against us, the beasts, the tribes, the volcanoes, all of this dark place. It does not seem sometimes that we will…

Anvil reached a finger to her lips. "Do not say…" He stared into her soft eyes, pausing to reflect before speaking, darting his eyes now and again into the moonlit landscape.

"We will make it. I will see to that." He looked at her with a new earnestness. She frowned deeply.

"Tara. I am just a soldier. I was here only to guard the gardens and the orchards. I was not involved with the botanical and institutional upliftment decisions, the planetary agreements, the management of the mission. I've never been part of the administrative scene over in Dalamatia. I don't like big cities. I am only trained in killing wild animals. So I don't have a lot of answers. And I surely never thought I would be trying to understand the intricacies of a rebellion against the One God. How could you expect it or prepare for it? We were only here to help the Dalamatians improve the lives of the evolving tribes, with foods from the earth, botanicals, irrigation, agriculture. Basic planetary ascension for our fellow mortals. That was all it ever was. And I do not think anyone had an idea that Prince Caligastia would get involved in something like this."

"Like what? Do you mean he defied the laws, the Ancients of Days, the Creator Son?

"It's much bigger than that, Tara. There is a major celestial administrator involved, Lucifer, perhaps you have heard of him."

"I'm afraid I did not keep up much with celestial politics, at least since we have been out here on Urantia. Since we cannot physically see many of the celestial personalities, I have not given them much thought. I have gladly left all this to the Inspired Connectors among us to work with them on our behalf, and just stay with growing the fruits and vegetables that nurture us. I always thought it was a noble enough calling."

"Yes, and I am as zealous a soldier as you are a botanist, and no politician, and hardly a leader. Who would believe we would lose so many others who were more qualified? I never wanted to be responsible for these lives. I am a trained destroyer, not a savior."

"And what is the appeal of this Lucifer?"

"Freedom. Complete freedom. Sweeping reforms. He says the One God is a fabrication designed to keep the Ancients of Days in power. He questions the right of Creator Sons to rule the local universes; they have delegated much of the creation, after all. He is apparently a brilliant, magnetic and very persuasive leader. They say he has a hypnotic and charismatic energy. He has taken more than 30 planets with him on this, already."

"It's madness! What's it about? What's wrong with God's plan? They've been successfully ascending mortals for a long time, have they not?"

"They question that premise. For whatever reasons, their audacity is amazing," muttered Anvil bitterly, pulling back his long red hair roughly behind his shoulders and rubbing his fingers vigorously through his grizzly beard. He sighed. "And now we are caught up in what should have been seen as painfully inevitable, even for arrogant personalities like Caligastia, Daligastia and Satan, that whole pompous court in Dalamatia. Quarantine. Any fool should know that the Ancients would cut off all of the energy circuitry, every way, every expression. It took only a few minutes. There's no way to get out of here now. There is no way. I have looked at every option."

"We had nothing to do with the rebellion. They have to get us out. They can't let us die here."

Anvil looked at her anguished face and eyes. He felt deeply for her, for her more than himself. He could kill or be killed. He could even appreciate, in a way, the dark light that seemed to pervade this whole savage planetary landscape since the onslaught of the rebellion. It would be a worthy challenge for a soldier. He worried for her however. She was of peaceful demeanor.

"They can leave us here, sweet Tara," he said gently, "and they will. It is evolution. That's all. We are just caught up in it, my sister, always have been truly. We were just on the wrong planet at the wrong time. As I can determine, the whole sector has been quarantined. Each and all of these planets are in official rebellion against God. It is unprecedented, to be sure, but reality nonetheless. And they will not let it spread."

"We are innocent," said Tara, "innocent." Her voice trailed away. "I love the One God. I always believed the One God loved me."

"When we ascend from mortality, we can, at least, look back upon all this in reflection," said Anvil. "Now, still as mortals, we have no choice but to deal with it in this time and space. We must be strong and bold for survival. Sometimes even cold killers. It is such an irony. I heard Lucifer on one of the last broadcasts. He called for individual liberty, freedom for the colonies, self-assertion, the inherent power and sanctity of the individual mind that allows us to choose for ourselves. He made it sound...glorious! But it never did feel right. It sounded like liberation in a way, but from what...order? We never have had to deal with questions like this in the Pleiades. At least I didn't."

"But in the Pleiades, we had earned the knowledge that was essential for full individual freedom," said Tara. "We had turned it into commitment. They could not have begun to grasp these greater realities here on this primitive place. They would not be ready for it. And so is that the reason for the chaos?"

Anvil looked at her kindly. She was full of questions, and did not fully comprehend that there were no more answers here. There was no more Control to provide total order. From now on, the denizens of this planet would only be able to speculate. They would know nothing of interplanetary life. By now, there may be no surviving bank of knowledge summations. May God help them for what they may do and how they may evolve from the ruins of Dalamatia.

How, too, could this planet possibly be ready to officially receive the planetary Son and Daughter who would be scheduled for bestowal, to build and biologically uplift from the foundation of Dalamatia? There would be no foundation, and they, all of them, would have been dead for thousands of years. He did not even know if it would be a good idea for them to somehow survive and bring children into this time of turmoil and danger. They were out of their time too.

Anvil heard a low guttural growl and turned quickly to see the shining eyes — cold, angry and confident. It sent his heart racing. It even seemed like exhilaration. The dark light. He heard Tara gasp quietly and felt her shrink away. He relished the life-and-death challenge; his eyes sparkled.

Without turning, seemingly even without moving a muscle, Anvil's arms flowed about him. He slipped an arrow from the quiver and loaded the bow.

The big cat sniffed cautiously at the carcass just below. Anvil eased himself lightly into a better position on the rock, to look down and get a clear stroke. The fur cape fell away softly, revealing his hairy, muscular arms.

The cat turned its huge head upward and lowered to a crouch, less than a hundred steps away but far enough for Anvil to fire the poised steel arrow. It was an eerie feeling to know that the cat's eyes were affixed on him. Maybe she would grab the smelly carcass and suddenly drag it off without a confrontation, the easier way. Probably.

No. Oh no. We must have a confrontation, thought Anvil, pulling the bow taut. He fired. We want the cave.

The missile split through the torso of the big cat with a rip. She unleashed a terrifying scream and leaped high, then fell hard and thrashed about on the bare ground, wallowing over the carcass, clawing desperately at the arrow, crying shrilly.

"Oh-h-h," he heard Tara wailing. "Kill her. Don't let her suffer."

Anvil had already re-loaded the bow, watching keenly as the big cat thrashed in pain below. But he had no such compassion any more. It was only in the cold, dark light that Lucifer unleashed here that they would survive at all now. Even gentle Tara would have to change to live, such a pity.

He held the arrow while the cat thrashed and suffered, the bloody shaft exposed at both ends through her chest, her tongue panting, blood coming from the mouth, struggling to drag herself away.

"Anvil, please..."

He didn't give a damn. He wanted to conserve the arrow. He remembered the cats that had attacked them, the painful claw marks on his back, the infection and fever. Perhaps life would be a continuing stream of vengeance and righteous indignation, and it would propel them forward from now, from this savage place. A society that would develop from all of this might be ruthless indeed.

He fired the arrow. It struck the beast's heart and, with a final trembling shudder, it was dead. It was 'it' to Anvil now, not 'she.'

Anvil finally looked to his side. His eyes had been riveted upon the prey throughout the deadly encounter. He looked into Tara's wistful tears and hurting face now and winced to know that he still felt a smothering compassion for her.

"I am sorry, dear Tara," he said. "There is a new reality here. And it is as basic as it can be."

She melted into his arms limply and he held her with strength and assurance. The brothers and sisters had made their way into a huddled mass near the entrance of the cave, hoping to know for certain that the animals they had ousted from this cave would not be able to retake it.

"Go back to sleep," said Anvil without emotion. "We still have dominion here."

ONE: A Recent Arrival -1999 AD

Mega awakened to the soothing strands of his most favorable harmonic sound vibrations, letting them massage and focus his energies for the day. In a moment, he came forth with a joyful smile even before opening his eyes. He immediately thanked the One God for the new day and began to assimilate the new language implanted during the...sleeping.

Mega pulled off the...headset, they might call it. His expanded mind bank told him that English wasn't the most widely spoken language on the planet, but it was the most dominant. It was associated with successful creatures here, or at least those who got what they wanted. From now through the mission, it was designated for usage by...what would be their word? We can call it...Mission Control.

The tall, broad-shouldered Zenithian lay quietly in the sleepframe and got accustomed to thinking in English, reviewing for full mindal implantation the translations with their native language. His large hands massaged and energized the chakra circuits in his scalp, tousling his long white hair into freefall over his bare arms. In moments, he had massaged his head into its daily productivity as an energy conduit, while also stretching the muscles of his sinewy and hard male body to limberness after the...transit sleep, we can say.

English was, as expected, simplistic, and that would be a handicap in communicating with the explorer team on the surface, but certainly that was often an important part of the challenge of these planetary visitations — getting it done in the native tongue.

As he relaxed with eyes closed, he could feel that the redirected mind circuitry was connecting ever-better, beginning to flow more fluidly with the translations he needed. The words emerged more easily into his genetically engineered mind as he needed them. Thoughts coalesced into new ways of expression.

After a few moments, Mega lifted himself gracefully from the deep cushion to do his morning exercises. They included stretching, flexing and three coordinated full body flips — forward, then backward, then to the side.

The word "cartwheel" slipped into the English layering of his mind as he deftly made a whirling circle around the sleepframe. The biology was all working well. His long white hair swirled in freeflight as his finely muscled and naked body activated itself rhythmically for the new day. He flipped up precisely onto his bare feet and breathed deeply several times.

Mega turned then to the control panels to order a morning meal, noticing that the menu had already been themed for the planet they were visiting. He ordered a Denver omelet and pancakes. After checking the composition of coffee, he decided on a hazelnut flavoring as well as the juice of what they called an orange. Ironically, it was also the name of the color. In a sidenote on the menu, he later noted that oranges were not, in fact, orange. It was a strange and deceptive planet. Things were often not what they seemed.

It was good to know that the lifedrives of the inhabitants seemed much the norm, however, the desire for wealth, power, intelligence, good food, and sexual love. And Mega knew from his mind bank that some of them loved adventure in the same spirit as did his people.

The spirit that brought them here.

Mega had loved adventure since he was a child, using his desire and talents to earn a position at the space academy. Now he was a Master Explorer, taking each adventure experience in stride and having enjoyed — he worked through his new mathematical programming — exactly 74 planetary visits, if he counted the abbreviated recycling stop on the Plus-2 moon of Grandfandalia.

Mega's experiences had mellowed him and expanded his mind up into the third layer of...PeacePower. He had the peace of knowing the ascension time and space plan in much of its grandeur, as a series of learning and growing experiences in the direction of perfected being, worthiness to be in the presence of...FatherGod...or Universal One...or First Source...or Universal Father? What name would be most appropriate here? They had so many, and ironically fought fiercely about it. Mega put the discussion onto his mind bank's agenda for a discussion.

As he worked his mind through final English translations, Mega routinely recapped the implanted mission facts that the ship's near 3,000 population had received earlier, before sleep transit. He now recalled it into one of his mind's higher layers, thinking to himself that given all the vast ethnic diversity here, it was going to an exciting adventure.

Now that their...mother ship (how quaint!) and...lightdome was in cloaked station in Earth's system, sleep state had ended, and everyone was awakening in their quarters at about the same time as Mega. More information would be forthcoming at his team's first meeting.

The early screen briefing in Mega's quarters gave more tantalizing clues to the new mystery-adventure that lay before them. Mega watched it while he slipped on his white robe with the blue bird of peace emblem.

> *Greetings. We give you: Urantia — known locally as Earth. You authorized to discover on your own initiative. Enjoy. Return with new perspectives and expanded knowledge if possible for Control. Minimal impact directed and anticipated. Caution urged. This is a dangerous planet.*
>
> *Random Clues: Mammalian upgrade. Semi-primitive. Alienation abounds. Food unstable. Wealth strongly imbalanced. Violent views rampant. Oxygen breath base. Technology progress rapid to slow. Spirituality fragmented and quarrelsome, often deadly. Intellectual capacity not focused on perfection. Emotional fear-dominated. Do not breath the air this month in Mexico City. Previous impact: unacknowledged but suspicious. Venturian UFOs have been abusive and ordered to leave the sector, at least temporarily. Frequency of tour visits: seldom. Learn the culture and store via E-Volve.*
>
> *Central Exploration Thread: Mystery trace the fortunes and misfortunes of one of our botanical colonies we lost in the Era of the Lucifer Rebellion. Timedrops scheduled as desired. Discover! Report your findings to DOMiNo.*
>
> *Incidental freedom upon discretion to energetically inspire selected humans. Leave some love and insight and do no harm.*
> *PEACEQUEST*

So a lost colony was the stimulus for coming way out here, Mega thought, and, as usual, his team would only have...pieces to the puzzle, threads of the forever interweaving tapestry of these time and space worlds. And he understood why fully. After these many missions, he understood very well how invigorating it was that they were given only a part of the vast store of knowledge on the planet that Control actually possessed, with more trickling to them during the mission from their own initiatives. This allowed them to rediscover and discover on their own in time and space, an ultimately thrilling adventure, and finally, in the end, expanding, updating and broadening the base of knowledge they were building collectively. The adventure was on! The experience itself was the thing.

Mega did not know, however, if the lost colony was indeed a mystery to Control or whether it was devised as an adventure rediscovery for their enjoyment. Indeed, he supposed, this was part of the mystery.

He called onto his screen and scanned geological information, as well as the names and profiles of the personalities chosen as his four Associate

3

Chief Investigators, especially configuring their subdivisions of responsibility that Control calculated to be optimum for the planet.

Control had chosen them all, of course, and the capacities in which they would serve. They trusted Control completely, for had they not personally and collectively stored within its intricate Divine Circuitry the knowledge of the universe.

In truth, Control did encompass extensive files and profiles of the ship's near 1,000 explorer personalities, considering their achievements, aptitudes, and abilities for dealing with this special kind of a planetary culture and, importantly, ways in which they could each best grow personally from the experience.

For some planets, Mega had been in a leadership role, at others just part of the team. Over the years he had matched wits with paranoid religionists with laser weapons, debated with self-styled intellectuals across the Andromeda belt, and had helped annihilate several swarms of giant prehistoric predators with brains hardly worthy of mention. Of course, he had served on many less exciting assignments as well.

In this case, he was chosen as Investigator One, somehow ideally suited for Planet Earth, and he would be making many timely decisions involving the hundreds who would embark for the surface for their myriad adventures in coming days.

Mega thought how he was indeed partial to worlds in this state of development because of the fast-paced mental ferment that was moving things along at a dangerous pace. It would be a welcome change from reptile-infested Centrus, their last exploration, where he had seen duty as a frontal commander and had almost drowned in a hot quagmire while exploring the volcano region.

For this exploration Mega was part of, they might say, management. His legs had been fully regrafted in the cosmetics lab and the muscles were attuned. He felt finely tuned all over from the expanded morning harmonics and the special day-one celestial energies, in good spirits and focused, centered, and intent upon an exciting, mind-expanding experience. Earth was everything he would want it to be, and he was easing comfortably into the language. It only had to be slowed into a flow, coordinating mind with inner accessment to oral expression...or something like that.

Mega walked lightly into the control center. The passage beam would trigger his associates to now join him.

The spacious control room for the Earth exploration expanded before him as a brightly lighted rock-floored dome of greenery and water, a garden with plants all about, a fountain and a pool of blue water in the center and a small, gentle waterfall and tropical plant setting on one side.

On the far side waited their five deeply cushioned, so very comfortable sensory expression seats and individual control boards, all with the newest upgrades. They lay in a half-circle, each with its own satellite screen, each facing a giant arched screen that would chronicle and master manage the mission.

The landscaping was a special touch for this particular investigation, produced overnight by the environmental team from the gleanings of their advance patrols. Mega looked up into the brightness of the simulated sundome and all around, feeling the sublime celestial energies of the scene.

On the huge screen, Earth information, true and speculative, would appear before them in the days ahead, as they searched through the history, current culture and likely fate of their host.

Mega turned to see a stream of smiling faces coming from the passageway to greet him, four statuesque, white-robed team members, three males, David, Atla and Jai and the feminine appellation, Blest, a known clairvoyant who was fresh from the academy and on her third mission, first time on the Top Team.

"Good morning," said Mega in good cheer. The four responded in near unison, and with friendly gusto. There were hugs and handshakes all around. Their bodies felt warm under the light robes as they shared their vibrational, loving energies and rejuvenated themselves even higher for the exciting new adventure.

"May we serve in love and glory," said Mega.

"Love and glory," they acclaimed in unison, as well they might, being cosmetically engineered to a near mortal material perfection in their advanced genetics laboratories.

Mega knew they would be among the more beautiful people on the planet. Yet hardly to be suspected as alien infiltrators for that reason. Certainly, it should prove an enticement for humans to communicate with them in their impending adventures here.

Most of the Earth people had been unduly influenced by the sporadic attentions of the neighborly but very curious Venturians as well, whose big-eyed, small-statured likenesses had even been emblazoned on shirt fronts and other material items on the planet. It had become a source of embarrassment for the Venturians, as had an unfortunate crash, and they had now been departed from the scene for a time.

It was interesting as well to Mega that the humans here and most other places did not know that they, themselves, represented the predominate pattern of animated biological matter in the time and space worlds. They might feel flattered to know this. The pattern, far and wide, is not dissimilar.

Mega led the team over to their work stations, feeling a mixture of humility and pride, a strong desire for a great performance here on behalf of

5

their own learning and growing, but also for what they could leave behind. Even after all these years, he could still be as excited as a child. It was a gift of One God.

His master control panel was a cornucopia of numbers and symbols that covered every nuance of this planetary and system spectrum. "I suppose it is expected," said Mega, "that we will use these…digital buttons, well, so be it. He accessed his mind bank, three fingers to his temple, pushing combinations of buttons with his other hand. "They have a saying," said Mega. "When in Rome…do as the Romanians. Yes. I think that's it."

The room dimmed and the large screen brightened into an illustrious white, reaching a zenith of pure, richly filled brightness, with sparkling sparks vibrating all upon it. An harmonic drone of sound rose up to fill their ears and minds.

A symbol faded up brightly before them, their acknowledged, energized and harmonized symbol for the ultimate expression of the spiritual fervor that they truly lived. Now, before their eyes, their holy symbol melted and translated into the equivalent in English: LOVE.

They closed their eyes and prayed quietly to the One God Eternal and Divine Source for safety, clarity, and the moment-by-moment guidance of Love.

They were soon refreshed upon opening their eyes from this reverent mission ritual.

"The translation word is simple again," said Mega evenly. "One…syllable, a very old word. But still apparently not understood or fully appreciated here," he said reflectively, still emerging from the moment of tranquility within their worship.

"They are still unfortunately bloodthirsty, are not they however?" said Atla. Like them all, he was handsome, muscular, with bright blue eyes and thick masses of golden hair nestled about his strong neck and shoulders. He was in charge of biology investigations, and his studies would soon make him an expert on all parts of the working bodies here.

"I enjoyed serving with you at Cretan, Atla," said Mega. "Do you remember those giant bats we found in the deep caves?"

"I could not forget those beasts," said Atla with a grin. "I checked here upon this planet at arrival to find there are only miniaturized advertisements of them here, unthreatening and dark necessitated at that.

"Love to you, Atla. Yet, you had best work on that English."

"And my love to you also, Mega One. I have found so far that the humans living here are of variegated colorizations. They war against each other for various illogical reasonings, especially greed, and even the…skin pigment factor seems to be a provocation itself. They often cover up their greed by cloaking it in religious differences, as if that were somehow a justification for war. They even have an incredible term, 'holy war.' Some of them will be dangerous if they feel threatened. We have a real, even a realistic, challenge here. We will, of course, accede...ummm...proceed."

Mega made a mental note to insist again on the remedial course.

"For their stage of evolutionary development, they are progressing much slower than the norm," Mega said, "but there are valid reasons. If you have not already, you will need to scan the history optical which will give you a time-sequence overview and summary of why they were quarantined from the celestial circuitry. Those circuits are even now being incrementally re-established. We will see why they were severed."

"Rebellious and arrogant leadership has invariably been the curse for them based on the history module," said Atla. "Their genetics are also kind of...unarranged. Anyway. I've drained a life picture, here."

Under Atla's perhaps precarious command, the screen turned into a mass of numbers superimposed upon a flattened Earth perspective. "This shows the density of various life types at different stages of history. Absorb please." They studied the compact jungle of numbers for a few seconds.

"Like all of our other information, the numbers are taken from computer, television and radio transmissions. These were collected and synthesized over the years by the superfluous station on Saturn moon Arapahas, said Atla.

"The surface has stabilized a great deal since the last ship was here," Mega observed, "but the internal heat still blows now and then. There are some dangerous fault lines too, I understand. Perhaps we can help with this."

"A very imperfect world," said Atla, "but beautiful. A little too much water. There are things called mosquitoes that are truly nasty." He pressed a button to present a new picture.

"These are population distributions related to climate and pornography. Then here (the numbers recycled) are educational comparisons. They relate heavily to these environmental factors, of course. There is much more suffering, you can see, across the tropical areas."

"I understand they're instinctive biological reproducers."

"Well, maybe," Atla mused. "But they are intellectualizing it a lot more in some places...here where you see these stabilized figures."

"Most of the children are being born where they aren't wanted or needed," said Blest.

"Well, there are a lot of peculiarities here," said David. "These people are pretty fragmented, after all. There are still lots of countries."

A button lighted on Mega's panel. He pulled on the sensory helmet to listen.

"A transmission from Control," he said, searching for the right button on the console. "The title is 2-com-DalamatiaArchive. 606. sat.neb. Umm. These ancient systems," he muttered. "Have to almost de-translate. It is…retrogressive. Okay. Here it is," said Mega, finally.

It emerged as a typographic report only. Kind of disappointing. He had understood the gardens were a botanical splendor. This black and white inventory report hardly represented the planetary garden he had heard about.

"Center upon the mission thread," Mega advised them. "This is the lost botanical colony. Connect this to the thoughtstreams archive for sharing. This is noted to be a standard establishment report with a list of supplies on hand and on order."

The team perused it for clues with lightning speed.

"It appears the colonists had considerable resources, at least for that time," said Mega. "How do you consider it, Jai?"

Jai was associate investigator for the material and institutional planet, soon to be proficient in geography, geology and botany, as well as the planet's governmental and social institutions and, hopefully, their most clandestine interactions, for that was of great importance on such a greedy and deceitful planet.

The young investigator was compellingly handsome too, but with his own distinctive differences, high cheekbones, wiry black hair and deep brown eyes that could focus into a penetrating, nearly mesmerizing stare. His nose was sharply angular and a little long. He replied to Mega in his unique variation of voice.

"They should have had ample resources to maintain a stable environment," Jai reasoned, "but the climate was highly unstable at the time. They could have been destroyed by a natural disaster. Or, maybe they are there, a part of the current population. It's also possible that others came here and interfered. Certainly, history records the celestial rebellion in this region at about that time. Are we being informed that this planet was a definite part of that? Or are they saying we should try to…find out?"

"Is often as is the case," said Atla, "they say naught at all. We is on our own."

"Exactly," said David, with a wry smile.

"I could not have said it no better myself," said Blest, unsuccessful in submerging a splitting grin.

Good, thought Mega. There is gaiety about. "We don't know this yet. Are there any comparisons to other gardens or orchards in this sector?"

Jai selected a button to project an overview of other seedings and service missions of the period. "As you can see, there was only one other in this solar system and that's about the…norman. There was so much garden to choose from out here that the most opportune environments were usually the only ones chosen."

Jai made another selection: "Here is a report of a brief...fly-by here some years later. Giant reptile creatures were observed...dinosaurs. The observed colony post was destroyed. No time for tracing, however. The ship had to leave quickly to obtain energy. That was more of a problem, you know, in 70 meterine."

"Well, we have, as they say, our work cut out for us," said David.

"It's too bad we can't travel materially...physically through time," said Atla. "We could just go back and do it again, like they do in the...cinnamon.

"The cinnamon?" asked David.

"That would surely be...spicy," said Mega, "but also a great deal more hazardous than timedrop visualizations under direction of Control and the spirit world. We must consider also that matter-based time travel would defeat the whole purpose of time and space in the first place," said Mega, "thereby making it impossible for celestial approval. It is truly like abrogating God's plan. I am surprised how few, so-called advanced planets in the local universe understand this, but I believe I understand how this can become an alluring scenario to some of the more rebellious, sometime scoundrels in the superuniverse."

"Too...lofty for me. I'll be content to just do a geographical overview," said Jai, pushing a button to reveal a new montage of illustrations on the giant screen. "Here are the date and time conversion tables. So 2zt converts to...approximately eight Earth hours from now. That's when I'll depart for the surface, after I've studied and, I will say, mind-photographed all of the available data."

"Your cruiser will have to be fully covered," said Mega. "Do not underestimate their extensive military surveillance. They are quite paranoid and prepared to act upon their fears, and who could blame them with all the savagery we still see there, and will see more of, my brothers and sister as we descend upon this savage place."

"They can't trust each other," said Jai. "It's highly improbable they would trust us."

"I presume Control will not allow any revelation of us to them," said Mega. "Logic shows that it has been very disruptive and...disorienting to such emotional creatures as these where it has been selectively tried. Perhaps you can tell us more about this after you've delved into the psychological components, Blest."

She sat to Mega's immediate right, her seemingly soft and beautifully sculpted face somewhat belied by the rippled muscles of her arms, shoulders and abdomen. Long, honey-colored hair cascaded upon her bare shoulders. Her strongly entrancing green eyes seemed to mirror a great depth of both

9

passion and insight, as well as a tightly harnessed energy. This was her first mission as an associate investigator for she was young, but Mega had heard she was gifted in special ways.

"Well, we know already that they strive hard for material comforts and pleasures at the expense of both their individual and collective welfare," said Blest evenly. A constantly changing stream of pictures of many kinds of Earth humans flowed in front of them, infants, the aged, the poor and starving, the wealthy, many colors, many shapes, many costumes, in a continuing and rapid stream.

"They seem to have an unusually strong dependency on foodstuffs and apparently have even made them necessary for survival," said Blest. "There is little ability to receive energy from light, air or water, partly because of impurities in all related to the wealth struggle, but also from decreased genetical ability. They should be able to do better," Blest emphasized, pausing. "These pictures are from a magazine called 'National Geographic,' by the way, which is one of the few reliable...periodicals."

She paused as more pictures flooded past before continuing: "They form and hold onto bad addictions and they have the disgusting custom of killing and eating their animals. This may be partly because of the rampant overpopulation — of humans anyway. They're beginning to tax and pollute and destroy their resources everywhere without any real idea of how they will be replaced. A bleak picture I suppose, but our explorers will not readily recognize it as such. It is a place thriving with activity, and, at this time, actually standing at the very threshold of some momentous changes. We don't know what, of course, but the celestials do."

"Well, they have virtually no planetary-wide infrastructure and only small hopes right now of...international initiative," said Mega. "And, though I would not presume to guess what specific mission questions may emerge in the course of this exploration, surely one of them will be designed to alleviate the threat to their finite environmental resources and some possible guidance...behind the scenes, as they say, to help clean up some of their toxins. That is the least we could do for the unknowing but nonetheless appreciated hospitality."

"That's a...cool word," said Blest. "I like serendipity too. In fact, that is some of what we have here." She laughed at her own good humor.

"Males and females have not reached productive communion, of course," she continued. "They haven't even considered, I will say, eye-depth communications, and lust still overwhelms love in most relationships, though they are beginning to see the folly of that. But, overall, fear is still the strongest motivational force. Somehow they must get beyond that."

"How can they when they are so dangerous to themselves?" asked Atla.

"Another good question," said Mega. "And what of you, David? Is your inspiration level high?"

At his far right, the young explorer was striking. Long, plaited blonde ponytails caressing his broad shoulders. Colloquially, he might be called the mission's trouble-shooter on Earth, being in charge of the traffic flow generated by well over a thousand explorers who might soon be on the surface. If and when emergencies were encountered, his quick wits and decisions to mobilize a rescue team under his direction would be responsible for dealing with emergencies quickly and effectively — while avoiding others.

"I'm anxious to get underway," said David. "Here are the mission...divisions. We will be headquartered in this area, a progressive English entity called the United States of America. We have an estate where we can truly blend in — a place called Beverly Hills. You will like this place, Atla, it is surrounded by the cinnamon business.

"You are on a <u>roll</u>," are you not, brother David?" said Atla. "I will heretoafterwards call them movements. That is another term for the Cinema. We will go...hang out at the movements." More laughter.

"Movements can truly be multi-faceted here, Atla," said David, turning again to the map. "Beyond Beverly, there will also be study cells here," he gestured to the screen with a directional beam, "in these countries around the Mediterranean Sea...also here in this large country called Russia, recently turmoiled into change by the Angelic Corps...also here in the so-called People's Republic of China...and this one in Europe...here also in India...here in Africa, watch out for this one...and here in a country called Brazil. Catch the festival in a place called Rio. It is in imminent arrival and will be listed on your calendars if you can get a free day or more. Dangerous but recommended. We will be alert there with more perfection for our sojourners.

"Protection," said Mega.

"Yes, protection...done perfectly," said David, rolling his eyes at his language foible and winking at Blest.

She laughed and massaged him with her eyes.

David continued: "We will also have a, I will say, quick run patrol on both the ice regions, north and south, but we don't expect to spend much time there, only drill probes to examine the, ummm, subterranean."

For a moment, the group studied and mind photographed the flattened perspective of the planet. Mega spoke momentarily.

"We will go now to organize the teams," said Mega. "Organize wisely. Contact your spiritual guides. Remember the corridors of safety parameters. Atla, do the remedial English. Each of you should also plan to intake a set of local encyclopedias called Britannica. A new version is being diverted to your mindbank holds from the, let me see, Roswell, New Mexico, Public Library."

"Cute," said David. "But the Venturians are not laughing."

Mega stood quietly and they each responded in unison, disengaging their control panels for now. At Mega's initiative, they symbolically gathered in a circle and joined hands in front of the screen, which turned again into their Love symbol.

"May it be a glorious adventure," said Mega, "and may it serve PeacePower in every way." They shed their robes to nakedness and stood in silence, looking at and within each other, in sharing, then locking hands to wrists securely in a circle, in the communion ritual that melted together their minds and bodies and spirits.

They stood fully nude as was customary in moments of deep sharing, warm in their space cocoon and in the glistening dome cities of their native land as well, no barrier physical or otherwise to the rush of collective spiritual and physical and mindal energies that vitalized and pulled them together from circuits not yet engaged in the backward, rebellion-torn planet of Earth.

As a unifying, mesmerizing, enjoining AdventYour exploration force, coming together in this moment, Mega's team could now remain strongly in each other's minds and telepathic conduits during the entire quest, not requiring physical presence, but by simply retaining and calling upon these special sharing vibrations they brought within them here. In these moments, the brothers and sisters effectively bonded the mission to these collective vibrations.

Later in the day, they sorted through and modeled the Earth clothes brought back by an advance patrol. Some of the hats enticed hearty laughter. Playing dress-up was sometimes fun on a new planet, if clothing were a factor at all there.

David especially liked the traditional word 'haberdashery' but could also appreciate the simplicity of the modern expression — 'rags.' It was symbolic of the way the U.S.A. culture had changed over the years.

They had fun interacting about the various cultural features of this many-faceted planet in the hours ahead, as did all on the ship. And that was a big part of it. The fun! Otherwise, there might not be enough incentive to come way out here.

Mega anticipated exciting adventures here for the explorers and the fare-paying passengers as well.

He was especially intrigued by stories of the Lucifer rebellion against the One God. It had been long, long ago, and Mega was not especially well-read about this part of the universe. He was certain of one thing; none of their Pleadian-7 colonists could have or would have rebelled against the One God — not knowingly anyway. Could they have been fooled?

He now recalled that he had heard stories of a strange and fearful kind of dark energy in these far reaches of Satania. They might even encounter it here.

Jim Cleveland

TWO: A Woman Out of the Sky

Jason Weathers awakened with a start. It sounded like...an explosion. He raised himself up on one elbow in the sleeping bag.

Flames licked skyward across the horizon. He blinked at it, all the while remembering he was on the ground here in a deserted west Texas canyon. There was now a huge fire somewhere out there in the mesquite and rock-studded wilderness that wasn't there before.

It was still dark. Jason sat up and rubbed the sleep out of his eyes. It was a roaring fire, across the sand creek and out there somewhere in the rugged valley. He figured he had to check it out. There was no one else out here that he had seen. Something had exploded, or maybe crashed.

He grabbed for his jeans, pulled them on hurriedly, strapped on his web belt with the canteen and knife, pulled a jacket over his tight muscle shirt, and furiously struggled with the boot laces. Soon he was splashing across the shallow creek and across the soft sand and rock bed, his slender 29-year old body moving lightly, lithely as the experienced backpacker he was.

He began jogging on the other side, shaking the water off his boots, hurrying on toward the flames. He ran too close to a cluster of cacti and heard their needles ripping across his jeans. He made a mental note of the maroon prickly pears he might return to peel and eat.

The sky was brightening in the east, heralding dawn. He was headed north. He hurried on. His watch said 5:47. He was getting out of breath, not in nearly as good a shape as he wished at age 26, too much office work and not enough of the outdoor life he loved passionately.

The sky was brightening a little. He could see a ragged gash in the shallow earth, a boulder unearthed and pushed out of the way, the shattered remains of mesquite trees torn away from an erratic upheaval of dirt to the fire scene.

He got there quickly.

Crushed into a wall of rock and splintered trees, the severely twisted wreckage was still aflame, a small plane it appeared but it seemed to be a strange shape, with a minimal wingspan. Scanning about, Jason saw shards of ripped metal, tattered debris.

The heat seared his face. He edged as close as he dared, shielding his face, trying to see inside, finally stepping away. So what could he do to save anybody in that living hell, anyway? Nothing.

Then he saw her and stopped short. She lay propped against a flat boulder, her pants ripped open and her leg a bloody mess, long honey brown hair hanging over her shoulders and streaked with the blood that had made rivulets down the side of her cheek.

Eyes wide, he moved steadily toward her. She appeared unconscious and — he could see more clearly in the brightening sky — she was beautiful, very beautiful! Slenderly fine facial features, flowing hair, a shapely body with ample breasts fitting into a tight blue and white shirt. A sleeve was ripped apart at her shoulder which was cut and bruised.

Jason stepped lightly, quietly, eyes affixed, to stand in front of her. Her eyes were closed, brow furrowed, it appeared, in pain.

"Miss…Miss! Are you all right?" He came close and squatted down to look at her. The leg was scraped and bruised and she had suffered a blow to the head. It was bluish and swollen. She appeared unconscious. Until he reached for her.

Her right hand moved up swiftly to clamp down hard on his throat, stifling his breath. Her eyes seemed to drill themselves into his. Her left hand came up swiftly to deliver a short burst of white steam into his face. He swooned dizzily, the scene melting to a quiet nothing of blackness. He fell away; everything dark and quiet.

He didn't know how long he was unconscious. When he awoke, he looked around groggily to see that the day was much brighter. She was standing there resolutely, staring at him intently. He realized he had been dragged across the bare ground and was propped against the same boulder upon which she had rested.

He tried to focus his eyes. She was looking at him hard, and didn't appear friendly. He saw that her leg was bandaged, that her face was now clean of blood and still the vision of beauty that he remembered until…something had happened and everything went dark. Actually, he felt rested and refreshed.

He thought it would be manly to get up, so he did, dizzily, and rubbed his head. She just looked at him still — quizzical, he thought. She was very wary of him, it seemed.

"Hey. I don't know what happened to me," he said. "But I came over here to see if I could help you, actually. And I wind up passing out. Ummm. Are you all right?"

"I'm fine. I believe you fainted."

15

"Not likely. I don't believe I've ever done that before," he lied, choosing not to remember the time he had mumps in the balls, or the time his head went through a windshield, the source of a jagged scar across his cheek. He was struggling in his mind with the question of whether he remembered anything at all. "What about this crash here? Were you in there?" His mind seemed unusually fuzzy, tentative.

"Yes, this is my...aeroplane. I was having problems with the engine."

"I can believe it. How the hell did you get out?"

She was now pulling on a snug silver vest jacket festooned with slitted pockets and featuring a circular emblem that featured some kind of bird. He had not seen that before. She limped slightly on the leg, but had managed to pull on a pair of long black, zippered boots. Her long flowing hair was still a little streaked with blood and the bruise was apparent on her forehead.

"Aren't you hurt? Is that leg hurting? How about your head?"

"I have to go. Thank you for the helpness."

"Go? Wait a minute. Are you just going to walk away?"

"Walk, yes, walk."

"No. You can't just walk away from a plane crash. Surely somebody is going to be investigating. Did you radio for help before you went down? There must be somebody on the way, huh?"

"No. It's really no...trouble. You stay here. Rest."

"You mean there's nobody that knows about this crash. Surely it has to be investigated."

"It was my craft. I am all right. There are reasons I don't have to explain to you. I will take care of it when I reach...a television."

"A television? Ummm. Well, I have a van about a mile over there," said Jason, his manner a little more clipped in response to her cold demeanor. "If you need a ride, I can take you. You need a telephone, actually, right?"

He thought she looked at him in a very peculiar way. She had something to hide. He was sure of it.

"Will you take me to a telephone?"

"Sure."

"Who are you?" she asked him.

"You mean, to see if it's safe to ride with me?"

"No. Not because that. I think I am safe with you," she said confidently, walking over to confront him face-to-face, and very close. She was bold and assertive. Unconsciously he almost took a step back, but consciously, with determination, he refused to do so. This was just a woman. Or maybe not.

Her eyes settled into his and captured them like a magnet, his own eyes almost popping from their sockets before settling back into captivity. He was mesmerized there as she reached up and touched her fingers to his cheek. He felt that they were very warm, but he couldn't respond, seemingly paralyzed. He was placid, but he could feel vibrational quivers moving up his back, across his temples, his short black hair lifting slightly, almost electrified, on its own. He was transfixed, he felt, in some kind of powerful but pleasant, smiley-faced energy. He couldn't help grinning at her and worried that he looked goofy.

She looked into him studiously, gleaning what she could from their limited first connection, deciding she could use him. Then she let him go.

He stood dazed for a few seconds before recapturing his senses. He did so in time to see that she was limping away. The wreckage smoldered on his left; she was moving away to his right, in the direction of his van. He didn't remember what happened and had no time to think about it. He followed after her, striving to catch up.

"So, you want the ride, huh? What do I call you?" he asked.

She frowned back at him. "I don't know if you call me."

"No, I mean what's your name?"

"My name is…I truly need a name."

"Well, yeah, so they can call you to supper."

"What is this place?"

"Texas, big old Texas. A camping area called Enchanted Rock."

"Then I'll be Roci," she said, contemplating and adding, "with an "I."

"Roci? R-O-C-I. Cool. Well, maybe I should do a new name too, but I've got no secrets so I'm just Jason Weathers.

She ignored the remark and walked on, seriously scanning all sides of the landscape as if expecting an ambush.

"You're pretty enchanting too, Roci. I have to admit."

She again ignored him and limped on.

"Well, I hope you have some insurance on that plane. Looks to me like you've got a pretty heavy loss. Matter of fact, it seems like a kind of unusual plane. What kind is it…was it?"

"Yes, all gone." She stopped abruptly to fondle the yellow blossoms erupting from a cluster of cacti. She looked at it closely, then moved quickly on, eyes darting left and right and even behind.

Jason's curiosity soared. "Where are you from? Anywhere close to here?"

She stopped quickly and turned to face him, her compelling green eyes capturing his full attention. She spoke clearly and evenly: "I don't want to talk while we're moving. But I want to talk to you later. Would that be all right?" Her eyes appealed to him earnestly, irresistibly.

"Sure." That's all he heard himself say.

When they reached the sand creek, she was still ahead of him by several strides, still limping slightly, but moving rapidly, even gracefully across the

17

landscape, not appearing to be in pain. Her eyes continued to dart here and there. Jason hurried to keep up.

Near the water, he saw it — a large snake — out for a morning sunning on a large boulder. "Hey! Guess you see that reptile at three o'clock, huh? May be a rattler!"

Suddenly, she turned and walked resolutely toward the snake.

"Whoa! I wouldn't do that."

She didn't slow her stride. "Are they fast?" she asked matter-of-factly.

"I'd say so. Better back off." He didn't have time to say more. She didn't even slow down.

The snake captured her movement, quivered and drew back, started to rattle and recoil for a strike. My God, it is a rattler, thought Jason. Her hand came forward steadily, slowly, toward the head, the slithering tongue. Jason was wide-eyed, frozen some ten steps away. She was encouraging a strike.

It came. Flying at her like a bedeviled rope, with an ugly, triangular head on top, white mouth wide open, two large fangs. But it captured only air. Her hands were quicker — one flying backward to miss the strike, the other curling around rapidly to grab the snake by the neck, in mid-air, and in a powerful grip.

She stood holding up the thrashing reptile in her fist, its horrible head thrust upward, mouth still open but paralyzed.

"The eyes are part of it too," she said calmly, "Very interesting." She stroked the body with her free hand, as it writhed about helplessly. "I would get a sample of the venom if I had time."

Jason stood there shocked, even more so when she disdainfully twirled the snake around her head like a whip and tossed it away. She watched it recover and scurry away, and turned to see that he was standing transfixed, amazed at the scene.

"That damned snake is loaded with poison. How in the hell can you do something like that? Are you a herpetologist? What?"

"It has nothing to do with herbs. I thought we agreed to talk later — later!" she said dynamically, and turned toward the creek. She stepped up to the shallow stream and stooped to examine it, reached into the gentle flow and pulled up a bulging handful of rocks, sand and gravel. After studying it for a few seconds, she let it wash away slowly, then stood to look at him again with a tight-lipped expression of wariness. Her eyes were cool, like a cat's. When they captured his, they seemed to gesture in the direction of the van.

"That is your...conveyance?" she asked.

"The very one," he said, snapping out of his stupor. "You seem to be pretty interested in this part of the country. Whew!" Jason felt a little dizzy.

"I'm very interested," she said, and finally gave him a slight smile — the first time. It was tiny and tentative, but enough to send quivers down his spine again. He knew he was irresistibly drawn to her, in a way he couldn't begin to understand. He didn't even want to.

His van carried them over the bumpy trail back to the main road, which was little more than a side road itself. He refrained from saying much, wary of just what he should and should not say to this strange woman. She stared intently at the passing scene, her attentions taken fully by the roadside parade of trees and mailboxes, cows and pastures and fences.

"Guess you've never been here, huh?" He was desperate for some scrap of information about her. He couldn't imagine the cool audacity just to walk away from a crash landing like that.

She ignored the question. "What is your occupation?" she asked.

"I'm director of public relations and advertising for a company in Dallas. FloorGem. We make tile, for floors, bathroom fixtures, you know. We're about the biggest in the Southwest. I'm just taking some time off. I love to hike and canoe and rock climb, nature stuff you know. I had some good memories from this place, so I decided to camp here overnight."

"You like to climb rocks?"

"Yeah. It's a great challenge. 'Course I'm not very good. I can do some things, you know. You have to know what you can do and what you can't. Rock-climbing teaches you patience, for one thing, and you have to plan and be precise. That's good. And you can't beat the scenery. That's for sure." He laughed and wondered if he sounded nervous.

"Those rocks there." She gestured outside to the rock-strewn landscape. "You climb atop them?"

He laughed. "Yeah, well, the high ones, like that big butte over there. That would be a nice climb, follow that crack on the left probably, most of the way up. Yeah. You like the outdoors?"

"Outdoors?" she mused. "Outside of doors? I think yes. Why do you climb rocks, Jason Weathers?"

"The challenge, I guess. I like adventure. Hell, I'm a Sagittarius."

"Adventure? You really do love adventure?"

"I sure do. How about you? Maybe we could have an adventure."

"Would you like that?"

"Sure. I'm free for a week or so. I've got some hiking plans, on up into Colorado, meeting some friends up there, two couples. But they're not set in concrete or anything. We could make a new plan. Or do that one." He hoped he didn't sound overanxious to be intimate with her but that was his supreme desire at this point. Everything else was secondary.

"Concrete," she mulled. "What kind of concrete adventure would you have in mind?"

19

"Hiking, I guess. Camping. I have a tent or, you know, one of us could sleep in the van. What would you like to do? I'm pretty easy to please."

"You may have to...take me somewhere, in a few days. Can you?"

"Well, probably, I mean, it depends on where it is, of course."

"Where it is I will have to find out."

"You don't know?"

"I can find out very soon. I will set up a meeting — to go home."

There was something strange going on, he had decided. She was on the run from something. It all had to be illegal. Drugs, maybe.

"You don't know where you need to go? Where do you live?"

"I can't go there now. But I can go with you if you want to adventure. For a few days."

"You'll go with me? For a few days?"

"Yes. And I want to know many things about you, and your life. Will you tell me?"

His laugh was surely nervous now. "Well, why would you be so interested, anyway? I'm just a normal kind of fellow."

"You are typical? Are you...average?"

"U-m-m-m. Well, I guess so."

"But you love adventure. Is that average?"

"Well, I don't know. Maybe not. There's a lot of fear around too."

"There would be much less fear if you could perceive reality. Can we go on now...to a nearby city?"

He looked at her curiously, wondering what to say. "Glenville Springs is close. But that isn't much of a city. It's a pretty nice town though, and I really had planned to stop by there and visit a friend for a few hours. We could maybe get you a room for the night there. You could make some calls...make some arrangements for your plane, whatever. I...uh...don't know what you're going to do for clothes and a toothbrush and stuff. I could visit Ellen, my friend, for a little while this afternoon. Shouldn't be gone too long. Umm...is that okay?" He wondered why he didn't quit blabbering, be cool, start trying to get some control in this strange new relationship, not appear an unorganized and uncertain questioner.

She thought for a moment, as if trying to understand his various meanings. He wasn't clear on them either, playing games as usual, but his libido was rolling and his mind racing. Could he possibly be so lucky as to score with this beautiful woman?

"We will do this," she said finally. "I will get to know you very well. We can stay together in the room."

"I think I'd like that."

She gave him another mesmerizing look, that incredible smile. "Yes, you will," she said with certainty.

"I know you've got some business to take care of — about the crash."

"Yes, I need to make some telecalls."

More strange language, he thought. "Your leg. I think we might need to see a doctor. And what about that blow to the head? It doesn't even look swollen any more though. How the heck did the swelling go down on that lick already?"

"It's all right. I don't need a doctor."

"You must have a damned good first aid kit. That's all I can say."

"I have what I need in my…shell."

"I beg your pardon?"

She didn't know what else to say. She unzipped the silvery vest a little and held it for him to see.

"Lots of pockets for lots of little stuff. You got everything you need in there, huh? Paper clips…caramel kisses."

"Not everything, of course. I don't have you in there."

"You need me?"

She smiled at him again, and it thrilled him once again. "You can help me if you want, and I will be a friend to you, a friend like you've never had. I had not planned on being with you but — you are here."

"That sure sounds enticing."

She just teased him again with the eyes, and turned again to the scenery. His mind whirled with speculations and anticipations.

They pulled into a service station in Glenville Springs and he asked her if she needed to go to the rest room. She said she wasn't tired.

He decided he wanted to appear like a tough and worldly guy to her, his usual role, but then wondered why he would want to do that. She got out with him and stood watching him fill the gas tank, turning here and there to study the traffic swirling around them, intently interested in everything but edgy, still wary, it seemed.

"We'll get checked in at the Southwest Inn over there, if that's okay, and then I'll be gone for just a few hours," Jason said. "Maybe we could go to the bar for a nightcap later."

"You are going to leave me alone for awhile?"

Her eyes had a hard edge, capturing his even with the service station hubbub all around them.

"That's really why I came through here, to see my friend," Jason blurted apologetically. "I've got to go. But I'm sure you'll be perfectly safe. I'll be back as soon as I can."

In truth, with this fortuitous and sudden change in fortune, Jason didn't hardly even want to go see Ellen any more, but he felt obliged. Jason always wanted to do the right thing, to be liked and respected by everyone, and Ellen had been his good friend for a long time.

21

"You can decide," she said. "I am…just visiting. I will see you again tonight to be friends."

He laughed self-consciously. That meant sex for sure — didn't it! "Believe me. I want us to be friends," he said. "Maybe we could set a time to go down to the bar."

"The bar," she repeated seriously.

She seemed confused to him. But no matter. The big issue in his ravenous mind right then was getting laid, not these amazing peculiarities in her behavior. He just couldn't help it. It was the raving beauty of her, the powerful eyes. She was peculiar but — that's it! — she must be foreign. Swedish maybe. They have legendary fair-skinned beauties, don't they? But there was no accent, none at all.

"Are you from overseas?" he blurted."

She shook her head slightly as if misunderstanding. "Over the sea?" She rubbed her head as if bothered by the question. Then, without saying more, she shook her head and limped purposefully toward the rest room.

So maybe she was having trouble with the language, the colloquialisms, he thought. He watched as she stopped at the two rest room doors, paused to examine them both. She chose the right one and disappeared inside.

There, she studied the bathroom equipment, filled a vial with tap water and placed it in a silver vest pocket. She tested the flushing mechanism of the commode and knew it was for bodily waste disposal. Thank goodness Zenithians were beyond that.

At the motel, she sat and bounced herself on one of the two beds. He noticed she was beginning to smile a little more. Those powerful green eyes appeared friendlier.

"I hope you'll be okay. Here's the phone number where I'll be," he said, handing her a note with Ellen Mackey's name and number. "Looks like a pretty comfortable bed. They got plenty of cable TV, looks like. I thought the barbecue place looked pretty good next door, or they had a prime rib special in the dining room, I noticed in the elevator."

"I will be fine. I have plenty of things to entertain me."

"Good. I just wish I was one of them, but I'll be back as soon as I can and we can really get acquainted. You like to dance?"

"I love to dance."

"Great. And a few nips maybe?"

She just stared at him.

"Maybe even a coupla hits of doobie. How would that be?"

"If that's your idea of entertainment, then that's what we'll do."

"You're sure agreeable."

"So far."

"So…maybe you won't be later?" he asked anxiously.

"I don't think you'll cause me any trouble."

"What are you talking about?" he asked.

No answer. She pulled open the drawer by the bed, pulled from it a Gideon Bible, and began thumbing through it.

"I don't ever intend to cause you any trouble," he said. "I just want to get to know you. I really…like you…okay?"

She turned to him with the penetrating eyes. "I like you too. Do you care about people, Jason? Is there love inside you?"

"Why, sure, I think so." He would agree to anything without thinking about it.

She continued to eye him deeply. "You don't seem very sincere."

"I think we could have a beautiful time together. You're very charming."

"You're shallow, I reason. I think you're only interested in the sexuality of the situation."

"That's a helluva thing to say. You know that's not true. You're a cool person. I mean sex is great, better than that really, but…" He knew that she really had him summed up, and he felt uncomfortable.

"You really should try to think before speaking, Jason. You should learn to decide things logically, then speak what you've decided."

"What I've decided is that you're very appealing to me. I think you're very beautiful and, okay, I admit it, I really want to go to bed with you."

"I want you to go to bed with me. I want to see you naked. You are attractive, but not too perfect. I can tell you have some of the good genes."

Jason's heart thumped. "I want to make love to you. I want to please you every way I can." He was standing awkwardly in front of her. She put down the Bible and got up from the bed to move toward him. Close. He stood his ground. Confidently, she met his eyes. He moved tentatively to kiss her.

She reached and touched a finger to his lips, stopping him. "We will wait until later," she said. "I have things to do as soon as you leave."

"Your hands are very warm." He took one of them in his, and she quickly pulled away.

"I'm sorry," he began. "I —" She zipped the vest and moved toward the door.

"I want to see the city," she said. "I need to purchase some things."

He watched as she pulled a fat roll of bills from the vest and shuffled through them. He saw that they were hundreds. She tucked them back into the zipper-laden vest. "I will see you when you return."

"Looks like you can buy —" She closed the door behind her. He stared at it. Suddenly alone.

"…anything you want, my dear."

Jason taxed his mind with questions all the way to Ellen's ranch. Was she foreign, without an accent of any kind, and having trouble with the

23

language? Was she spaced on some drug? Was she on the lam? Was she a foreign drug addict on the lam? Was the plane stolen? Was it full of illegal drugs? Why did she want to go camping with me? As a cover? Are we both in danger? Does she really want to see me naked — and why? Is she horny like me? That would be a lucky break. Is she rich? Who else but the rich fly their own planes? Maybe she was a zoologist. How else could she handle a rattlesnake like that? He decided not to tell Ellen about her. Why complicate things? Anyway, he wouldn't know what to say that made any sense.

In the end, it didn't really matter; his cock was always the final arbiter anyhow. He wanted to get laid above everything; he didn't care if she was a Russian spy or a drug dealer or a runaway heiress. He realized he was a pretty shallow guy, but didn't much care. The world was basically a shitty place anyway; you had to grab for gusto wherever you could find it.

He still hadn't decided anything for sure about Roci when he pulled onto Ellen's long gravel driveway. Sex would be the priority, he decided. It seemed a logical plan for a horny young bachelor who also liked adventure.

Ellen came out with her usual exuberant smile, bountiful hair tied back in a rag, bulging breasts exploding out of a halter top, faded and patched jeans and sandals, painted toenails, just a little bit fatter than she had been.

"How you doin', promo man?" she called to him. "It's been too fuckin' long." The old friends embraced and kissed, and were soon smoking a joint, drinking a Lone Star beer and catching up on times and acquaintances.

She gave him three more caps of organic mescaline, and he was glad he had decided to come.

"I want you guys and gals to trip your socks off, now," Ellen said. "I'm sorry I can't be there."

"We're gonna miss you, Baby. Have you tried this batch? Is it good shit?"

A friend in Brownsville, down on the Mexican border, had a clandestine laboratory which turned the awful goop of the peyote cactus into clear crystals.

"Well, Tico and Betty and some of their friends tripped over at Edge Falls a few weeks ago and said it was heavy duty. They loved it. May be better than the first batch."

"No joke?"

"Said it was really something. Said the clouds looked like they were rolling down in your lap. They did some rafting over there. Had a ball."

"I guess we'll just camp at Loch Vail. It's a big, beautiful lake about nine miles from the road. It's in the Rocky Mountain National Park. And right on up from there is a place called Timberline Falls. Big waterfall. It's beautiful country. Wish you were gonna be there."

But Ellen's mother was sick and she couldn't come. Now, maybe Jason had fortuitously found a replacement for his longtime friend. All he had to do now was convince Roci to do organic mescaline, that fabled Indian hallucinogen that she might reject, figuring it to be hard drugs.

Ellen had made a stew and they devoured it. Later, the kitchen table, crumb-strewn and bedecked with dirty dishes, lay before them while they talked.

"I guess you decided not to sell the ranch, huh, and move back to the city?" he asked her.

"Naw. I've gotten to love the country life. You know, Stuart and I had made plans to come down here eventually. We both liked horses and wanted a little bit of land to grow stuff on, especially a little weed. So much for long-range plans, but it's okay down here. There's not much hassle. I got a job in town, at the Dodge and Plymouth place."

Jason often thought about Stuart, her man, a jovial, dark-bearded guy, overconfident, who got mixed up in smuggling weed and maybe more in Mexico. He had carried Ellen down to the border to claim his body, found tied to a post with his throat cut, up in the mountains and out from San Luis Potesi.

"Well, maybe there's a man around these western parts for you, Baby Doll. You seen anybody interesting."

"Cowboys mostly. I swear I think some of 'em are trying to make it through life with one brain cell."

He laughed. "I'm sure you're being too hard on them good 'old boys in these parts," he twanged.

"I am," she said. "There's some pretty nice guys around. They just hadn't been anywhere much, you know?"

"Fortunately, we're world travelers."

"Oh! You know what I mean," she protested. "I mean we've been out trying to get our kicks, expanding our minds all through the years, keeping our minds open to new things, new ideas, going places like concerts and campouts and pot rallies. Some of these people have done good to get up to Austin to the Armadillo. And they sure can't rap about Gurdjeiff and Gibran and Jesus stuff like we used to."

"Then why do you like it here?"

"I don't know, man," she said, running her fingers through her tousled brown hair, flipping her cigarette ash into her stew bowl. "I feel like I'm at some kind of a crossroads right now, you know. Stuart's been gone about eight months and I think I still haven't been able to change directions in life, you know, shift into some other gear. It's like this place is very peaceful and all and I like it, but I'm not really doing anything with my life. I'm not contributing. I'm not making anything better for anybody. And I don't mean

25

a j.o.b. either. I mean we used to talk about how love and brotherhood and the Age of Aquarius and all that was coming. Well...hell, it's like I <u>still</u> believe that. I never did get over it and I'm not doing anything about it. I want to do something, but I don't know what I want to do."

"Be a good person. Care about people. Do things to help people, not to hurt them. That's all. Don't worry about it. Have a good time. We're on our own down here. God'll see what we did with it all down the road sometime."

"Well, you know, I don't get much chance to do nothin' down here in the boonies. What about you, though? You said you got in a crack with your company about smoking weed or something?"

"In the damned parking lot. Security guard saw me taking a hit — damned fool thing to do in the car but...I did it. I still don't know where that guy came from."

"So what's the deal?"

"The carpet treatment, slapped my wrist, told me to take a couple of weeks off and come back with a new attitude. Acted like I still have a job if I get some rehabilitation."

"Rehab? Are you kidding? For marijuana?"

"These people don't know the difference between pot and heroin, believe me," said Jason.

"So what you gonna do?"

"Beats the hell out of me. Maybe it'll come to me out in the wilderness, while I'm tripping." He laughed derisively.

She laughed too. "I wouldn't count on getting any practical help there. That stuff'll put you in a whole new dimension."

"If we were to get busted with organic mescaline, they'd put us <u>under</u> the jail," he said.

"Just see that it don't happen. You guys got to be super cool. I mean like, they're just capsules. They don't look suspicious if you're cool. I wouldn't do over three-quarters of a hit, by the way, maybe a half later in the day when you start comin' down. Better do it on an empty stomach too, you know, or you'll probably be callin' Huey for a little while."

"Yeah, I don't relish pukin.' Think I'll be as empty as I can, but I think the other guys were talkin' about something easy, like cereal and milk."

Dunno, man. It's your trip. What I do know, dude, is that these babies will give you maybe six or eight hours of really cool trippin' and, like I said, you might want to punch 'em up later in the day. You gonna try to get spiritual with it?"

"Well, you know how I feel about nature," said Jason. "It's all spiritual out there in the mountains. I'm kind of a pantheist guy, still. This place we're going is knocked-out beautiful, peaceful, you know. It'll be like our

Enchanted Rock trip all over and but then — wow! — the Rocky Mountain grandeur washed all over everything. Those peaks are just about too much, Sweets."

"It's gonna be a mind-blower, promo man. Those clouds are gonna be comin' down for you, the wind, the creatures, everything. You're gonna be an integral part of a cosmic scene."

"We're always lookin' for that ultimate trip, aren't we?" Jason mused, "even if it's just temporary."

"Well, it's the closest I ever got to feeling TBG, you know, truth, beauty and goodness," said Ellen. "It's like some kind of preview of something fantastically better, loving vibes that you can feel all over, a oneness with everything, even if it's just for a little while. You remember how it was at the Rock. We just had to get naked; there were clothes strewn all over the landscape." She laughed heartily.

"Yeah, I know you're dragged out most of the next day, too," said Jason. "Down at the Rock, we weren't good for much of nothing except laying around."

"It's a real downsider, that's for sure. I wouldn't plan anything but R&R the day after. Your mind's full of cobwebs. But it's worth it, for sure."

"I guess," said Jason a little uncertainly, his mind secretly troubled how Roci could fit into all these drug doings. Questions emerged out of his mind and there was no time to think about them now.

"Well," he added. "I'm sure it'll be — real." He grinned at her, winked and passed the joint, took a hit of his longneck beer and wondered what things might happen in the days ahead.

It was near nine and, with anticipating penis, he wheeled the van into the motel parking lot, put the mescaline caps in the glove compartment and locked it. He walked to the room, intent to see her, freshen up, gargle and wash his face, apply some cologne. She wasn't there. One of the beds was filled with paper bags from the Wal-Mart. There was a new green backpack on the floor. The red message light shined on the phone and he called the desk.

"Yes, Mr. Weathers," said a woman's voice. "I'm afraid there has been a little bit of trouble with your wife. Could you please step down to the office?"

He arrived there quickly to be confronted by two uniformed policemen, with black-holstered sidearms and dark ties tucked into their blue shirts.

"Where is she?" he blurted. "Is she all right?"

"Mr. Weathers, you're going to need to come down to the sheriff's office with us. Your wife is all right, but she's being held down there for assaulting two men, and I think one of them's been carried over to the hospital."

"That's a helluva note. She assaulted two men?"

27

"Yessir," the officer said stiffly. "That is a helluva note, ain't it?" He was trained to be deadpan and make few comments, Jason knew.

The sheriff of Glenville County was craggy-faced and overweight, a gut hanging over his gun belt and crow's feet pushing out from his weathered eyes.

"I reckon it may be hard to believe, I grant you," he told Jason, "but we're gonna have to abide by the law just the same. Did you know your wife doesn't have a single stitch of identification of any kind, Mr. Weathers? That seems mighty peculiar."

"Well, maybe she left it at home."

"Well, she wouldn't say much about it. In fact, she won't say much about anything. She acts like she's pretty scared and mixed up. I've got one of our female officers back there trying to talk to her right now."

"I want to see her, and see about getting us out of here. What do I need to do?"

"You need to listen to what I'm telling you. Don't you want to know what she did and what we're charging her with?"

"Assault, you said. That's hard to believe. Tell me what happened."

"Couple of gentlemen staying there at the Southwest from Besco Industries. That's over in Waco. One of them says they talked with her at the bar, even bought her a drink. Says they walked out to the pool later and she was already out there swimming. She had this little ol' bikini on. Still had on the price tag, from the Wal-Mart. From the looks of your room, looks like she bought a whole bunch of clothes over there.

"Now they said they were just trying to be friendly, and, so they said, she went crazy and threw both of 'em in the pool. One of 'em followed her to her room — he said just to find out what was the matter — and she proceeded to knock him down and then throw him into one of them big hedges in front of her room. He took several stitches on his eye down at the hospital."

"Seems like to me they were trying to put the make on her. You can't always trust traveling salesmen, you know, sheriff. Were they drunk?"

"I think them boys was pretty drunk if you wanna know the truth about it, but that don't change what happened. I'm here to tell you, though, they are about ready to forget the whole thing."

"Then we can get out of here."

"Well, just hold your horses. She wadn't through by a long shot, Mr. Weathers. One of my deputies tried to get her to come down here and she refused, locked the door and wouldn't come out. They went in with a passkey and she still wouldn't agree to come. Acted like she was mighty scared or upset. Kneed my man in the balls and doubled him up. Made him draw his weapon."

"Oh, come on now, sheriff."

"Now don't gimme no indignation, sir. Your wife has already about wore out my patience for one evening."

"He drew his weapon?"

"Yeah. And by God if she didn't take it away from him. He can't remember what the hell happened."

"Maybe he got overly excited and fainted."

"Not very likely. When he woke up, she had a wet towel on his forehead anyway. Two more of my officers arrived on the scene and she came on down here. By that time, one of the housekeepers had been talking to her, and apparently got her calmed down a little."

"Was she scared or what?"

"I don't know if that's what you'd call it. In fact I don't know much of anything at all from talking with her. But maybe we can call her in here and we can get this mess straightened out. Give it a try anyhow." He gestured to a tall deputy with a hawk nose and high cheekbones, who turned and left to get her.

Jason tried to think fast. She was supposed to be his wife; they were on vacation. But how could he explain how spaced out she was? And was it going to be too late to get laid tonight?

"Now when she gets in here, Mr. Weathers, you see if you can't get us a little more cooperation. I'm not necessarily adverse to ya'll getting out of here tonight. Neither one of the men wanted anything to do with pressing charges. I'm just going to have to ask your cooperation in answering a few questions and assuring me that we're not going to have any more ruckus in town before you fine people can get gone from here."

"We'll be gone in the morning. We'd just like to get to bed if we can stay away from any more drunken salesmen."

"Mr. Weathers. I would prefer you didn't get too specific about whether them fellas was drunk or not 'cause we really didn't give 'em a test. That really wadn't what we was concerned with at the time. And, like I done told you, they're ready to forget the whole thing, stitches and all."

Roci walked into the room confidently, eyes alert, with long strides, followed by a matron and the tall deputy, who curled back into a corner and stood erectly curious. She came directly to Jason and reached out, melting into his arms wordlessly, surprisingly. The grip of her fingers was strong across his back. He imagined he felt her heart beating against him through her brand new jeans and shirt, unusually warm skin, feeling her breathing with him, coalescing with his breath in some kind of lustful affection. My God! He suddenly realized again that she had a substantial power over him. But be cool, he told himself. Be in the moment.

She pulled back. "I'm so glad you're back, Jason. Two awful men said dirty things to me. I was scared. And these men act as if I did something wrong."

The sheriff's face dropped an inch or more at Roci's sudden change of personality. The tall deputy's beady eyes opened wider and cut toward them. The matron's tired stare suddenly grew perplexed; her eyes bulged in wonder.

"Well, I hope they're just trying to protect you from those two lounge lizards," said Jason. "And I think that's the case. Isn't it, sheriff?"

"Mr. Weathers. I've got the concern of this lady disarming a police officer. When he woke up, she gave him his revolver back but she hid the bullets. We still don't know where they are."

"If he let her disarm him, I don't know if you can trust him with bullets," Jason deadpanned.

"He just fainted," said Roci softly.

"I beg your pardon," said the sheriff. "Deputies don't faint!"

"Unless they are kicked in the...scrotum. Do you see, I don't like guns, so I disabled him, took it, emptied the bullets and threw them away. That was my room and I didn't want a loaded gun in there."

Jason and the others just stared at her.

She spoke again: "I trust this is all right. I just don't like guns. That's just the way it is."

"Ma'am. My deputy is an officer of the law. He is supposed to carry a gun. He uses it for the protection of the public. He would use it to protect you."

"I don't want him using it on my behalf. I don't know why you...manufacture these things. They serve no useful purpose."

"Only if you need protection from the criminal element that's out there. Then I believe you'd be happy to get our help, little lady."

"I wouldn't be happy. No."

"Well, hell," said Jason. "If the man fainted, that's surely not her fault. Can't you help us get out of here? Seems like this whole affair would be best forgotten. It's been totally overblown."

"Well, she assaulted my man first. I reckon he might've had good reason to pass out. He's down at the hospital being checked out too. Got a knot on the side of his jaw the size of a hicker'nut."

"She was just upset," said Jason. "She didn't know what she was doing. She had almost been assaulted by the boozeheads. We need to get out of here and let's forget the whole thing." He said it but he didn't think they'd buy it.

But the sheriff looked suddenly confused, blank-faced. He rubbed his forehead. Jason turned to Roci. Her eyes were staring at the sheriff intensely.

"To tell the truth, I think we've all had enough hassle for one night," the sheriff said, still rubbing his furrowed brow. "I'm plumb tarred out, and I'll personally be happy to help you on your way, Mr. Weathers. But I have to have some identification and some information in case the two…victims decide to press charges later. Probably just a matter of bookkeeping, but it's gotta be done. Then you can be out of here pretty quick."

Pretty quick? Jason thought he might still get laid. He unfolded an accordion of identification cards.

They didn't seem to mind that none of them included her name. In fact, the more they talked with Roci, or tried to look in her eyes, the more disconcerted they all seemed to be. The matron searched confusedly for word processor keys. The sheriff lost his stream of thought twice. Jason looked at her each time, and noticed that she was staring intently at them when they fritzed out. There was something about that look, that stare, he realized. She could do things with it. And the more it worked on them, the more he realized they were going to get through the whole affair without showing any identification on her at all.

Who in the world was she? A woman who fell out of the sky.

The car was dark on their way back to the motel. There was a rainy wind coming up out of the south and a few drops speckled their windshield as he drove back deliberately, trying to put all this together in his mind, in some new way that made more sense.

He looked over at her a few times before speaking. She was quiet, looking out at the row of neoned businesses, a beer joint called "Lou's Lounge" surrounded by mud-splattered pickups and a red Cadillac convertible with a white top. Finally he said it: "Roci, you've got to tell me what's going on." He used his most serious tone. He was glad it was dark; she couldn't work him over with those eyes.

"We are going, aren't we?"

"What?"

"We are going on," she said earnestly. "Aren't we?"

"Never mind," he said finally.

And a few blocks later: "Has anyone ever told you you're a very unusual person? I mean, like, extremely unusual?"

"Yes, they did," she said reflectively. "They did tell me that."

"Is something bothering you? Are you all right?"

She turned to him, reflections of the lights outside glistening in her dark eyes. "Yes," she said. "I am fine. And are you?"

31

"Sure. Because, well, I don't really know you, but I'd do anything I could to make things...good for you. I'm just a little...confused by the way you talk, the way you act."

"I know that you're sincere in your desires," she said without hesitation.

"I...I really don't know why I'm so taken with you. Maybe it's your incredible beauty. Maybe I'm just lonely right now. Maybe I see that you really are somehow...very different from anyone I've met, and that's good. I'm just kind of...mesmerized, I guess, by your very presence, somehow. I don't really understand it."

"I understand it. Everything will be all right, Jason. I want to put your heart at ease."

"You do?"

"I know that I have a power over you. I must be honest with you also and tell you I am going to use it."

"Wait a minute. What do you mean?"

" I will speak to you more directly — in my way. I know what you want. You want to be with me intimately, in the flesh, and this will give us both pleasure, I think, so we can do it. I want to share this with you because you are...exotic to me, very exotic, like a magnetic, strangely primitive human animal. It will be exciting."

"I...don't know. I would love you with unbridled passion. My hormones are flaming when you're nearby. I hope I'd be what you want. But what kind of power are we talking about? And what will you do with it?"

"I need your help for a week," she said. "I am telling you that I am a writer on a research trip. I will go with you to the mountains according to your plan and observe. I may have some personal needs from time to time with which you can assist if you choose. In a week, I will need to meet my friends at a designated place and perhaps you can take me there."

"And then?"

"I will go home."

"And that's it? It would all be over between us?"

"What would be over?" she asked. "It?"

"I mean, you'd take off and forget about me, is that it? Wouldn't there be a chance for something permanent between us? We might just make great lovers and great friends, maybe even great life partners. Who knows? We could give it a try — for the long term."

She laughed and it took him aback. He was pulling into the parking space in front of their room. "Jason," she said, "there are many thousands of possible sexual partners for you if you people would only act out your loving desires. But you can't come home with me. I will have other adventures to live."

32

"Fine," he said defiantly. "That's cool with me." He shrugged and killed the engine.

She eased over to him in the dark van. "Are you afraid of me, afraid of my power?" she asked as she began to breath on his cheek, brush her lips over his face. Warm breath. Warm kisses. Very warm.

"I believe you," he said firmly, trying to hold himself in control. Her hot mouth and tongue engulfed his, though, and it swiftly took him under control. He quickly fell into a whirlpool of eroticism that surged his mind upward into intense vibrations of sucking, strained breathing. He felt buttons popping open, smooth and rounded peaks of her warm, open breasts, reflecting in the motel light. There was unzipping, grasping, kissing, a moaning sound escaping from him, then suddenly ecstatic spewing. His penis, uncontrollably, exploded in rigors in her hand, there in the car.

In sweating, near breathless delight, he reeled and quivered, and fell limply, relaxed, before suddenly recovering his composure in time to see a strange sight. She was spiriting a palmful of his semen into a small bottle. What? It had all required only a minute or so. He felt deflated. And what was she doing?

He could only stare at her, and then at his spent cock, exposed there in soft repose.

She smiled slyly at him. "It's all right, Jason. I just have to see what we're dealing with. That's all."

He shook his head tiredly. "That's all?" Embarrassed suddenly, he pulled in his wet penis and zipped, wiping his hand absently on the seat. "This is crazy. Crazy! What are you up to? What's going on?" Maybe he sounded panicked.

"I just have to get a laboratory analysis. I've made a call. I can get it picked up in Austin tomorrow. We're going that way, aren't we?"

"You're taking my semen to Austin?"

"They'll meet me at the corner of Second Avenue and Larabee Boulevard at one p.m."

"Maybe I don't want my semen left there. Did you ever think of that?"

"You shouldn't mind. If you're okay, we're going to be sexually intimate for awhile. In fact, I want to test your stamina."

"Is that what you're using then? If I go along with the plan, I'll get fucked regularly, right? Trouble is, I want to know what you're doing this for? It's the damned most peculiar thing that ever happened to me in the course of lovemaking. I'm sure of that."

"I thought you loved adventure."

"Yeah but, good Lord, I need to know what you're all about, lady. I mean…this is crazy."

"I'm not crazy. Are you?"

"That's not what I mean. I mean, I don't want to be some damned guinea pig or something. Do you understand that?"

"I don't know much about pigs."

"How can you take a specimen like that? Are you a medical technologist? What?"

"I told you I'm a writer."

"So you think that explains everything. I want to know what you're all about."

"If you don't want to be with me, I'll leave. I will do well without you."

"That's not what I said. I just think you ought to level with me, that's all."

"We have some time together, Jason. I will tell you some things. We will be friends if you still want, but you have to quit being…upset. This is a great opportunity for you whether you realize it or not."

He thought about it a few seconds. "An opportunity, huh? Do you mean just for sex, or what?"

"Much more. I don't know why you put so much emphasis on sex. It's only a pleasure activity and procreation method. There is much more than this that could be revealed to you if you could get beyond the lust."

"And you'll reveal it?"

"Some of it. Enough to open your mind to some glorious new things that have nothing to do with sex. You're preoccupied with pleasure activities."

"And part of it is getting my semen tested, huh? I don't know why you're getting this done in the first place. And secondly, I'll tell you that I don't have AIDS or anything else."

"We'll see."

"Who will see?"

"My friends. Maybe you'll meet some of them."

"Semen testers. What else do they do?"

"I know you don't understand all this. Can you not wait until I can reveal to you over time? I will be part of your adventure too. Do you have friends?"

"Yes. I have friends too. Maybe you'll meet them. Two other couples. We're planning the hike up in the Rocky Mountain National Park. Will you go with us?"

"Yes. I told you I wanted to go with you. I would like to meet more friends."

"Fine. And what about your plane? What about your family, your other friends? Don't you need to tell them?"

"I have already telephoned. It has all been handled."

"Just like that. You're not even upset about the plane. Your leg looked bad. It doesn't seem to be bothering you either. The limp has gone. Your

34

forehead looks…fine. What gives? You just don't talk like or act like anybody I've ever known."

"You keep repeating that. I'm not! Okay? Let it go!" she said, pulling open the door, slipping outside, slamming it hard and making her way to the motel room. She was gone again. He had no choice but to follow.

He locked their door while she was stripping nude. She seemed suddenly impatient with him. He thought that she had the most gorgeous body he had ever seen, perfectly shaped and tanned brown all over, ample and upright breasts, a smooth and flat stomach, and a thin narrow tuft of dark pubic hair.

She had no reservations about being completely naked in front of him. She hardly noticed him and said not a word, slipping easily onto the other bed while he fumbled about more slowly.

He undressed to his briefs, climbed into the other bed and turned out the lamp. She had pulled the covers neatly to her shoulders, fully naked, and lay quietly on her back, eyes closed, seemingly at peace.

"Goodnight," he said mildly.

"And you," she said softly, calmly, without moving.

Lying on his side, he peeked at her in the sliver of light that slipped through the drapes. She seemed in peaceful repose, perfectly still. He turned to his back, not sleepy, and lay there amazed at all that had happened, turning over thoughts in his mind that came to no solid conclusions. He knew that he had to have some answers. Answers! Not to mention more sex.

He suddenly resolved also that he needed to be a lot less shallow and pleasure-seeking in his life, hedonistic. He felt like, in large measure, he had been wasting his time here, frittering away his life.

No matter in this moment, though. He suddenly felt very tired, deeply tired, and was momentarily asleep.

THREE: *An intimate integration*

Jason awakened slowly at first, collecting his thoughts, remembering the motel room, Roci, a sudden flood of incidents from the remarkable previous day. That awakened him quickly. He pulled back the covers and whirled himself upright, sitting on the bed a little groggily. She was gone. He read 7:14 on the clock.

He made his way to the bathroom; she wasn't there. He splashed water on his face and wiped it with a towel, wishing for a cup of coffee, and wondering where she was — hopefully not tangling with the law again.

On the counter, he noticed that his electric razor had been disassembled. Holy Cow! It lay there in pieces, rotary blades and plastic case and screws. He heard the door open and turned to see her coming in, dressed again in the jeans and plaid shirt and hiking shoes from her shopping excursion, with a newspaper under her arm and a paper bag from the motel coffee shop.

"Good morning, Jason," she said cheerily. "I didn't know what you would want for breakfast, but I brought coffee with things to put in it, and a doughnut. I know they're quite popular."

"Great. What are you having?" He walked to her and took the bag.

"Nothing. I don't consume much."

He didn't reply, just took the bag and pulled out the coffee.

"So…do you still want to hit the road today for the hiking and camping trip?"

"We will climb rocks?"

"Sure," he said. "We will climb rocks."

She read the newspaper in an unusual way, scanning the columns consecutively it seemed from page one. She was either reading faster than anyone he had ever seen, or else she was catching the gist of the stories and moving on, but she was intense about it, methodically following every article with a guiding finger, moving it rapidly up and down until she finished and pulled back the page to begin covering another.

She wore neither nail polish or make-up. Her complexion was smooth and free of hair, evenly tanned and contoured with tight muscles. The bluish bruise on her temple was much smaller. He supposed her leg was still bandaged under the jeans but he had noticed no limp at all.

He sipped coffee and reached for the sports section while clandestinely studying her every move. She seemed intently interested, even wide-eyed, at everything she read, everything she saw, as if seeing it for the first time.

"You sure read the hell out of a newspaper."

She looked up. "Hell?" she said.

"Never mind," he replied. Another odd question. He resolved again that it would be his vocation to solve the mystery of her. He had to know, he had to find out what she was all about. And apparently he needed to stay with basic English, no colloquialism or attempts at wit.

"Yes," she said seriously. "There is much hell in the newspaper. Misery and suffering throughout the world. Wars, killing, famine, disease, hatred, greed. Children and innocent people suffering and dying constantly. Murders and atrocities are being committed somewhere every minute of the day and night. How do you face it every day without…hurting inside?"

She seemed to be hurting now, her face contorted to show the pain of her empathy.

"Well, you'd get depressed if you thought about it a lot."

"So you…don't think about it then? You refuse to be concerned or involved."

"Not exactly. I'd like to do something about all of it. It's just that there isn't much an individual can do. We just have to live our own lives as best we can, care about people, you know, but I learned some time ago that you can't really solve people's problems for them, tell them how to live. We can't suffer for everyone in the world. It's just not possible to take on all the world's misery."

"Do you think of your life as an obligation, or an opportunity, Jason?" she asked him.

"I guess it's both. You have to take the bad with the good, maybe."

"Your planet is cursed. Your planetary prince, Caligastia, betrayed you, and then the default of Adam and Eve. I have read of it."

"You know about stuff like that? But what do you mean 'your planet.' It's yours too, isn't it?"

"Sometimes I think I don't belong here."

He laughed. "Sometimes I think you're right."

"Do you really care about people, Jason? Do you have empathy for those who suffer? Do you have compassion for those who do wrong because they can't help themselves with their…deficient minds?"

"I try to. I really do."

"I believe you do."

37

"Yeah, sometimes I moan and groan about not doing anything truly worthwhile with my life. Advertising is an okay job, but it really doesn't contribute anything of lasting value. And there's lots of bullshit and greed and misrepresentation in the business, I guess like there is in most everything else. What I'd like to do is write, maybe a novel that really has a point-of-view, that really cuts to the heart of what's wrong with things and offers logical solutions, something a lot of people would read that would make a lasting and positive impression, how we've got this great responsibility here that's also a great opportunity, a great challenge, a great adventure, to make things better for everyone. If I could influence people to love and nurture one another like God intended, that would be something. But every time I sit down to write, I never get very far. I guess it just hasn't all come together in my mind well enough to write yet. Maybe I can do it when I'm older, when I have enough experience and maturity and insight to get the job done."

She listened intently. "You're a good person. I'm glad I met you instead of someone else. I think we can be good for each other."

"I hope so. I think you're as fascinating as you are beautiful."

"If you could write well, if you had something to say, then could it be...published?"

"Well, it would have to be sold to a publisher. Some people say it's tougher to get something read and published than it is to write it, especially if you're not saying what the book business expects you to say, something that fits their way of thinking, or fits into some genre, some formula or other. I don't know if that's true. I'm just cynical about things sometimes, too much of the time. There seems to be a confounding mix of idealism and cynicism in here." He punched his head with his finger.

"Thank you," she said. "You've been very helpful."

"Thanks? For what?"

"I wanted to know all about you. And you're telling me. Thank you."

"Why? Why are you so interested in me?"

"Well, why are you so interested in me?" she retorted.

"Because you appear to be...a truly amazing person. I know I'm sure as hell not."

"You're fascinating to me. You can believe that," she said.

"I'm very glad you think so."

Her broad smile revealed perfect white teeth. "We will have adventure," she said, overjoyed, flinging the loose newspapers all over the room, standing and whirling around and around. "Adventure! Adventure!"

Her joy spread quickly to him. He got up and hurled the sports section across the room. "Adventure!" He reached his arms to her.

She embraced him. He clutched her warm body tightly. My God, he thought, what am I getting into? Maybe something momentous, maybe a turning point in life. It was crazy but he thought he loved her deeply, not possible after only a few hours. But what is possible? What is unfolding? How will the adventure shape up?

She looked into his face. "All your questions will be answered," she said.

"What questions?"

"The ones you are asking yourself. When I am very close to you like this, I can get into your mind. I can feel what you are thinking sometimes."

"That's quite a power. How is that possible?"

"You are full of questions, aren't you?"

"Overflowing."

"The answers will come," she said, "and perhaps you can do something with them."

"Right now, I wonder about my razor. Did you take it apart?"

She laughed. "Yes. I was just curious about what made it work. I'll put it together again." She stepped over to the counter and picked up two tiny screwdrivers, held together on a small chain.

"Why are you so curious about things? It's like you're seeing everything fresh, like you've never seen it before."

"You're perceptive," she said. "And your mind seems open. That's a good thing. We'll see what we can do with it." She began reassembling the razor, swiftly and surely.

"You act like I'm a project of some kind."

"You are perceptive," she replied. "Do you mind?"

"Will it be good for me?"

"Beyond your imagination, I think."

"That'll take some doing."

"Good. I love a challenge."

"So do I. Maybe you'll be my project too."

"Yes," she said. "That's fair. Do your best." She handed him the razor she had rapidly reconstructed. She had handled it as expediently and deftly as she had the snake.

They were soon on the sun-swept highway to Austin, talking about many things. She was enthusiastic, asking about everything she saw, and it was contagious.

In Austin, they asked directions to the designated street corner. A white van on the street captured her eye. She directed him to park and went over to it, knocked a couple of times on the door. It slid open, revealing only darkness, and she stepped inside. Waiting in the van at her request, he

39

strained his eyes to see anything at all but couldn't. The blue emblem on their vehicle appeared to be a circle with a dove or bird inside.

In less than five minutes she emerged again and made her way back to Jason, gliding gracefully across the street, no limp at all now. She eased into her seat gracefully, and looked at him with a peaceful smile.

"Don't I get to meet your friends?" he asked.

"Not yet."

"I can't believe you're having my semen analyzed. This is crazy."

"I had some other samples as well."

"More semen? The desk clerk, right?"

"No, just other things I'm curious about."

"What's really going on, Roci? I thought we were friends and in all this together. Why can't you talk to me, tell me what you're really up to? I know you've got some kind of agenda going."

"You just have to be a little patient, Jason."

"I just want to know what I'm getting into with you. That's a fair question, isn't it?"

"We just have to wait until I can give you a good answer. You deserve that, and it should be soon. I'm just counting on your physical desire for me to keep you interested until you can learn the whole truth." She wouldn't say anything else, was content to look at the scenery and scan the radio stations.

So that was Jason's fence to straddle — an intense curiosity about this strange woman and an intense desire for sexual union with her. Was it the traditional cock vs. brain dilemma? He just knew he was compelled to stay with her — in anticipation of a thrilling adventure. But she was certainly in charge here. He admitted that to himself. So he knew he should just drop his usual, phony macho lover demeanor. He was a good person down deep, without the airs, he felt. This might be an opportunity for once, to have a sincere relationship with a female, just be himself, whoever that was. He would just have to be cool here and go with the flow, find the answers maybe like gold nuggets in the stream, as he explored. It would require time and patience, and he would have to be ever-perceptive.

They talked, listened to music, had lunch in a fast-food restaurant. She chose a salad plate. He found that she had some interesting viewpoints, and the peculiarities in her speech and behavior seemed to be going away.

Regarding his job promoting and advertising floor tiles, she wondered why people had to be persuaded to buy something, why they couldn't just decide on their own. She couldn't accept his rationale of consumer education if there were schools and homes for that purpose.

And the environment. She couldn't believe that there were no lakes and streams where people could still drink freely since people had been here only what she considered a short time. She thought the air was acceptable here but said she had been warned to be cautious in cities.

And the mountains. Spectacular, she thought. She was from a place of grassy hills, plains of grain, fruit and nut trees and often cold wind. He guessed it must be Nebraska and she told him again that he was perceptive. Still, he didn't know about fruit and nut trees in Nebraska. She was noncommittal.

Looking at the snowy peaks of the Rockies on his Colorado highway map picture, she became more enthusiastic. "I want to go as high as we can go, Jason. Can we do that?" she asked anxiously.

He wanted to say no several different ways, but then he couldn't. "We just might give it a shot," he said.

"And that means?…"

He just had to quit using colloquialisms. "It means we'll do the very best we can — working together."

She smiled at him so spectacularly that he almost drove off the road. "I like that," she said, and his heart wailed out in hope that she would fall in love with him. His mind was twisted with ways he could make it so.

They stopped at a fresh produce stand on a roadside. She was fascinated with the pot-bellied Mexican farmer who sacked the goods and his weathered wife who took the money. She bought some of almost everything, cherries, apricots, plums, peppers, apples, and two kinds of squash. They washed them in a stream by a roadside park and then, for good measure, with a bucket of water from the rest room, laying back and eating the raw food and trying to coax down an especially loud bird, a large gray squawker who had been to the garbage cans here before.

"Do you like this kind of food?" she asked him earnestly, plum juice wet on her petite chin.

"Sure, I like it. It's natural. It's good." He would still agree with anything she said without thinking about it. He was pretty much hopeless.

"You eat a lot of dead animals, don't you?"

"Yeah, well, nobody eats live ones," he said, with a grin. She only looked concerned.

He quickly added: "What I mean is, they do have to kill them. It's a mean, distasteful business. I'm not into it."

"Do you eat them?"

"Well, yes, I'm guilty of that. Nothing like a good cheeseburger, maybe a BLT.

"It's none of my business," she said quickly. "I was just curious about why it persists."

"What?"

"Cannibalism."

41

"Wait a minute. Whoa! I don't think there are many cannibals left."

"But you eat many kinds of animals, mammals, birds, fish, reptiles."

"We don't eat people. I kind of try to avoid reptiles, too," he joked again.

"Don't you feel any kinship toward the other animals?"

"Well," he said, brow furrowed. "I don't know. I know there are animals we don't eat, like horses, dogs, cats, apes, field mice. The ones we do, I guess we figure we have dominion over everything, you know, all the animals, earth and seas it says in the Bible, so I guess we human animals, so to speak, we decide. Maybe primitive man had to start eating meat to survive at all. Maybe God intended for cows to live awhile and then get made into steaks and ground round. I don't know."

"Where did you get this...dominion over everything, do you think?"

"It's God-given, I think. I'm a religious person, if you want to know, and I think God created man, man sinned and fell from grace and is still paying for it. That's the way things are. You wanted to know about all this bullshit in the world — and that's it. That seems to be where it came from."

"Do you think you're to blame for what your ancestors did? How many of them? Do you think everything here is...not of grace?"

"Not all of it. I love the natural part. People have fucked up, excuse me, most everything they've touched because of greed and selfishness, lack of a spiritual center. Shit! Me included. But I don't think of all that when I get up in those mountains. To me, it's like fresh and clean and pure and beautiful up there. Those snow-covered peaks are like cathedrals; the streams are like holy water. Sometimes I'd like to just get lost up there if there was any way to survive without heavy-duty hardship. Then I realize that's not possible. We've got the ball down here, people I mean, and we've got to play the game day after day. There's no way to escape except for a week or so every now and then. We don't run the world; it runs us."

"But you said you had dominion."

"Well, maybe dominion means we have all the responsibility and none of the authority."

"You don't need the authority. You have a very wise and loving and compassionate God. You all know the way. It's to live in love. Then the way will be readily shown to you. You are all just determined not to do it. It's too hard for most of you. So you take the hard way, ironically, of doing everything on your own."

He thought about it. "You're right. It is all up to us though, isn't it? And then, too, I might live in love and get my ass shot off by the guy down the street, who lives in shit."

"Have you ever heard of celestial protection? You have the one supreme and perfect gift from God. That gift is life itself. For good measure, he gives you free will. What more would you dare ask for? It rests on you and your brothers and sisters as to what you do with it. And there's a tiny spark of God inside to show you the way."

"Ummm. Like a pilot light, huh? How do you know so much? Are you a Ph.D. or something, or a minister?"

"Does it matter? I doubt that you want my advice, however. A mere woman. I don't know why I present it."

"I appreciate your advice very much. You have a perfect sense of the way things should be. I can see that. And I wish to God it was all reality."

"You have to work for that reality. It isn't given to you, Jason. Giving you…the Garden of Eden didn't work."

"Boy, that parable has been twisted into a lot of contortions to suit the needs of organized religion."

"What do you think about it?" she asked.

"Man disobeyed God — and paid the price."

"And woman."

"Yeah, her too. I meant mankind."

"Do you think about that story much?"

"As a matter of fact, I do. Sometimes I think if I could get to the kernel of that story, understand the real truth of what happened, without all the heavy-handed interpretation of all the power-grabbing churches over the centuries, maybe I'd understand everything. Seems like the whole thing might be explained right there. It might even give me something to write about."

"Do you need something?"

"Sure," said Jason. "All I have are ideals. What I need is a story, a little bit of plot, some conflict, a few interesting characters."

"Well," she said, "you never know who you might meet. I might even introduce you to a friend of mine. He is like a mentor to me. I think he might enjoy meeting you, and sharing what he knows about publishing."

"Is he like you?"

"You know, we're all different, Jason," she said thoughtfully. Did you know that no two people on Earth are alike, or ever have been, or ever will be?'

"So is God just trying to get it right?" he said flippantly, and then regretted it.

"Well, you know, in all the billions of worlds in time and space, there are surely no two personalities exactly alike either. Did you, perhaps, ever think of that?"

"Ummm. Talk about being broad-minded. Yeah, sure. It's incredulous to think that we're in the universe alone. And yet, we're really alone in our uniqueness. That's pretty heavy."

"Heavy," she mused, eyeing the passing scenery and drifting again into her own thoughts. "I thought it might be considered light." She shrugged to herself.

They rolled on up into the mountains of northern New Mexico, through Taos and onward. The air grew cooler and lighter. The campers and motor homes of retirees and tourists increasingly clogged the highway. Pasty-skinned sojourners in bright clothes lined up at service stations and gift shops to see the mountains.

Sundown filled the western sky with colors of burnt orange, violet and bronze, heightening in splendor and then fading slowly to black. They pulled into a motel in Pagosa Springs, Colorado, in the heart of the San Juan Mountains.

By that time she had plundered through all of his outdoor gear in the van and was even looking at it by flashlight. She had a massive curiosity for all things. She brought up a final something to show him.

"One more question. What are these?"

"Snowshoes. Makes it easier walking in the snow. Don't know that we'll see any, but who knows? How does this motel look?"

"It looks much like the rest of them, I think." She may have wondered why he asked.

"Great! Then maybe they have beds too," he quipped, grabbing the door handle and shifting to step outside.

"Jason," she said evenly. "We will only need one bed, a large one."

"Did my sperm pass the test?"

"My associate examined it. It looked clean and healthy."

"I think I'll do a cartwheel out here on the parking lot. How do you know?"

"I am telepathic when focused," she said. "Whatever that means to you. I suggest you save your energy."

He looked at her to catch her mood. Instead, her eyes caught him magnetically, hypnoticallly, and a subtle ecstasy thundered inside him — a powerful desire mixed with fear that she would find him wanting as a lover. Outwardly, he just returned her sweet smile, then stepped out to go after the key.

He knew that anything else he might have said might be wrong, so he said nothing. Don't mess up a good thing. She's gonna do it already! Then, while he did business with the desk clerk, all he could think about was the curse of premature ejaculation. It had happened before but...with this ravishing beauty, he felt almost confident of getting a second wind given the opportunity.

In the restaurant, he remarked how her mood seemed to be getting brighter all the time. She attributed it to gaining self-confidence with him. Somehow that put him more at ease.

She loaded a plate from the salad bar, then went back for generous seconds. Conscious of her dead meat ideas, he ordered a trout dish instead of a steak. She talked about using aquariums for growing seafood, varieties of shellfish and mollusks reproduced specifically as food for consumption and pretty much oblivious to the pain and suffering associated with killing animals. Pretty radical ideas, he thought.

"Surely they don't have those things in Nebraska," he said.

She acknowledged these were only ideas for future food generation provided the waters could be kept clean.

"You're not really from Nebraska, are you?" he said.

She looked at him with a penetrating hardness. "No," she said. "I'm not from Nebraska, but I'm not authorized to tell you where I'm from."

"You're on the run from something or somebody, aren't you?" he asked, swelled a bit from his success with the last assertion.

"No. I don't ordinarily run from anyone or anything. Only if there's danger."

"Who would authorize you to tell me who you are? Do you have a boss out there somewhere, somebody calling the shots? Is this a remake of 'Charlie's Angels'?"

"We are not angels. They are celestial personalities. But perhaps you would like to meet someone at least as interesting tonight."

"Would I?"

"Yes, he has great wisdom."

"Should I?"

"We will see. In fact, I will go now and use the telephone."

"You mean tonight? Can he possibly be in Pagosa Springs?"

"He could...drop in, perhaps. There might be some time later. He has a busy schedule, however. I will ask."

She was off to the phone. As soon as she disappeared, he left his after-dinner coffee to head toward the rest room, which was close to the phone. When he saw her at the phone, dialing, he turned quickly in another direction, circling around a partition and planter to get close to the phone and eavesdrop. He could hear most of her words from behind his camouflage of greenery.

"Darien...yes, it's Blest...I'm glad you've gotten established. Do we have all the connecting links?...I have a message for Mega. I want to know if he'll join me in a...(sounded like some kind of visit)...but can we complete a relay?...Pagosa Springs, Colorado...still have it...activate it

45

at...o'clock...p.m...It's there on the Earth map that says Exxon...BP Oil? Sure. They would be the same. Thank you, Darien...Love to you, brother."

Jason hugged the wall, heard her hang up. He waited a second longer then looked up — shocked! — to see her standing right in front of him. She appeared amused.

"And you talk about me being curious about things."

He could only laugh. "You're the biggest mystery I've ever run into," he admitted, shaking his head at his own foible. "I'm just dying to figure out who in the world you are and what you're all about. I apologize though. I'm sorry. I'm just too damned curious. I'm just...really taken with you."

"We'll see how much you want to know, Jason. I believe we can give you all you can handle."

"Whoa!" he said, still good-naturedly.

"Too late for that," she said, giving him a mischievous smile as she headed back to the table.

He was burning with questions about her but decided to junk them all for the night, the better to get laid without complications. She forgave him this shallowness given his primitive nature. After all, she was burning with questions too, and a growing desire to tear away these cumbersome and primitive clothes and ravish his body into hers.

In the room, he hardly knew where to start, but he needn't have worried. She pulled the drapes closed and put the chain latch on the door. He stood there a little uncertainly, removing his windbreaker and hanging it up as slowly as possible.

She clicked off the lamp by the bed to darken the room and made her way toward him, as he stood in the dressing alcove next to the bathroom. "A little romantic lighting, huh?" he said, as she stepped past him and clicked off the bathroom light as well.

"I have a candle in my backpack," he added as she glided past him again to the small round desk by the door and pulled the chain to douse the last lamp, filling the room with blackness.

When she turned to him, he gasped and fell back. Her eyes glowed brightly in the dark, an emerald green glow like he had never seen before. He stepped backwards against the dressing table, then sideways, knocking coathangers askew. The glowing eyes moved forward slowly. He finally retreated back into the bedroom into the corner on the other side of the bed.

"What the hell, Roci? What's going on?"

"Adventure," she said calmly. "I have to generate the energy for it."

"Oh no. Oh no. You're doing some kind of trick. What are you trying to do? What's the deal with your eyes?"

"I have a high energy level, higher than yours. It's okay. We can use it, both of us." She took a step toward him and he tried in vain to melt into the wall.

"Jason, look at me. You will see there's nothing to worry about. Can you look in my eyes?"

"I don't know if I want to. I don't know if I should. You have too much…control, or something."

"I have to be in control of this adventure. You wanted to meet Mega. I can take you to him."

"None of this makes any sense. It's too weird." He continued to avoid her eyes.

"Adventure is exploring the unknown. I thought you were ready."

He tried to squint into her eyes, still worried about the consequences, but it was too bright. "I…can't handle it. Too much glare."

"Yes, I thought there might be, but I had to see. I expected to start on a more…basic and material level anyway." She moved toward him. He stepped back and held up a hand.

"Wait a minute," he protested. "I want to know more about what's going on. I want to know where we're going and how, and I want to know who you are and what's your plan."

"I don't mind telling you the truth, Jason, but according to our information you people can't handle it."

"Don't worry. I'd believe anything at this point."

"We are extraterrestrials," she said. "Our plan is exploration. We are going to see my group's chief investigator and we will do so in an altered state, a mindvisit during which time our physical selves are still here, safe in this room. It will be real in that your visit will be one of genuine correspondence, with a fabricated physical reality added to give you a sense of security and identification.

"You're serious, aren't you?"

She laughed. "Well, we try not to be morbid…gloomy…oppressive…taciturn…stoic. We enjoy what we're doing."

"This is all pretty hard to believe, you know."

"Do you have a better idea? All you have to do is unify with me emotionally and sexually, and that should create a sufficiently strong bond to realize Mega. Do you think you can reach the precipice before orgasm so we can break the threshold together?"

"Well, we can try…" Jason was feeling better about it all the time.

"We must achieve penetration and maintain our orgasmic strength together, our bodies fully locked, in order to achieve a mindlock with

Mega," she said. "It will not be easy this first time. We may even fail, but I don't think so."

"So…we can do it?" he asked tentatively. She was unbuttoning his shirt.

"I think you can avoid a overly rapid semen explosion if we are perfectly still."

"Yes…I'll try," he enthused calmly.

"Do you think you can?" she asked pointedly.

"I think so. Yes. I think so." His heart pounded. In fact, he didn't know. He had no control when she really got after him. Seemed like it might be up to her. "I…maybe I'm a little nervous," he said shakily. "Maybe I can't even get…anything to work with."

He felt her warm breath and kisses tickle and vibrate his bare chest. Her lips lifted to warm his neck, kissing him gently, again and again. She pulled away when he gasped, leaning against the wall.

His eyes had become accustomed to the darkness and he watched her unbutton, then strip away the plaid shirt to stand bare before him. Her eyes were now a cooler green, more reassuring. Her naked breasts reflected in the light of her eyes. She grasped his head, his hair, in both hands in a firm grip and brought her breasts to his face, pressing them gently into his eyes and nose and mouth. He felt a penetrating warmth and softness. He kissed them, again and again, boiling to a near frenzy, and powerfully aroused.

Then her eyes were upon him again, close upon his face. He perspired before her unusual heat. The green eyes pulsated now, drifting him upward, inward, downward into some kind of lightness, airiness, paralysis.

Hypnotized, he closed his eyes softly in the intensity of the green glow, trembling as she embraced him lightly, aglow in calmness. They were both fully nude somehow.

In deep, interlocking embrace, they kissed furiously, then lightly, warmly, slowly, her warm mouth and hands inducing a steamy heat over his nude body. His mouth turned again to her breasts and they soon writhed naked together in the bed, his control steady, her hands exploring him ravenously, fingernails tickling his huge erection.

Soon, she slowed their lust with a finger to his lips. They rolled over to his back and she smothered him in her embrace, their mouths clasped firmly. She thrust his shaft inside her, in delicious heat and wetness. He felt their muscles working, tightening and pumping in rhythmic flow, in deep and sensuous embrace.

They did not move. They held it there, on a breathless ledge of shattering passion. Their hearts beat together; it was quiet and still. He lost control and fell helpless to a paralyzing convulsion and expulsion of climactic, vibrational ecstasy. It poured helplessly from him. He felt her body tighten into rigors as well; she quivered all over, let out a whimpering gasp, and fell heavily upon him. His head felt dizzy. He lost his balance into a dizzying whirlpool and fell away. He heard a giant sucking sound and they were suddenly swept away.

He opened his eyes to a soft kiss on his lips, seeing clearly the room around him, Roci standing there in jeans and shirt as before, the room mostly as it was but him fully clothed too. He felt remarkably rested and alert, fully calm and comfortable. She looked at him benevolently.

"Do you feel all right, Jason?"

"Yes, I feel fine." He sat up on the bed, which had been made-up and covered with a green spread.

"It appears you had a nice nap, Jason. We're going to see Mega as soon as you're ready."

He worked his mouth, felt his hands.

"You will feel numb," she said, "and that may be a little strange, but it's the way it should be. You shouldn't worry. This is only real in the mental sense; your physical body is at rest beyond the alternate reality of this fabrication."

"If you say so." He felt a little weird.

"You'll feel better in a few minutes. We're going to walk out of the motel and over to see Mega. It will be good for you to walk. And remember, the numbness is good. It gives you a feeling of strength, of being impervious to anything at all that could harm you. You feel that you can't be hurt."

"Can I?"

"Only by accident," she said, reaching out to take his hands and gently pull him to his feet. "You'll need to get your shoes on," she said. "We wanted to leave something for you to do."

He sat back down and put them on. It seemed to go okay. And he knew his even disposition would give him the control he needed with a strange, new kind of confidence. He was anxious to get on with it.

"So, is this kind of a dream state? Is that why I feel…kind of light but also numb…like a big old, lightweight boulder."

"Well, actually for your particular life form, you'll just have to tell us," said Roci. "We're all of the same pattern but there are differences."

"I feel strange, but actually I feel good about this. I'm kind of energized."

"You seem to be suitably impressionable, Jason," she said. "That's good."

They stepped out the motel door, her leading the way, and across the open balcony to the back of the lot. There, they descended the stairs, past the drink machines where a fat man jiggled the coin return and beat with the heel of his hand, seeking to recover his lost coins. Why is this all happening, Jason wondered.

They climbed over a wire fence and walked out across a dark field. Moonlight washed them as they left the lights of the motel and the boulevard of restaurants and stores behind. They crossed a dry creek and climbed up the other bank into a large open pasture.

"Why are we doing this?" he asked her. "I thought this was a mind experience. It's been quite a walk."

"We think it should be real for you, Jason, convincingly real so that you can understand that this is truly happening. Mind experiences are as real as physical ones. Also, we're studying the various linkages and what we can do with them. Don't forget. We're new here, and learning too."

"What? I don't understand."

"Of the different realities, it's the physical that is most real to you. So we make the mindvisit complete by creating a full scenario. It's a greater adventure if it all seems very physically real. The element of danger even appears, as a thrilling embellishment."

They were on somebody's farm, an imaginary, mind-fabricated farm, he supposed, and soon enough there before them was the proof of it — cows — black-and-white spotted ones, Holsteins, he knew, imaginary Holsteins, standing placidly and chewing by moonlight. Who was fabricating all this if they were physically back in the motel?

The big moon cow faces showed some curiosity about them but they didn't seem inclined to inject themselves into the scene any more than as backdrop.

"Cows!" he said. "This is cool."

"They're wonderful cows." The deep masculine voice behind him turned Jason around to see a tall and solidly built man in a pair of bib overalls and plaid shirt, and an Anaheim Angels baseball cap. Long, straight hair, shining white in the moonglow, hung on his shoulders and he looked resolutely at Jason as he stood with an arm draped over one of the Holsteins. He was maturely handsome, with dancing, perceptive eyes, and a wry smile.

Jason couldn't say anything.

"The cow has a gentle, loving disposition that you all could learn from," said the man, leaving the placid cow to come and stand before them, his eyes still firmly on Jason. "I know, of course, that their docility has led to their enslavement and slaughter, he said, "You are smarter and stronger than these beasts, but you are also more evil."

"Thank you for coming, Mega." said Roci.

"I'm pleased to give you some time," he responded in his kind and assuring baritone. "I wanted to meet this individual whom you believe may have potential." His eyes searched across Jason's face, looked inside the eyes.

"Are you a farmer?" Jason asked uncertainly, quickly realizing it was a stupid question. "I guess you aren't, actually."

Roci and Mega were both amused. "In some ways, yes." he said. "I'm Mega 117 and I work with the resourceful woman who brought you here. I only hoped that my imagination would provide you with an empathetic and appropriate heartland vision that would prevent your being unduly startled by my presence. Do you like the farm?"

"Yes. I'm just trying to comprehend all this."

"I like your farmers very well. They're plucky, resourceful, and mean no one harm as a rule. This is why I chose this scenario. We're trying not to move too fast, Jason," said Mega, "but maybe you're ready to move on." They both looked at him quizzically.

"I'm okay. I'm all eyes and ears."

Roci and Mega looked at one another for a second, then burst out laughing.

Jason couldn't help laughing either.

"What a vision," said Mega in good humor. Nothing but eyes and ears. A rather cluttered montage of a scenario."

He raised his hand to his mouth to reveal a small mechanism in his palm. "Lights up," he said softly, and suddenly across the field there emerged a huge bank of lights, bright white, red, yellow and green. Jason squinted and looked with shaded eyes to the large form of a compact and circular alien spacecraft.

There were several strong supportive legs, three of them holding mounted spotlights that shone onto the main body. The ship contoured in layers, robust platelike cylinders, the largest in the center. It contained a row of round portholes, many of which reflected variously colored lights from within.

The ship rather resembled a colorful spinning top. The topmost circular compartment could have been a control module, Jason thought. On its side, he now saw an emblem of blue — the familiar circle encasing a bird in flight.

"This is my personal cruiser," said Mega, "with the emblem of our PeacePower mission. Perhaps you would like to come aboard."

"Yes. Will we fly away?"

"Not tonight. I had in mind a conversation to let you ask whatever questions you have. I'm curious as to what they will be."

"I have a million questions."

"We don't have time for all of them, but we'll get to a few. So let's go inside."

Jason turned to look at Roci, but found she had disappeared.

Before he could speak, Mega did so: "She delivered you to me and has no need to be active for awhile, so she leaves you in my care."

"She's gone?"

"She'll be waiting for you. Come follow me." Mega turned and walked toward the light-encrusted spacecraft and Jason followed. From underneath the craft, a panel opened and a smooth walkway rolled down to meet them. Mega walked up into the interior and Jason followed. In this state, whatever it was, he felt little apprehension at all.

Inside, he watched as Mega seated himself in a large cushioned Early American easy chair. He was now suddenly dressed in a long white robe, the blue circle emblem and bird in flight centered on the front. The room was decorated in traditional Early American pieces, with another easy chair there for Jason, a magazine rack and coffee table, shelves of books, and a modern home entertainment center of sturdy oak on one side, containing the most modern of home electronics. Plants and hanging baskets here and there made the small room cozier. It didn't remotely resemble an aircraft or spacecraft.

"Have a seat, Jason," said Mega. "As you can see, I have been indulging in various earthly pursuits of reading, watching, listening, learning. These things reveal much of what you're about, and it's our custom to explore these things fully on each planetary visit."

"You go to other places? This is just one of many?"

"There are tens of thousands of worlds to visit, although most of them are expecting our visits. The universe is very much larger than most of you know or even imagine. You are only a small part of a massive intergalactic administration. We explore these worlds for adventure, enjoyment, enlightenment, in fascination, and often to implant positive gain in your continuing evolutionary march toward oneness with God. On this particular planet, we have to be...undercover, as you would say, since you're not aware of the interplanetary system.

"God? You believe in God then."

"Of course. A universe of universes such as ours can't happen by accident. You would know this much as do many thousands of other worlds but for the unusual circumstances here, which involves the quarantine of your planet because of the rebellious disobedience of your planetary prince, not to mention a few other unfortunate events of history. These are really too complicated for you to get into at this moment and they aren't of great importance right now. They're history."

"What will you do here? How will you change things?"

"We get our ideas for action from what we will call Mission Control. Much of what is to come remains to be seen, to be revealed to us, but it's very likely that we won't inspire or effect any significant changes at all here.

You are supposed to evolve much as you are. We've generally been instructed to leave citizens to their own situation, even if evolution has suffered some deviations, as it has here. However, we've been into universe exploration for a long time, and we've made some subtle contributions here and there."

"Well, you could help a lot. We have many problems. You could cure disease, perhaps stop our senseless warring, destruction of the environment. Why wouldn't you help?"

"It's your adventure, not ours. You're like babies in the universe. You've ascended from implanted life here to achieve what you have so far, and it's been remarkable, but there is a vast distance of ascension for you that you cannot imagine. When this mortal life is over, if you have spiritual value, you will move forward into more enlightened adventures beyond this one in a succession of mansion worlds specifically designed for you. You won't be flesh then, you'll have new and, shall we say, streamlined bodies."

"Eternal life, then? That is a reality?"

"If you want to be part of the adventure, then you can be — living, learning and serving in successive worlds for ascending mortals of time and space. It's not that novel here. Your Christians know enough about this for their salvation, and so do other religious faithful, and even people who aren't religious. The message has been sometimes distorted and opaque, deliberately and inadvertently, but it's basically sound. And our loving God wants to make it as easy as possible. Faith is the key.

"You already know that, and that's remarkable because you have no physical evidence of these hundreds of other worlds of even your local universe, no contact with them, no absolute proof that there is a great deity on the Isle of Paradise, as there surely is."

"The Bible has it right then?"

"Generally speaking. The message is there, though it may be time that you were given some major corrections to it, less reverence for it, and a far greater amplification of the truth about your world, your history and the divine plan for each of you. It will be a kind of…Correcting Time, I believe the Melchizedeks call it."

"Perhaps you will give us some…truer paths then."

"There are as many paths to God as there are souls to walk them," said Mega. "We will see. Of course, we're only mortals, like you. We don't put together celestial plans, and that's where much of universal guidance resides.

"I want to know my part in all this. Have I got a part?"

"For now, show your guest around. Pretend she's a friend, no more. Although I'm well aware of your intimacy. I admit that this surprises me a little, that she would take her adventure this far."

53

"I guess I'm inferior, huh?"

"I wouldn't think you're tuned into all of the sensory circuits of the human body, even as undeveloped as it is. I doubt that you orchestrate sexual ecstasy very well, but I really don't know."

"She's a beautiful and insightful, umm, person, of course," said Jason. "Maybe I can learn something."

"Far beyond lust pleasures, I hope. I must tell you that this has all happened by chance, perhaps even divine chance, and it can be a wonderful learning experience for you, Jason, if you can level and center your thoughts about it. Can you do that?"

"Beats me. I'm not on your wave length yet. I…just want to say I'll work with you. Maybe you'll be generous and give us a cancer cure or something."

"We're not authorized to make that kind of a population shift but maybe we could leave another species of fruit tree or a more inclusive microchip or something — an innovation that couldn't be traced, probably through some, shall we say, inspired humans."

"I just want you to know I'll help. And I'll surely be glad to carry Roci anywhere she wants to go."

"Just remember, Jason, that she's never been out on an exploration like this before. This is all a new experience for her too. She graduated from the space academy in late 21z, about an earth year ago, served on an asteroid blaster for…awhile, and qualified at a regional audition for this tour. It's her first, so everything is very new and especially exciting for her."

"She's exciting. Believe me."

"So I'm counting on you to take care of her."

"Me? You're counting on me?"

"You're the host."

"Okay. I'll take care of it. She's safe with me."

Mega perused him with a serious eye. "She sees goodness inside you. I trust that her confidence is well-placed."

This tall host in the long white robe seemed more ominous now. His eyes hardened on Jason and sent his mind scurrying with questions about a possible dark side to this cosmic scenario. Jason worried…is this all goodness and light or…

"She can count on me for my best effort," he told Mega. "We're going to avoid any more problems if we possibly can. We're going to the mountains to see a few friends if that's still okay. She said she loves the mountains."

"Ours are mostly worn down," said Mega. "We have a lot of hills."

"The Rockies are…nice," said Jason.

Mega stared at him for a few seconds. "Even I can find a better complimenting adjective for the Rockies than 'nice'," he said. "I believe this conversation is effectively over. I'm going to send you back to…Roci."

"They're better than 'nice,'" said Jason. "I've got better adjectives, and I want to know more about what's going on, much more. Do we have to call it off?"

"I have other appointments," said Mega. "Getting established in a new place is always a busy time. Do you want to walk back to the motel with Roci, or get an instant transport…something like a wake-up call."

"What's better?"

"It depends on whether you want to test this dreamscape a little more with another moonlight walk. You could pet the cows. Or whether you want to wake up in the motel room and maybe…who knows, go to the bathroom."

"Let's try the quick way. Will Roci be there?"

"Sure. It's you and her. Hope you enjoy yourself. Are you ready?'

"Guess so," said Jason.

"This is crude but effective," said Mega, reaching over and slapping Jason across the cheek.

Jason awakened, feeling a sting on his cheek, blinking a moment and looking about the motel room. Roci's beautiful nude body lay beside him on the bed, the crack in the drapes carrying a shaft of light across her peaceful face, looking upright in calm sleep. She was a vision of perfect and beautiful repose.

He remembered the visit, the conversation — Whew! — but was too tired to think about it. He got up, went to the bathroom and returned to bed, overwhelmed by the desire to sleep.

Mega, at the other end, pulled the sensory helmet from his head and rubbed down the tinglers. If Blest had to be down there on her own, he reasoned, the situation could have been a lot worse.

He began to think about allowing Jason to visit the lost colony with them.

FOUR: *Into Separate Realities*

She pulled open the drapes and flooded the room with sunlight. The rays embraced Jason's sleeping form and roused him.

She had been up since 4:40 and had been out exploring the brightening townscape, collecting the first newspaper of the day immediately after the delivery truck pulled away, walking up and down the streets of Pagosa Springs and wondering why more residents were not out enjoying the coming of the new day. The denizens she had encountered had grumbled and looked unhappy.

He squinted to look at her against the light flooding in from the window. She sat at the small table, smiling, her arm lifted and forefinger pointing down at a steaming cup of coffee and a styrofoam-encased breakfast complete with plastic fork and spoon. She didn't speak, but somehow he knew that she was wishing him a good morning and inquiring if he slept well. Not bad, he thought, without speaking.

From the bathroom, Jason came back to sit in front of her, sampling the coffee.

It's still hot, and so is breakfast. She was communicating to him through some kind of mind opening, he realized, and he thought about thanking her in his still sleepy mind. You're welcome, he received. Scrambled eggs and something called hashed crowns, she thought further to him.

"We're growing a little closer," she said aloud. "If we can communicate scrambled eggs via thoughtwaves this soon, I have hopes for being able to feed you...powerful intellectual sustenance as well."

"I'm receptive. I guess. You know...I remember last night. I remember some kind of trip we took, out in the pasture. A man was out there, in a white robe, with a weathered but handsome face, very peaceful eyes, hypnotic. This was all coming to me while I was washing my face just now."

He looked at her with a question in his eyes. "Maybe I should have looked in the mirror to see if I'm really all here?"

"Do you feel it really happened?"

"Yeah. I think so. Did it?"

"It did in the sense of internal reality, yes," she said, "though your body was able to remain here and be refreshed by sleep after somewhat superlative and...exotic sex. Only your mind traveled. Mega was pleased with you. He wants us to carry you to Edenroot."

"To where?"

"Edenroot, an ancient garden and orchard we tried to establish here, believe me, a very long time ago. We can speculate together there on your so-called fall from grace. We can see if it ties together with our efforts here. We will be there to watch some of it. Should be exciting!"

"Whew! Sounds like a pretty big trip. Wait a minute. You mean you really are from another planet. I'm supposed to believe this?"

"I would say that's your first order of business. Then we can move on."

Jason sipped the coffee. He remembered the green eyes now...the deep sensuality of the sex...the explosiveness of climax, a threshold of some kind...Mega, the Holsteins...The Early American den fashioned inside the spacecraft...Mega's personal cruiser, he had been told.

"We only have to explore our ideas and imaginations," said Roci, "open our minds to the spirit personalities who will guide us, who are always there for that purpose, to help in mental transit. We know that we were here to help your planetary prince civilize and develop the evolving tribes. This is the way it is in the universe. Those who know and have more help those who have less. But Urantia, this is what your planet is called on the official registry, was very young, and a major challenge. Today? We are optimistic about your coming progress. The celestials have promised some new energies will be opened to you soon."

"Are you saying we're going back to the colony? We're going back in time?"

"Sure. I thought that's what you would want."

"Yeah. Right. We'll do it."

"You said we would be at the campground at mid-afternoon. Mega suggested that he come visit us after dark for an after-dinner drink and another visit."

Jason laughed. "Yeah, maybe we'll have brandy and coffee after our cheese and crackers. Maybe he'll bring it."

"Mega is very resourceful, and kind of theatrical too. He likes to play roles. I'm sure he'll find a way to dramatize a little. But we will have to effect another bodylock and enter into an altered state to bring him in, if you approve."

"Yes, I remember."

"Is it all right?"

"It's more than all right," he said calmly, digging purposefully into the scrambled eggs.

Then he thought about all of the other plans, the other reality — the hiking and mescaline trip with his friends at Loch Vail. He blurted out his concerns to her; how could they do it all. Could they fit all this and his friends and the hiking and camping into a finite amount of time.

"Give them your waking consciousness," she said with a wry but confident smile, "and give me your, we will say, alternate reality. We will use the rest time. There is much of that available."

At a nearby pharmacy, she peeled off another hundred dollar bill and bought an armload of magazines. She devoured them cover-to-cover, not missing a page, as the van rumbled north from Pagosa Springs. They fell before her, page after speedy page…Psychology Today, Newsweek, Time, Playboy, Sports Illustrated, True Confessions, Police Gazette, Better Homes and Gardens, Outdoors, Backpacker, Rolling Stone, Organic Farming, Prevention, Vogue. He drove on.

Soon she had finished them all and announced with a sigh: "I haven't been to many places, Jason, but this one is surely exciting — wild and untamed people throughout the world doing aggressive things, power struggles among governments, businesses, ideologies, all permeated with drive and desire. One could spend a lifetime here."

"Yeah," said Jason. "I guess so. I always thought that's what I'd do anyway." He couldn't believe that he knew what he knew, or thought he did, and was taking it so calmly. He felt he was imbued with some kind of numbing, yet mesmerizing, sensually opening, aura. He hoped she wasn't going to turn him into a zombie.

"I'm sorry you can't travel elsewhere in the local universe," said Roci, "but I think you can stay amply entertained here. And there are challenges here that are found nowhere else in the system."

"Well, that sounds pretty good, I guess, or does it?" he replied. "I think we have plenty and enough challenges. I'd like to get a little more of that peace of mind stuff I've been reading about."

"You didn't tell me why you were sleeping there alone, by yourself," she said. "We know that you usually go into natural areas to kill animals, but you told me you personally don't do this."

"It was just a place I had been to before, with friends," he said. "I had good memories of it. I needed a place to camp for the night after I left Dallas, so that was it. A little out of the way, but I like the natural outdoors, away from noise and people sometimes. It helps me think and kind of get my life together, my purpose in life."

"What is that?"

"Well, actually, I don't know yet," he said with a laugh. "That's what I'm always asking myself. I don't really like my job, to tell the truth. I went to journalism school, I used to be a newspaper reporter, a feature story writer, but I kind of just gravitated out of that into corporate journalism. I edited a company magazine for a utility company first. Then I went to FloorGem and got into advertising there. The company needed a program and I wound up developing it."

"Advertising the company? Telling people about it?"

"Our product lines. The stuff we sell to make a buck. We talked about it. The more we sell, the better off the company and the people working for it."

"Do people need these products, these floor and wall tiles?"

"Yeah. They're useful. They're attractive. Easy to clean, you know. A lot of things go into making a home, you know. I guess you do."

"I think you could take pride in producing and providing tiles, but I don't understand the necessity of selling them, or anything else. People working together could provide everything all of you need if there was a central authority to establish order in the fulfilling of needs. You would not need to sell the tiles if you were being provided food, shelter, adventure and entertainment."

"And how would we get these things without money? How would they be divided by need?"

"Collect your greatest intelligence and bestow it upon a mind network, of course, incorporating all or most experiences. You should be trying harder to avoid all the competitive clamor and establish order based on the authoritative wisdom you have. Working together you could expand upon it with incredible speed. One of the first ideas is to balance production and consumption and plan for each of your selves productive schedules of work and play for your mortal days here. You'll help to achieve that after you have put down your doomsday weapons and devoted more resources to cleaning and safeguarding the environment."

"Maybe," he said doubtfully. "Maybe you should stay here and help. I would work with you with my best effort. You could count on that."

"We will see what happens," she said cautiously. "We have other things to do. This is your planet, not ours."

"You never told me what happened to you. You crashed in that wilderness. What happened?"

"I think I should show you," she said, "so that you will understand more about me and so you'll know that our mission is more than just an exercise in creative imagination. It can become a matter of life and death."

"I don't imagine I could think of it in any broader or more serious terms, to tell the truth," said Jason.

"But in more real ones, I'm sure you can. Perhaps we'll take a nap after lunch. In intimacy and closeness, even without the sexual climax, I think we can effect this readback, ummm, in other words, a reading of my memories

59

of what happened. I will relive and dramatize it for you, even though it will be somewhat unpleasant."

"Well, I don't want you to ever suffer anything unpleasant."

"It's okay," she assured him. "It's actually okay." She gave him a smile.

"Well, then, let's actually do it," Jason said with a shrug.

They stopped at a roadside park and he lugged the ice chest over to a picnic table, which they covered with his rain parka. They shared a meal of cheese, nuts, fruits and lettuce. Later, they walked down beside a stream and watched the water flow in the shade of a large cottonwood, she lying romantically in his arms. He was learning from her the beauty of silence and observation.

"I can imagine I died and went to Heaven," he said. "Is there a Heaven then? Would you know such a lofty question as that?"

"Of course. Everything didn't happen by accident. There's an amazing cohesion in the time and space worlds. Once you understand how the creation works, then you know how God works. And you know God."

"Well, what's the ticket to what they call salvation anyway?" Jason asked, a little flippantly.

"To accept that God is your Father for all that means, and love your brothers and sisters as a Father would intend, for all that means. Everything else flows naturally to goodness out of that. Of course, you're not supposed to be anything close to perfect. You're ascended from lower mammals except for some strains introduced from celestial biology projects."

"What about Hell?"

"No such place. It's amazing what primitive people come up with. And since it's very old, you automatically think it's good. This is illogical."

"So there's just one place to go — no Hell?"

"If you decide to go at all. You can give it up at any time. The ascension plan is there for mortal personalities who want to strive forward. The opportunity is there."

"Well, then why wouldn't anyone choose to go on? I mean, once we pass over and understand the whole picture?" he asked.

"Indeed. But once you know the plan you need to all the more live in love. It is more of a rejection to the God Father since you are knowing. You need to honestly strive to do it, no matter how imperfectly. And when you fall down, just get your Father's constant forgiveness and go for it again."

Jason felt very sleepy. "Boring, huh, my struggling earth man. I am inducing a stupor." She pulled herself up and rolled him gently over on the grass. He was too weak to resist.

"I'm just wasting my life here," he mumbled, "looking for good times all the time. Why don't I…" He yawned mightily and was asleep.

"I think not," said Roci, looking into his peaceful face. "I think you can do better than that."

Some time must have passed, but not necessarily.

He opened his eyes in darkness, listening to a steady, low-pitched whirring sound. He raised up from the cramped floor and realized he was lying behind two people sitting in a cockpit, close quarters, with an array of lighted controls in front of them. They did not notice him at all.

A male pilot was on his left, Roci on his right, both with helmets, blue zippered suits, and firm grips on the controls.

Outside the window, he saw the craft's short, swept-back wings streaking through the night, glowing slightly in a strange, soft light. The craft was moving at a rapid pace.

A radio squawked with static and a nasal voice talking about an unidentified aircraft. Jason looked closer at the pilots. Their helmets were connected by multi-threaded cable to an array of colorfully lighted controls in front and above them in the cockpit.

"He's underneath, five hundred feet. I will take command," said the man, flipping a switch. The craft settled down to a duller whir, deeper, slower. They were streaking across the night sky. "We have him. Quick now — drain all codes and commands."

Roci immediately reached for the panel with both hands — pressing three buttons simultaneously with her stretched fingers. The squawky voice on the radio continued: "I can't control the plane," it said in a panic. "I'm…being carried forward by something — some force! I've got no controls. None!"

"He's getting agitated," said Roci. "I've got what we need. Let's turn him free."

"Fine," said the other pilot. "Disengage." The ship seemed to break into another dimension, cruising easier now, with a lighter drone. "Circle back. We'll extend speed to leave his radar field." The craft rolled upward, turning them bottom-side up. Jason grasped the seats hard, hanging on desperately, dizzily until the ship righted itself again.

"He has turned to pursue us," said Roci calmly.

"Call up his command sequences," said the other pilot. "We'll pull one that calls him off. But be careful. It's fully armed. Don't get the wrong — No!

"Emergency!" the man called. "Activate shield! I've accidentally triggered a missile. Evasive —"

A ripping, clanging explosion tore sparks out of the control panel and opened a gaping hole from the top of the cockpit. The rush of night air thundered through the gash that exposed them now to the sky. Jason flinched and gripped tight. Sparks and rushing noise blew all around them.

Smoke gushed out of the floor, swirling up into the turbulent rush. The craft rolled and dove out of control.

Jason struggled to get up. Roci fought desperately to get out of her helmet. The other pilot was slumped unconscious, his helmet cracked open and blood trickling down his face.

"Donello! Wake up, please!" she pleaded. Jason's knuckles gripped white on the seat. He had no physical energy, no real presence here, was helpless to intervene.

She was gradually getting the ship slowed and under control, on an even keel, but it was pouring black smoke. "We are stricken. Missile. Going down. Mark location. Donello hurt," she called into the radio. "Shield not sufficient. Fire. Will try to eject."

Jason saw that they were going down steadily. The tree-studded, rocky landscape was looming up larger, whipping past. No doubt to where I found her, Jason thought. How the hell do I get out of here!

She was trying a succession of switches and buttons, but nothing seemed to work. "Donello!" she called again, trying to revive her co-pilot by shaking him with her free hand. She pulled off his helmet to see that his head had been smashed. "Don-o! Please!" She shook him in vain. Blood trickled from his lips.

"I've got to help. What can I do?" Jason hollered in frustration, but she didn't hear or see him, it being only a re-creation. He realized anew that he was just an unseen observer. But could he be killed? That was the crisis of the moment. He pinched his arm. Still numb.

Fire was engulfing the wings now. She again talked hurriedly into the microphone. "Say again. Satellite 4ee to Control. We're damaged. We're going down. Controls out. Ejection out too. Donello critical. Need best idea."

"Manual takeover," said a calm, clear voice. "Try a low drop with a rocket booster if operable. Maneuver 12. We'll sight your elevation and give you a go-buzz. Do it well, Blest."

She reached back past Jason. He stared wide-eyed as she pulled from a compartment a kind of backpack with heavy crossed straps and a single cylinder that appeared to be a rocket. But there was a crack. Gas spewed from it. She examined it quickly and with a frown, but hurriedly pulled it onto her back anyway, then unfastened Donello's belt and pulled his limp body against hers. Leaking or not, it appeared their best chance. They would leap out and ignite the rocket when they were lower.

The craft was growing very hot by then, flames leaping from the wings, the acrid smoke choking Jason's throat, burning his eyes. From somewhere she had pulled a small cable, which she encircled around Donello's unconscious body and then fastened it onto her own belt. Jason could make out the outline of the rocky plain coming up fast.

Then the buzz. She pulled herself and her heavy burden up from the seat and, with a strong blow from her forearm, tore the rest of the top away, igniting a burst from the rocket pack and sending the two of them soaring out the top.

Jason rose also, lifting upward like a spirit, magically, out of the smoke and watched from his weightless flight as she struggled to hold onto her companion, keep them aloft with the sputtering rocket pack. But it faltered, spewed loudly and then died. They began falling.

She clung desperately to her stricken co-pilot as they dropped earthward in the dark sky. The rocket re-ignited to slow their descent again and start a precarious climb, but only briefly, then choked and faltered again. She held more tightly to the slumped, bleeding body as they fell again.

The craft crashed and exploded into flames up ahead of them and they tumbled faster, harder, the cable slipping. She finally lost her hold on Donello when they plummeted hard into a mesquite tree.

She came crashing through the foliage, branches cracking, and quickly landed with a jarring thud down on the dark ground.

Soaring on unseen wings, Jason's dreambody circled the flaming wreckage and sailed back to where they had fallen. He dropped lightly onto his feet on the ground. For the first time, he noticed his body seemed to be at least partially transparent. With his hand, he reached right through himself.

He saw her writhing on the ground there in the gathering dawn, glided up beside her, feeling with her some of the tragedy of the experience.

In a moment, she tried to lift her head, look at the flames up ahead, licking up into the night sky and dancing over her face. She squinted and stared groggily at the bright blur of the wreckage as it came slowly into focus. It was being devoured by fire. The pain in her leg grew more intense as she tried to roll over, and she felt, for the first time, the aching pain of her head, the soreness of all her muscles.

Leaping spears of light illuminated the bulk of Donello's dark body lying nearby. She struggled to get to her knees and crawl toward him, fighting to regain her full senses and devise a plan of escape if the inhabitants came. They were volatile; she had to worry. And she knew she wasn't scheduled to be revealed to them.

She reached Donello and rolled over his body to see that his skull was truly crushed. He was dead. The rocket pack delivered enough power to slow her descent or her body would have been smashed too. Breaking down, she fell over against him, crying in anguish, wailing suddenly and loudly into the night air. Watching, Jason's body quivered with feeling for her. His

63

heart ached and seemed to fall empty into an empty darkness. She was in deep pain.

But, face streaked with tears and blood, Roci quickly recovered. She struggled to her feet and moved toward the flaming craft, dragging her leg.

The heat seared her face, but she reached the craft, jerked open the rear supply compartment and pulled out a field vest — a valuable survival tool in this primitive land. It was already smoking. Trying to run, she fell to her knees with a painful gasp, and strained to crawl away from the fire, finally stopping to recapture her breath, clutching the vest.

There seemed to be no one nearby, but she couldn't take a chance. She mustered enough energy to pull herself to a sitting position, propping herself against the boulder where Jason had found her. From the field vest, she pulled a small vial, uncapped it and put a tiny pill on her tongue. It would soon quell the pain, she knew, and give her a temporary burst of energy and calmness.

Jason watched from his cocoon of unreality, aching inside that he couldn't help. He couldn't stand to see her hurting.

In a moment, she seemed calmer to Jason, but also a bit dazed. She pushed herself to her feet and made her way unsteadily toward Donello's body. She knew she couldn't communicate with her people, that she was largely on her own for awhile, but knew also they would be here when possible. And she had to hide the body in case the humans came sooner. She might be able to wait for a rescue or might have to make an escape if the humans threatened.

Soon she was dragging his dead weight across the bare earth and into a brace of trees, rolling it onto a large flat rock and pushing it over behind. She held his limp hand and, tearfully, spoke to him with her thoughts: Blessed Donello, love and peace to your mind and body and spirit as you move forward toward perfection. May the power of peace be yours.

Her pain lessened now, she pulled a site navigator from the vest, a small red ball that she squeezed hard in her palm, fixing her mind intensely, eyes tightly closed, to send her energy charge into it. In less than a moment, she loosened her gripped fist and the device had become a glowing red orb. It would lead them to Donello and perhaps to rescue her if she could stay here long enough. She placed it behind the rock and hidden from the crash scene, she hoped, should the Earth denizens come swarming.

They would surely come soon. They must have heard or seen the crash, seen the flames and smoke. And she realized she would have to deal with them in English if she couldn't get away. She pulled a tiny object from the vest and clutched it in the palm of her hand. Jason remembered his face had been sprayed by some kind of gas; the first time this fact had resurfaced in his mind.

"I can do it," Roci said aloud to herself. "I can do it in English." She scanned the landscape, retrieved the rocket pack she had shucked, struggling forward to face the fiery, collapsing craft again, and hurled it into the inferno. "I can do it," she kept muttering to herself, making her way back to her former resting place.

"In English…I can do it…A…B…C…D…E…F…G…" The pain was duller now but she felt exhausted. "H…I…J…K…"

Her mouth was dry. The air was a little denser than she had expected. "L…M…N…O…P…Q…R…S…T…

"I know they will not leave me here," she said in cautious English. "Hello, my name is…what is my name? Hello, my name is…I have had an accident. But everything is…fine. Yes. Everything is fine." She steadied her breathing and began centering her psyche. "The…what?…medicines in the…vest will heal my wounds."

"U…V…W…" She was slipping into a rejuvenating sleep, could thankfully talk to Mega then. He would advise her, encourage her.

"W…X…" She would rest and then be strong again. Strong! Resourceful! She permeated her thoughts with positive reassurance. She continued to grip the…gas pistol.

"Y…Z."

Jason jerked awake. He was back under the cottonwood tree, lying in her warm arms. She lifted her head from his chest and looked into his eyes.

"I'm sorry," he said. "I didn't know about your…partner…Whew! I was there."

"It's all right. He has ascended," she said. "I just thought you should know what happened.

"The jet. The missile. You must've been reported. They must have found the crash site by now. Maybe they know you're here."

"Even if they could convince themselves of anything, they wouldn't report it, believe me," she said. "And they will strive for any possible explanation, however illogical, before they accept the fact of extraterrestrials. It's rather preposterous actually that many of your people consider you're all alone in the universe when they can look upward and see thousands of stars and planets and know the existence of millions of others"

"Guess we're hopelessly provincial," he said. "Maybe we should put a little white picket fence around the whole place."

"I have never known anything to be hopeless," she said. "And every fence must have a gate."

"What about your co-pilot? What's to be done?"

"Don't worry," she said. "We already have nearly three hundred explorers on your planet, and we'll soon have a lot more. We've been planning this mission a long time and an advance team has been making the way."

"I…We've known nothing about it?" Jason asked.

"Well," she said, "I wouldn't say that." Most of the time, though, we program the people we personally visit to think we look like something else entirely."

"Really?"

"Right," she said, "There's a pattern we use, borrowed from the Polarian galaxy, which is nearby. The Venturians there are kind of small with very big eyes, and they have visited you from time to time anyway. Curiosity, you know. We had rather you think we look like that."

"Instead, you're all perfect physical specimens. You look like us, only much better built."

"Sure, we are both from the predominate local universe pattern. We've just mastered a higher level of genetics. That will take you a while longer."

"We can't all be beautiful. That's what we say."

"I didn't say that," Roci replied. "You shouldn't say it either. There is a lot more to beauty than you can comprehend."

"The missile…getting shot down. What were you doing? What was your mission?"

"Curiosity, adventure, and the quest for knowledge, of course," she said, as if he should have known it. "We wanted to lock onto a jet fighter and extract all of the codes and commands for Mission Control. They could prove useful for PeaceQuest."

"I'm not sure we want to mess with the Air Force, Roci. You see what can happen. We may be primitive, but we can be deadly, even deadlier than you've experienced."

"We will have to monitor the situation with new explorers at the crash site," said Roci.

"What happened?"

"We may have accidentally triggered a missile. We may have been simply shot down. The shields on our craft were not sufficient to fully deflect the blast. Your military has enhanced its firepower since our last report."

"So, have you been keeping tabs on us for, what, eons?"

"Certainly," said Roci. "We have television, radio, your Internet. We get movies, newscasts. Wouldn't you want to be prepared if you came to visit us in the Pleiades?"

"For sure," said Jason. "What channel are you on?"

"You will need a new cable service, Jason," said Roci with a mischievous smile. "You are on a waiting list."

The van rolled up into the high country, approaching the Rocky Mountain National Park and the Long's Peak campground. Jason finally told her about Kevin and Susan, Chuck and Sandra, the couples who would meet them in two days — on Friday.

"It's about a nine mile hike up to Loch Vail," he said, "and another four miles up to Timberline Falls, if we decide to do that. It's a very beautiful area. I've been there and we've been planning to have this get-together up there for most of a year."

"I anticipate with…fondness," she said, "and of course they won't know who I am. I'm sure we can conceal it."

"Sure," he agreed. "But the thing I have to tell you is that we're planning something of a mind-expanding trip. I have some caps of organic mescaline, pure crystal, which is a kind of hallucinogenic drug processed from the peyote cactus. It gives you a fascinating new perspective of things. We call it a 'trip.' I don't know how you feel about such things."

"I could have had it analyzed if we had left a sample in Austin. I guess you've consumed it earlier."

"Yeah, a couple of times. In fact it was down in Texas, where I was camping. It made the whole place come alive, vivid colors, and an incredible…euphoric state that makes you feel like you're one with nature. Of course it's illegal. The establishment is pretty damned paranoid about drugs of any kind. We have to be pretty cool…like secretive and undercover about any kind of drug like that."

"So it's like a tool for you to expand your vision, your consciousness…alter your perspective?"

"Yeah. That's it exactly."

"Is it illegal because they think it's dangerous?"

"Right. They worry about addiction, and brain damage or some other kind of physical damage, short or long-term."

"Well, that's the role of established authority, and it should be. But it's best to make restrictions and laws based on intelligence. There are chemicals which are very beneficial in doing what you want, and they should be provided to people — not sold. But it appears you're sometimes still making laws partly based on ignorance, mythology and fear because that's all you have."

"So do you want to do some? There's a couple of extra hits."

"It would be good research, but I shouldn't, since I don't know what kind of effects it would have on my body and mind type. But I assure you my mind is already…expanded and can further expand, as you say, naturally, which is the best way when you achieve the power. You'll discover that many of the chemical inducements you uncover here will function primarily as a pathfinding tool, carrying you temporarily to a threshold of enhanced awareness and understanding. It isn't a permanent improvement but it does show the way to altered and advanced perspectives that you can, one day, achieve on your own through spiritual connectedness."

"A natural high," Jason responded. "One that you can stay on most of the time if you can get away from all the hassles of life. Yeah, we talk about that."

"But you must have the maturity to control your lustful habits, Jason. Having ascended as you have, this tends to be a problem for you."

"No joke. Lots of bad habits around. Dope, coffee, cigarettes, TV, movies, playing games with the other sex. Seems like I'm never really going to contribute anything to this life. I get wrapped up in all that shit, I really do. And I sell damn floor tiles for a living. I mean…really."

After a quiet pause, he spoke again: "I just hope one day I can do something worthwhile, something that helps people. I'd hate to think I lived and died and never did anything of any real value, made any kind of positive impact. I could help you and your people. I could do that. I could even go back with you. How would that be?"

"I doubt it. You have a purpose here. You're part of the overall evolutionary plan here, whether you realize it or not. And we're not here to make any impact upon the evolutionary plan. I think that may be the main reason why we're allowed to come here repeatedly, our assurance that there will be…minimal disturbance and also just a little bit of help from time to time."

Jason looked disappointed. "Well," he said with a shrug. "Guess I'll hang down here then and let you guys explore the galaxy. It's kind of a letdown though now that I've considered the possibilities."

"You won't remember we've been here. That can be arranged."

He looked hard at her. She betrayed no emotion. "Bullshit!" he said. "You gonna take my memory away or what?"

"It'll be painless. And it'll be for the best, believe me."

"I…don't know what I think about that. I don't like that idea. I want to remember you. Hell, I don't want to forget you."

She stared into him, studying him outside and in. "It's not for us to decide," she said simply. "It's not our decision to make so there's no reason to think about it. It will be nothing to endure. You'll be fine, just as you were before."

"I still don't like it. I thought we were sharing something. I thought we were building something together, something I could be part of."

"You are. We will have a fine adventure together."

"And then it'll be as if it didn't happen."

"It'll be fine, Jason." She reached over to him as he drove the van and caressed his cheek with her fingertips. "We just can't question summed intelligence," she added. "Mission Control is the ultimate authority. Our minds can be at peace in our adventure because the best decision will always be made, each one considering all of the factors we couldn't possibly consider as individuals."

He pulled back from her and looked into her face. "But how can you know that? How can you know it's the best decision? I've never known a central power authority that had all the right answers, that knew everything and knew exactly how to use it."

"Certainly, you wouldn't," she said firmly. "You've been disconnected from the interplanetary circuits for a very long time. This is a treasure beyond your conception, a code of ethical justice based on summarized knowledge handed down through the ages, and certainly not one to be questioned by a single material being like yourself on one of our most primitive and violent planets."

"Guess I'm just a speck in the wind," said Jason resignedly. "Sorry. Do whatever the hell you have to do. You've got the power anyway. I'm just along for the ride."

"We trust the universe circuitry. We've always been well cared for," she said. "We receive what we need — learning, productive service, adventure and pleasure. That's exactly what you need down here too."

"I guess we're just grasping down here, reaching for things we don't really even understand."

"Don't worry about that," she said. "So are we."

They reached the park campground near sundown, searching out the most secluded part and pitching the tent before dark. He lit the lantern, gathered and chopped firewood and started a blaze. They snacked lightly on nuts, cheese and fruit, then cooked a batch of cream of wheat on the fire and ate bowls of it with butter in front of the flickering flames.

Most of their talk around the fire was about things she was curious about, and there were many. Jason soon felt he was doing too much of the talking and learning too little.

"So are we going to see Mega soon?" he asked her across the fire.

"He will be here in eleven minutes," she said.

"But...don't we have to be...in sexual union? Isn't that the way?" He wondered if he sounded lustful.

"We shall be," she said mysteriously through the flames. "I thought that we would...seize the moment, so to speak. I've seen it done in your movies. In fact, I would be pleased to lead the way." Her green eyes started to glow softly in the night.

"Uh-oh" he replied uncertainly. "You know what Kermit the frog said. It's not easy being green."

She looked at him hard for a moment, her eyes growing in intensity, a steamy heat prickling up on his skin across the campfire. She stood up, and her mind screamed softly at him to stand up too...stand up...stand up...He did so.

She walked past the fire toward him, reaching out to take his face gently in both hands and urge him a step backward, one step, then two. He felt helpless in her onslaught, feeling his back push firmly, grittily against a large fir tree. Her lips touched his with soft kisses, then clasped to him warmly, sucking, her arms engulfing his body, carrying his mind away lightly. In a few seconds, he felt her nimble fingers scrawling his zipper down. He felt warmer, then hot, his passion growing to bulging hardness as her hand ripped open his briefs with a loud tear and freed his erectness.

He managed to open his eyes for a second to see her unzipped pants, she pulling them open, taking her panties in strong fingers and ripping them apart too. The hard tear again split the night silence. Still clothed, they were sexually exposed, and her eyes glowed stronger. She was even more aggressive tonight.

She pushed closely to him again, breathed hotly against his trembling face and with sure fingers thrust him smoothly inside her vibrant, warm wetness. It gripped him, snug and tight. His back was pinned hard against the tree trunk, his breath erratic.

"Sh-h-h-h!

The command of her voice stopped his labored breathing. Her lips smothered his and they were both still, sexual muscles taut and frenzied but holding together in their steam-heated and melting cocoon, their muscles pumping softly, cohesively, quietly but holding back his explosion. He quivered hard and fell unconscious just as the release burst open in full flower.

Somehow a soft loud voice was calling to him, asking him. Do you want to? There is more to discover here. Over and over. He exulted in his mind: "Yes!"

The climax exploded a second time, from deep inside him, like no other he could ever recall, spewing his lifeforce inside her, his body caught up in rigors of ecstasy that wouldn't quit, but finally did. Then the wave from her swept over him as well — reciprocal. Her passion engulfed him with a gasping whimper, his whole body swooning in total release. He slid down exhausted.

When he opened his eyes, he found himself slumped to a sitting position under the tree, the familiar campground trappings around him, his wet and flaccid penis hanging from his pants. He struggled to regain his sense of awareness. Roci wasn't there; neither was Mega.

But as he started to get up, the voice came from across the way.

"I think this calls for a celebration, Jason, my friend. That was surely a spectacular sexual climax."

He walked out of the darkness into the lantern light, a tall and muscular man in faded jeans and white, open-necked shirt, with a leather vest and heavy hiking boots. He had a neatly cropped white beard and long white hair cascading down his back from under a broad-brimmed and battered brown felt hat with a leather neck strap.

Mega carried three shot glasses deftly with the fingers of one hand, a wrinkled brown bag with a bottle inside in the other. He sat down at the picnic table and spilled the bag to reveal four bright yellow lemons and a salt shaker, which fell out of the bag abruptly and inexplicably sat itself upright on the table.

"When on Earth, do as the Earthlings, they say," said Mega wryly. "And I know it's customary to celebrate things with a bit of alcohol. So in the spirit of Earthiness..." He flipped open a knife he pulled quickly from somewhere and sliced three of the lemons with lightning strokes. The quartered pieces fell out upon the table.

"This seems a ceremony altogether fitting of your world," he said philosophically. He flipped the knife and it stabbed upright in the table, then he lofted the bottle of clean white tequila.

"This could be called the essence of your material lives, he intoned dramatically, "because humankind everywhere loves to get high." He pulled the cork, which "pooped!" loudly as if heralding a kooky spirit. He sprinkled a small mound of salt from the shaker on the back of his cupped hand, and held a lemon quarter up with two showy fingers.

"Ah-h-h! All three elements present," he said, "or should we say four. The essence, this hard stuff here, its salty and sour mortal embellishments, and the vessel itself — ourselves. The intestinal fortitude which we seek to bring forth." He turned up the bottle and took a hearty swig, bit firmly into the lemon and tongued the salt. He winked mischievously at Jason as it all went down.

When he had savored it and rubbed his stomach, he announced: "That's about like your mortal life, and it lasts about as long, leaving only a warm spot inside. You'll look back fondly at this primitive world if you choose to continue your ascension toward perfection."

While all of this was happening, Jason was sheepishly zipping himself, first looking bemused at the ripped flap of his briefs, tucking it inside. He didn't have the mind to be embarrassed by it all.

He had more important questions. "Of course I want to ascend toward perfection. Is that the plan?" he asked.

"You may choose it through faith.

71

"You've got to help us, Mega. There's so much horror here. You've just got to help those of us who want to change it, who are willing to work for peace on earth."

"We don't have to do anything. You're getting pretty confused, Jason," said the burly mountain man. "Here. Have a shot."

"Sure." He grabbed the neck of it. "Jose Cuervo, a good brand even. Is this real?"

Mega just shrugged. His smile was only a hint.

Jason shrugged too, and belted down a swallow. Whew! It did, in fact, burn. He grabbed a lemon and bit into it, grabbed the shaker and shook a pile furiously and licked it down too.

The warmth settled into him, adding more calm. "Seemed real to me," he ventured.

"You don't seem to understand yet that it's not our place to interfere here, to get involved in your evolution" said Mega firmly. "It's entirely your adventure. We don't have the authority to try to alter the divine evolutionary plan. That would be absurd and foolhardy. It's not so terrible that you suffer and die anyway. That's the only way mortals can get into the divine ascension from here. Believe me, your life here is just the beginning of things that can be far more brilliant and gratifying." He reached for and took the tequila.

"So we're bound to suffer and die then."

"Pay your dues. See, death is your only effective means of shedding this body type. It's your ticket to a better place, as you say." Mega lifted the bottle again and did the trilogy of hits. He passed it back to Jason.

"I guess it's a small price to pay, huh?" Jason asked.

"Indeed. Look, Jesus showed you the way, taking on earthly form, suffering and dying just like you, all the while teaching you the divine way to eternal life. If he can experience your mortal life plan, through empathy, before earning full control of the local universe, then so can you mortals who are only destined to be students in the first mansion world when you pass on. Take it easy. Cool it. Go through evolution."

"You've sure got a lot of answers there. Now you've even got Jesus involved. It all sounds pretty simple when you rattle if off like that but I'm going to need you to go a little slower." Jason sprinkled salt on his clenched fist.

"Ah-h-h, I don't mean to sound like an arrogant know-it-all," said Mega. "But the point is that we're only mortals too. We're from a neighboring planet. We've been tuned into the universe circuits for a very long time though, and we know what's going on. We are ambassadors of service here and there over the local universe. But we don't have any special dispensation to effect things here. We're approved to visit only on the provision that we follow certain rules, some parameters."

Jason belted down the hit, then lemon and salt.

"But you said you might do something positive. You said it remained to be seen," he protested mildly.

"If Mission Control says it's okay. But I can't imagine anything major that would affect the orderly progression of the system. You had best face it. You're in for thousands of years of problems and challenges and sequential development before you enter the era of light and life. You learn more by doing it experientally; some lessons can't be learned any other way."

"But we'll get there, I hope," said Jason, growing more confused. "I hope we'll eventually get there before we destroy ourselves."

"Sure," said Mega. "You don't think the universe powers would allow the destruction of a perfectly good planet and all you children, do you?" He took the bottle from Jason and downed another large hit, swiftly cutting another lemon twice even as he swallowed, and speedily completing the trilogy with a salty lick and the plop of the shaker.

Mega's dexterity, like Roci's, was amazing. He could move his hands with lightning speed, faster than Jason's earth eyes could follow.

"So we won't destroy ourselves," said Jason. "That means we'll avoid nuclear holocaust, right?"

"Sure. The world is beginning to see it makes no sense. There may be some trying times ahead, though. You, personally, will be ascended long before the threat is completely gone, I would guess. And it'll be a long time, also, before your people's imagination and insight can accept the benevolent reality of visitors like us. You're still a fear-based society after all."

"Do you really have hundreds of explorers here?"

"And many more to enjoy your hospitality in coming days. Since we look and act, I will say approximately like you," said Mega, "it all should be, as you say, low key. And, as Roci told you, we have methods to help you forget much of what you see or experience so that you will not be troubled by it."

It all came back to Jason suddenly. She had told him his memories would all be obliterated. Here was a higher authority saying the same thing.

"Does that have to happen? Isn't there another way."

"It depends on Mission Control. It's not our concern. You've been told that. Why can't you accept it?"

"Under what circumstances would you actually do us harm?" he asked.

"We don't mean you any harm," said Mega, "and we surely don't want to dispatch you too swiftly from this mortal realm. You're supposed to stay here and struggle and learn and grow like the rest of your kind. If you make the most of it, it can be quite an adventure. If you learn to struggle in loving service and not fear, then you will really have succeeded."

Suddenly Roci walked up to them. Jason had forgotten even to inquire about her, being absorbed so completely with Mega's insights and persona.

She spoke before he could collect his thoughts. "I guess you guys are solving all the world's problems, huh?"

Mega spoke: "I think we've expanded your love partner's horizons a bit. Don't you think so, Jason?" He passed Jason the bottle.

"How do I know all of this is some kind of revelation, all this stuff you're telling me?" asked Jason, the tequila reaching his brain.

"You don't have to accept it. Like everything else, it's up to you. We are certainly not here to preach to you. We're here to learn ourselves and you can learn with us — just possibly for a purpose you will only discover later. That's why we want you to go to Edenroots with us, mindtravel with timedrops back to the colony that we had here, speculate and perhaps see what happened to it."

They were always catching Jason off guard. Just when he thought he had them figured out, they made a quick turn.

"I'll go too," said Roci. "We'll see what happened to my people here — and maybe yours." She reached out and took the bottle from him, took in a hefty mouthful which she held in her jaws. She dusted her fist with salt, deftly grabbed a lemon slice and chewed into it, and licked the salt slowly, fully…it seemed to Jason a little seductively. Her tongue seemed to quiver at him. Sex, alcohol and celestial revelation was a discomfiting mix for his embattled psyche.

"Visit? A colony you established here? Well, we wouldn't be really there, would we?" asked Jason. "Would it be really what happened back then or just imagination…speculation? What good will it do?" He watched as she sucked on another lemon slice then ate it, peel and all.

"Well, you're all wrapped up in the physical sense," said Mega. "An event doesn't have to happen physically in order to be a valid happening. Bodies aren't affected by such events at timedrops, but everything else is. The drops are gleaned from the archive of experiences that have been carefully recorded in a vast library maintained by the celestials. You could call it a…celestial archive. Humans ordinarily can't delve into these archives, these experiental glimpses into the past, without help from celestial spirit beings but, fortunately, there are many out there to help, in other words to facilitate transmission of these episodes that are played out in our minds."

"So we're supposed to really and truly be looking into the past? How can that be? Do we go back in time or don't we?"

"Let me say it differently, Jason. We will return in re-created experience episodes, presented to us through spiritual inter-connection, allowing us to enter a picturization from the experiences archives. I think you call them the Akashic Records. We can stand in and watch events transpire, but can't affect them. The time and space plan is inviolate.

"We often can't be completely accurate about which timeframe we will be dropped into initially, but over time we learn to attune the visits more precisely to what we need to find out," said Mega. "You see we're always given just pieces of the overall planetary puzzle, not the whole picture. The adventure is in finding and assembling the rest of the pieces, or clues, or reality perspectives. Mission Control always knows much more than is revealed to us in these adventure excursions. At the same time, we invariably bring forward the total knowledge."

The tequila seemed to have robbed Jason of his capacity to follow all of this, but, inexplicably, he understood in that instant that the knowledge had been implanted within him for recall later.

"We're sure of one thing," said Roci, handing the bottle to Jason. "It'll be adventure — high adventure."

Jason took the bottle, rallied his equilibrium, and took another lusty hit, grabbing up a lemon slice deftly and following with the salt. He was feeling light-headed. He managed to hand the bottle over to Mega. "Let's do it," he said. "I'm just a mortal too, but count me in! Maybe I can just ride in the back."

"We didn't think you'd pass up this opportunity," said Mega with a sly grin, "especially since you have become intimate with one of our leading explorers, it seems every lustful evening now." He lifted the bottle for a hit, ritualed the lemon and salt, and handed it over to Roci. It was getting low.

"I think you should find yourself a primitive," she said to Mega. "They're very exciting. I recommend them highly." She took a solid hit and passed the remainder to Jason. She swallowed and didn't bother to touch either the lemon or the salt.

She twinkled her penetrating eyes at him; they flashed green. "How did you like that new dimensional orgasm, Jason?" she asked matter-of-factly.

Jason took the bottle and eyed the half-inch or more of tequila that remained. "It was better than sex," said Jason, "and fairly similar. I hate to get the last drop," he said wryly to each of them, "but...well, what the hell?" He downed the rest of the bottle, sighed loudly and fell over softly, unconscious on the ground, his lips twisted in a smile, his hiking boots pointed up to the night sky.

This proved to Roci that tequila, an interesting Earth drink, worked on both the mind and the body.

75

Mega only found it an amusing aside to an otherwise busy and unsettling day of setting up with new study bases here and there on the planet, and coping with several more adversities.

"I hope you don't mind…incapacitating him so we can talk a few minutes, "Mega said to Roci. "I hate to cut things short but I have a great deal of work to do with the Asian connections. We have an explorer in captivity at one location, and another was wounded in a government demonstration in a city called Rangoon. I think it is actually full of what they would call 'goons'."

"I should be up there helping you," she said.

"Such is fortune. We can take care of it easily enough. Zemblia has stepped in for the psychological project. All is in hand. Just enjoy your visit, Blest. You'll be back at Control, as they say, soon enough. Meanwhile, I believe this young man may actually serve you well."

"Yes. I like him." She scanned his peaceful repose, stretched out on his back on the ground with one hand on his chest.

"You had best control your natural affections, Blest. You are young in the service. Don't be too impressionable because we are certain to leave him here and you must deal with it all, they would say philosophically, and go on with us to Jezhume and beyond. The rules are to put each mission behind you. Completely."

"I will leave him readily," she said without hesitation. "But I feel I can empathize with him safely for awhile. I know there are other worlds. And he is just one small universe personality, after all.

"Beyond that," said Mega. "We aren't likely to give them much direct help either, as he keeps insisting. Invariably, our orders are to leave them to their evolutionary plan."

"It doesn't seem right. Coming here to enjoy them, exploit them, and not helping them overcome some of their major problems, which we could solve so easily. There are people dying constantly here, horribly."

"Often, problems are not as easily solved as you would perceive, dear one," said Mega. "They learn best through experience, living life themselves. Don't question divine authority, my precious sister. The collective wisdom we have centered above our world has to be trusted. Just as you told Jason. These are all divinely inspired worlds on their own and must evolve as they were intended under the time and space plan."

"Maybe the plan includes us, though," said Blest. "Maybe whatever great good we would do on these visits would actually be part of the divine plan in the first place. Couldn't it be? After all, we're here. That's a reality. We're here right now. We're a legitimate part of their evolution, no matter how we affect it. If so, maybe we could upstep it, save some lives, because we're part of the plan."

"Earthlings who dote on God's will might even call that blasphemous," said Mega. "and, in some ways, I might agree with them. We're not divine and it would be presumptuous for us to claim so. If the One God wants us to help them, it will be so directed via the Celestials. To my knowledge, it has not been. Still…I will think about our conversation and let's talk again. I sure love the friendship times we've had together, my beautiful sister."

"I know I'm young and have a lot to learn" she said, not letting go of it, "but maybe we should begin to assert ourselves more in the universe. Make things happen."

Mega chuckled. "Young explorers like yourself always think you have some new answers. Sometimes, it turns out that you do. But if we don't follow the dictates of our highest, collectively established intellectual authority, which is imbued with all the facts and ideas of all the universe circuits, then it would seem we're stupid indeed. Individually, we may not understand all the reasons why but we know they are there. And they are there for us to find if we study the archives."

"I know you're right," she said softly. "If we mess up God's experiments, there is no way to know how they would turn out."

"We just have faith that they will from experience," said Mega. "Why don't you put your lover friend to bed and I'll see you tomorrow night — in Edenroots."

"Can he handle it?" she asked.

"Yes. His circuitry has been adapted. He can take it in stride."

"Then…we have already been of great assistance," she mused. "And we are making changes."

"There is an old saying from Quomoni," said Mega. "The lightest footprint will preserve the path for others. But there will always be change."

Ellen Mackey was at home alone. The darkness had settled in around her small ranch house and the horses were safely in the barn. She sat under a lamp reading a novel until she lost interest and sat there staring across the room at the cat licking herself by the wood stove. She heard the wind rustle through the trees outside, the leaves of the poplars gently swaying and singing their quiet song as the night breeze rolled through.

And then it was all suddenly quiet. Strangely quiet.

She got up and walked to the screen door and looked outside. She could see a dark figure walking up the driveway, his feet scrunching against the pea gravel, getting closer. Her fingers jostled the latch on the screen door as he stepped resolutely toward her in the dark. It was latched tight and she thought quickly about moving to the bedroom to get her pistol.

"Hello," she said. "Who are you?"

He stood facing her and she saw that he was tall, handsome, muscular in a tight-fitting t-shirt, his windbreaker tied around his waist. He could have been modeling sportswear.

"My car broke up about a half-mile from here. Could I use the phone?" he asked in a clear bass voice, his eyebrows arched appealingly.

She flipped on the porch light and looked into his eyes.

FIVE: A Few More Imaginative Interludes

Jason emerged from the tent, scratching his tousled, sleepy head. It was daylight and Roci was missing, and nowhere around the campsite did he see evidence of their tequila revelry of the previous evening.

Why? Because it didn't happen, thought Jason, making his way to the camp stove to make coffee. He really didn't know if it did or didn't in these awakening minutes, being incapable of serious thought. But there was no hangover, and he felt rested.

On the open stove on the picnic table, there sat a pan of water under a low flame, smoking and just hot enough for the instant coffee in the jar beside it. Her note was held down by a spoon and two bags of sugar. "Good morening," it said, and she had drawn a sun with a big smile inside. "The anemals are all out very early, so I've gone to see." She signed it: "Roci."

"I hear that you could be called a 'sleepy head.'" He turned at her voice. She had walked up silently behind him, bare feet on the clean ground, and stood radiantly there with her long flowing hair upon her shoulders. She wore shorts and a halter top.

"Did you see the animals?"

"Yes, a beautiful group of deer over there in a meadow earlier. And I saw a large furry animal. It had two big teeth in front and was in the water. You know this beast?"

She walked over to the ice chest and pulled the orange juice from it.

"A beaver perhaps. Or a marmot. Do you like our animals?"

"They're fascinating. I hope to see as many as I can."

"Thanks for the coffee." Jason poured the hot water over the dark crystals. "How'd you manage to have all this here?" He surveyed the coffee service before him.

"I'm pleased to be your friend, Jason. Thank you for all the help you've been to me. I'll be a friend to you."

Jason's thoughts were circuitous trying to arrive at a proper reply. He knew he had to go to the core — honesty!

"I...don't know why I feel so close to you. At first it was...it was a lot of lust...you were so beautiful...<u>are</u> so beautiful. But it's so much more than that now. I'm telling you, as I stand here with this coffee cup, I've fallen completely in love with you. I don't know if it's the idea of seeing perfection in front of me — what I think is perfection. Or whether it's some hypnotic state I'm in, maybe that you've put me in. Maybe it's a spell. But I feel deep compassion for you and I think I would fight, do anything to protect you and to forge some kind of...lasting relationship. My heart's going to be torn open when you leave. It's going to be like the...ultimate loss."

She looked at him and shrugged. "Whew! It's too early in the morning for that intensity, Jason. I thought you woke up slow."

"Sometimes I wonder if I'm awake at all." He shook his head and took a sip of hot coffee.

She smiled and looked at him benevolently. "What shall I call you?" she asked, as if to herself. "My good friend. The Earth guy?" She laughed delightedly and whirled away. "I'm going swimming in the creek," she said, pulling off her shirt to reveal her naked breasts.

"Better keep those under wraps," said Jason. "There are laws against being...nude, you know. Maybe it's weird, I don't know, but we got 'em. They'll arrest us."

"Nakedness can be beautiful; it's a release gift," she said, "but I won't rush things for you. I purchased a suit, as you know, at the Walled Mart. It seems to hide just enough for legality. I think that's...cute."

As usual lately, Jason didn't know what to think.

Later, after their swim, at the camp store, he reached Ellen on the phone.

"Hey! Sweet Lips. Just wanted to call and tell you we're in the Long's Peak Campground, Rocky Mountain National Park, U.S. of A. How are you doing, and your mom?"

"She's much better. My new friend and I went up to see her yesterday and she perked up while we were there. Her blood pressure went down, everything's looking up, and I think she's coming home tomorrow. Dr. Whatshisface said it was kind of a miraculous recovery, really."

"That's great. I know that's a load off your mind. Maybe you ought to come up here. We're still going on that adventure with Captain Mescalito."

"Naw, I'm kinda busy, really. I met this guy last night. His car gagged down the road and he came in to use the phone. Well, he turned out to be a real nice guy, good-looking, well-built. But nice as he can be. He went up with me to see mom this morning, and we've been talking about this and that. He wants to see a little of this part of the country."

"Yeah? Sounds pretty exciting." said Jason, "Perfect specimen of a man, huh?

"You bet," she said. "I mean, this guy can even cook. He's in there knockin' out a Spanish omelet right now, if you can believe it. He wants to make tacos tonight."

"Well, sounds like you guys can have a lot of fun together. What kind of business is the guy in?"

"Steve. His name is Steve. He's a student somewhere, didn't catch the college, a graduate student I think, doing research for something he's going to write."

"Maybe a thesis or a dissertation."

"Yeah, one of them, I think. Heck, man, he's just a way out cool guy. But, shit, I didn't tell you the bad part, though. Bummer! When we got back to where his car was, it was gone — stolen! So...I guess he'll be spending some time gettin' that straightened out. But he doesn't seem too worried about it. I think he must be well-fixed for money from all accounts."

"That always helps. Maybe he's got a big roll of bills tucked away somewhere."

"Maybe."

"Why don't the two of you come up here, meet us in the park?"

"M-m-m-m-m-m-m-m," she pondered. "I guess maybe we'd just like to take a little short trip, if we go anywhere, maybe just the two of us," she said, "if mom keeps gettin' better."

"Sounds romantic," he replied blandly, his mind whirring with questions. She was laughing on the other end. He was frowning, putting two and two together.

Roci was sunning by the creek when he got back, her long wet hair tied into a ponytail, her bikini exposing more than he believed prudent. He was ready to confront her about it now, before he got mesmerized again by that face, those eyes.

"What are your people trying to do with Ellen, my friend Ellen?"

Her stare was a little harder than usual. "She won't be harmed in any way. We are very loving and benevolent people. You need to realize this." She reached for her towel, shook her hair free and rubbed the towel through it vigorously.

"But what is your...man, whatever he is, doing down there? She's my friend, one of the few friends I've got. I don't want to see her mind messed up by all this."

"We're not messing up your minds. The rest of you don't even know we're here, and won't. Just you, Jason. Just you. Can you handle it?"

"Indeed. What about <u>my</u> mind? I don't want my mind taken away. You're going to blot out my memory, aren't you? Mega confirmed it. What else are you going to blot out? What's the real deal here? How does Ellen fit into your master plan?" He said it all resentfully.

"I'm disappointed at your emotional reaction," she said." There are several reasons Steve is down there."

"I'm listening."

"The military people are swarming over the crash site. They're all over the area asking questions. Steve can keep an eye on that situation and maybe point them in another direction. He is tuned in to the police and telephone frequencies."

"Are they looking for us? Did they find the body, your...ship?"

"As of this hour, they are tracing our tire and feet, umm, footprints which are all over the area. Donello's remainder was...spirited away by...one of our service vans. They have gathered a few material objects at your campsite. Did other humans see you there?"

"No. The area was deserted. Of course, people may have come by and seen the van. So do you think they can trace us?"

"They know my craft isn't an airplane. And they will find a number of strange things when they sift through the rubble. The fire wouldn't destroy it all. Of course, they won't announce any of this."

"Do you think they're after you — after us then?"

"Sure they are. Remember what happened at the motel? The salesmen I threw in the pool — they deserved it! It was great! — and then getting involved with the law. They've got a fix on us, identification on you, your van, and the knowledge that somebody got out of that crash. There was no body on the scene but plenty of blood, and it was definitely an alien craft."

"And...what about Donello's body. I hope it's not still in a 'service van' somewhere?"

"Steve and Cassandra took care of that," she said matter-of-factly. "They said the ascension rites and incinerated him up into the spirit circuits. He is moving ever onward toward perfection."

"Obviously, we're not. Conversely, we're getting into deep shit with the authorities."

"They may have reached your home by now, the place you work. Can you be traced to where you're going?"

Jason thought about it. "No. I told no one anything beyond a hiking trip in the mountains, maybe in Colorado. Who are we running from anyway?"

"Internal security officers at the U.S. Air Force training and testing facility near Palo Verdes, Texas. They have great freedom of authority, secrecy and movement, believe me, and don't mind using it when they think they're after one of their imagined enemies."

"Surely your behavior at the motel wouldn't be enough to link you to that crash. That just doesn't..."

"Jason, we hear everything your people say on the telephone and on radios, any kinds of circuits, computers, faxes. We're tuned in to all of this. I'm telling you how the investigation is progressing down in Texas, not speculating whether there is one."

He stared at her hard. They truly had their fingers on everything.

"Yes," she said out loud, "we do. We haven't needed to visit here often because we've kept surveillance in other ways. The right antenna here and there in this area can do wonders for communications. Our listeners produce scannable information from all transmissions and we're constantly using it to protect our explorers here."

"Well, if we're on the lam, we'd better do something to avoid being picked up. The van may be hot, then. We'd better get some other wheels."

"Wheels? Perhaps," she said quizzically. "I'm really sorry you got mixed up in all this, friend Jason. Perhaps I should not have…adjoined so closely with you. I should've left instead of waiting for you to regain consciousness. I almost did. And then I began thinking what we possibly might accomplish together, how you could help until I was ready to go back, and how interesting you are, in fact, and the joy we might find in energy cohesion." She paused and reflected. "Then the next thing I knew I was at the Walled Mart, adorning with clothes and then decided to immerse in the pool and then on and on…in this enticing place!"

"Whoa! Roci," he said. "You're a lot like we are. We humans get carried away sometimes too. I'm sure you've noticed."

"Alike," she said, "but opposites attract as well. We'll carry it farther, friend Jason, but for now, let's get the van unloaded."

"I beg your pardon."

"I've just heard this information I relayed to you. Did you know there was another telephone down by the bath house?"

"No, I didn't."

"There was a fat woman in there. Her body was horribly deformed by fat. In her case I can understand how nudity could be…problematic."

"Yeah, well, we have a saying: Fat happens. But why do we unload the van? Why?"

"We're changing vehicles because this one's being sought. You said it yourself. We had planned for it. Let's get busy." She squeezed his hand and gently pulled him toward the van.

"Wait. Wait a minute. Why do we unload it here? Where are we going to put the stuff?"

"You know what I would like?" she said lovingly, reaching to grasp his hand and pull him to her there by the side of the van. "I would like for you to learn to trust me. It would feel good if you would trust me implicitly. I would like that."

He shrugged and grinned. "I…think I do, actually."

She grinned back. "Well, hang in there then. Get all of this stuff out of here. Let's go."

"I would like to…I would really like to…not lose my van," said Jason, with a resigned sigh.

"Get busy," she said.

It all soon sat in piles out at the campsite, their luggage, the box for the tent, the tools and snowshoes, the glove compartment cleared of maps and matches, tapes and a coffee mug fished out from under the seat, and everything sitting there waiting at 11:45.

"What time did you say they'd be here?" he asked her.

"Right about now," she said.

A white van pulled into view, moving slowly on the campground road, the sun reflecting brightly off the windshield so that Jason couldn't see inside. It rolled up to their campsite and pulled alongside Jason's van. The doors opened and out stepped a man and woman in white coveralls, their backs and front pockets emblazoned with the blue circle emblem, this one with a crossed "X" designed with a wrench and screwdriver inside it.

Wordlessly, the man began deftly began removing the license plate of Jason's van with a screwdriver, laying a substitute on the ground beside him. The woman came up to Roci forthrightly and handed her the keys. She was very attractive, with long black hair, a wiry frame and olive complexion. Both of their coveralls were soiled with garage dirt.

"Baby Blue's Paint and Body Shop, 5th and Main, Crystal Lake, Colorado, at your service," she said to Roci, who took the keys and smiled broadly. "Not really," she added, "but of a sort."

"We'll probably paint this one blue," said the woman, turning slightly to face Jason. "So you're the fascinating Earthling we've been hearing about, huh? Do you have the keys?"

"That's me," said Jason. "Guess you folks have taken over the planet's garage business by now." He handed her the van keys from his ring."

"It's a dirty job," she said wryly, "but somebody's got to do it."

She turned to Roci: "Here's an instructional module for you," she said, handing her a small round silver ball. "Just some additional information Control thought you could use."

The man had switched the tags and was now standing beside them. He was swarthy, muscular, handsome too. He stared at Jason as if he were profoundly curious. "I don't mean to stare," he said, "but I just haven't been down long. I'm anxious to spend some time with one of you."

"Will you?" Jason asked.

"Maybe a female, actually. I should be approved for that by next week," he said.

"We have to be going," said the woman, "tight schedule."

They climbed into Jason's van and pulled away, he following it nostalgically with his eyes. He almost waved to them. Things were happening pretty fast, but they seemed to be in amazing control. Now he had a new van. There was eleven miles on the speedometer.

"So you people are very curious," he said to her. "He's going to get his very own Earthling next week. Is that what you're doing with Ellen? I guess he'll seduce her, of course. I know that's got to be part of it."

"Sure, the sharing of affection is a basic need, one that your people haven't come close to understanding yet. We much appreciate exotic lovers and know secretly that you do too. Maybe we should try to teach you to be open about that."

"You said there were other reasons — I remember now — other reasons why he was at Ellen's — Steve, whoever — other than helping us cover our trail.

He wanted a human to befriend and study, of course, and Mission Control wanted more information and opinion about you. It worked out both ways."

"Why? Why do you want more information about me? Am I consequential in some way?"

"I don't know," she said. "I guess we'll both find out, as you say, soon enough."

"I'd like to be…consequential. I'd like to make some kind of positive contribution to humankind. But I can't imagine what it would be."

"You can get some firewood," she said, with a wink and a smile, "but hadn't you rather check out your new van first."

The Colorado registration and plates seemed to be in order and the interior was customized with a soft and expansive couch that he quickly imagined as the scene of their next lovemaking.

After a light lunch, she encouraged him toward a streamside hike, on the trail where the camping tourists meandered their way to a waterfall. The trail was paved and they passed by oldsters and youngsters in short pants and baseball caps and even pushing strollers. The tiny cameras hanging from their necks would record their presence there, gaily in front of the rushing torrent, and doubtlessly blocking much of it from view.

When they reached the scene from the brochure, Roci stood seemingly mesmerized watching the menagerie.

"They're all going back," she observed. "Why is that?"

"It's the end of the trail," he replied. "There's even a sign there, see, that no one should climb up the side or get in the water."

"You surely put a lot of restrictions on yourselves."

"If someone gets hurt, they sue the park for damages. The park has to have all their prohibitions to protect against lawsuits"

"Do you mean," she asked, "that if someone decided to climb up the falls, fell and was hurt…or killed, that the park would be held responsible?"

"That's right."

"But the park had nothing to do with it."

"Sorry, Roci, but don't ask me to explain the judicial system. I can't do it to where it makes sense. I do know that a lot of people who get hurt try to blame someone else for it, especially if they think they can get a court settlement."

"We won't sue anybody, Jason, and I think we're...nimble enough to make it up there, don't you?" she said quickly, already making her way up the steep bank, reaching for a handhold on the first boulder, then a foothold.

Jason looked around at the loitering tourists, who had no interest in any of it, looked up at her steady climb, shook his head and started to follow.

Up they climbed, careful hands one after another on the driest rocks they could reach. The wet ones were dangerously slick. It felt good to Jason, scaling the rocks, recalling how he used to admire the skills of excellent rock climbers and wanting to do it too. He would always wake up from such daydreaming though, in the reality that the skill took many hours of practice and preparation, not a possibility down in Texas, and with the time available.

But now he imagined himself being more proficient than he was, following her lead up the rock wall right next to the rushing waterfall, feeling the cool, swirling mist on his face, reaching for cracks when the solid handholds disappeared, puffing out-of-breath by the time they reached the top, where the soft, flat stream dropped sharply off the ledge. They stood confidently on a flat boulder in the middle of the flow, looking down at the cascade, Jason feeling self-satisfied. He could've fallen and hurt himself — but didn't. That was somehow satisfying.

Then he turned quickly and saw that she was now leaping expertly across the boulders and heading upstream. Maybe she was challenging him, he thought. Yeah! Let's do it. He was off too, in a burst of energy, following her up into the highlands. He felt invigorated.

Soon they lay side-by-side on a sun-washed boulder in the middle of the stream, far from the tourist trail and hearing only the nature sounds of birds and rushing water, the gentle rustle of the wind in the surrounding fir and pine trees.

"It's so beautiful and peaceful up here," he said to her, "away from the hassle of humanity, all scrambling around trying to get their greedy hands on this and that. It would be great to get back to some kind of communion with the Earth, a kind of peaceful relationship with nature."

"Nature is impervious to anything you want, Jason," she said. "It doesn't even guarantee that you will survive. Only the fittest and the fortunate do. I'm told that our people had to struggle hard to carve just a small piece of the wilderness of your emerging world into a garden sanctuary."

"And you said we are going there. When?"

She rolled over and looked down into his eyes, her face close to his, her body against his and he lying flat on their large flat rock. "Look into my eyes," she said. "Tell me what you see there."

He looked into them and they mesmerized him quickly into a near hypnotic state. "I see...I see a power like I've never experienced before. You...have a depth of knowledge...compassion...insight. It just seems more than I can...But, wait a minute, I see that you do have love for me. I know that you do. I don't know why you do, but..."

She interrupted him with a soft kiss on his lips. He felt her warm breath. "So you can know the truth of situations, you see. But what you don't understand is that I also love all of God's creatures for the fragment of God inside them, and for the potential that it gives them. We can all be worthy children of this first and divine source and this is what we strive to teach and to display on the path to spiritual perfection. And it is so natural to share this beautiful intimacy together."

"I'm just...not as advanced as you. I just don't..."

"You just have more distance to go," she said, "but I will help you. And we are much closer now. We are progressing. I can even now carry you to Eden roots without bodylock — the sexual orgasm trigger."

"I...actually don't know if that's good for not," Jason grinned. "But I'm sure...well, I'm just...sleepy...So are we..."

And this was all that Jason could say. Roci's green eyes engulfed him again and he fell into a dark quietness.

Jason awakened to the loud nasal squawk of a large bird. He opened his eyes to see that his face was resting on a clean, warm blanket of green grass. He raised his head slightly to look upon a new scene — a surrounding profusion of exotic green plants and flowers. Colorful orchids and bromeliads hung from the branches of the trees. Warm sunshine cut through the foliage and brightened the green carpet beneath him, which felt tender and soft under his naked body.

Naked!

Jason rolled over and sat up and realized fully that he was completely nude, out in some primeval forest somewhere — not in Colorado. There were huge ferns to his left, the green fronds of rugged cicads protruding upward, the twittering, whistling sounds of many birds up in the treetops which blocked much of the sun. His bare skin looked too white and out of place there and he suddenly felt terribly insecure. Without clothes! Damn! What could he do? What could he do without clothes?

A bird's guttural squawk again captured his ears, then his eyes. He was conscious that he had actually heard the sound. The bird sat there in front of him on a thick, low-lying limb of a huge oak tree. It was large and colorful, rainbow-like with red and green and yellow patchwork feathers, a huge yellow bill and a tiara of white feathers rising from its head. Its large eyes were fixed on Jason and it clucked softly now, looking at this new and naked and strange sight in the garden.

Jason got to his feet and again perused his awkward nakedness, turning in circles to scan the luxuriant garden landscape. It was all manicured neatly, like the grounds of a mansion, but there were no buildings in sight, just a deep green, misty forest on every side. Neither Roci nor Mega was anywhere to be seen.

The large bird sat there eyeing him as he ran his hands self-consciously over his nakedness. He did feel his skin, it wasn't fully numb, but he felt neither cold nor warm.

He suddenly felt strongly that he had to be clothed, though. He had to get something on his body, and he looked intently at a huge plant with giant leaves. He had seen a similar one in Kevin's greenhouse and it had been called a fiddle-leaf fig. He resisted the temptation to rip off leaves and try to fashion some kind of cover, at least for his genitals.

No! He said to himself. That now seemed foolish. For some reason he didn't want to now. Instead, he began walking toward the bird, stepping with increasing confidence. Maybe I am pure and clean again, he thought to himself. Was the thought his own?

The rainbow bird did not move. He walked quietly up under the limb, his bare feet feeling the soft grass, and reached his arm up to it. The bird stepped lightly onto his fingers; he felt the rugged claws wrap around them. He looked into the bird's eyes and, in amazement, saw more than the wild blankness of familiar animal creatures. The bird seemed to be thinking, wondering about him. But Jason realized it could be his imagination, no more real than the rest of this — a mindtrip or something, they called it. But then it all might be real too. That still remained uncertain to him. Did he even have an imagination in this state? Or was that all it was?

He heard a rustle behind him and turned to see Roci emerging from the foliage, carrying a huge leaf weighed down with what seemed to be food. She was naked too; his eyes fixed on her perfect brown breasts nestled among the colorful vegetables and fruits, and her small tuft of brown pubic hair. She was smiling kindly.

The bird stepped off his fingers and, with gentle flaps of its large wings, was quickly on the grass beside them. She took a sprinkling of seeds from the leaf and dropped them for the bird, which promptly began pecking them up.

"I have some garden food for us," she said, "a blend of vegetables lightly boiled in the warm waters coming out of the hill, some fruits and seeds and lemongrass seasoning. We can talk while we eat."

She sat down cross-legged on the grass and, wordlessly, he sat down in front of her. She showed him the exotic fare and it tasted vividly delicious to him, real or not.

"Is this Eden then? Is it as perfect as it looks?" he asked.

"Not perfect but well-balanced. We came here and took dominion over a great profusion of plant and animal life, all struggling for survival and reproduction. We established beauty and order for awhile."

"And were there people here?"

"Primitive, evolving humans, divided into tribes, with more hair than your later versions, and often tree-dwelling. They are ancestors to more resourceful and admirable humans. The Dalamatians were helping them learn things, like health, sanitation, agriculture and irrigation, animal domestication and management, language, some spiritual values. Our concern at the bases, though, was the development and maintenance of a self-supporting food supply, safe from predators, for Dalamatia and the outposts. "

"What kind of predators?"

"We will go for a walk in a few minutes," she said, "and we'll see."

"But the world is predatory, isn't it? Everything feeds on something else. Living things destroy other living things to survive."

"On this planet at any rate. Once the delicate balance was lost here, it all came to be that way again," she said. "When the natural plant foods were scarce or gone, it became a stringent competition to survive. The garden's electrical barriers were lost and the savage world outside came in to consume and destroy it. But we still don't know precisely what happened or how. We will search for these answers together."

"Quite a history lesson," said Jason.

"With shortages would come selfishness, the hoarding of food and the pulling-apart of brotherhood and sisterhood in favor of competitive alienation, private property, even violence, killing. This is likely the disintegration that came. Also, the exacting demands for survival, for a strong body and clever mind, were likely much to blame for your loss of spiritual direction and emotional stability."

"Paradise lost," Jason muttered.

"And difficult to regain," she said, "in view of your depressingly large numbers now and the worldwide fragmentation of ideologies."

"What do we need? One-world government?"

"Of course. You all have a great stake in planetary progress and you will eventually resolve your differences and work together. But we know now that an intervention such as ours is not advisable. As we've said, the evolutionary worlds have to work out their own destinies over many generations. You would be unprepared for much of what we or others could

89

give you. The divine plan is to achieve it on your own, at your own pace, to let you cling to foundations of falsehood even, superstitious and self-serving primitive religions and the animal-like bellicosity of your animal ancestry until you are absolutely ready to give them up for something better. The children of advancing generations will do that."

Jason was thoughtful and quiet for a moment. If this wasn't all real, it might as well be.

"Of course it's real, Jason. It's not physical, but it's real."

"I don't want to lose this knowledge. I don't want it wiped out. I want to use it. I want to be part of the plan to make it better. Okay?"

She looked at Jason with what he interpreted as worried compassion.

"I will speak to Mega about it," she promised. "Now, let's go for a walk." She rose to her feet nimbly, with strong smooth legs, lifting the leaf that now was empty of food. She reached a hand and helped him get up.

He stood there naked beside her, not as uncomfortable as before.

"There is such a freedom to nakedness," she said with a smile, reaching to run her fingers over his chest. "Perhaps it's partly symbolic, but the idealistic love it sends to the heart and the cool air that touches the skin, the feel of the sun and wind, and the gentle underthought that we can love together and feel the exquisite touch of one another's fully opened nakedness too is such an intensive pleasure that it will always prevail upon us."

Jason was speechless.

Suddenly, she bleated like a sheep, or goat, nasally. "Ba-a-ah!" He looked at her, dumbstruck. A small white goat bolted out of the foliage and stood before her. She reached and gave it the large leaf, which it tore away from her joyfully and, tail-wagging, ran back into the foliage, chewing it up all the while.

"Might as well enjoy a few imaginative interludes, Jason," she said. "Did you get that?"

"I guess so," he said, blinking.

"Let's climb the hill," she said, "and feel the aura of the place."

He found quickly that his energetic walking energized him more. He strode behind her through the fern-studded woodland and up the side of a tree-draped, grass-covered hill and higher from the deep shade into the sunlight. It was most exhilarating in the nude, and he felt like a pure and innocent spiritual being. That, of course, wasn't so — except for here!

He was puffing slightly when he came up alongside her on a sunny, knoll of high brown grasses, wafting in the wind. Their open bodies were exposed to all the world, perspiring gently in the warm radiance of the primeval sun.

"It's hotter now than it is in your day, of course," she reminded him. "The sun is stronger. Look, there, over the landscape."

Jason turned to look across the expansive green valley across the way, studded with an orchard of trees, neat rows of garden crops, fields of grain, all laid out in rectangular and circular order. A large, shining dome sat in the middle of it all, approximately the size of a stadium.

The top third of the dome was framed transparent panels, open to the sun and reflecting its rays brilliantly. Inside, Jason could see a mini-forest of green. The encircling gold base portion of the structure appeared to be a full two or more stories high and he could only imagine what was inside.

"Living and serving quarters," she said aloud. "You can see most of the exterior garden from here. What you can't see are the underground laboratories for genetical and botanical enhancements, and the supply centers."

"Why did you come here in the first place? Why not...stay home?"

"We have many of the same motivations as you," she said, "adventure, discovery, knowledge, wisdom, challenge, sometimes danger. It was a place to explore and, beyond that, we wanted dominion over this world. No one else had it. And it was right in front of us. Caligastia said he represented the Celestials. Perhaps he did at the time. We came from the Pleiades to help them uplift the place."

"We <u>are</u> alike," he said. "Maybe we're partly evolved from you — your people."

"We don't know," she said, "but we will search for that answer, among others."

Jason heard a rustling in the grass behind them, whirled to see a single file of men, laden with burdens, dressed in zippered blue body suits, oblivious to them as they began climbing higher on the trail. Jason turned quickly to see Roci's reaction.

"Don't worry. They can't see us, she assured him."

Jason moved backward a couple of steps anyway, watching wide-eyed as the men made their way beside them, moving lithely and purposefully, with faces of determined confidence. The man in front was heavily muscled, with flaming long red hair and beard cascading around his fearful head. He had a long and large-barreled weapon strapped over his shoulder.

They trudged upward, six of them behind the red-haired leader. Two of them carried a large round cylinder, seemingly of metal; two others carried backpacks from which emerged what appeared to be artillery shells. The remaining two men carried smaller hand weapons. None of them paid any attention to the these two nude people watching the parade.

"I have a thought wave that they are pursuing a large creature that invaded and damaged the colony last night," said Roci. "I believe we will see them on the attack. Come on. Let's follow."

91

They followed a respectable distance behind, plowing through the deep grass and climbing to the sunwashed top of the hill. When they arrived on the scene, the men were already planting tripod legs into the ground. The legs whirred noisily for a moment, drilling themselves tightly into the rocky slope, a firm base for the barrel and chamber they deftly assembled atop it.

The red-bearded leader looked down into the other side of the valley with a small set of binoculars. There was a lake there, at the other end of the valley, and the water was steaming warm, its smoke rising and casting a gray haze over the jungle landscape.

"A fissure opened in the bottom of the lake a short while ago," said Roci. "The colonists found that there were eggs buried under there, giant ones, possibly planted from elsewhere, but they made no effort to bring them up from the lake. Now, some days later, the heat from the earth has apparently begun hatching them."

"How do you know this?" he asked.

"These are just thoughts coming into my mind," said Roci. "Either they are inspired to be there, or they are only conjecture. But this is the usual method for celestial input if we are centered spiritually."

"Wait! What's all this 'if' business?"

"Jason," she said firmly. "I can trust my impressions. You need to work to this point."

The bearded man's booming voice commanded their attention. In a strange language, he was conversing with the men manning the artillery. He turned, unslung the long-barreled weapon from his shoulder and took dead aim at the lake.

A burst of thunder and smoke exploded out of the barrel. A short, straight projectile of laser light streaked downward into the valley and splashed resoundingly in the lake far below. Jason could almost feel the electrical impulses quaking through it. The waters heaved and churned, electrical charges popping and sparking above it. The men stood ready.

Then he saw the head, dark and huge, pushing up out of the smoky waters. A loud shriek split the silence. Its huge, gaping mouth was filled with rows of sharp teeth. Jason was thunderstruck, watching it emerge fully from the deep, a gigantic prehistoric beast pulling itself out of the water with short, powerful legs and clawed feet.

"A dinosaur. My God," he breathed.

"A similar form," said Roci, "but they have huge lungs which serve as airpockets. They emerge from their eggs, or cocoons, and seem to migrate to the surface to replenish the air, but they can survive underwater for a long time."

The men were sighting the larger weapon by this time, one of them wearing a headset. He adjusted the barrel. Far below, the giant beast, staggered by the electrical charge, struggled to pull itself out of the lake and into the jungle. Jason could see now that — massive as it was—it was probably only recently born, or hatched, from the mysterious cache of eggs.

"Zipke!" called the man at the cannon, which was now pointing at an upward angle. Two of them stepped up, dropped a large shell into it, and fell to the grass. It boomed in fire and smoke. Jason realized it was like a mortar.

"Yes, it is," said Roci aloud. "They're extremely accurate with it and have to be. Their weapon energy is limited."

Jason stared again at the beast, pushing its way into the trees with a long flapping tail. It was quiet for a second.

Then the projectile struck and an explosion blew its body apart in a burst of fire, smoke, dirt and bloody pieces. The beast's shattered head flopped over and fell motionless, awesome rows of teeth in a grotesque grin. The bloodied stump of a leg fell on top of it. Jason had to tear his eyes from the incredible scene.

The men were all celebrating now, surrounding and hugging one another with laughter and camaraderie. He could sense that, though they did this violent deed, they were caring and intelligent people. And they were proficient. One shot to stir out the creature; another to destroy it. He looked back at the smoking carnage below and then to Roci.

"They've won for the day," she said. "But we think there are more of them than you can ever imagine."

"How did these beasts get here? What kind of quirk is it? What is this time, before or after the dinosaurs?"

"They are not supposed to be here, Jason," she said. "And we don't know the secret of the eggs either. Where they came from? These beasts weren't here when the colonists arrived."

The men were now assembling their gear, then soon were moving at a deliberate pace down into the dense valley, in the direction of the beast.

"I'm sure they'll learn what they can down there, but if there are many more of them, and if their limited number of shells and charges are exhausted, they may get overwhelmed here. That's what we're thinking we'll find. When our supply ship arrived at the colony some time later, they found it overrun with those creatures. If there was a final transmission from the colony, it was lost on the spacewaves. Perhaps we'll find it here."

"A message? You think we might find a message?"

"They searched before, but found nothing. Much of the underground had collapsed though. They didn't reach every part of it and they were too busy eradicating those beasts. Who knows what might have happened in the final days? Did they retreat successfully? Perhaps not. I know our discoveries could be grim for you."

"No…I'm actually elated to be part of it." Jason said thoughtfully.

93

She smiled broadly at him, her incredible beauty filling him with boundless energy. "That's the spirit," she said, walking toward him. "I think you might have it in you to be a spirit warrior."

"A…what?"

"Sounds romantic, doesn't it?" she said, moving her soft face and orgasmic eyes close to him. She kissed him hotly as they embraced, feeling their bare skin, clasping hungrily to one another there under the ancient sun.

Then he blinked his eyes and he was back on the rock, lying fully clothed out in the warm sun, the Colorado stream rustling gently on either side of him. He looked over and saw that she was just awakening too, rubbing her eyes and pulling her fingers through her long flowing hair. Their eyes finally met. Her look was kind, rested.

"Wow!" she said. "What a nice trip."

They talked about it later by the campfire, the beauty of the colony gardens, the threat of the giant beasts, the origin of the eggs, the earth heat that may have finally hatched them, whether there was an underground civilization that conspired to unleash these beasts, whether they were preserved for a long time there in the water, having been laid there or carried there by some ancient mother or other. She told him that Mega would be along later.

He was bursting to know where they would go next. She just smiled there in the fireglow, stirring the potato soup, and saying it would be Mega's surprise. "He really is very talented, you know," she told him. "He worked in entertainment before joining the space academy."

"Are you all explorers then? Did you go to school to…learn to do this?"

"Those were wonderful days," she said with a faraway smile. "Sometimes I dream about them."

"And at the academy, you learn to be…spirit warriors. You said that."

"We aren't truly spirits, of course. We're mortal like you. But it's more that the spirit inside us, inside all of us, is especially strong. That essence, that spirit, that soul, that kernel is the energy that presses outward toward discovery, adventure, knowledge, wisdom. I told you before about that center, that spirit, and I'm telling you again that you yourself have it — and I have it. And I developed mine through the academy and became a skilled adventurer, a warrior going out to do battle with any forces of evil that we can reach."

"Evil? But you aren't fighting evil here. You said you were here to observe, not to seriously affect anything."

"There are more ways to fight evil than you can imagine," said Roci. "Evil hasn't much power here after all. Not one of you is compelled to do evil; it emanates from your own mind. There has been an evil prince here until recent times, in the spirit world, but he has no power over you unless you let him have it."

"So the devil didn't make me do anything?"

"If you did it, it was your choice," she said. "Maybe your conscience, your angel, your thought adjuster, your voice inside, your soul, your name for it, knew you shouldn't do it and told you so. You listened but did not hear. Your problem is that you're seriously overpopulated with subnormals and deviates who don't or can't listen to the spirit."

"But all of us know right and wrong, don't we? Even the jungle pygmies and outback aborigines. Is that what you're saying?"

"It's inside each of you. Each of you is part of the divine plan, companion to a fragment of God."

"Whew!," Jason exclaimed. "You should write a book."

"No," she said. "You should."

After their meal, they sat by the fire sipping hot tea. The darkness around them was pervasive with night sounds. They could hear an occasional laugh or clanging of pans from the campers just down the road. Jason's mind swirled with speculation over the winding turns of his new life. How could he possibly get into the upcoming trip with Kevin and Susan, Chuck and Sandra — after this?

"Is Mega coming soon?"

She looked at him across the fire. He again thought he saw love in her eyes —love! — could he be loved by an extraterrestrial? How would that be? It had been spectacular so far. She didn't speak, only sipped again from her tea mug, sat it gently on the picnic table, rose and came over to lie with him on the sleeping bag.

They snuggled, her warm head on his chest, and were soon asleep.

At some later time, he opened his eyes, looked about at his surroundings warily to see if they were still alone. Roci was asleep beside him. He raised up and looked across the smoldering fire to see the dark outline of a large standing figure.

It was Mega again, wearing only a loin cloth. He held a double arm full of firewood.

"Hello, Jason. I think it's time to stoke your fires."

"Are you really here?" Jason looked down at Roci, who was still asleep.

"She needs her rest after your busy day. We're on our own tonight, just us guys." Mega squatted and dumped the wood and began rekindling the fire.

"Are we going back to the colony?" Jason asked, pulling himself up from the ground and looking about anxiously.

"No. We're going in another direction tonight," said Mega, pointing his finger skyward. "I thought you'd like to see how we run this operation."

95

Jason looked up into the dark sky, seeing nothing but stars. Mega had quickly gotten the fire going again.

"Here," said Mega, holding out a pair of stylized glasses. The lenses were gold. "I want you to see everything when we rise up into the clouds."

Jason took them cautiously and examined their smooth, rounded design. "Go ahead," said Mega, so he put them on and looked upward.

Everything took on a shade of gold but he could see for a great distance. Far up in the sky, he saw a large dark object, absolutely stationary and absolutely quiet. "Is...that your headquarters there, a space station?"

"Just my personal carrier," said Mega. "I've come down to get you and carry you to Mission Control. You should feel honored getting this kind of, what do you say, V.I.P. treatment. We want to see what kind of reactions we get from an ordinary and typical mortal. You did profess to be one of those, didn't you?"

"Whatever it takes to get aboard," he replied.

He took off the glasses and examined them again. The night sky again enclosed its secrets.

"So I give you glasses to see and you deliberately take them off. Stand just a little to your left," said Mega, motioning him to move with an outstretched hand. He did so.

Within seconds he knew why. Moving down swiftly and very silently from the sky came a large round silver cylinder, suddenly levitating there in front of them while he scrambled to put the glasses back on. It glowed brilliantly in the light of the campfire and Mega stepped forward to open its door for them. The cylinder was small but roomy enough for both and there was a window on the other side. It rather resembled one of those outside elevators at the Hyatt Regency.

Jason looked at Mega, his white hair cascading down his broad, bare shoulders, his white beard closely cropped, looking at him with what seemed to be fatherly affection. It calmed his mind and he stepped inside. Wordlessly, Mega followed him in and closed the door. The cylinder began rising.

Jason watched the golden campsite and campground receding below them as they rose up into the golden sky, watched the wooded terrain expanding underneath, the lights of nearby Crystal Lake appearing in the distance. He felt invigorated, anxious for the adventure.

"You're making great progress," said Mega. "She tells me that you want to help us." Jason was almost uncomfortably close to the large naked man.

"I do, very much. I want to make things better here — anyway I can."

"I have no doubt that most of you would say the same thing."

"Maybe I don't have the ability. But I would use everything I have. And I can learn. I'm a fast learner."

"Your learning capacity is quite important," said Mega, "considering the base from which you begin."

Suddenly the rising cylinder was engulfed in a dark gold nothingness. A soft white light came on to reveal the interior of Mega's cruiser. The cylinder had fitted neatly into a custom-made compartment. Mega opened the door as Jason removed his glasses, and they stepped out into the cozy quarters where he had sat before. He followed Mega's lead and sat in the same soft chair, eyeing again the books and music the explorer had gleaned from the planet.

"Ah! It's nice to be home after a day out on the planet," said Mega, as he stepped over to his easy chair. "Please. Sit down." Now the cruiser seemed to be rising.

"We're still moving," said Jason.

"Yes, up to what you would call the mother ship. I want you to meet my associates."

While they traveled upward, Jason followed the details of the interior, scanned the books in the shelves. There was "Moby Dick," "Absalom, Absalom," "A Tale of Two Cities," "Zen and the Art of Motorcycle Maintenance," "Your Erroneous Zones," "Future Shock," "20 Years of Rolling Stone," a world almanac, an atlas…

"You've read a lot about us," said Jason.

"It was easy and entertaining," said Mega. "I like your English alphabet. It works as well as any I've seen in this local universe."

Jason thought about thanking him but reconsidered. He had no part in structuring the alphabet.

It seemed now that they had stopped. Mega got up and Jason followed him to a sliding door. It opened to reveal a long hallway, all in white, with an arched ceiling.

"We will visit the dome first," said Mega. "It's on top of the station and will give you a good impression of our lifestyle here."

Jason followed him past a series of sliding doors, all with colorful circles above them, shades of purple and red, green, yellow and blue in various combinations and thicknesses of stripes, a color-coded language, it seemed. Suddenly a naked explorer — a man — appeared in front of them, running swiftly, raising his open hand in greeting, which Mega returned. He was quickly gone.

"Fitness training," said Mega. A naked woman came up behind them and ran swiftly past. Jason marveled at the uncommon speed and agility of the runners.

They stepped onto an open platform which rose upward into a vertical tunnel. In a moment, the broad vista of a transparent dome opened before them. Jason looked in amazement at a huge garden of small trees, green foliage and flower beds, a flowing water fountain of silver and white and a number of naked explorers, all with resplendent physiques, sitting and lying around on soft chairs and pillows and the shiny green grass, some of them in loving embrace.

In the center of it all, rising out of the floor, was the giant trunk of an oak tree, disappearing below the floor and rising up to command the scene with its huge limbs and canopies of leaves which seemed to reach the top of the dome. It was the centerpiece of a well-lighted arboretum, and he looked up through the foliage and the transparent ceiling into the night sky with its thousands of bright stars.

But Jason's eyes soon turned downward. He was more captivated by the nude explorers, who seemed to be curious about them. This was not like a timedrop; he would get to talk to them maybe, as more than an observer.

"They're all as handsome, as beautiful as you and Roci," said Jason.

"We have long ago mastered the genetic and cosmetic sciences," said Mega. "We could have evolved into some other more mind-oriented countenance but we preferred to maintain our strong bodies and compact heads and our general physical features which, I admit, we find quite attractive. This is how we choose to look. We didn't want to become little green men or something, and we also wanted to remain…physically fit." He laughed softly, "not let our intellects make our heads too big, so to speak.

The others paid casual notice to them as they walked across the garden landscape. It reminded Jason of the garden colony, which he and Roci had seen that afternoon. He saw two more rainbow birds, sitting together up in a tree which sprouted a full bunch of yellow bananas.

"Do these…people all have work to do?"

"Yes," said Mega. "We have schedules much as you do for fulfilling responsibilities and utilizing the mind and body. We also have an equal measure of what you might call leisure or pleasure time. In our view, it could be called interpersonal and recreational relations. You know what you say about all work and no play."

"And you…have sex and reproduce like we do?"

"We not only have maintained and refined sexual unions, we also revere them as a sacrament on occasion," said Mega. "The supreme power allowing us to taste just a tiny bit of the creation of life. And we reproduce much more easily than you. The fetuses are transplanted into laboratory settings where they are developed quite efficiently. Childhood can be accelerated greatly if desired through nutritional engineering. That's a matter of genetics to you too, I suppose."

They arrived beside a flowing willow tree and three explorers rose from around a small, circular table to face them. He saw Roci first.

"I believe you know Blest 20," said Mega. "or Roci as she calls herself on your sphere. And this is Jai 47...and David 111...and Atla 83." Jason shook hands firmly with each of them. They were all perfect specimens and all nude. They sat down again and an equally beautiful woman with amazingly full black hair cascading to her knees walked up to them softly and handed Mega and Jason large frosted glasses. They contained a blue beverage filled with shaved ice and with a green sprig of plant life on top. He noticed the others had the same beverage.

Mega raised his glass in a toast and they all followed. "To adventure," he said, "and to our new friend, Jason."

They drank. Jason found the taste vivid and satisfying.

"It's a mixture of berries and grapes, with a little spice," said Blest. "Nothing as dramatic as that cactus liquor we had last night. We have business to conduct. We wanted to interview you for a possible assignment."

"I would like to have an assignment. I think you want to help us, so I want to help you."

"Do you have the attributes we need?" asked Jai, "wisdom, courage, fortitude, honor?"

"I hope that I do. How much is enough? I believe that I can do a lot, especially through your example."

"You'll be alone here when we leave," said David. "You will only have yourself for reliance and for inspiration."

"But if I know all this," said Jason, "if I understand what we have to do to save ourselves, then that knowledge can be my power. Maybe I can start a movement. Maybe I can get others to help."

"I don't think that's possible," said Atla. "I think you've got it all wrong. We aren't a movement; you and your people are already a movement. And you're all progressing just about on schedule considering some of your past history. What is it you think you could do?"

"Live by example. Care about people, about getting us to where we can love and nurture one another and stop all the war and hatred and greed, the disease and starvation and destruction of the environment, bring people together and help them understand that there is a supreme and benevolent power, a God, who wishes us to strive to be like him."

"Or her?" said Blest.

"Of course. Whatever," said Jason.

"You could certainly be doing those things without any participation or inspiration from us," said Atla. "I hope you will after we leave."

"Maybe I could even go with you."

"You contradict yourself," said Mega. "I thought you wanted to go to work here."

"I would gladly go to work here but...going with you seems to be the ultimate adventure. Maybe I could come back, knowing more, able to do more."

"We probably won't be back," said Mega. "There are so many other places."

Jason looked around at the explorers facing him. He felt like a guinea pig, a job applicant rapidly sinking in failure. "I guess you'll obliterate my memory then. I guess I won't be able to do anything," he said dejectedly. "I was just hoping for something better. I hate the idea of being born, living and dying without creating anything of lasting value, not making any positive impact at all on society. I really was hoping to do something good with my life, not just for me but for other people."

They seemed to be communicating silently with one another. Jason followed one face to another but they were all opaque, revealing nothing, at least to him.

"We'll consider your request, and your needs," said Mega. "Now, I think we had best visit Mission Control. He rose and each of them followed suit.

Jason shook hands again, firmly, and all around, including with Blest, who seemed strangely aloof to him, neutral and noncommittal. Jason felt he had flunked the test. Mega was soon leading him away before he was really cognizant of it.

They walked to the trunk of the large oak and stood on a small rectangular platform at Mega's direction. It began sinking with them, slowly, into the floor beside the oak.

For a moment they were in darkness. But quickly a giant room of busy activity opened before them around the massive base of the tree. Again the behemoth was in the center of the scene, disappearing from here into both the ceiling and floor. Explorers ringed all sides of a circular wall, sitting at control panels, monitoring and responding to what seemed a rapid inflowing of information with a cacophony of strange verbiage.

All across one wall a giant electronic map of a flattened planet was marked with lights of many colors, spotlighting hundreds of locations on both the sea and land areas. The panorama dominated the scene and held the rapt attention of a double row of statuesque, bare-skinned explorers with personal control boards and talking into headsets.

"They are in touch with our explorers in many parts of your world," said Mega," collecting their information and impressions and feeding it into Mission Control, the vessel for all of our accumulated findings. Naturally enough, it is all stored inside the giant oak."

"A tree? Why a tree?"

"It's symbolic and it's beautiful. The oak tree is one of the finest of the One God creations. You will eventually learn this. It is also symbolic of the ecological potential and limitations of our work. In the course of the mission, it grows as our knowledge grows. The expanding rings inside it are like the rings of our mission symbol. Do you understand?"

"I...don't think so. Not so well," said Jason.

"I'm sure you don't," said Mega, "so I suggest we get to the root of the matter. Just step back on the conveyor here." He and Jason descended again on the mobile platform. The floor again opened and they were into darkness.

Momentarily, another room opened to them, engulfed in blue light. The base of the oak was even larger here, the room was deserted of explorers or equipment, but there were numerous pillows and soft couches all over the blue-soaked room. Jason seemed to be standing on bare hard earth.

"The light warms the soil and nourishes the roots, and has an energizing effect on the explorers who enjoy coming here for repose," said Mega. "The blue light is very powerful when you learn to access it."

"The roots. Where do they go?"

"Follow me," said Mega, stepping around the side of the tree. Jason followed.

On the other side of the giant trunk, he watched in surprise as Mega squatted at the lip of a small round hole wedged against the huge trunk. "If you like adventure," Mega said with a wry smile, "try this." He eased his nude body down into the black hole, waist-deep, lifted his arms up above his head, and quickly slid out of sight. Jason's eyes widened.

It was his turn and he thought it would be best not to think about it — just do it. He eased his slender body down into the blackness, felt nothing, then managed to find some kind of smooth, cold surface with his left foot. He eased further down, neck deep, then turned loose.

Down he plunged, on a short sliding board that circled twice around the oak trunk and plopped him down on soft, cool earth. An amber light washed this new scene. He saw that this tiny compartment was circular, Mega was there observing him, and the compartment's centerpiece was the huge taproot of the great oak.

"This is the Source," said Mega, his hands passing gently over the smooth hard surface of the giant exposed root. Jason reached to touch it too, in some holy way he didn't understand.

"This is the source, where our sensors are connected, just below here, in the soilbed."

"Yes, but is it the source of the tree, or is it more than that? Are you saying it's much more?"

"Our knowledge is all stored here," said Mega. "All that we know and all that we learn comes here, to be protectively encased inside the living tree, a tree of life, similar to the one you have heard about in Eden. It is safe here from the strange and erratic magnetic forces of space as we travel. Those forces can destroy entire files. This infusion into a high-level biological life form gives technology a true communion with nature and strengthens its fruits."

"Are you saying it's like a computer, storing information? Protecting it from magnetism? Then you're all connected to the tree, right?"

"There are monitors all over the ship, putting information in, taking it out, integrating it to arrive at conclusions based on an ultimate and supreme logic. It's all in here," he patted the root, "in the core here, in the various roots all around us, carefully…trellised through the earth soil, or up inside the trunk, in the limbs, even the twigs and leaves, based on the information's vitality. It's concentrated as tree sap and it permeates the whole natural structure. And it grows as our information expands, as our knowledge grows."

"Until what? What happens when it outgrows the ship?"

"We will send it back and plant it in an appropriate place of learning on Pleiades-7 or nearby. We will grow another when we visit the next planet. You see that your Earth store has already grown quite large here. You should also try to learn here, tonight, that this is all highly symbolic of your individual life quest. You can think back upon this visit and glean continually expanded understandings."

"Amazing," Jason muttered, trying to take it all in, fondling the massive root in front of them. "And what of the oak itself? Does it reproduce?"

"Let's go check the fruit," Mega replied. He grasped the rails of the silver slide and pulled his muscular body upward, leading the way up and out again. As he disappeared above, Jason fumbled to get a grip on the slide rails, which actually had handles, and struggled to pull himself back up and out of the amber room.

From the blue room, they rose back up into the methodical activity of the control center. "So this is what we call the Front Line team," said Mega "They are busy, but of course they work in rotating teams. We have just about all the explorers on the Earth surface that we can manage right now. Others can descend when we have more returns."

They continued to rise, up into the garden dome and to a stop again in the area of the relaxing explorers. Jason noticed that a couple was making ravenous love on the grass near the fountain.

"I'll never look at an oak tree in the same way again…or people either."

Mega laughed. "Let's go up," he said, looking upward and whistling loudly. Startled, Jason looked at him.

"Whistling," said Mega. "It's an interesting thing that you do. Like a universal or intergalactic language — for calling attention. There are many forms of it."

Jason looked to the domed ceiling to see two long ladders of rope falling before them, flopping and flouncing until Mega grabbed them both and held one out to him.

"Get a good hold," said Mega. "They'll pull us up. I like to make things interesting...okay?" He smiled wryly at Jason, and winked.

Jason got a good grip with both hands and pulled his feet up to the first rung. Up through the ceiling and floor they began rising, above the lounging explorers in the skydome and on up the side of the giant oak into the masses of limbs and leaves. It was a perfectly manicured specimen even up high, and Jason realized why as they soared past workmen on the huge branches. They were misting the leaves with sprays of liquid.

Mega and Jason came to an easy halt near the top, from where Jason could look up and see an incredible skyscape of sparkling stars. A slender young woman on a slender limb, her nude waist ringed by a busy tool belt, exchanged smiles with Mega.

"Perhaps a fresh fruit, my beautiful sister," said Mega. She responded by handing him a firm, nicely shaped acorn. He took it as he stepped out onto a small limb. Jason clung precariously to the rope ladder.

"This is why we call it the tree of life," said Mega, holding up the acorn. It still sported its cute cap and a short curved stem. "I'm sure you've heard of the tree of life."

"You said it was like the one in Eden. This is it?"

"Ours...for the present. There was exactly one, your allotment, on your planet once — but not any more. We eat one of these fruits each day, and it's all we really need for nourishment."

"Acorns? You eat acorns?"

"If your metabolism is attuned and the oak is properly nurtured, it's the best food for your body, your mind, and your emotional and spiritual growth," said Mega evenly. "This is arguably the finest material product our civilization has yet produced." He looked intently at the acorn and then at Jason.

"Of course, we will have to give it up," said Mega somberly.

"But...why?" asked Jason.

"We have the acorn...but no pockets in which to carry it away," said Mega with a hint of a smile, and noting their naked thighs. They laughed together.

"And so you know now what's inside the tree, sum knowledge in the form of running sap," said Mega. "And you see that this is fruit that comes from inside. Just remember this as a metaphor."

Jason ventured to step out onto the limb now, did so with Mega's help, holding another limb above him to keep his balance. "I've heard of the…tree of knowledge, of good and evil. Is this part of all that then?"

"Well, you know the expression," said Mega, "you are what you eat." He and the slender girl with the basket of acorns began laughing heartily. Jason tried to laugh too.

"But I have a lot of other things to do, if you'll excuse me," said Mega. "I'd better get you back to your camping trip and let you think about all this. Hope you've enjoyed the audition." He reached out and slapped Jason smartly across the cheek.

He quickly awakened there on the sleeping bag next to Roci, his cheek stinging, or so he imagined. He touched it lightly.

She remained asleep. He sat up and tried to collect his thoughts, finally getting up to add more sticks of wood to the fire. The load of wood brought by Mega was not to be seen.

It was all just about too much. He sat next to the fire and watched it catch up with the new fuel. He looked back up into the night sky. The stars still twinkled quietly. There is a giant ship up there, a huge dome. Why can't anybody see it? The word "cloak" entered his mind. Who put it there? "Cloak?" He guessed that the ship, the dome, was all covered up, cloaked, from primitives like himself. However, this could all still be dangerous. Already, humans had killed at least one of them. What else could happen?

What a day. He found out they were being pursued by military types, and that Ellen had an alien visitor too. He met some more of these visitors, got a brand new van, went to a prehistoric agricultural colony and saw a kind of dinosaur get blown away, then went up into the night sky to an…extraterrestrial headquarters and learned that Earth knowledge is being implanted into a huge oak tree possessed with superfood acorns, and growing to accommodate what they are now learning here. And those were just the high points. It was like an educational pleasure cruise, or adventure excursion, for them.

He also had flunked a job interview, he supposed. But Mega said he should remember all of this. That's what he said. Ummm. Jason was encouraged. He was being asked to remember.

And another day would soon be dawning. Having all of his good friends show up might be boring after all of this. What would they think of Roci? How could they fit into this galactic picture?

SIX: The Serpents of Eden

When Jason awakened to the sunlight, he struggled to turn over in the sleeping bag and see if she was there. Again, she was gone, the perennially early riser. He hurriedly pulled on his pants and, partially clothed, holding his boots and socks and no doubt sleepy-eyed he emerged from the tent to see her at the picnic table. Coffee had been made again, and she was reading a newspaper and eating an apple.

She turned and looked at him with a clever glint and wryly curled lips. "Well, aren't you a sleepy head once again, Earth friend," she teased.

"And so did you have to get up and milk the cows?" he teased back. Uh-oh, she wouldn't get that one.

"Ha!" she said good-naturedly, wiping apple juice from her chin. "I had forgotten you did that."

While he drank coffee and put on his boots, she asked about his friends. Jason had to collect his thoughts and bring them back to his comparatively mundane Earth life. He had never tried to describe them before so it wasn't easy.

Kevin and Susan were the ones he truly admired. From a small plant nursery business, competent Kevin, a former Infantryman, had gotten into exporting from Mexico — cacti, ponytail palms, other exotics. He hired Mexican collectors now and he trucked large numbers of plants across the border, through the government's inspection and fumigation, and on to Florida for wholesaling. Jason admired him for his physical prowess, his fortitude and courage.

Susan, his woman, was admirable too — petite, pretty and smart, like Kevin a partaker of some recreational drugs but highly responsible and now making money selling silver that Kevin helped her get from Mexico, as well as with her plant maintenance business. They were both resourceful entrepreneurs.

Chuck and Sandra were different, more negative and cynical in attitude compared to Kevin and Susan's upbeat and positive demeanor. Chuck was slightly built with little wire glasses and a craving for all kinds of mind-altering drugs that Jason thought could be dangerous for him. His paying

105

work was as a hairdresser but he longed to be a painter, had taken art lessons and now produced some art, mostly oils of abstract things, sometimes neon sculptures, in his spare time.

Sandra, too, was a gentle and caring person at heart, but she frequently complained that the world was a shitty place and totally unfair to her, mostly because of their struggles for money. She did office work at a loan company. They often bitched together about drug prohibition and narcs, the political power structure, straitlaced and stuffy people, and other things that they seemed to feel were conspiring to hold them down economically, spiritually and otherwise. They still called the source of most misgivings the "establishment," or simply "them" or "they."

Jason felt their infatuation with drugs was risky and that their attitudes were unnecessarily negative at times. But they were all friends and they all seemed to commune more cohesively because of their common appreciation for cannabis and occasional trip drugs. These recreational adventures had involved LSD, downers, uppers, magic mushrooms and now this special treat that Kevin and Jason had conspired to extract from the peyote cactus.

"We did it down in Texas, at Enchanted Rock, the place where we got together," Jason told Roci. "We rambled out into the wilderness that day and it was really a profound kind of experience. A couple of folks up-chucked early on. That often happens. But when the mescaline took effect, it opened a whole new dimension of intensified sights and sounds, a deeply felt communion with nature, like an altered perspective on the whole creation and how we fit into it. We skinny-dipped in a pond, saw the deer and jack-rabbits and dragonflies, climbed over the rocks, laid in the sun, watched the big, puffy, white clouds. It all felt spiritually uplifting, free, euphoric. There was never anything like it before."

"And afterwards? You told me it was the..."

"Downside," said Jason, "that's the hippie word for it. Like...a downer. We all were lost in a kind of a deep melancholy for most of the next day. Our minds seemed to have turned to ashes and it took a while to get our equilibrium back."

"Was it worth it?"

"Yeah, I guess so. Just a hangover. If drugs like this can open up some new vista for us to take a look at, and try to learn something from, then it's worth a little downside, I think. I don't regret it. In fact, I was looking forward to doing it again."

"You're using past tense — was."

"I guess I am," Jason admitted. "It doesn't seem so important any more. It seems like not much of anything in the face of what I've experienced with you, what I've learned. I don't care if they even show up or not. I guess I wish they wouldn't, and we could go about whatever adventure we have left.

You're the most important thing in my life right now — the only thing really."

"I want to meet them."

"You do?"

"I want to know them a little, see how they're different from you, how they're the same, perhaps give them some encouragement."

Jason realized he hadn't sufficiently considered Roci's wishes. Now he did. "Sure, that's what we'll do then. It'll be my pleasure helping you get to know them. And...can I ask you something? When are you going back? How long do we have left?"

She looked at him with feeling. "I'll be picked up Monday night — at midnight — Rocky Mountain time."

It didn't seem to him that she was happy about it. Was there any way he could change it? She must have read the thought.

"I live in a grand and glorious place," she told him gently. "There is so much love and compassion there, true togetherness as communities. We live in large arboretum cities, self-contained and protected from the frigid season. At other times of the year, we go out freely onto the plains. The deep sweet grasses there provide much of our food. But...life there isn't completely grand and satisfying. The elements of high adventure are no longer there. There is a sameness. That's why I wanted to be an explorer, to get beyond the peace and love of the planet and into the dangerous and thrilling cosmos."

"Then maybe you could stay here. We could stir up a bit of excitement from time to time." He grinned.

She laughed. "Remember, I've been seeing the newscasts from here for a long time. I know what it's like here, and it truly isn't...universally appealing. I've even seen some entertainment presentations."

"Do you get our television there?"

"Of course, but I've never bothered to watch it much. We get a great many better things from the enlightened worlds."

"What do you remember — from our broadcasts?"

She thought a minute. "A lot of people playing roles. A lot of requests to buy and consume things. Remedies for pain. One would think you are a very sickly people. Laughter that sounds and is artificial. Killers and thieves, real and unreal. Not much of interest. You all seem to dote on conflict. I'm not sure I understand that. That is a constant aura here, and it needs to be spiritualized. But there isn't enough spiritual unity."

"I wish I could know your world. What is it's name?"

"There is no name for it in English. We would have to fabricate one. Sorry."

"I understand."

"I transmitted a request on your behalf to Mission Control, Jason. I asked that you be allowed to contribute."

"To...the oak tree? You put a request into the tree."

"Yes, a reply should be sprouting from the top very soon."

"I...beg your pardon."

"The sap in the newest leaves emanates from the deepest root, and considers all of the information — logical, emotional, spiritual — in every part of the tree. An answer to my request will be forthcoming. Of course, the sap is electrified."

"Electric...sap."

She laughed. "Sometimes your people are so preoccupied with symbols that they fail to see the essence of your lives and the simplicity of the powerful energy forces you have been given."

"I'm sure that's right," Jason said, thoroughly confused.

"Perhaps you'd be surprised to really understand what can be contained in tree sap, or what you could achieve by a stronger communion with nature. There are essences in your world that you haven't begun to discover. Perhaps you'd like to see some of the essence of ours. I can take you there in an altered state. You will dream about it with me if you like. I will give you mind pictures from my life."

"Like a timedrop. Or like that scene where you crashed."

"Similar. You will see."

"Fine."

"Do you really care about my life?" she asked him suddenly. "Are you sure that you really care about me, or are you just infatuated with a beautiful...thing?"

"I'm infatuated," he said. "But, believe me, it goes much deeper. You've put reality into things I've wondered about and dreamed about for a long time. I'm so deeply committed to you — the idea of you, the reality of you, every nuance of you — that I think I would die for you. I know now that I'm bound for a greater life beyond anyway. I would just wish I could share some life with you — any kind of life."

It had all gushed out of him, and he was profoundly sincere. She stared at him, sharing his love, and her large green eyes misted with her own feelings. They came to each other and clutched hands and eyes. She motioned him inside the tent, where they stripped nude and wrapped themselves deeply into each other's warm bodies.

The scene materialized for him out of a fog and somehow Jason knew that he was being carried on a tour, was viewing reconstructed scenes and hearing silent explanations from her mind — transmitted to him so he would understand something of her life. Images came upon him and faded into others.

She materialized in his mind at a younger age. He saw her running up a green and rounded hill, fresher of face, willowy thin. Deep rich grasses blowing in the breeze, her looking back at the massive clear dome, a tropical garden inside shining lustrously in the sun across the open plain below. The landscape was an impressive panorama of long grass and smoothly contoured hills, blending with giant clusters of boulders.

The images melted into newer images.

A glistening single rail carried a sleek, silver train very slowly across the landscape, her there inside with friends, talking in indecipherable, rapid tones, laughing together. Outside, for the viewing pleasure of the passengers, masses of foliage and flowering plants comprised the passing scene, a menagerie of exotic animals living in customized, sometimes rock wall enclosed landscapes, each with a flowing fountain and pool for water. Education, entertainment and beauty for the travelers.

"I am Blest 20 and I am seven tribs old," the voice whispered to him, directly into his ears as the pictures continued. The monorail train moved casually across the landscape; there was no hurry here, no stress.

The space academy loomed up ahead. Silver pointed spires of towering buildings shining in the sun, the historic and symbolic sun pinnacle glowing bright atop the highest structure, the familiar blue dove of peace emblem beneath it. To the left she saw the rocky peaks of Alzatore, lifting out of the long wildlife valley. To the right she knew they would train also in the tropical swamps of the Tarpean low country. "My heart is thrilled," she whispered. "I will be an explorer, perhaps a spirit warrior." He saw tears in her eyes.

He saw her with friends, colorful living quarters, a soft couch, pillows and plants and nude lovers embracing. The clear blue pool was part of the interior and she was swimming down inside it, a deep grotto filled with rainbows of fishes, her beautiful body arching and turning, immersed in the shiny blue, illuminated with lights. She came nose to nose with a large orange fish, big-eyed and curious.

The couples rubbed their wet bodies with towels. All was gaiety. The food came out of the wall, steaming warm, piles of green and brown objects, a white lumpy soup and red liquid.

She chose a gown for the evening, a sheer, free-flowing and transparent fabric. My lover brother's name is Mast, her soft voice told him. He is tall and gentle and strong and golden.

She untied the red ribbon on her leg. This symbolic signal told him he could come to her now, when he was ready. It was clear that he was erectly ready. His face and lips disappeared upon her body; her thin fingers ran through his hair as they embraced in gasping abandon.

The sun was shining suddenly. With a running start, she races across the parade grounds as the crowd cheers, her momentum carrying her up the slanted side of a stone wall, gasping and grasping at the top in her final burst of energy, there grabbing the large and shiny gold ring that had been implanted by professors over two hundred epochs ago. She was grinning broadly, clinging to the ring, bare toes clasped to the stones of the wall, one arm lofted triumphantly. The crowd cheered good-heartedly.

There fades into Jason's mind a cloudy day in the swamp, rich green and misted in cool rain. The cadet ahead of Blest climbed precariously across the precipice, legs dangling, small female fingers grasping to the large, roughly twisted rope, suspended, dangling and moving one hand in front of another. The river was running silently, some 200 yards below. Halfway across she falters, clings helplessly for a moment and falls, arms and legs flailing. A net rises up out of the water to catch her fall, sagging her gently back into the water as the class claps and whistles for her effort. Blest poises confidently to take her place at the rope.

He heard her voice. "I am brave. It is invigorating to be brave, good for self-reliance and confidence, good for growing ability too, good for all." She sounds younger. She begins climbing, arm-to-arm, strongly, in confident strides. Her arm muscles rippled and wet.

The scene fades to an open field. She and Mast, both helmeted and ready for another space academy test.

He is first and she watches anxiously — a test of comprehensive dexterity, a milestone, a merit badge, a stimulating competition.

Mast is brown-skinned, has lean muscles, ridged hard across his bare stomach. He wears only a loin cloth. The crowd is anxious, as he is, now taking wing on fleet, bare feet, running across the courtyard, beginning to swing over his head the steel anchor at the end of a long rope. He unravels the rope, ever longer, as he swings. The arc grows wider as he runs faster, on and on toward the testing tower.

Finally, he leaps and throws with all his might. The anchor soars skyward and catches cleanly on the rail of the second-story balcony. He quickly scales the wall, sure-footed. The applauding crowd can hear the jetflyer, pilotless, approaching. He must have precise timing.

Mast swings himself surely over the second story balcony rail, pulling up the anchor and rapidly rolling much of the rope around his arm. Quickly, he is swinging the anchor again, in a smaller arc, careful not to whack into the tower. Time was getting close. He swung the anchor upward, with a back spin, up to the roof, hearing it clack, then bounce, then catch hold on the rim. He hears Roci's soft voice say: "Great! But hurry."

Mast tests the rope, pulls himself over the edge and climbs upward again, muscles straining. He struggles to pull his legs over the top, rolling over twice onto the bare roof. He sees the jetflyer approaching, cruising smoothly, arriving at just the right moment and at just the right altitude to be challenging. Mast rolls up the anchor, begins swinging it again, furiously.

The jetflyer is coming closer, flying steadily twenty feet above the roof. It soars toward him as Mast lets the anchor fly. It clatters against the side, missing the loop and falling free as the flyer reaches the roof and glides quietly on. Failure! But he still has the second chance — the rope ladder. It dangles down enticingly, but the flyer will be quickly past the roof, in seconds! He runs after it at breakneck speed, desperately, to catch it before it reaches the edge. He leaps there at the precipice into the nothingness above the street.

One bare hand catches the rope firmly, his arms and legs dangling over the nothingness down to the courtyard and the failure represented by the net. Jason watches him clutch at the ladder once, twice, with his free hand, and finally grasp it hard with a final lunge, just in time to relieve the aching muscles in his other arm. He climbs the rope, commandeers the jetflyer and brings it onto the landing pad smartly.

Cheers and laughter. Hugs and kisses. Classmates acclaiming his fine showing. The scene fades into another.

Blest 20 puts on her spacesuit in the new scene, with a transparent globe helmet to protect her from the hard chill which would hit her above the cloud layer. This was a major academy test for her.

While the piloter carries her up into the sky, she plots the exact location of the pinnacle light on atmosurveillance equipment, then sights it with her portable tracker. The piloter opens and she ejects smoothly, the backpack rocket propelling her straight up into the wet clouds, teeth clamped onto the breathing line. Jason seemed to feel the dark wetness inside the clouds.

Momentarily, she bursts through the cloud layer, her suit wet, helmet dripping, up into the sunlight above. But it was bone-chilling cold up here. Jason, too, felt a chill. The pinnacle orb floated a hundred or more sphactants to her left. She had miscalculated and barely had enough rocket power left to make it there. The gauge read 52-low.

The large transparent ball reflected a pale blue light, clearly visible even in the full sunshine here above the cloud level. "The pinnacle is a containment of light energy that can change into many colors to direct my people's priorities," Roci whispered to Jason's sleeping ear "It is encased in the large round circle of unity, clear and transparent, and is comprised of perfectly pressured airmatter and lightenergy. It is a symbol of the space academy mission."

Jason watches as Roci squeezes the hand controls to provide a burst from her rocket, and arches her body horizontally to glide in the direction of the light orb. Closer and closer she floats, teeth clenching the breath line, face tensed with the stress of making an exact connection.

She feels the rocket sputter as she nears the shining orb, quickly loosening the strap in order to jettison it, jaws gripped, eyes strongly focused. Timing is critical. She reaches with both arms and allows the pack to fall away, grasping and embracing the huge ball quickly and surely, wrapping her body around it, arms, legs, body, and all.

This tandem of epic lightsource and grasping, embracing mortal tumbling and rolling over and over and, in its added weight, beginning to fall downward, Blest's weight pulling it down faster and faster, rolling like a giant marble and falling down into the clouds.

What a sight it was! And Jason was somehow falling with them. Her body wrapped around the light ball, plummeting through the dark wet, swirling clouds again, but this time the light turned the interior into a magnificent luminous scene of billowy white, filled with glistening and streaking crystals.

Bursting down and out of the clouds, they fell faster. Now, the cheers of classmates and friends could be heard below. Clutching hard onto the falling blue ball, she checks the meter on her shoulder.

She had spat out the breathing line; now she clenched her teeth tightly on the shoulder control, pulling the lever to unleash the huge mushroom chute from the waist pack. The chute filled quickly with air, puffing open to jerk back her descent to a soft floating, carrying her gently downward to the field, arms fully embracing the light, tears of joy in her eyes.

Cheers abound. Well-wishers cover her gloriously, showering her with affection, carrying her jubilantly over their heads to the presentation area, holding aloft the great blue orb too, and singing. Voices high and low-pitched and all together, strange and intense but ecstatic, harmonic, exhilarating.

He saw her and Mast back at their quarters, celebrating with friends. "We have been granted a child request, came her whisper in his ear. He saw her with friends, sitting together, and love seemed to permeate the room.

"We will continue our studies and bequeath the child to a fortunate pair," she told him. "There are so many who delight in child-rearing, such a noble calling. And they are blessed in many ways for their service."

The scene faded into a kind of laboratory. She and Mast and several others admired the fetus on the support system, growing there, with tiny fingers and outsized eyes. Connected to the system. "It is surely a very fine little personality," he heard her whisper. "All the tests were positive and they will give her all the good virtues to her capacity to embrace them. We are told we should be proud of the creation we have achieved. God has allowed us to create a bit of life too." There is happiness in the air.

She is ministering to Mast in their quarters, his body cut and bruised from exploding fragments at the firing range. He is soon well again.

They are together in another scene and they are parting. "My love is assigned to a mining team. His engineering knowledge and aptitude recommends this service but does not absolutely require it. He will go, anxious to get out in the local universe. I will stay. I may become an explorer. They say I can do it."

He sees her walking with Mast to the jetflyer, which will carry him to the transport ship. "We smiled and laughed and recalled to each other joyful things we had shared," she recalled, speaking silently to Jason's mind. "The parting is not tragic. The memories will always be there. But there are so many others to love too. All of us. We are all much the same, so it is self-love, our species. Yet we are each fascinatingly different, each of us, often in subtle ways, as we were created to be."

The jetflyer burst away, her holding an open palm after it.

Jason continues to see Blest in the remainder of this day, having a meal with friends at the Rosewall commune, swimming with them in the grotto, returning to her apartment for several hours of rest and mind transmissions on geological dating. She bathes, tends her plants, records a message for possible callers or visitors, and enjoys a visual presentation on the exploration of Dardamunde, hoping she can go there someday and meet those electrical, non-breathing life types. Jason hears her whispering her thoughts to him.

She recalls a variety of memories with Mast, to ensure their permanent retention and recall, she tells Jason, and then she can purposefully move on to new adventures the following day.

He sees her fall asleep, and Jason slowly begins to feel that they are together again in the flesh, flowing together as one, slumbering in the tent in Colorado, on planet Earth, in the warm morning sun.

They awakened, rolled deeper into each other's perspiring embrace, with lustful sweat and sensual abandon. Then they got up, went to the shower house together and began preparing food for their incoming visitors. Jason drove in to Crystal Lake to get more beer and two bottles of tequila for the occasion, and try out his new van.

Waiting for his friends at mid-afternoon gave them the opportunity to handle campsite chores, prepare for their evening meal of stew and salad and for Jason to take further stock of his new realm of thinking. He was anxious to return to the Edenroot colony and Roci promised him they would timedrop there with Mega when they turned in to sleep that night.

He saw her gazing at Long's Peak, highest point in the park at 14,700 feet, snow-capped and rocky, well above the tree line and wrapped now, as it often was, in a shroud of cloud and mist.

113

"They say the weather can be fine down here but can stir up a pretty bad thunderstorm or snowstorm up there in no time flat," said Jason, "The weather can change in a hurry on the top."

"Have you ever been up there?" she asked.

"No. Always wanted to climb it though. There's a way to get up there, they call it the keyhole route, where you can make all right if you're not an experienced climber. But I'm sure it's tough too, especially if you aren't used to the lower oxygen level up here. It's just hard to breathe up there if you aren't used to it. Saps your stamina. Of course, maybe you would be different."

Roci walked forthrightly to the tent, where she pulled her special vest from the canvas bag she had bought at the store. She came back and reached out something to him. He took it, saw that it was a large green acorn, shorn of its cap and stem.

He stared at it as if it were magic. "It is magic, I suppose," she said, responding to his thought. "If there comes a time when you need energy very quickly, then break it open and eat the nut inside."

"Is this from where I think it is?"

"Yes, it is," she said. "This is our special diet — one a day — which maintains our optimum level of physical strength and mental clarity. I think it may work the same for you. Keep it for an emergency."

"What kind of emergency? What do you anticipate?"

"I only anticipate that you may need it," she said. "It is in my mind. I don't know why."

Jason gripped it hard, looked at it again as if trying to see some hidden power inside. He laughed. "An acorn. It seems like just an acorn, but I suppose it's much more."

"Your acorns here haven't been infused, so don't bother to use them. But keep this one in a safe place, and on your body."

"As you wish," he said, tucking it into the inside pocket of his denim jacket. "It'll be next to my heart."

Soon, Kevin's gold van came rolling up to the campsite. The four of them piled out amid greetings, smiles and laughter, and introductions went all around. The camaraderie was on, food was unloaded, two other tents started up, an ice chest of beer appeared, and a clandestine marijuana joint began circulating between them. They were caught up in the revelry of friendship, and for the rest of the afternoon, Jason, still somewhat withdrawn because of his extraordinary experiences, remembered mostly a series of visions and comments.

Kevin, tall and lean, sported a ponytail and an Indian headband these days, wore a buckskin shirt and jeans, a huge belt buckle of mottled turquoise and high-top hiking boots. Jason had always greatly admired him for his bearing and bold demeanor, and his physical abilities doing things like barehanded rock-climbing and skiing on one ski, and then barefooted!

"Jason, you old stud dog," he kidded. "You got yourself a damned beautiful woman this time, ain't you? Man! Ain't she something?" Jason couldn't help beaming with pride, but tried to hide it a little. He couldn't lay claim to her.

Other scenes were to come:

Chuck, peering over his little wire glasses and stroking a tiny mustache, said: "Yeah, Boulder is all right, I reckon. The hair business is pretty good. They're pretty laid back about drugs in most places, but there's a real blue-blood society there, the old families that have been there a long time. They think they're hot shit and they look down their noses at the hippie types. I say…hahahaha…fuck 'em if they can't take a joke." Obligatory laughter all around.

Sandra commented, holding a cigarette aloft and nursing a Budweiser: "Just the same old thing, office work, a finance company. Helping the assholes hound decent folks for their money, charging high interest rates. Them that got is them that gets, as they say, and they're still shittin' all over the people who ain't." She seemed unusually negative to Jason; he realized that her and Chuck's bitching had never bothered him much before, but did now. In fact, he bitched with them. He had been too angry, too cynical, too much without any faith in anything." He no longer had the inclination to bitch about anything.

Susan said: "Yeah, things are okay right now. I'm making pretty good in the silver business, more than I ever made in the plant business. I just hope it holds out. I can just about sell everything I can get and wish I could get more. It's a nice little cottage business."

Susan was still positive, Sandra still negative. Susan still partook of health foods and natural vitamins, herb tea and the ministrations of an octogenarian naturopath. Sandra and Chuck still smoked cigarettes and talked too much about "playing with our heads." If they weren't actually doing drugs, they were talking about them, it seemed.

Chuck still said "Wow!" and his head and eyes rolled skyward when he talked about some new speed or downer he had tried. Sandra seemed to follow his lead; conversely Kevin seemed to follow Susan's lead in social and domestic matters, devoting his enthusiasm and energy to his entrepreneurial adventures.

While Chuck could get wide-eyed talking about some mind-drug, Kevin was excited when he talked about his forays deep into Mexico, and the idea of putting some money into a gold mining adventure in Ecuador. And going down there — presumably with machete in hand.

115

He and Susan had a self-reliance and gumption that Chuck and Sandra would never have, Jason thought. It seemed to him that they turned their energies into more positive directions.

"Hell," Kevin laughed, "I don't know how much money I'm gonna make sometimes, but I been making enough to eat and pay for the adventure anyway. Maybe that's the main thing."

He talked to Jason and Chuck about taking a trip to Mexico with him. Chuck was most interested about the quality of the marijuana found there, and how to get it across the border. Kevin was more interested in the types of cacti and succulents he could collect and how well they survived during trucking.

After dark, they sat around a roaring campfire, passing joints and tequila. They had plenty of limes and salt, and the remainder of a case of beer. Jason couldn't help thinking about Mega with each hit from the bottle. He found it difficult to keep his mind on the casual conversation.

Kevin was saying: "I think I'm gonna do a whole cap this time. I just did three-quarters last time, down in Texas. It was fuckin' great — whew! — might as well do a whole number this time. Go for it, right?" He turned up the bottle.

Chuck said: "Yeah, they say you might need a little more the second time anyway. Isn't that what they say?"

"Who's they?" asked Susan.

"Who?" Chuck repeated with a sarcastic laugh. "How the fuck do I know who 'they' is? I don't guess we got any experts on this stuff, have we?"

Kevin replied: "The Indians down in the Southwest used to do it, the Yacquis, I think. I think they still do. It's a big-time religious ceremony, you know. They all paint their faces and eat the peyote. They turn it into this goddawful mush, man. You can't eat it without gagging. After you throw up and get your system all cleaned out, you get these amazing visions, really weird, supernatural stuff. The Indians believe that's the way to make contact with the spirit world."

Chuck was bleary-eyed and still jolly. "Well, fuck, I'd never be one to pass up a good hallucination. You think it's as good as the windowpane we had at that Joe Cocker concert, Jason? You remember that shit?"

Sandra chimed in: "Hell yes, I remember it. We went out in the park, about midnight, swung on the swings."

Kevin agreed: "That was some good shit."

Jason felt he needed to comment: "It seems like more of a nature thing to me, the mescaline. I felt like I was really part of the whole natural wilderness experience down in Texas, you know, the sun and the clouds, swimming in the pond, remember, where we saw that snake, the animals, climbing over the rocks. That windowpane seemed more of a rush-rush thing, not as mellow, the kind of thing you'd want to do in your apartment with some friends and food and music and lay back and get all those rushes but not have to get out and navigate too much."

Kevin said, "Oh yeah, man, you're right. This mescaline's really pretty mellow, isn't it? I think that's what I like about it. You can do it and still get outside and truck around."

"After you puke," said Sandra, with a chuckle. "But it's worth it. 'Cause you're high most of the day."

Susan said: "I think we ought to eat very lightly or not at all before we do it. Maybe a little cereal, maybe not even that. It'd be better to have a completely empty stomach, or at least something really bland on it."

Chuck interjected: "No coffee? Naw, better not risk it."

Kevin said: "We might upchuck a little. Hell, that's part of it. That's the way you get your system purged so it can work real good and get those outstanding rushes comin' at you." He is animated, dodging imaginary rush waves. Everyone is amused. Everyone is also very stoned by this time, mellow-stoned with the mix of the tequila.

Jason was mostly bored. He began to see how shallow he and his friends were about most things.

As if on cue, Roci spoke: "Do you guys and girls just try to reach these altered levels of consciousness on special occasions like this, or do you try in your everyday lives, the natural way, by getting your mind at absolute peace?" Jason's attention perked.

Susan spoke: "It's so important to do that. Like, every day, I take time from whatever I'm doing to lie down and meditate and breathe deeply and just get myself centered again as to who I am. And sometimes, when my system is particularly clean I can sometimes get into a real cosmic state. I actually think I left my body once."

Sandra had heard it before, but replied: "Astral projection. Wow! That's neat."

Kevin added: "Yeah, I know what you mean (nodding to Roci) about a natural high. It's just that it takes a long time, maybe even years, to get to the point where you can get high naturally. Fortunately, (laughing demonically) we have a quick way to do it — with Captain Mescalito." He held up a capsule and twisted his face into a devilish glare. Laughs went around.

Sandra asked her: "You ever done mescaline…or acid?"

Roci replied: "No. It'll be a new experience. I hope you'll be kind enough to help me do it well."

Kevin was quick to reply: "Don't worry about a thing. We got you covered, Babe.

Sandra said: "Stick close to us, Roci. It'll be good. You'll like it. I guess Jason's given you a briefing too, huh?"

"He's been a wonderful companion," said Roci, "and a good lover too."

Uh-oh. Jason, caught off-guard, listened to the loud laughter around him. Kevin slapped him across the shoulder; Susan smiled impishly. "Watch out for that wonderful companion stud!" called Sandra. Jason couldn't help but be pleased at the revelation. How vain and shallow of me, he thought.

"Oh, I'm sorry," said Roci. "I'm not supposed to be that open around people I don't really know." Jason thought that she looked a little dazed. The tequila! Jason remembered seeing her take down two good belts, maybe another, and she had hit the joint a time or two also. This time, he reminded himself, the tequila is a real, material thing, the better to mess up their heads."

"Actually we're quite pleased to know that Jason is a good lay," said Susan gleefully. "And I'm glad to know you two nice people are gettin' a little bit from time to time," she said kindly.

"I sure try to get as much as I can," said Chuck. Sandra, grinning, slapped him playfully across his tousled dark head with a rolled-up trail map.

"I think if we'd all learn to be more loving and affectionate with one another," said Roci, "we'd have less need for drugs to reach some kind of altered state."

Everyone laughed and seemed to agree, but no one knew whether to take her seriously, including Jason. He felt he really needed to say something about all of this.

But she spoke again first, cutting through the confused silence. "That's the most pleasurable thing I can think of, anyway, sharing our bodies in sexual ecstasy, that is if we really care about each other and find each other attractive and have love for all brothers and sisters to share."

"That sounds like an invitation," said Kevin, smiling broadly.

"We could all lie naked and make love here by the fire if we were able to," said Roci, "but I'm very sure you're not inclined to do it or ready to do it. It's too...radical, I think."

Jason could hear the flicker and pop of the flames, saw his friends exchanging looks as he was around the fire. There had suddenly emerged a gigantic pregnant and awkward silence for someone to fill.

Roci broke through it with authority: "There's no reason you need drugs in order to have that carefree abandon. "Get your mind free of fear and judgment and that will be a trip. And get your body free, and that will be a trip too." She unbuttoned her sleeves and pulled off her shirt smartly, revealing perfectly beautiful breasts that seemed to pull his friends' eyes from their sockets.

"Do you think we can all fuck one another and enjoy it?" she asked. "I try to keep myself fit for it — physically and mentally." She tossed the shirt on the table and stood before them with bare breasts and hands on hips. She reached for the bottle of tequila from the table, grabbed it by the neck.

Jason saw that her equilibrium was wavering a little. He worried that those green eyes would start glowing.

He just sat there motionless, with a small, bemused grin, outwardly calm as the rest of them wanted to appear to be. But he suspected they were all too dumbfounded and uncertain and confused to open their mouths. Not knowing what to say, whether she was serious. Hoping she was — or wasn't.

In the instant, he rapidly surveyed the scene. The guys — Kevin and Chuck — looked mischievous, fearfully ready for the kind of free love that they, and hippies in general, had long yearned for, but rarely found.

Susan and Sandra stared at each other. They seemed perplexed. Sandra raised her brows at Susan and gave her a little wide-eyed nose scrunch that said: What the hell is going on here? Susan looked wild-eyed, like a trapped doe asking for mercy.

"We might go for it," Chuck said softly, hesitantly, exchanging a furtive glance with Sandra, whose bemused face at that moment reminded Jason of the Mona Lisa's enigmatic smile. Maybe Da Vinci was propositioning Madame Mona at the time of the painting, he thought. No, actually, he had heard that Da Vinci was homosexual. That would be another appropriate reason for such a bemused smile.

"I don't know," said Susan. "This is pretty weird. We've been friends a long time. I don't want anything to mess that up." She looked helplessly at Kevin.

"Oh, I don't know," said Kevin. "We _are_ good friends. So maybe we could all just get into it. He laughed as if trying to talk them into it —no big deal. That was Kevin. No act of physical courage or forthrightness was ever a big deal to him, with his extraordinary prowess. But he remembered that Susan had once told him disdainfully that Kevin could only find physical solutions —not those of other kinds.

"It sounds like fun to me," said Kevin. "I think we're gonna need to pass this bottle around a couple more times though. Give it to Susan here, Roci. Hand it over here." Lots more laughter rolled out, especially from Susan.

"Fuck! Better light up another jay too," said Sandra. She seemed almost ready for an orgy — looking for reinforcements. She pulled a roach from the ashtray and began lighting it with her zippo. It started smoking and flaming. She blew out the flame and began sucking the smoke through her nose.

"How about you, Jason?" asked Kevin. "You ready for a little love-in?" Eyes were on him. Roci stood there, bare-breasted, amused at everything.

119

"I'll tell you what," said Jason smoothly. "I've always thought each of you fine women to be beautiful and sexy. It would be my pleasure to try to bring each of you to a climax. I'll pass on you guys though." He lit a fresh joint. Laughter rolled again.

"What are the rules for this game, anyway?" asked Chuck. "Who's the leader here? Got to be Roci — our guru."

Roci stood there uncompromised by her partial nudity or slight sway in her stance, amber and luscious in the firelight. She took Jason's proffered joint and sucked it loudly. They all waited breathlessly while she held the hit. In a few seconds, she blew out the smoke loudly.

"Well," she said. "If I'm the goo-goo or who-roo tonight, I will suggest that we all sleep upon this weighty concept of heavy lovemaking. It's much too sudden for sheltered earthlings and captives of evolutionary religion to come upon and accept this plateau of sharing upon the majestic mountain of ecstatic spiritbeing."

Uh-oh, thought Jason. We're in trouble now. He looked any second for the glowing green eyes, and his friends to start shrinking back and knocking over their lawn chairs.

"I suggest," said Roci grandly, "that we simply kiss and hug each other...fratomically, umm, plutoniumly, no, umm, platonically...a very sleepy goodnight and become more familiar with the gift of intimacy before we move into body-sharing. We need to, as you say, get used to the idea."

"I think that's a great idea," said Susan, seeing the escape.

"Yeah, maybe we ought to play a little doctor first," said Sandra.

"Well, nevertheless, I think we should be proud of our bodies," said Roci, passing the joint to Susan and taking the tequila back from Chuck. "We should try to make ourselves beautiful without and within and choose times to share our bodies in love and affection — and make them all very special times."

She turned up the bottle. Her bare breasts and petitely cute navel peeked skyward. Smoke from the campfire rolled up into the night sky. It was quiet again for a few seconds. She wiped her mouth from the hit and squinted at him across the fire. "One of your nicest words is pussy...pussy. I love that word," she said absently into the night. She really looked woozy now, and was getting some disturbed looks from his friends. Wow! Even extraterrestrials can get crocked and horny. What a revelation!

"Tomorrow we'll be up in the mountains," announced Kevin, as if to get the group back on a logical course. "Maybe a love-in up at the loch would be a good way to really get back to nature, like, you know, the Garden of Eden or something. Except this time in the Rocky Mountains. We've got all day with Captain Mescalito coming up, after all."

"Are you kidding?" said Sandra. "It's gonna be cold as hell up there. We're all gonna be bundled up with everything we got. No place for an orgy. We shoulda stayed in good 'ol hot Texas for that."

"When the sun goes down up there, the bottom really drops out," said Susan.

"Guess we can't do it if our peckers are drawn up into our belly buttons," said Kevin with an uproarious laugh. They all laughed.

"Looks like this scheduled love-in is gettin' to be too much trouble," said Chuck. More laughter.

"Well, it wasn't that important anyway," said Roci, somewhat recovered. "The important thing is that we love each other and support each other as brothers and sisters. Sex is always secondary to that. The true secret to minute by minute happiness is living in love for ourselves and each other. That creates positive energy that can make us feel great even without pharmaceuticals, natural or otherwise."

Damned! Jason thought. Get it together! She was amazing.

She smiled broadly, as if to confirm it. "I love you all. I want to hug you all," she said, reaching out to kiss Sandra on her cheek, then pull her and a wide-eyed Chuck into her embrace. Jason reached to hold Susan in a strong and loving hug and reached to grab Kevin's hand. They passed this pleasurable sharing around the campfire, to each and every one of them, and it was good. Friends, thought Jason, are one of a person's greatest assets.

Jason wondered what this had all been about. Adventure, he reckoned. She must be studying human reactions and behaviors.

When they had turned into the tent later, Jason asked her why she had decided to hit the tequila and weed. "My associates checked it out for me," she said. "They seem to be relatively harmless except for habitual abuse. And the mescaline is all right for me too. None of your cacti contain anything harmful that we could find."

"So you'll do a hit then? Maybe…part of a hit?"

"Doubtful," she said. "I see now that these things can do nothing for me that I can't do for myself."

"Well," said Jason, surprised. "Lucky you." He thought about it for a moment. So…the mescaline is worthless…or could be…in a real sense anyway.

"Are we still going to the colony tonight?" he asked. They were lying together in the dark tent, the glowing embers of their campfire reflecting on the sides and showing him her uncannily relaxed body in repose, lying on her back, her face sculpted in stillness and beauty.

"Yes, it will be exactly six weeks later than our last visit," she whispered without opening her eyes. "I think things may be growing desperate by now. Are you ready for it?" She rolled over suddenly and kissed him softly upon the lips, looked down into his eyes.

"Are you looking for the answer in my eyes?" he asked.

"They are mirrors, but you have to know how to see into them. It is not with material eyes."

"We seem to be working together well." It was another of his barely cloaked hints at their having a permanent relationship.

"The man-woman team is the strongest cooperative enterprise in all mortal creation," she said. "If you only could imagine the heights of ecstatic energy opening that the male-female linkage can achieve. You have briefly experienced it. But you will just have to wait, I suppose. In the meantime…"

Her warm breath touched his cheek, his whole body vibrated and trembled, and they were soon naked, clasped in a quiet, lustful embrace, body heat permeating each other in a deep, womb-like warmth. Their loins came finally to burst in mutual climax and they fell away into darkness.

Suddenly, there was bright light. Jason blinked to grow accustomed to the harsh brilliance, managed to sit up and look around, shielding his eyes. He was out in the sunshine. The landscape on his left looked like a shattered battleground, a stricken badland scattered with debris and pocked with small craters, piles of splintered tree trunks, stumps and brush lying here and there over the desolation. Some of them were smoking. To his right, Jason saw the golden dome glistening in the bright sun. It was hot out here, steaming tropical hot.

Jason didn't see Roci anywhere, or anyone. Surely she wouldn't have left him alone. Surely she and Mega would be here somewhere. But he saw no one on either side, only the scorched earth, what seemed to be left of the garden colony. But there was the dome, undamaged. He decided to go there alone.

But then he heard something in the opposite distance, across the spent plain, an ominous rumbling. Some giant mass of something was furiously beating down toward him, growing louder, pouring a sea of dust into the hot air. He turned away toward the dome and — stopped short!

Mega stood there facing him, having appeared from nowhere, standing tall and imposing, with short white beard and long white hair tied into a ponytail. He wore a stately, white robe with the hood turned down. A large pendant around his neck was held by a thick silver chain. It was a mosaic of blue and white stone — a white dove of peace on the blue background, all too familiar for Jason — through the ages.

"I think help is coming, Jason," he said confidently. "We can let the action come to us."

"Mega! Where's Roci?"

"She's resting her head," said Mega. "That tequila is really…influential stuff."

"What's coming?" The noise was getting louder. Jason looked back at the dome and saw a brace of men rushing toward them, long-barreled weapons on the ready. They came close by and dropped to their knees in a firing line, just ahead of them, except for the red-bearded leader, who stepped two paces to the side of his soldiers.

Jason stared hard at him. His left arm was now missing, a bloody clot of bandage replacing it at the shoulder. His face was even more weather-worn, blistered ruddy and traversed by a deep jagged scar, cutting a swath across his cheek and the tangled beard. Hard times had visited.

He turned back at the noise and realized what it was — a stampede. Bearing down on them was a thundering herd of four-legged denizens, antelopes perhaps, and dark-skinned, horned creatures. He saw a clique of giraffes peering over the others in the mad flight, zebras as well, a menagerie of plains beasts bearing down on them rapidly.

The leader said something Jason couldn't decipher. The men fired. Lightning bolts streaked from the barrels, exploding the earth across the front of the rush. Bare dirt blew skyward. The animals bolted left and right, stumbling, several run over and crushed under the horde. Several more lightning blasts finished parting the panicked creatures.

In a moment, Jason saw what had panicked them.

It loomed out of the swirling wall of dust in front of them, a huge and hideous head, gaping grin glistening with sharp fangs. Its green reptilian body took long methodical steps and quickly stood barely a hundred yards ahead of them. Eyes of steel. Cold evil emanated out of the monster and chilled Jason's blood.

Then he saw the large antelope-like animal lying helplessly on its side, struggling in vain to get up, its bones broken. The dinosaur lumbered forward on huge, clawed feet, one heavy step, then another to the stricken animal.

The bearded leader stared but made no command. The men remained in firing position, weapons aimed at the massive creature.

Mega stood quietly by Jason's side, seemingly unexcited by the confrontation. "They have very little electrical energy left for the weapons," he said calmly. "They have already had to close down the electrical barriers. If the creature would go away, they could save their power now. It takes a lot to even disable one of them."

Jason had already unconsciously backed up a few steps; his eyes remained riveted on the behemoth. Mega was unperturbed.

The giant beast eyed the tiny band of humans coldly, then took another plodding step closer to the fallen animal, which was now wild-eyed, panicked, struggling in vain to get up, wheezing a pitiful braying sound. The dinosaur stepped forward quickly, jaws open, massive teeth clamping down to cover the animal's head with a bone-shattering crunch and ripping it off, blood-spewing, from the torso. The headless neck spurted red and Jason fell thunderstruck to his knees, a trembling down his back and spine, unable to extricate his eyes from the ghastly scene.

The men waited imperviously, weapons ready. The monster in front of them ripped another part from the animal. Blood dripped from its horrifying fangs.

The leader said something softly, and the men responded by moving backward steadily, long weapons still at the ready, but retreating warily from the scene. "They are hoping to reach the dome," said Mega calmly. "We had best go with them."

Jason had already started moving, eyeing the beast furtively, anxious that Mega was following. He was, walking in large, calm strides, majestically in his white robe as if presiding over some dramatic ceremony.

Then the beast perked its head higher, opened its cavernous mouth and uttered a belching roar. It stepped forward slowly but with long strides. The red-bearded one was speaking again now. One of the men threw something small into the air toward the monster. It fell to the bare earth and burst into flames. The beast halted and reared up, momentarily stymied.

Jason paused to look and saw the enormous tail for the first time, swinging wildly and tearing through a small pile of debris. All of the men were running by now, and Jason started running too. Mega still walked calmly, steadily, and Jason passed him up again.

He heard the beast shriek and saw that it was racing around the flames they had put before it, faster than he would have imagined. The leader lofted a large handgun with his single arm and fired a bolt. It struck the enormous body and sent it into electrical rigors. The men ran harder now, as did Jason, the monster stumbling briefly, claws tearing up bare dirt. It was quickly up again though, and after them with giant consuming strides.

One of the men turned to his knees to fire another bolt. But he wasn't quick enough. The monstrous reptile was upon him, giant mouth engulfing him, lifting his thrashing, screaming body. Jason was paralyzed, aghast.

Lightning bolts struck the beast from left and right, scorching its thick hide with burning shafts, forcing it to relinquish its prey and fall lethargically to the ground. The bloodied man tumbled in front of them and a rescuer ran boldly toward him.

The beast's eyes rolled skyward. Its huge body thrashed weakly. Another man was struck by the heavy, swirling tail and sent tumbling. The bearded leader stepped closer, very close, while the beast struggled to recover its senses. He had another small ball in one hand and he flung it hard into the beast's horrible mouth. He nimbly ran backwards to get away.

In a second, the ball exploded into flames, enveloping the creature's mouth and head in a furious blaze. The beast writhed helplessly for another moment, head ablaze, then jerked crazily in a death spasm before finally falling still, its head burnt ludicrously black and still burning. It seemed dead at last.

The men were already ministering to their stricken comrade, two of them carrying his shattered body between them as they hurried on to the dome. The leader followed closely, scanning the horizon behind them, weapon ready.

Jason hurried to follow them on to the dome, looked ahead to see that Mega, still calm in his pure white robe, was waiting for them at the open door.

They all clamored inside, Jason searching out Mega to stand beside in a quiet corner of the room. He surveyed the new scene quickly.

The room was in disarray, piled high with transparent boxes, a stack of weapons, some furniture pieces pushed to the wall. It appeared as if they were packing to leave, retreating. One wall was lined with a massive control board, lighted and operational it seemed, with a strip of picture screens across the top showing various outside scenes. These landscapes were as ravaged as the one he had already experienced.

The one-armed leader was examining their fallen comrade closely, looked up from the battered and unconscious body to inquire something of another. The man spoke a few words and shook his head with a sad frown.

The leader's head drooped, trembling also in sadness. He stood more erect, tiredly, pulled the weapon from a broad belt around his waist and aimed it at the stricken man's chest. A high-pitched squeal of sound was joined by a quick flash of light. The body flinched once and was still.

The leader replaced his weapon and stepped over to the control board, flipping a succession of switches. Mega spoke softly to Jason: "This has to be part of the permanent record. I will auto-translate for you into English as he speaks."

The man spoke into a recorder. "Update to Dalamatia, if and when you are back online. Attacks continue periodic and unabated. The wildlife panicked into a stampede today. Beloved brother Tyran was mortally wounded and I relieved him from hopeless suffering. We killed another. It required too much energy. They completed the destruction of the north garden yesterday. We destroyed three of them there without casualties. We have precious little energy left. I will call us together and we will decide upon the trek to the mountains. From there, we can replenish and wait on any word — hopefully from you. Out. "

Sadly, he turned off the switches, and spoke rapidly to one of his comrades, who quickly moved toward a stairway Jason hadn't noticed before. The man disappeared down it. The leader rubbed the bandaged stump of his arm and stared down at the floor; he was haggard, his eyes burned deep with anger. His tangled red beard and hair gave him the look of a blazing fire. His intense eyes gave him the look of being just a little out of control.

"The dome," whispered Jason. "What is up in the dome here? The tree...of life that you mentioned?" He pointed upward.

"You don't have to whisper," said Mega. "No, this is Pleiadian Mission Control. The revered Tree of Life came to Urantia, Earth, with your assigned planetary prince, Caligastia, many thousands of years before Eden. It was transplanted from the garden planet, Edentia onto the surface, as is customary," said Mega. "It would be centering the city of Dalamatia, in the courtyard of the Universal Father's temple...if it is still there. There are rumors that a group loyal to the celestial administration have taken it and transported it up into the north mountain country. Dalamatia is under siege by the natives."

While they waited, Jason searched the line of monitor screens in vain. There was no giant oak tree on either of them, only the ruins of their former botanical splendor.

"This is the agricultural colony. You will not see Dalamatia on these screens," said Mega.

"Can we go there to see what's happening — to Dalamatia?" asked Jason. "So this is the same Tree of Life that was in Eden then? Or...could it be destroyed?"

"So many questions. Yes, it can be destroyed. It has been subjected here to mortal dominion. But loyalists to the celestial administration would protect it at all costs and save it for Eden," said Mega. "As with the Caligastia regime here, the Tree of Life would be preserved to be the energy sustenance ages later for your celestially-assigned Planetary Son and Daughter, your Adam and Eve. At least, this is the celestial plan — barring something such as rebellion. Your Adam and Eve, also from Edentia, would be genetically engineered to sustain eternal life and service on your planet from the fruit of the tree and engage in their mission of biological and botanical upliftment."

"But how could anyone take the tree with them, from Dalamatia? How could it be moved?"

"They would have to take the core only, the tap root." said Mega. "It would be a long time bearing fruit again. Quite a sacrifice. Even at that, its eternal life fruit is worthless for mortals, though I doubt that the invading primitives will discover that for some time yet. It is truly 'food for the gods' only as you say. It provided the eternal energy sustenance for your planetary prince, Caligastia, and the materialized so-called Caligastia One Hundred who were assigned to uplift the planet long before the scheduled arrival of a Planetary Son and Daughter.

"But," said Mega, "what they may not fully comprehend yet is that the rebellion caused all of the celestial circuitry to be severed immediately — to quarantine these 32 rebellious planets for the plague that they are. The Caligastia One Hundred can no longer get sustenance from the tree; they have been mortalized. And the primitives who seem to be clamoring for it never could."

The men were stirring again, following their leader outside, holding for now Jason's myriad of questions. Mega and Jason followed them.

When they were out in the sun, the bedraggled soldiers with the big-barreled weapons lined up single-file again. There were only six left to serve on the firing line. The bearded man paced back and forth impatiently in front of them, holding the red-soaked bandage where his left arm used to be.

Jason noticed for the first time a large flat expanse of brown to the left of the dome. He heard a low-pitched hum and saw the surface split open from the center, opening a large hole in the earth. Dust showered down within and swirled up into the hot air.

From inside lifted a multitude of dirty faces, rising out of the ground, men, women, children, all fair-skinned and well-built, but worried and tired-looking, eyes darkened, bodies bruised and bandaged. Most of their clothes were tattered. There seemed to be thirty or more.

The carrier reached up to ground-level and stopped. The leader stepped forward and looked at the gathering coldly.

He spoke in a husky but weary voice. "We have lost beloved brother Tyran. Say a prayer for full spiritual release," he said evenly. He paused before speaking again: "We have very little power left to stop these horrendous beasts so we have to decide now about the retreat to the mountains. I think we must go there immediately. The gardens and orchards are effectively destroyed. We have recovered all of the food that we can, plus seeds and roots."

A worried woman spoke rapidly, "What of Mission Control? Is it still operational?"

A man called out: "I hear that there is war in Dalamatia. Who is fighting?

The leader spoke more loudly: "Dalamatia continues to be under siege by the evolutionary tribes. They have reverted to the savagery which we first encountered here. Dalamatia was evasive, gives no reason for this. Neither could they offer advice or assistance against the beasts, or explain to us how they came to be unleashed. They are equally evasive about the status of the

Tree of Life." He paused again, as if to let the colonists think through their dilemma with him. "And now they are offline. We hear nothing at all.

"We believe that many of the interplanetary energy circuits have been severed," he said. "It is unclear why, but there is rumor that our planetary prince is at odds with the celestial administration. Everything has been shut down, perhaps, by the Ancients of Days, perhaps by Caligastia himself."

He paused again, before resuming: "This is all hard to believe, I know. Certainly it is for me, and I cannot confirm it. I only know there is fighting in Dalamatia. I only remember vividly recent...rhetoric from there. There were challenging words. You have heard some of them. Each of us has to believe what we will of these...pronouncements. We do know that we are in chaos and we must struggle just to survive."

He paused yet again: "You know that our administrators have all died. I have therefore reluctantly assumed full command of our limited forces. My security guards support me," he said gruffly, certainly. "I want you to understand that Control would be useless in making decisions to stop this scourge even if it were operational. It is unprecedented. It is a crisis that Control was never equipped to meet. The Control concept is an intellectual tool of advanced peoples, anyway, a grand design of the Ancients of Days. But I, Anvil, say to you, as Caligastia has said, the Ancients have never known what it was really like out here. For their grandiose seats of celestial authority, they cannot and do not understand many things that are reality on the frontier."

Anvil paused again before continuing: "There have to be other, more basic, powers in play to hold dominion here, not simply the passive kind of spirituality that they may have been selling us in order to keep us meek, keep us under their control. I have heard some of Caligastia's ideas, and Satan's and Daligastia's, and they seem to make sense to me. I think that these worthy ideas, for more freedom out here, more autonomy and control, the liberty to work out our own problems, take advantage of our own opportunities, without the ethereal grip of the Ancients may just have prompted them to embark on destroying us — all of us. I heard this from Satan; I cannot confirm it.

"And now...where are we?" Anvil resumed dramatically. "Our colonists may have just gotten confused into this rebellion, unfortunate enough to be here and perhaps assumed to be in league with Caligastia in promoting these...radical ideas. It is about power," said the man confidently.

"If we must choose in this confusing picture," he continued, "I am inclined more strongly than ever to believe that we must support the powers in Dalamatia. There is no choice really. We could hardly support the primitives, and we have no means to communicate with the celestials since they seem to have deliberately severed communications. I am also told by

Satan, remember, he is Lucifer's most trusted associate, that the Ancients' anger with Lucifer and Caligastia and the freedom fighters may even have resulted in these damnable beasts appearing to destroy us. I cannot say this either, for sure."

"As for here, there is no longer anything to protect," the man reasoned. "We have to make it into the mountains to be safe from these monsters. We can find places where the creatures can't follow. We can hope for renewed contact with Dalamatia through the portables, or contact with a passing ship. And so — deliberate now and decide."

There was a general rustle of agreement that they all must leave.

The people were forlorn, mothers grasping several small children to them, men comforting their women. Jason looked at the distant range of mountains, shrouded in fog.

"It will probably be a perilous journey," said Mega. "There are many wild creatures, and the volcanoes are quite active. The walls around here are mostly destroyed."

"Walls?"

"They were built of stone, encircling the whole garden project here. But they were not built to contain such as what we've seen and, as was said, the electrical barriers were abandoned also with the power shortage."

The platform of people lowered again into the ground and disappeared under the sliding floor. The guards moved back into the dome. The retreat would soon begin. Jason and Mega stood alone, out in front of the dome. Jason looked again at the desolation, the shattered body of the giant beast.

"Where did they come from? Why didn't they know about them — those monsters?" Jason asked Mega. "They had made so much here…like a garden paradise really. Then they lost it all."

"We will find out more as we modify our timedrops," said Mega. "We will learn with each episode until it becomes more clear."

"What else can we know? Are they going to survive?"

" We shall see," said Mega. This is our principal interest. The rebellion in Dalamatia is in the library anyway."

"The — what? I never read about it," said Jason.

"Not your library," chided Mega with a wry smile. "You don't even have a clear picture of Eden, which will not appear here for another 165,000 or so years."

"So where will we go now?" Jason asked anxiously. "Let's go there — Eden."

"You're going back to the campground," said Mega. "We can't leave Blest alone with that motley crew of self-indulgers for very long."

"My friends," said Jason, with mild indignation, but then saw that Mega was smiling in good humor.

"You are certainly giving our sister, Blest, a wonderful exploration," he said with an amused wrinkle of a smile. "Thanks." He reached out and tweaked Jason's nose.

Jason suddenly came to his senses in the dark tent, touching his nose which he felt had been mashed. Roci...Blest slept calmly, beautifully, beside him.

It had been another eventful day. He had experienced some of her world, an academy, a glorious place of adventure and daring. He had watched the colonists' desperate struggle to survive, seen another frightful prehistoric beast up close, heard more about the rebellion in Dalamatia, their decision to flee. And the red-bearded man, seemingly a focus of the story. Who was he?

Roci stirred sleepily, rolling over gently to face him, eyes still closed.

"Anvil," she whispered into the dark. "His name is Anvil."

"What? His name is what?" Jason whispered.

"Anvil," came the whispery voice from her unconscious. "Anvil 66. He might be anyman; he might be everyman. He may have survived; he may be of a lost strand in the life tapestry." The voice came out of her but she remained in sleep, eyes and lips closed...enslumbered peace.

He could only stare at her, at this new perplexity of communication.

Then came some final words into his head. "This has been a pre-sleep message. And offered with my loving vibrations. Goodnight."

"Goodnight," he thought hard, hoping it was getting into her. He stared at her peaceful repose, and a powerful feeling of love and ravenous desire rose up in him. He could never let her go.

The name echoed through the caverns of his mind. Anvil? Anvil? And he had taken command. He told them he had taken full command. Representing what?

"Are you awake?" Jason whispered to her peaceful face.

"No," she whispered with her lips. "Rest."

So he rolled over and lay there on his back thinking for a while, trying to assemble the jumble of interplanetary confusion that had swarmed upon his life, a table full of jigsaw pieces sprawled before him.

Did she really say she was asleep?

Yes, he sighed to himself. She did.

SEVEN: *Behold the Prehistoric Life!*

They trekked single-file up the trail, beside a roaring creek and its occasional waterfalls, under majestic firs and pines and a warming sun. The fellowship was good, and Roci had taken a genuine interest in befriending and talking with each of his friends.

They were tired at their mid-afternoon break, lying back on the bare earth and boulders while the air rustled gently through the trees. At last Jason found a moment alone with Roci.

"So, what do you think of my friends?" he asked her.

"They have the same inner goodness as you," she replied. "But it's sad the way Chuck and Sandra are growing more dependent on drugs to alter their consciousness. It's constantly in their conversation. It will be the cause of much trouble, I think. When you get used to crutches, you can't walk alone sometimes. And you can surely be addicted to entertainment, often at the expense of learning and service."

"So, they're grown-up people. They've got to make their own decisions."

"They'll be doing what they're here for in any case," said Roci, "learning and growing experiences. Experiential learning is often the best kind.

"It's just hard to be as upbeat and philosophical about it as you are, reality being what it is." Jason protested mildly. "Everybody's out there struggling to make a living, competing hard, making ulcers…"

"Your people contribute strongly to making the reality what it is," she said with authority. "Creating the reality is your responsibility, Jason, and it is certainly not our place to interfere with your time and space evolutionary plan. You can live with each other however you please. At least you're not in open warfare here, as they are in so many parts of your sphere at this moment. But you're really not nurturing yourselves very well anywhere at all. People seem strangely alienated from one another compared to normal worlds. It is a…dark energy."

Later, the group puffed up a steep and narrow incline, their tired legs sagging, lungs clamoring for air, except for Roci, who appeared to suffer no strain. Jason puffed up beside her and asked her to stop for a minute.

"The dark energy?" he asked, out-of-breath. "What is it? Exactly what is it?"

"We will have to discover that together. Caligastia, the one they now call the dark prince, called it self-assertion, self-determination, self-rule and individual liberty, the power and infallibility of mind, concepts you know well today. And that is much of the reason for your planet's problems. Those energies are still residual in this place. Observe the violence and greed upon this small planet still, the suffering you bring upon yourselves because you clamor for these things."

"I would be part of no rebellion against God. You can be sure of that. Hey! There's no history about it. Maybe you've got us mixed up with some another planet.

She laughed. "That would be…convenient."

"Well," he pressed on, puffing between words as they climbed steadily, "Maybe if we're still cursed by this thing, this rebellion by this dark prince, you could just show me where we're going wrong today because of it. Just give me some pointers about what you think we need to do to make things right, maybe a new way of looking at things. You've been places, done things — to say the least."

"I told you it's not our responsibility. We aren't here to make changes; one of our purposes most of the time is to avoid changing things. We've told you that. All of your changes will be directed by the celestial spirit world and the evolutionary plan of the One God, not by us. We are mortals too, remember."

"Sometimes," Jason puffed, "when I'm trying to keep up with you…it doesn't seem so."

In late afternoon, Kevin led the thin line to its destination. Beautiful Loch Vail came into view as a giant deep blue expanse, materializing slowly through the fir trees and growing larger until they came fully upon it in its rippling splendor.

The clear blue water stretched out before them, calm but for a few running ripples skittering with the breeze. It was capped on its shady side with a thin crust of ice, and backgrounded with the billowing snowy peaks of the vast snow-capped Mummy Range.

The gray rock behemoth to their left, and much closer, was Long's, rising triumphantly into the cloud-spotted blue sky, and again speaking silently to Jason of a challenge in his mind that he had never undertaken. Long's. Kevin had climbed it, and talked about it. He had not. But it was still far away from here, from this lovely lake which he had recommended to his friends.

They were pleased, and Jason beamed. It was as beautiful as he said it would be. They enthused in awe and were soon at work pitching their tents and gathering firewood for an evening blaze.

The bonfire was a good one. Kevin, ever-resourceful, had located a downed tree and, hatchet swinging, had forged a pile of sticks and limbs for Jason and Chuck to draw from and service the campsite. It was his usual guise of physical leader, the same role he had struck by being the first to reach the loch.

He wished fervently that Roci could be his woman, could forge with her the same kind of earthy and fun loving relationship that Kevin and Susan enjoyed, seemingly so much in balance with one another and their environment. Roci...Roci...Jason and Roci...Blest...My God, he thought to himself, she is an alien being, he supposed. A few days ago, he doubted that he would ever see or hear of a real extraterrestrial in his lifetime; now he wanted to spend the rest of his life with one. What an incredible turn of events.

Somehow, it seemed funny, like everything else seemed to be on this good night of laughter and light rapport. The warm heat and the fireglow, the star-filled sky, their happy moods, even the hot chocolate and the limited, humorously doled-out marshmallows made it an especially warming time.

And there was no mention of the previous evening's sexual frankness. It was as if it weren't important or provocative any more. Jason thought that they all seemed content to leave it in some amorphous past, not bring it up, that it wasn't something anyone wanted to get into on this perfect night. This seemed a good lesson learned. He wondered if Roci was affecting all of their moods somehow.

As they were tucking themselves into their sleeping bags, he asked her if they were going on another timedrop, if she would join them tonight.

"We're going to find the refugees," she said. "We'll find out if they made it to the mountains."

"You'll be with us this time?"

"I will," she said, "and believe me, we are going to have to...indulge Mega on this one. He is a dramatist at heart. You'll see."

Before he could reply, she was in his arms, her warm fingers caressing his neck, warm breath fluttering his cheek. Her eyes glowed green in the darkness, engulfing him. It was easier for them to fall into this glorious whirlwind now, required just a moment.

But before he fell away, he managed to say what he most wanted to say: "I love you, Roci. I...love you...Blest. I love you across all the cosmos."

When he opened his eyes suddenly, he expected the scene to have changed. But it had not. He raised up in the tent and thought that he was still at the loch. But then he realized she was gone. He patted all over the dark tent, hurriedly, to confirm that she wasn't there.

Then he heard a peculiar snort. Some kind of animal. Nuzzling the tent, sniffing, snorting. Jason drew back. Was it carnivorous? The shadow of a huge bulk rose over him from the lantern light outside.

"Jay — son! Git 'yo mizzable ass out 'chea and let's go find that lost colony, pilgrim. "

It was a rough, masculine voice, somewhat aged, with a colloquial drawl that smacked of the South...maybe the Southwest.

He poked his head out of the tent uncertainly and stared at the strange couple there confronting him. It was undoubtedly Mega, but much-changed, and it was indeed a mule, a pack mule loaded with provisions.

Mega's white beard was long and scruffy this time, his tangled white hair in furious profusion all over his head. He wore dirty overalls and a ragged blue work shirt, work boots and a floppy red bandana hanging down his chest like a bib. His eyes and the mule's were intent on Jason.

"Is it really you, Mega?"

"You darn tootin' it's me. It's show time!" He saw that Jason's eyes were fixed now on the two nearby tents of his friends. "Ain't no need worryin' 'bout them. They still in there snoozin' far as we're concerned. If they ain't there, well, that don't make no difference neither in this here con-structed scenario." Mega rared back his head and spat a long dark stream on the bare ground. Jason saw his bulged cheek for the first time. Chewing tobacco? This was too much.

"Why are you dressed like this? Is this all...functional for some reason?"

"Well, bein' as it's Colorado, I figured I'd get into the spirit of it by bein' a pioneer gold miner. Used to be lots 'a ol' farts like me up in these mountains, lookin' to strike it rich."

Jason was standing outside the tent now, noticed for the first time that he was fully dressed. The mule was sniffing at his leg.

"So you're playing the role. Roci told me you used to be in...Did she say the theater?"

"Performance art. It's big over our way. I think Argentina's took a likin' to 'ye." The mule had nosed forward to smell his crotch.

"Or she thinks I smell funny. Come to think of it, I don't smell anything at all, not even your mule."

"Well, it ain't easy workin' in th' olfactory stuff in trips like this," said Mega. "It ain't no treat smellin' a mule anyhow and Argentina, well, I just got her actin' like a natural mule, and sniffin' and snortin' is a couple of things she naturally is gonna do."

"Where does her name come from?"

"Well, they's a story to that. I thank I could probably be a'tellin' it while we head out into the valley to walk a spell. We got to go ron-day-view with Roci Sue out yonder a ways."

"Roci...Sue?"

"Jason, boy, lemme tell you sumpin'," said the grizzly Mega. "We just tryin' to be funny tonight, okay, entertainin', 'cause we gonna havta get sobered up soon enough tonight. So don't be so gol-darned, whattya call it, in-cre-du-lous." He had begun walking deliberately, the mule following along, and Jason too.

"You like to have a good time, Jason, boy, 'an we like to have a good time too. Gonna be a doggone good 'un if we can pick up some nuggets on this trip."

"Gold?" Jason asked.

"Wisdom. Gonna have to see if these colonists are gonna make it. It's a long haul to the mountains." They were walking resolutely now.

"Well, so who's in charge in Dalamatia? Rebels? Loyalists? The primitives?" Jason asked.

"We hear tell they's still a lot 'a conflict up there, and we don't rightly know who's in charge. Heared tell that the Melchizedeks showed up in Jerusem, quarantined the whole system, cut off the broadcast circuits to all the rebellion spheres, and locked up Lucifer sommers. Reckon Caligastia and his bunch may be on their own down there."

"And...which side are these colonists on?"

"Good question. Sounds like Anvil's sidin' with the rebels. Guess we're gonna hafta pay 'em another call in a little bit." He spat again, the brown stream splatting against a boulder.

"Looks like this Anvil is pretty much running things," said Jason. "Well, who's this rebellion against anyhow? Who is the celestial administration...once and for all?"

Mega arched his eyebrows. "Why...the One God, fer sure, and all the spiritual legions. You don' know mucha nothin', do ye?"

"Well, who would have the audacity to rebel against God? Wouldn't they know they would be — like, crushed or something?"

"Well now, Lucifer ain't no slouch," said Mega. "He's way on up there in the ranks. An' he's about as sharp and slick a feller as God ever created. Fact of the matter, I thank his ego just got the best uv 'em. He jus' got too big for his britches — if them celestial fellers has britches."

"Well, why doesn't God just...end it. Surely God has the power. What's the point of putting up with some hot shot pretender, no matter how sharp he thinks he is."

"Well, then folks couldn't learn as much from the experience. I figure God's gonna let it play out, let folks make up they own mind, see jus' what happens when the inmates take over the asylum, so to speak." He spat theatrically again, and let out a cackle of a laugh.

Mega had become occupied with a flashlight he had picked up from the campsite ground, flipping it on and watching the stream of light play over the landscape.

"Lordy mercy. One of these thangs woulda sho' come in handy back durin' the rush," he mused, plodding on. "Probably coulda scared the shit out of the Indians too, and coulda got way up in some of them caves around here without worryin' about 'che torch goin' out."

"You can have it," said Jason. "I got it at the Wal-Mart."

"Naw," said Mega, turning it off and laying it gently on the ground. "We headin' back to the prehistoric out yonder a piece. It wouldn't fit in a'tall. Les' be a goin'. Come on heah, Argentina."

"Is…the mule gonna help us do this thing?"

"Naw. She's just part of the scenery. And she's carryin' what we goin' be wearin' in a little bit. But I did wanna tell ye' that story about this fine li'l four-legger. It's a purty good 'un. Made it up myself."

"So it's not real. Just like the rest of this. It's a story."

"Well, you keep interruptin' my mule story. If you'da been around, it woulda took the Lord eight or nine days, I reckon.

"See, it's like you been told ever time we do this, it's an episode in time we're droppin' in on. We trust the celestials to let us see it accurately. But, you oughta know that speculation is a pretty good tool for humans, too. You gotta realize when you speculate, somethin' is puttin' that speculation in your head. Just what that somethin' is…well, it's a matter for speculation too. In fact, it's whoever you's asked for guidance. That's who it is. I'd ask God myself. "Another brown spit as they trudged along. The mule was still unconcerned."

"Now, that's sho 'nuff sumpin'fer you to thank about 'cause they's a process a'workin' heah if ya can see it. It's mind over matter, ya know. Whatever you put your mind to is invariably what happens. Thoughts has a power to make things, change things."

"I'll…have to think about all that," said Jason. "I hope you let me remember it. I hope you will." Jason was still nagged at the idea of losing his memory.

"We just liable to cut you some slack on that one," said Mega. "I wouldn't be a'tall surprised. But about this here mule, Argentina, I got 'er from a Mexican feller down near Pueblo, feller by the name of Caesar. He got in a mite 'a trouble sellin' weed and had to hightail it out of the territory, so he sold 'er to me fer a real good price."

Mega spat another brown stream onto the dark ground as they walked languidly, the three of them, in the night. A three-quarters moon and the multitude of stars helped light the way.

"Caesar said the mule didn't have no name. He jus' bought him off the folks over at the dog food factory 'bout a hour or two 'fore they was gonna knock her in the head and grind her up. He 'us usin' her fer some work around the house, workin' the garden, ya know, ridin' his two kids around the yard. He said he done clean forgot what them kids named that mule, so he reckoned I could name 'er what I wanted.

"Never will forget. 'Ol Caesar was a' loadin' up some stuff in a ol' ramshackle GMC pickup when I come by to give him the hunderd pesos. I said, 'Whur you goin', anyhow, Senor.' He said, 'Why I shore don' know. I'm just lightin' out. They wantin' to send me to the joint about this little 'ol bit of weed. I may not stop 'fore I get to Argentina."

Mega laughed raucously. Jason only smiled.

"Well, hell, feller," said Mega. "I thought it 'us purty funny. If you ain't havin' a good time, then what you doin' here?"

"Trying to figure out what's going on most of the time," Jason admitted. "I thought you should have named her GMC, or Jimmie C."

"Figurin' things out ain't too danged easy," said Mega. "But I like Argentina. It has more…romance. Life is what you make it."

"I know this is a part you're playing. This old geezer fellow," said Jason. "Well, what makes him tick? What makes your character tick? What does he think about the creation?"

"Well, best I can figger," said Mega, "they ain't too many things I need to be happy. Needs that's purty simple is purty simple to meet. Depends on what kinda…conveniences you get used to, what kind you think you gotta have. Some 'a you folks is like me; they'll take that all-out freedom instead of a VCR and a auto-mo-bile. Doin' what the hell you wanna do ever' day and dreamin' about strikin' it rich so you can buy the stuff you gave up in the firs' place so ya kin be free." He laughed again in a cackle.

"Is it important to strike it rich?" asked Jason. "Is that why you mine?"

"Naw. I don't really think so. I got a fine little woman for a friend. I go all over this beautiful country foragin' for food and findin' it most times. She sleeps with me at night. Never did wanna settle down. Too restless. And I'd surely be bored in the same place. I surely would. I'm jus' lucky I got a woman that likes the foragin' life too."

"It gets cold up in these mountains. Need a woman to sleep with, I reckon," said Jason.

"Well, I'm liable to be headin' down South to the high desert 'fore winter sets in. It's a mighty fine place too, purty warm. Shoot, you got all kinds 'a seasons and all kinds 'a ways to dress fer 'em. This here's a big and fine country if you didn't but know it. Tell you how I figger it, an' I give it a lot of thought. I figure they just ain't nothin' as great and gratifyin' as self-reliance. That's the ultimate. An' the perfect com-ple-ment to that is this purely fan-tas-tic country God give to us. See, it's easy to think that way if you know you goin' to a greater re-ward after you've cashed in your chips here. All we doin' in a way is jus' makin' a good record for the Lord to look at."

Somehow the scenery had changed. They were walking in a valley of grassland, mountain ranges on either side. The sun was a giant red ball protruding over one horizon, washing the landscape in a reddish glow.

"Is it sunrise or sunset?" he asked Mega.

"Don't rightly know. It don't really matter. We gonna let the sun stay right there a spell in this here speculation, if it's all the same to you." He spat again, then pulled the remainder of the tobacco cud from his mouth, staring at it disdainfully.

"I'm 'bout to get tarred 'a this nasty stuff. I don't see why anybody'd wanna chew it."

"Well, then why did you?" Jason asked.

"Well, 'cause I'm tryin' to get in the skins 'a you people, walk around a while, figger what makes you tick, why you do this, why you do that, how'd you get an attitude about sumpin'. I figgered a character like I'm puttin' together here would likely be a chewin' man. But we 'bout to get into sumpin' else anyhow."

"What? Are we going back to the colony?"

"What's left 'uv it. Things ain't been too pleasant since them big critters showed up. What's left 'uv 'em is up in the hills yonder. Roci probably done spotted 'em fer us. It's dark, so we'll see their fire."

"What about those giant beasts? Shouldn't we be concerned out here? Could we be…killed or hurt? I don't really feel anything physically, when I pinch myself," said Jason, "but emotionally I got fairly well scared shitless last time that creature showed up."

"You ain't gonna be hurt 'cause you ain't here in the physical sense," said Mega. "Anyway," he chuckled like Walter Brennan, "it ain't like you can't see 'em comin'. They don't mess around much at night, and, anyways, I ain't gonna knuckle under to them devilish varmints. I'm too proud to hole up in some nasty cave and be scared to poke my head out. I got work to do."

"What kind of work?"

"Well, ever' body's got to have work, responsibility, some kinda contribution to makin' things better. This here idea of doin' what ye' damned well please an' jus' gratifyin' y'self is shore devil talk to my way 'a thinkin'. If I was this character I'm actin' out, I'd be a' lookin' for gold, get the wealth outta the ground, but do it in a responsible way. Don't leave too much of a mess behind. If I was one 'a them colony people, like I'm gonna be as soon as Roci Sue shows up, then I'd have another responsibility. You'll see in my next performance."

"Well, it's hard not to be concerned. I've seen what those giant creatures can do, and I'm kinda used to being physical myself."

"Once a feller gets to be afraid, and lets that fear get the whiphand on 'im, I've seen what that can do too," said Mega. "Got to use your head. Got to use your cunning, your courage, all them talents God give you, to good purpose. If'n 'you don't, then you ain't doin' what the Lord ast you to do, give you the opportunity to do, when he put ya here. I think you better use what you got and fulfill that trust. If you don't turn out to be a re-sponsible person, what's the use in lettin' you carry on in the next world? Might as well just let you die on out if you ain't worth savin'."

"Sounds like you're on a real mission," said Jason.

"We all got the same 'un," said Mega, motioning for Jason to look with him to his left. There, Jason saw a dark figure running toward them, lightly over the grassy plain. He strained his eyes to see against the huge hanging sun.

It was a woman, a hairy dark skin wrapped over one shoulder, her feet and ankles tied up with sandals, and carrying some large object under one arm. As she moved closer, he recognized Roci, Blest, and as she slowed to a walk and stepped up beside them, he saw that her beautiful face was grimy with dirt, bright, wild eyes shining through it, her hair long and tangled over her shoulders, her legs and feet muddy and scarred.

Her cold and steady gaze centered on him. He couldn't tell if she even recognized him. The object under her arm was a huge egg. It looked to Jason to weigh several pounds.

"Vittles," said Mega. "Hot damn! This little woman done stole us a big 'ol egg. Too bad we ain't got time to rustle up a far and scramble it."

She held it out to Mega, wordlessly, like a gift. He raised an open hand to gently push it back to her. "Hang onto that thing a spell, sweet thing. Sometimes the future gotta wait, and we got to wait on it."

"Roci," said Jason, trying to get her attention. "Do you remember me? Are we still partners too?"

She looked at him with hard eyes, not so friendly, wary, like an animal. He could see that she was sinewy and strong, a creature of the wild, likely with the cold guile of a fox, the lifesaving alertness of the other animal denizens of this danger-fraught primeval land. She carried what looked like a sharpened stone or stick in a sheath hanging from a rope on her waist. She didn't speak, only looked at him without flinching, with a knowing, confident gaze. Her fingers brushed at the handle.

She made Jason uneasy. He turned from her to Mega: "I can't grasp the future either," he said. "Sometimes I just hope there is one."

"Well, it's our'n to shape howsomeever it turns out to be," said Mega. "We got to work together to get it done. 'Course, rat now, we got to see what them colonists is up to." He was already rummaging into Argentina's saddle bags. The mule stood languidly.

From the bags, Mega pulled two other bulky animal skins, dark and hairy like Roci's. He tossed one to Jason. "These here skins is purty seasoned. Fresh 'uns kin be 'sho nuff o-di-fer-ous. You ain't used to puttin' that kinda stink on your bodies like them prehistorics."

"We're going to wear these?" Jason held his up uncertainly.

"Yep. We got to get into the spirit of this thing. You got 'ta get the ex-per-ience in order to learn for yourself. Me tellin' you sumpin' ain't you learnin' it. You rememberin' what I told you ain't you learnin' it either. It all gets in ya head a lot deeper when you discover it fer yourself. You got to know what it all feels like."

Mega was already stripping his dirty clothes and Jason followed his lead, still eyeing Roci, who watched them calmly. She seemed to have no desire to speak, if indeed she could in this primitive guise.

The skin was uncomfortable, ill-fitting, wrapped around his body loosely and tied with grassy thongs at the shoulder. He felt the scratchy roughness of its underside on his bare skin and imagined how tough and leathery the skins and feet of these prehistorics must have been, how the idea of "comfort" had to be greatly modified, or dulled, in order to survive in this hostile land. He believed he was beginning to know a little of how it truly felt to be a human mortal in this ancient wilderness.

He looked at Mega the primitive, now standing in hairy splendor, tall, muscular man of the primal realm, white hair and beard pouring from his head. He was no longer a grizzly miner; he was a patriarch of prehistory, holding now a large wooden staff like Jason would have imagined Moses to have. Maybe he was like Moses on this night.

Jason looked at himself. He appeared too clean and white and weak to be in company with this rugged duo. He longed to be stronger, tougher, fully self-reliant, with feet less tender and prone to hurts on this hard earth. The weak would not have survived in the clutches of the cruel nature all around them. The survivor, building strength, would have lost much of the civilized nature.

"Behold the prehistoric life," said the new Mega-like personna with authority, a clear, new and deep voice establishing his authority, without the hint of accent, drawl or colloquialism, putting down his staff as he squatted and scooped up a double handful of the ancient soil, rising up again and throwing it into the air. It came down and blew swirling dust in the wind, settling all around and over them and also dancing away on a whirlwind over the grassy plain, like the plaything of a genie.

Jason went down on one bare knee and scooped up the gritty soil, flinging it upward as Mega had done, watching it blow away in the night wind. He followed Mega's lead.

"From this point on," we are in a participatory experience," said Mega with authority, "so watch your steps."

"Wait," asked Jason. "What does that mean? Is there danger then?"

"We just want to do some interaction," said Roci, speaking for the first time. She walked up confidently to stand next to him, her eyes penetrating his, and continuing: "In an immersion exercise, a step beyond a simple timedrop, we are allowed to take on personas of others who might actually have been in the scene, that is, when it physically happened back in time."

"Whew!" said Jason. "Whatever you say. Okay, let's just do whatever."

She reached to touch his cheek with her dirty fingers, capture his eyes in her own wild ones. He was suddenly sexually aroused for her, for her abandon, her savagery, the anticipation of powerful passion with her. She looked at him teasingly, eyes coy, seductive. Jason was almost breathless.

"Break this emotional reverie," Mega commanded them firmly. He stood these imposingly, like Heston as Moses, lifted his long stick and led the way again across the primeval valley. The scene was washed amber in the constant glow of the hanging sun, which had not moved.

A gentle breeze was cool on Jason's bare arms; the warmth of the skin was welcome. He was actually feeling with his senses as Mega apparently wanted him to do. Argentina stood passively behind them as they walked away, leaving her in another time. Roci walked alongside them, still apparently feeling no need to communicate, carrying the large egg lightly under one arm.

In such a time as this, Jason realized, there was little to communicate about. It was basic survival here — food, shelter, gratification of urges, nothing like social relations, politics, or entertainment to prompt conversation. He wondered if the colonists, with few resources, had survived, would survive, and how would they be changed?

As they walked, he felt increasingly like a man of the earth, a self-reliance growing in strength inside him, little need for conversational chatter, little need for anything beyond survival and gratification and a wonder of what the whole creation was about, how the ancient evolutionary man and woman must have felt in this time. Priorities in his mind were being swiftly and surely re-arranged and he felt he was learning from it.

To his left across the plain, he began to see creatures, a variety of four-legged beasts grazing or lying in the valley grass. Above them he heard the flapping of huge wings, turned in time to see a giant bird swoop down nearby and seize a small animal. It squealed and thrashed helplessly in the claws; the predator and prey lifted away together into the shadowy sky.

Jason was wide-eyed, looked at Mega and Roci to see that they had observed this but were impassive about it. They walked on. Jason realized anew the threat of sudden, horrible death to those trying to live here.

He stopped suddenly at the sight in front of them. Mega, just ahead, brandished the long stick. In his face stood a huge, lizard-like creature, just a few yards away. It stood seven feet or more high, with heavy scaled shoulders and a squatty torso, sinister eyes looking right at them, four short, strong-boned legs and clawed feet, a long, whiplike tail. A long forked tongue slithered quickly out of its mouth and disappeared back inside. Jason felt a chill.

Mega's eyes were intent on the creature, as was Roci's, but they showed no fear. Mega was already stepping even closer, holding the stick as a weapon. He must be crazy, Jason thought. Roci was cradling the egg in both hands, as if this was what the creature wanted. She stood her ground.

The beast opened its mouth to show a profusion of ugly fangs, but only for a second. Mega lofted the large stick and swung hard. It caught the giant lizard flush on the head with a loud thud. Its eyes walled back as it fell over with an enormous guttural grunt, forked tongue slithering, tail swishing.

Adeptly, Mega swung hard again, crashing the stick against the creature's head again. It struggled to right itself. With claws tearing furiously at the ground, it backed off to stand dazed.

Roci stepped forward quickly, lifting the large egg over her head with two hands, flinging it toward the beast. It crashed into the creature's head, exploding jell-like protoplasm and shattered shell over the horrible face. The beast slithered frantically away, dripping the goop behind it.

"Bon appetit!" hollered Mega. He turned back to them. "Those creatures should have been gone from here millions of years ago. We need to figure out why they're even here," said Mega. "Someone had to re-establish them. Someone in the laboratories of Dalamatia had to take the life plasm and implant it."

"They implanted those creatures then, underwater? Where they could hatch? Who would do that?"

"Caligastia. He wanted the Pleadian colony to fail because the leadership refused to side with the Lucifer rebellion. Anvil's predecessors had been staunchly loyal to the celestials. It was easy enough to do. The plasm was still here, from the time they ruled here a long time ago."

"Dinosaurs? Mysteriously implanted, re-introduced, to destroy the colony. Are you just speculating?" Jason asked.

"No, we have other explorers at work. They are discovering information all the while. The Oak grows. Control grows. Knowledge grows. Everything is reported to me. I am now reporting to you."

He pointed to his right, in the direction of the mountainside. Jason looked and saw the glow of a fire. "They're there. We must go talk with them," said Mega.

They struggled up a boulder field toward the firelight. It was hard. Jason's sweat sent rivulets of the primeval humidity down his forehead and he wiped it with a dirty hand. They strained upward together.

The rock field soon changed to a steep hillside of stubbled grass. Soon they could see the high, dancing flames of the fire just ahead. Jason realized it was under the canopy of a large, overhanging cliff of rock.

A dark figure came into view, silhouetted by the flames. Other dark figures appeared, facing them as they approached. A black cavern seemed to lead back under the rock, shelter for the embattled survivors from the gardens. He saw a woman emerge, bedraggled and dirty, in the ragged remnants of the clothes he had seen on them before.

Now other figures facing them materialized fully, rugged, bearded men with spears and one with a bow and arrow at the ready. Jason hoped suddenly that they wouldn't be attacked.

"We have returned." A voice from behind them called out. Jason turned to the darkness and saw nothing.

"We thought you were likely dead," said a strong masculine voice in reply.

"Stay close," said Mega. "They won't be able to see us."

Before Jason could ask, he heard footsteps behind him and whirled to see a new visitor to the scene stepping resolutely up to and past him as he stared in amazement. It was one of the colonists, a muscular male, clad in a tattered blue body suit, wearing one of their utility vests and a belt from which hung a large holstered knife. The stranger strode confidently, walking up to confront the group by the fire. It was comprised of perhaps a dozen or more men, a handful of women and two young boys, with fearful animal eyes, faces masked with dirt. They seemed to know the stranger, and as Mega had said, paid no attention to the trio of time visitors.

"What did you find?" asked one of them.

"There are many wild grains in the East. I think we could make much bread there, begin our agriculture again."

"And what of the wild beasts? Are they there?"

"They are here and there. We can subdue them with fire. The soil is very rich, no volcanoes threatening. I must talk with Anvil about it. Where are they hunting?"

"Anvil says we will settle here. He will be back soon with the warriors, with food and skins. We are safe here, he says."

"We came here to establish a garden. You've forsaken the mission. We must get back to it. I have many seeds left, although I have also sown many seeds all over this vast valley. They will grow and multiply and bear fruit."

"Fruit for the beasts, not for us. The mission is hopeless now. Don't you realize that? We can't survive down there any more. The steep mountainside is our only place of relative safety. Anvil and the warriors kill animals and bring them to us."

"We came here to be gardeners, not killers. You have subverted the mission, shattered our ideals, and succumbed to fear and malice."

"We have had to survive. You surely won't with your foolhardy missions across this savage place."

"The First Source, the One God, will send a rescue ship. I have faith in it. We have been loyal. When the rescue ship arrives, we must have made a good accounting of ourselves, maintained our ideals, pushed forward the mission against the odds, planted many seeds, controlled the creatures with the natural fire that we have here," the visitor pleaded. "We are not part of the rebellion. They will see that."

They had taken turns speaking to him. A woman with great hurt in her eyes spoke next: "Anvil says we must support the prince and his staff, whoever is in charge. There is no other choice. And indeed none of us see one. Who else is there to support? The Ancients of Days can surely come and exert their power. If they succeed, we will simply support them. "

The visitor responded forcefully: "If the prince and his staff are in rebellion," we must be wary in giving them support. You have each heard of Lucifer's philosophies. You can see that they are dangerous to our spiritual survival. But it seems apparent now that the whole system is involved in one way or another with this rebellion, maybe beyond."

"Lucifer has always been a very able and loyal administrator," said the woman. "He has been a pillar of support for the staff members who have worked so hard here. His brilliance of rhetoric and reason is well-known."

"But he has been outspoken against the Ancients, and even forcefully questioned the existence of the One God," said the visitor. "He believes fervently in more self-assertion and freedom for all of the worlds, and he has also been very critical of the entire ascension program of spiritualizing the ascending mortals. He believes it too time-consuming and resource-intensive. And, worthy of mention, he seems to have fallen in love with himself, too, I think. Did you not observe his arrogance at the amphitheater during our last visit to Dalamatia?"

"Free discourse is one thing. A rebellion is almost without precedent," one of the men mused. "And surely we would have heard of it through the universe channels before we lost the connection."

"Why do you think we lost connection? Anvil said it was a power shortage, but I think he's part of the rebellion on the side of Lucifer," said the visitor. "To aid the cause, Anvil would have had to take control of the colony, as he has surely done, over the backs of our departed leaders.

"If Lucifer is in charge of a rebellion, then he won't abandon us. I wouldn't sell him short. He has some powerful ideas and a mesmerizing presence."

"To the contrary. Lucifer couldn't succeed in any way," said the visitor. "My friends, you have been out here too long, and are a little too dazzled perhaps with the seeming brilliance of personalities like Lucifer, Caligastia, Daligastia and Satan. The Ancients of Days simply have to assert their authority here. Rebellion would be quickly thwarted. Caligastia may even be out of power now, and so we may simply be in the hands of...Anvil. Have you considered that?"

"They are in my hands," came a booming voice out of the darkness.

Jason turned to see a line of five fur-clad men, armed with strong bows and quivers of arrows, spears, hatchets and knives, with dark, neatly combed beards and plaited pigtails of dark hair hanging down either shoulder. They stood hard-eyed, their muscles sunburnt brown in the fireglow, but clean. Unlike their downtrodden comrades by the fire, they seemed to take pride in their stature, the lofty and brave countenance of warriors.

In their center stood the red bearded one, Anvil, his eyes intently fierce upon the bold visitor. He carried the grisly remains of a small hog over his shoulder, his other arm, or where it should have been, completely cloaked by the fur. He dropped the dead animal with a thud. The field beast lay open-eyed, dead, throat slashed. Two others dropped furry remains in front of the encampment, by the fire.

All of their eyes were hard upon the interloper.

"I'm glad you were successful, Anvil," said the visitor calmly. "Food and clothing maintenance is still moving along, I see."

"We are still doing well here, Adam, while you struggle to strew about your tiny seeds," said Anvil sarcastically, "and I see that you are still fantasizing about some kind of celestial conspiracy. I'm surprised you haven't turned up as fresh meat for these reptile devils you continue to taunt with your...singular adventures, you and the woman."

Anvil strode purposefully over to the fire, warming his blood-spattered hand.

"I'm too clever for them," said Adam. "I've found a wonderful place for a new garden."

"How many mitres?"

"Forty, maybe a few more."

"We will stay here," said Anvil forcefully. "I don't want to hear any more about it."

"Maybe <u>they</u> would," Adam motioned at the forlorn group around them.

"They know what's out there. We've been out there and the price was too high. You wouldn't know, Adam. As an arrogant runaway...renegade, you and...your woman managed to avoid the harrowing march to this place. I think they'll be pleased to stay here with me. I feed them. I clothe them. We can assert ourselves in this high place. If killing and malice are the way of the land, then we will command it."

"You can assert yourself by helping regain dominion over this wild world. That's the mission. All of us together can re-establish the garden in the East. I know that is the best place. Grow food from the ground."

"Aren't there volcanoes?"

"No. Not a one."

"Forty mitres is too far. Lucifer will send for us when he gets these wild primitives back under control. That's the only problem. We can wait here."

"You can't wait here, Anvil. I know now that what I believed was true, that you have led the colony to one of the most dangerous places on this continent. On the other side of this mountain, you could see it plainly from the top, there is a huge volcanic inferno underground, causing the earth tremors that we feel frequently. I believe there is a gigantic eruption coming. The mountain will explode from there and likely come crashing down on you."

"And where do you get this astounding piece of information?" Anvil boomed at him. "It seems you would tell anything to convince us to follow you to that...joyous, imaginary garden. Can you not tell the difference in a fresh roasted carcass for sustenance and a handful of seeds? The garden mission is over, and you are over. This is not a place for botany. It is a place of beasts and beastmasters. When you failed to join us on the march, you forfeited all rights to membership in this group. I think you should leave our fire and do it now."

His face shone sinister, shadowed by the flames, eyes glinting cruelly over the slash-scarred cheek.

Adam was not cowed. "I tell you the truth. The fire will burst open the land. This place is not safe. I can lead you through the beasts. I've been there. I know that we can do it. I know how to do it. Agriculture is the mission. Agriculture is how we will eventually prevail.

"So! You want to be the leader then," barked Anvil, "spouting philosophies. It all becomes clear now. You want to lead now that we are safe. You want to lead them back down into the valley for forty mitres or more to start growing fruits and vegetables. Your ignorance and blind loyalties are despicable! Get out of our camp — now! — or I'll have you thrown over the side."

"And would you do that then?" Adam asked him. "Are you now killers of men as well."

"Self-determination and self-reliance mean nothing to you, do they, Adam? What about bravery, courage?

"Yes. It will take a great deal of it to reach the new garden. But I'm certain we can make it and that we can defend it easily. I now know how to harness the fire. We can use it to protect us from the beasts — all of the time. I have found sources for it under the ground. I can show you. We have to work together, Anvil. We have to fulfill the mission. That is our responsibility and also, as it turns out, our salvation."

"Maybe the men and I will check out this…inferno. Perhaps on our next outing. In the meantime, we have no need for a new garden. We can eat meat far easier than we can grow food plants in this predatory wilderness. We failed in that too, Adam. So many things you forget. Must we rail about this endlessly as before you left?"

"I remember what the mission is. That is why we're here in the first place."

"Was! The mission is no more. It's time for us to take hold! Do you not have the courage??

"You had no authority to change the mission. I want to know what you last communicated to Lucifer and when?"

"I tell my people everything," said Anvil, growing angry. "I have said truthfully that the circuits are down. I tell you nothing more. You are an outsider now and the woman you took with you as well for choosing to flout my proper authority."

He suddenly lifted another arm out of the fur and lofted it high. It was muscular, hairy, lofted in a fist.

It was the arm of an ape.

Anvil leered proudly at them, pulling an arrow smartly from the quiver on his back and taking a proffered bow from one of his soldiers. He took aim with the huge beastly arm and fired the arrow hard up into the night sky.

"And so you see one of our last medical miracles," said Anvil with a sneer. "We control the beasts. We will use the beasts. We will have dominion. Indeed, we have harnessed another strength for our welfare. Let me show you."

Anvil picked a flaming stick from the fire and carried it past them and into the cliff cave. The upheld torch illuminated a huddle of tortured faces in the darkness. Jason counted six or more hairy faces, saw their arms and legs bound tightly. They were apes, now apparently slaves to Anvil's team.

147

"I am training them to do much of the work. They can easily be controlled. We are smarter; we are stronger. That is the law here. That is the law you don't seem to understand."

He tossed the flaming stick into the cluster of apes. They shrieked and grunted in fear, jerking in vain against the grass ropes, struggling to avoid the flame lying in their midst.

Anvil laughed. "There is a great satisfaction to achieving power here," he asserted. "Our hearts have been sufficiently torn by defeat. Now we will be strong, and I am the strongest of all. Much stronger than you."

"That remains to be seen," said Adam. "Brute strength is not the only kind we need here. We need strength of character, strength of will."

"It is precisely the same thing," said Anvil coldly. "You will leave now. I won't have you disrupting the system, the order that we have created, and the sanctuary I have provided. You are a traitor here and you are no longer welcome."

"I will go," said Adam. "We will do what we can without you. Dawn and I can do it alone if we are fortunate. We will create a place where all of you will be welcome." He surveyed the hapless faces to see a sign and saw none.

Anvil's eyes flashed. He grabbed a spear from a nearby soldier and raised it back as if to throw it at Adam's chest. He held it there poised, eyes cold and hard, filled with hatred.

Adam stood facing him for a few seconds, defiantly, meeting his eyes resolutely, then turned abruptly away and walked quickly into the darkness. Mega led Jason and Roci to follow, looking back anxiously at their angry antagonist, and the cluster of embattled aliens isolated in this savage land.

Jason caught up to Mega's rapid step, saw that he was intently thoughtful. "Will they survive?" he asked. "Are these our ancestors here?" Mega and Roci walked on and Jason hustled to keep up. The man they called Adam had disappeared into the darkness ahead of them and was nowhere to be seen.

"Where is he?" Jason asked, whirling to look around and about them.

"In pursuit of an agrarian dream," said Mega cryptically.

Jason fired more questions at Mega while Roci walked beside them, silently. "So who is this Adam? Does he have good information? Who is right here?"

"There are differences of opinion," said Mega. "Will they farm or will they hunt? Will they go here or go there? Will they trust in the planetary prince or will they defy him in an unseeing, unknowing faith in a celestial authority, a great spiritual idea which, unfortunately, has not yet presented itself clearly? These are indeed weighty questions," Mega mused.

"They can have children. They can continue on. They could be our ancestors."

"They don't believe they can reproduce," said Mega. "For a long time, our Pleadian-7 children have been removed during pregnancy and genetically birthed and developed in laboratory environments. This is a superior way that you will learn in time. The same kind of laboratories were brought here. But they are gone now, deserted or destroyed. They were underneath the dome. Anvil, of course, was able to graft a limb before they departed, no doubt, with some poor beast out there paying a price."

"They…can't have childbirth then?"

"We don't truly know. We had already developed much beyond that experience of pain and suffering at the time, feeling that we had learned sufficiently from it. But Adam and Dawn were engaged in an experimental childbirth just before the fall of the colony, a research project sponsored by our research academy. This is why they didn't accompany the rest of the colonists on the retreat. They stayed behind, underground, and tried to carry the birth through before leaving. Anvil advised a termination and immediate retreat, and they resisted it."

The trio continued to struggle down the rocky slope.

"Were they successful?"

"No. Their new child died. But they may be next time, if they're abandoned in this wilderness and forced to make another effort."

"And so there are two threads to follow," Jason reasoned.

Mega stopped short and turned to Jason. "We will not pursue all knowledge on this sojourn. We will understand more, however, on our next mindvisit. We will go to Mission Control, see what is left of it. Look." He pointed across the broad landscape, brightening now with the further rising of the sun. Jason could see many miles to a distant array of high silver spires. Black smoke could be send rising from the faraway ancient skyline.

"Dalamatia," said Mega, "a modest city of some 6,000. There is much turmoil there. We will go later and see what this rebellion has wrought."

"Perhaps we are all descended from these two, or even Anvil's group," said Jason. "Maybe we're all even related to one another."

"Of course we are," said Mega. "But that's another story, and one requiring a far more cosmological perspective."

"I…want to understand," said Jason, still confused.

"We will find more answers at Mission Control, in Dalamatia" said Mega. "For now, I have an urgent call about an emergency in Bangkok. I suggest you keep your mind clear and clean in the meantime, if you will be adequately prepared."

He reached out to Jason and touched two fingers to his forehead. Everything fell sleepily to black.

Jason opened his eyes and saw that he was back in the darkened tent, Roci sleeping beside him. Again, he had much to think about before sleeping. He thought too about the coming day. How could the mescaline trip serve any purpose any more, except perhaps as a detriment? He didn't even want to do it. Mega asked him to keep his head clear. He would have to do so. He couldn't take the fun time tomorrow; for the first time he could recall, he had something important to do, to learn, to understand, and there was a strong reason not to take the easy way.

He was invigorated just thinking about the next mindvisit. He lay there wide-eyed in the tent, energy soaring. He tried to imagine what it was like in Dalamatia.

She turned in her sleeping bag to face him. "I saw you out there with that…dirty woman," she said. Jason could see her smirky, cute smile.

"I thought it was you."

"Nominally," she said. "But certainly another episodic adventure from Mega's fertile, imaginative and theatrical mind. I enjoyed it all actually."

She reached out sleepily and touched his cheek. He was suddenly relaxed, dreamily happy. He kissed her hand and feel quickly asleep.

Down in Texas, Ellen Mackey lay beside her remarkable new friend and lover, thinking about her life there in the peaceful night. She could hear the crickets outside.

She yearned to the core of her heart to do something splendid with her life, to love and nurture and influence people to higher purpose. Her friend seemed to have solidified these thoughts in her head. She glanced over at him, in calm, sleeping repose. He looked peaceful and this gave her a comforting peace as well.

Ellen resolved that she would begin to take more positive steps in her life in the morning. She wondered if he might be there beside her, sent by angels to help, stay with her…from now on.

A premonition told her that he wouldn't.

EIGHT: *Naked in the Storm*

Jason sat and contemplated the capsule in his hand. On this early Sunday morning, he was revisiting his decision to abstain. It actually seemed like a big step in his life.

There was no hot coffee at the campsite, too harsh on the stomach, and he could use a cup. If he took the mescaline, however, he had to be careful to avoid puking if he could, risking only a bit of cereal if that. He might skip that too. He kept thinking that what he really needed to skip was the capsule itself.

Kevin walked up to him with confident strides. "You done yours yet, Jason?" He was slipping a hunting knife through his belt, looked rugged with the beaded headband and a t-shirt with the arms ripped out, accenting his muscular shoulders.

"Waiting to do it just before we strike out, I guess," Jason replied. "And trying to decide whether to eat a little something."

"Not for me. I've had a good shit this morning and I feel cleaned out and good, real good. It should take about an hour to get up to those falls. That'll be about the time it's taking effect."

Kevin, the natural leader, had led them in planning an addition to the trip this morning, a hike on up to Timberline Falls. The cascading water could be seen with strained eyes from Loch Vail and the group thought it would be more secluded there, away from at least those many hikers who made it as far as the lake.

Jason's mind was on the other mindtrip, the real one, the one that made the mescaline seem rather insignificant by comparison. He wanted a clear and clean head for it as Mega had admonished, if it indeed mattered in that altered state, and he knew that after taking the mescaline he would be dog-tired that night, stomach empty and craving food, and that tomorrow his mind would be fuzzy and unfocused. He would have no incentive for much, only a lazy lethargy, a mind-messed torpor that he didn't like at all — the so-called downside.

He put the capsule in a film canister and put it in the pocket of his jacket. Noticing the acorn there, he pulled it out, considered it a minute and returned it to his pocket. He renewed his decision to save those nice clean crystals and maybe use them somewhere down the line, when the time was more right.

The acorn? He wondered where and when it might be of use.

He wondered what the future would bring for him, embattled and unfulfilled as he was on his job and undecided about staying there, enamored with Roci and her team of explorers but not knowing what would come of it. The time was drawing close for her departure, midnight Monday. They would have two more days.

He looked up to see her walking up beside him, her smile radiant. He was overjoyed to see it.

The others made ready for the hike in various ways. Chuck was at the bathhouse; Sandra was zipping up their provisions in their tent. Roci had been a personable companion to his friends, asking more questions about their lives than discussing her views about it, and they all seemed to like her a lot.

Her style seemed to fit with a longtime belief of Jason's, that most people, even your friends, were only moderately interested in your life. They would prefer and would enjoy talking about their own lives and their own ideas, and a great way to make friends was to indulge them in this, take an interest in them. This is what Roci seemed to be doing, but he knew there was a stronger purpose, probably comparing the various personality types on this particular world. They were all research subjects in a very real sense.

Roci sat beside him. She snuggled close and they kissed gently. she showed him a kind and caring smile that he still could not fathom. How could she really care about him? And if she did, couldn't they…wasn't there some way…they could be together?"

"Did you swallow the drug?" she asked him.

"I'm not doing it. I'm afraid to do anything to mess up my head. It seems like we've got some important mindtrips of our own happening. I don't want the hangover tonight and tomorrow. Do you think that's wise? I wanted to ask you."

"Sure. There's a downside to most of your pharmaceuticals. You haven't been able to produce purified forms yet. There is also some foundation chemistry that you haven't discovered, and you haven't learned much about balancing chemical relationships and the varying body chemistry that exists in each individual."

"So are you still not doing it? Or are we both abstaining?"

"I have no need for it. I received a more complete report this morning by phone and find that it wouldn't be anything new for us. We have produced hallucinogenic and visionary effects before in our studies of altered consciousness. There is a large file on it, and we did some mind expansions at the space academy."

"I just want to be with you all that I can today. It's going to tear me apart to let you go."

She smiled pleasantly. "So many of you here to love and nurture, and you want to cling to me any way at all. That's very peculiar, Jason. There is so much for you here, so many people who need your love so much."

"But you won't be here, and you are the one, the only one, I have ever loved this deeply. I just can't help the way I feel about you. I'm…just…"

"I also love you in a special way," she said softly, "and that is somewhat strange. I never thought I would have such a bond of affection with…one like you. It is a surprise for me as I'm sure it is for you. Like you, I don't quite know how to deal with it. But I know that I have to leave. I have responsibilities, obligations. We both need to accept that as a certainty, and go on with our lives with a full and fond memory of this time we've had together."

"So that's it. You're resolved that it's all over for us, at midnight Monday."

"You must release this, Jason. When you and your friends go down tomorrow, I will stay here for a while, she said with calm certainty. "Then I will go to the meeting place and they will pick me up."

"I want to go there with you. How about that? Please."

"I don't think so. I chose the place in order to have one more splendid adventure here, a challenge somewhat unlike anything I could experience on my world."

"Where? I'll go too. Why not?"

"Because it's on top of Long's Peak, straight ahead, up there." She motioned to the gray, snow-blanketed peak, made famous by legendary stories and climbs over the years and a rugged test for either hiker or climber, depending on the route.

"I know about Long's Peak. I've read everything about it, wished I could climb it a million times. I told you that."

"That's where I got the idea, I guess. Anyway I'm going. They'll collect me there. It appears to be a safe place, especially late at night."

"Maybe…maybe I could make it."

"I can surely make it, Jason. I'm very trained for it. I have had the muscular toning and developing, the power nutrition, the breathing supplements. I have the hereditary attributes and laboratory enhancement. You haven't been fortunate enough to have any of this. I don't want you to take any risks."

"I think I can make it. Can't it be my decision to try?"

"I thought you wanted to fulfill some worthwhile purpose here. I thought you wanted a mission. That is still being decided, but I know it wouldn't be rock-climbing, and I know you would be risking that mission by putting yourself in danger."

"What about you? If I decide to go, is it all right with you?"

"You guys about ready to cut a trail?" Kevin walked up to them, ready to take the helm. Sandra was helping Chuck adjust his pack. Sweet-eyed Susan was wearing a Mickey Mouse t-shirt and a cute straw hat. Jason didn't get his answer then.

They trekked upward for a while, stopping to wait on Sandra and Susan while they vomited over in the bushes. Chuck was nauseous too, but with relatively nothing in his system, he was racked only by a few dry heaves.

"You guys ain't feelin' puny?" asked Kevin, who seemed all right.

"No. Looks like you're still the strong man in the crowd," said Roci, "along with Jason and me."

"I'm kinda queasy, if you wanna know the truth. It'll be passing in a little bit though and everything'll be brightening up. Man, the colors you're gonna see. They're outta sight."

"The colors are already here," said Roci. "What's missing now is your feeling of intensity about them."

"Yeah, Captain Mescalito just takes over and puts it all out there in front of you. Like you've never seen it before. Just wait. He'll be arriving with some real big rushes. We may take a break up here a little ways and light up a number. That'll help our stomachs and kind of take the edge off. I always like to smoke a little doobie with whatever I'm doing. It's a good mixer with anything."

The trail was rocky and steep. Roci made it easily, but the others puffed and strained before arriving at the falls, a cascading torrent that leaped over a rock wall and crashed into a cold blue pool, its beauty somewhat besmirched by the presence of downed timbers. They were tired, and they sprawled down there on the warm rocks, even then coming under the influence of the mystical mescaline.

Each was soon tripping in his or her own way. Kevin, without takers to his invitation, climbed atop a rocky butte and sat like the king of the mountain looking out over the distant horizon, lost in his own thoughts of grandeur which Jason knew to be self-reliance, physical achievement and an ingrained amazement with the natural wilderness and the challenges it offered, to test one's self, see how far one could go, how much could be achieved.

Susan lay in the shade of a wind-rustled fir, seemingly in deep admiration of the tiny flowers around her and the clusters of greenery and the friendly intrusion of a big gray bird that pecked at the crackers she scattered. She was dreamy-eyed, with a beatific smile.

Chuck and Sandra huddled together, relying on one another's support as they always did, sometimes laughing at some inside humor, sometimes walking over the rocks by the falls, gazing at the water's powerful crashing, then later skinny-dipping in the chill water. Kevin joined them, then Susan, then Jason and Roci, all naked, all soon chilled to the bone, laughing and joking and shivering in the cool, thin air.

They rushed for the towels and lay naked on the warm rocks in the healing sunshine. They compared notes and enthused about the brilliant colors, the exquisite natural setting, the rainbow in the mist of the falls, the puffy white clouds that seemed to be alive with faces and activity.

After a while, Jason and Roci made their retreat up into and behind the falls, slipping back of the torrent into a cold dark cave and looking out through the resounding crash at their friends below.

"Are you cold?" she asked him kindly.

He replied that he was a bit chilled and she came to him, wrapping him in her arms and holding him in her supernatural warmth until he was comfortable again and his shivers had subsided.

Her soft, warm lips were on his, and she told him that Mega wanted him to visit again now, that time was running out, and Mission Control of that ancient age was still to be explored. Within moments, he was asleep in her loving embrace.

It seemed that the roaring cascade of the water never ceased, but when Jason opened his eyes, he found that he was lying cheek-down on the muddy earth. His eyes gradually focused on the miniature scene just in front of him, mud and spattering raindrops and an intense feeling that he was unprotected or helpless under onslaught of something relentless and powerful.

It was a storm, and as he lifted his head uncertainly and looked around. Raindrops were beating on his face. He heard the clap of a thunderbolt, looked wide eyed at a crackling flash of lightning. He saw that he was completely nude and being pelted by a torrential thunderstorm. He raised his head to look around at the deluge, as best he could as water from his drenched head rolled down his face and into his eyes. Naked — and in a storm. Why?

He saw then the dark figure standing stolidly in front of him, in a dark hooded robe, face almost hidden from view, impervious to the drenching rain. More thunder resounded and a lightning bolt slithered and skittered down across the sky behind the black and still apparition. Straining his eyes Jason saw that it was Mega's face and white beard inside the hood, staring at him as if awaiting his awakening.

155

His body was muddy all over but the pouring rain continued to wash away the brown. The water streamed down from his cheeks onto his bare chest. Trying to shield his eyes, he wondered if Mega would ever speak. He did not, only lifted his hand and pointed for Jason to see. Jason looked around to see that they were surrounded by the weathered, moss and vine-covered rocks and collapsed walls that appeared to be the ruins of an ancient city. Looming up before them in the center of the desolation was the massive, towering and fire gutted remains of a tree, still dominating the landscape in its death, as it must have, gloriously, in life, when the city was alive.

The trunk's jagged, bare limbs protruded haphazardly A fire, perhaps lightning, had burned down the behemoth long ago, leaving a majestic natural artifact that rose above them into the storm-darkened sky. It stood huge and stark against the massive thunderclouds that filled the sky.

Though dead the tree seemed mightily impervious to the assaults of the elements, lifeless but still magnificent.

It must have been the vibrant living oak that was Mission Control, Jason reasoned. Without a word, Mega was already walking in its direction. Jason hurried along behind him.

Another thunderclap rattled the sky, joined by a rattling crackling of lightning. Jason and Mega walked hurriedly. A gust of wind rolled up against them, blowing through Mega's dark robe, almost tripping Jason who followed close behind him, feeling weak and unprotected in his nakedness, yearning for cover.

As they drew closer, the remains of the tree became a true giant, towering up into the tumultuous sky, taking the pounding rain in stride, without a visible tremble. Already dead, it could not be harmed, its naked limbs protruding on every side like defiant probes, daring the storm to inflict further damage, knowing itself to be free from destruction for it had already been sapped of sustenance.

They reached the behemoth and he stood with Mega on the sheltered side, partially protected from the fury of the rain and wind. Jason reached out to touch the rough bark.

"We are here, my friend," said Mega, speaking for the first time. His face and robe were saturated with rain but he was unmindful of it, perfectly calm in the face of the raging storm. He motioned for Jason to follow him as he stooped at the base of the rotund trunk and pulled away a small flat plate to reveal a dark hole at the tree's base. It was like the one Jason remembered from the space station, which they had entered to see the core.

Down into it Mega disappeared without a word, and, without hesitating, Jason slipped his nude body down behind him, submerging himself in the darkness. His hands gripped a wet ladder. His feet dangled helplessly, scrambling to touch something. His stretching toes touched nothing at all. He gripped the rungs, daring not let go.

"You may release yourself," said Mega's deep calm voice. "Have courage and faith. We are here."

Jason gripped his lips with determination. It would indeed require faith. He closed his eyes and loosened his grip. He dropped a foot or more, splashing into a few inches of water, his toes mushing into the muddy floor.

He stood there in pitch blackness for a second, then saw a dull light gradually building power to his side. Mega was standing there with both hands flat upon it, empowering it with energy. He recognized it as a large, round pinnacle light, from the dream that Roci had shared with him, a large globe of warm bluish brightness that illuminated the cavernous room around them, floating freely, and revealing to him dark walls of dirt and rock, buried boulders laced with roots that crawled in and out like petrified subterranean serpents, squeezing into the rock and holding the whole mass together. Water from the storm outside dripped here and there through the softening earth.

There where the giant tree's taproot should have been was some kind of implanted mechanism, seemingly of metal, with a monitor screen above a panel of controls. Covered with the grime and dust of years, it appeared to be long deserted, likely left by the fleeing colonists, standing as a cold, dead sentinel over what was left of Mission Control. Mega was already stepping toward it.

"Is the core gone?" Jason asked. "Is this where it was?"

Mega stood at the control panel as he replied, with his robe and hood resembling a monk at an altar, about to perform a ceremony. "Perhaps there is enough residual power to hear the message they must have left behind," he said, pressing a button, then taking the wet sleeve of the robe to wipe clean some of the aged dirt from the screen.

A picture gradually materialized on the monitor. It was the red bearded one, Anvil, belabored, standing and giving the message he had heard before. "Update to Dalamatia if and when you are back online. Attacks continue periodic and unabated. The wildlife panicked into a stampede today. Beloved Equal Tyran was mortally wounded and I relieved him from hopeless suffering. We killed another. It required too much energy. They completed the destruction of the north garden yesterday. We destroyed three of them there without casualties. We have precious little energy left. I will call us together and we will decide upon the trek to the mountains. From there, we can replenish and wait on any word — hopefully from you."

The picture dissolved into a blur for a moment, then another picture came on. Again it was Anvil, his face hard with determination, his eyes afire with fury. He faced them directly as he spoke:

157

"I am alone. This is my parting message to Caligastia, Satan or other of our forces who would access. I know that you will come to rescue us from the curse of these monsters when you have subdued the tribes. I have to trust you for I have pledged you our support; we are now in great need of reciprocation. We are moving to the mountains to the north, the high ground, at 828zTwR12, with every brave hope for our revolution of self-determination and free will, and from the domination of the Ancients of Days, and their shackles of servitude and restriction, and slavish labor on behalf of upstepping these miserable specimens of barbaric life. They have even unleashed these demons from another time upon us. We leave these gardens in ruin because of them, from their arrogant petulence that we would desire at least a modicum of self-government. We will anxiously await word from you in the mountains.

"And should you encounter the colonist Adam and the woman Dawn," Anvil added, "be assured that they know no facts concerning our fight for freedom. He is only suspicious, but I choose to deny him." They are both likely beyond logical persuasion, being blindly ignorant to the higher purposes of this noble crusade, and naively trusting of all of the celestial leadings. Both are stymied by an illogical faith in the rhetoric of the Ancients of Days and the pious personalities of the Creator Sons.

"The two have chosen to remain here, are involved in a foolhardy attempt to bring about a full womb birth. The man is persistent about establishing a new agricultural garden — foolhardy with so much meat to eat here, and so many predators to kill at the same time.

"The two have constantly questioned my wisdom. Should they complete the birth experiment and then venture to find us, they will not likely survive at any rate, especially if they have a child. I am certain that you will deal with them in a just and deserving way. My group needs to know little of this situation.

"Neither have I informed our surviving band of the official Lucifer Manifesto or our plans, awaiting you to arrive and impart your superior wisdom in a more convincing manner. I am a man of deed, not word. It would all prove too disconcerting coming from me, especially in the face of these many hardships from the attacks the administration has undoubtedly instigated against us.

"Finally, I implore you once again to destroy the reptile devils and save us from this forsaken wilderness. We await you. I remain your loyal soldier in the revolution."

The transmission faded to black. Jason was amazed, lost in thought.

The screen was dark again. Mega spoke: "It appears that Anvil did not take it upon himself to fully apprise the others of his deeper involvement in these matters. He would leave that to Lucifer's legions when they arrived.

Apparently they never did. The Melchizedeks stopped it all cold on Jerusem."

"My God," Jason said, "a rebellion against God. Anvil was part of it but kept the rest of the Pleadians here in the dark. They had nothing to do with it. Or...did he get involved with the rebels in order to try to save them from destruction — from the beasts? You said you had history books. What do your damned history books say about it? I mean, this has already happened for God's sake. What happened?"

"The historical fact, of course, is that the rebellion failed, that Lucifer's communication channels were promptly severed throughout the universes, but that the 32 planets involved have been paying the price in their evolutionary plan ever since, a heavy price that was eventually paid, in part, by Adam and Eve and now through the ages — by you! We know now that Lucifer himself has been in detention for some thousands of years waiting on final dispensation from the judges of the universes. They just happen to be those same Ancients of Days. High-powered administrators of the One God, the highest court. And here is where Lucifer's case is still being argued, even today."

"Today? And what of Anvil?"

"Should we care? He was only a soldier — like you. His tiny band of unfortunates are in full retreat anyway. We would expect them to have a minimal impact on the future, likely die out altogether. Let him rail about liberty and self-rule all he wants out here in the wilderness."

"Their philosophy actually sounds pretty familiar today," said Jason. "Guess that's why we're still in conflict. And so maybe the genetical seed of these lost colonists did spawn future generations here. Maybe they are our ancestors. But they said they couldn't reproduce, that a fully physical childbirth was...outmoded, something their bodies could no longer do."

"Perhaps they only chose not to do so. Mankind has always wanted to be delivered from physical pain and hardship."

"And there was Adam," said Jason, "and Eve. They had tried and failed but they said they would try again. I recall that. But what's going to happen? Maybe they were our ancestors."

"We are here to discover much as you are," said Mega, "But don't confuse them with your assigned Planetary Son and Daughter from Edentia, who come to effect biological upliftment on every inhabited planet of time and space at an appropriate time. Had Planetary Prince Caligastia and his materialized superhuman uplifters not defaulted in the first place, you would be enjoying their company and the superiority of their genes even today."

"Then, perhaps these colonists all failed at this point in history. Perhaps this was all a failure, Dalamatia, the gardens," said Jason. "Is that what you're saying?"

"Much of what was achieved in the 200,000 years of Dalamatia was lost again," said Mega. "You have recorded that Adam and Eve defaulted as well. This is true but not in the sense that you understand it."

A sudden trembling of the earth around them stopped the conversation.

"These walls are precarious," said Mega. "The storm above seems not to be abating. We had best see the recent views of Dalamatia, see what is happening in the streets and the amphitheater."

"And so we are leaving?" asked Jason anxiously. The walls about them seemed to be lurching back and forth. A stream of water now began cracking through the dirt to Jason's left. It splattered into the water that covered his bare feet and had risen above his ankles. The pinnacle light nudged against the creaky soil ceiling, spinning about and becoming streaked with mud.

"We shall stay here for a while," said Mega, to Jason's disappointment. "We must scan the city from these monitors, if they are still working."

"If we don't get out of here, we may not be working," said Jason. "This seems awfully real in here, Mega, close quarters."

"A close encounter, I should say," said Mega. "My information says that we should have a visitor very soon."

"I'm not sure we're ready for company," said Jason.

Mega had the monitors working now. They looked to a panoramic picture which was the streets of Dalamatia. There were numbers on the bottom of the screen which Jason couldn't decipher. The streets were full of people, some arguing viciously, loudly, others crowding against a huge, heavy door, trying to push it in. The camera was scanning from a high location.

The scene was melee. Fires burned here and there across the cityscape. A band of naked and hairy men rampaged up and down the street, screaming to all sides. Another man preached loudly from a small rise. Scores of men and women surrounded him, cheering his words.

"The streets have become a wild place," said Mega calmly, as they watched the multitude of conflicts on the streets, an orgy of violence and screaming, dead bodies stacked here and there. The hairy men were now being sent into retreat by a band of very tall and heavily muscled men, each standing over nine feet tall. They hurled rock-like missiles with uncanny accuracy. A tall warrior with long blonde hair threw hard at a retreating hairy one and struck him solidly on the head to drop him dead.

"What the hell," said Jason. "All hell has broken loose."

"These particular primitives, some of a great many, managed to break down a wall and swarmed in to ravage the city. It activated the recorder atop the Spiral Center. They are being beaten back by a fire team of Caligastia's superhumans."

"Superhumans? Yes, they're big. They're hairless too." The camera continued to circle the city. From the new perspective, Jason could see that parts of the city appeared deserted, except for looters climbing through smashed windows.

"There's quite a genetical difference here," said Mega. "The legendary Mighty Men of Old as your legends call them, highly advanced materialized personalities who came with the planetary prince to uplift, and eventually became part of your ancestry, all the while juxtaposed with hordes of evolving savages from almost the other end of the spectrum. It is a fascinating clash, is it not?"

"It's horrible," said Jason. "There is a woman being raped and murdered in an alley!"

"Very crude. The celestials, of course, fight at a different level. The War in the Heavens was fought in the vigor of ideological debate." Mega flipped on another screen. "Here, at the same time as the violence of Urantia, we see the celestials debating the merits of the Lucifer Manifesto."

Jason looked up anxiously at the dirt walls which were beginning to pour water, but couldn't keep his eyes from riveting on the screen.

The amphitheater was enclosed, a dome, and filled with rows of inclining seats. They were filled with an array of beings as Jason had never seen. The glowing white light emanating from their bodies blocked to Jason's mind hardly any detail of them at all. They were just too bright for his eyes to penetrate, but he could see them moving, swaying slightly, like bending beams of light, arms and legs and faces with large expressive dark eyes. It was the most incredible array Jason had ever beheld.

In the center, a tall man in a white translucent robe, sparkling with light, spoke in smooth, melodious, harmonic tones, in words Jason could not begin to understand. It seemed to be a series of tonal vibrations that continually leaped and danced rhythmically. It was the most incredible, persuasive and harmonic blending of sounds Jason had ever heard. It was a day, a powerful moment, for superlatives.

"This is Gabriel," said Mega, "the Bright and Morning Star. He is debating against Lucifer's ideas. It will all be quite...civilized I will say, within this arena. There is war outside and inside, different levels, higher and lower consequences. Amazingly enough, Jason, while empires rise and fall, institutions emerge and crumble, this debate will go on. It is recorded that the Lucifer Rebellion was not adjudicated until the early 1980s of your time."

"What? I was here. Why didn't I hear about it?" asked Jason, incredulous at this flood of revelation.

The cavern walls vibrated and cracked with a rumbling tremor, loose soil shaking from the earth ceiling all about them, water gushing from the storm above. Clots of dirt crashed down on his left; a gash opened in the root-laced wall to his right. It seemed that it would all come thundering down upon them.

A pang of fear struck through Jason's heart. Could he be killed, could he not die in this mind state? How could he? He was afraid. It was so much more intense than it had been before. He surely felt the fear; perhaps he could now feel — pain?" He looked about and — what! — Mega had disappeared. He wasn't there. He made his way back toward the portal; maybe he could stand on something and get out.

Then Jason heard a clumping noise above, heard the sliding panel come apart. He looked up at the dark hole, moving several steps back in fearful anticipation. Jason had said they would have a visitor.

Now, two strong naked and hairy legs appeared from where they themselves had come. Jason splashed away, standing there naked, with no weapon.

They were the muscular limbs of a man, feet wrapped in some kind of fur-lined boots, caked with mud and descending slowly.

Down they came, revealing the fur-clad body above them, and an angry face shrouded with a long and tangled red beard — Anvil! — staring viciously at him, holding onto the ladder with that one huge beastly grafted arm of hair and muscle, hanging easily, no sign of stress with the powerful arm, drilling him with those powerful eyes, then dropping with a splash onto the cavern floor. They were alone together.

That triumphant beast arm reached and pulled up a jagged ax, fashioned from stone and tied onto a split wooden handle. He stood facing Jason with eyes of hate, brandishing the ax, his face shadowy and sinister in the soft light of the pinnacle.

Jason heard Mega's words come from somewhere. "He is here. Perhaps he is evil incarnate, Jason, and as we all must do at some key point in our lives, we must face it. We must choose."

In near panic, Jason turned to either side. Though he had heard him speak, Mega was not there. He was here alone.

Wide-eyed, Jason faced his protagonist, still naked, still feeling inadequate, unprepared, afraid, no weapon at hand. Anvil lofted the ax menacingly, moving it from hand to hand, from the bare hand of his superior alien form to the long-fingered, hairy hand of the physically superior ape that had been grafted onto his person.

"Why are you here?" Jason asked uncertainly, hoping to reveal no fear. "We mean you no harm. We are here from time ahead to learn what happened to you."

"We. I see no one but you, helpless you." rasped Anvil. "And I see that you must have the answer I seek. I must have the core. You will tell me where it is."

"I search for the core as well. I am only searching for truth. I only want knowledge. I want to understand from where you came, from where we came, what should be our purpose here."

Anvil began moving in a circle slowly, splashing one foot after another. Jason felt compelled to maneuver with him, stay away from his wrath, the primitive ax he held threateningly, wondering if at any second the barbarian would rush upon him and kill him. Desperately, he taxed his mind, trying to think of a way to turn back the hostility. The storm had stopped; all was silent now. The walls and ceiling seemed to have stabilized a little. But then Jason felt an earth tremor. Everything shook slightly. A large clot of dirt fell and splashed into the water between as they circled each other warily.

"Surely there is no accomplishment in killing me," Jason said with all the self-assurance he could muster. "It would only produce a dead body, of no value. I have empathy for you. I have seen how you and your people have suffered. If I could, I would deliver you from your torment, I would cast away the devils, but I implore you not to become like them." Jason could hardly believe he was saying these things; they seemed to be channeled through him.

"Perhaps you are the one who sent them," Anvil charged raspily. "You are not part of the colony. There is no reason for you to be here. You are out of time sequence as are they. There must be a connection."

"I only came here in search of you. I came to tell you that you must not descend to the level of the beasts in your adversity, that you must preserve the values of spiritual virtue, love and mercy. My compassion for you is boundless because I have seen your great suffering and I realize that, even though you joined in a rebellion against the One God you did so out of conviction and your commitment to save the colony, and that the continued love and mercy of your creator will prove to you that it was wrong. You will see this and you will be saved to grace and salvation. You are a beloved child of God and there will be every opportunity for you to be part of this family."

Anvil's eyes blazed at him. "You can stand here facing torture and death and say you love me. You are mad," he screamed. The cave echoed with his booming voice. A large crack appeared in the ceiling to his left and a gush of water poured from it.

"Love is the power of the One God," said Jason calmly. "Our quest is to learn to embrace it in our lives, for sustenance and power. But there cannot be peace when vastly imperfect, animal origin personalities have absolute freedom. You see the chaos that has resulted. God has a plan for the universe. You will be at peace when you learn to align your will with God's, not swallow yourself in false pride. I love you as a child of God. Honor God with the life and free will given you." Jason was speaking methodically and surely, preaching mightily, wordily, but he didn't know where the words were coming from.

"It is a lie! It is impossible that you could love me, that you could face me with that preposterous tale which you believe might save your puny life."

"Our mortal lives are only temporal," said Jason. "You put far too much value on them and far too little on your potential spiritual ascension after this mortal flesh is dead." Jason marveled at how fluidly the answer came.

"You speak from fear of taking action only, you helpless fool," Anvil accused. "You are weak and I am strong. My way then is undoubtedly the best for I am in control."

"You do not appear to be in control. And you see no fear in me, my brother," said Jason. "I am far stronger and braver than you realize to stand here and face you with these words and without weapon. If you will look into my eyes openly and honestly, you will see this truth. You will see the joy of knowing we are both God's children and we will ascend far above this temporary mortal life. This is just a school for material experience."

Jason knew that his eyes must continue to meet Anvil's as he spoke, that he must not flinch in the face of evil, must prove his words, show his strength, turn away evil with good, dissolve fear-driven hatred with service-driven love. As he had spoken he had fully realized some profound truths for the first time, in his own heart, and amazingly, somehow, they were coming from his own mouth.

Their eyes held together, Jason's compassionate and empathetic, Anvil's embittered and defensive — a test of will, of logic, of power, for only a moment but of interminable length, through all of time.

"God is love. And so you have lost God," said Jason calmly. "God is love and love is the opposite of fear."

Anvil's eyes gradually turned from malice to terror, then pain, then some kind of realization. He must have known he could not kill the intruder now. There was no reason to kill one who offers you love, and, in his conscience, his inner spirit, which remained an indelible part of him, he could not have lived with it. He could never have forgotten that he had done so, or forgiven himself for an act of horror against such an empathetic creature. He realized something he had lost, that true love can indeed vanquish evil, hate.

Anvil's eyes widened as if in a frustrating, horrifying trance, then softened to acceptance. He lowered both arms helplessly and dropped the ax with a splash into the water. He stared at Jason as if pained but resigned, still strong of will but helpless, anxious but contrite. Jason reached out his bare hand to him. Anvil stared at it and almost seemed ready to reach out as well. He looked at Jason. His face was filled with a call for love.

But then the deep rumble began again and they both were taken aback. The walls trembled, shaking loose huge clots of earth. Water poured out of the top in a gush. All of the earth shook around them and a huge mass came tumbling down to smother them, and someone was shaking Jason, shaking him awake.

It was Roci. He opened his eyes and they were again under the waterfall. He realized he was back in Colorado. He looked into her face and saw again that she was beautiful, and she seemed very pleased.

"Welcome to the mission," she said. "You now have an assignment. Congratulations!"

They were all tired and subdued around the campfire. They resolved to spend this night at Timberline Falls and to return to Loch Vail the next morning. Jason's friends talked of the visual imagery they had experienced, and the feelings of weirdness they experienced during the day. He and Roci interjected themselves only modestly, more curious than not, still maintaining the secret that they had not indulged in the mescaline.

They talked of tiredness too, mental and physical fatigue and the fact that they would be "fuzzy-headed" the next day as well. And they talked of returning to their homes and jobs, their plans for the trip and the following week and a time when they might meet again.

It all seemed pretty mundane to Jason, who could not get his confrontation of the day out of his head. In a quiet moment with Roci, he had asked her if she knew about it. She had only smiled and said that she did.

And in the night, they walked together away from the campfire to look at the multitude of stars above them.

"Can you show me where you are from?" he asked her.

She scanned the horizon and pointed in the lower eastern sky.

"It is all so incredible," he said, "as if this has all been a dream."

"And incredible for me as well," she said. "I have found a deeper understanding of the universe forces that bind us all, the divine purpose behind all of the creation. I am anxious to apply what I have learned with other lifeforms, those not as similar to our own."

"There are many kinds of life?"

"Of course. Some air-breathing, some not. They are of various colors and kinds. They thrive under a variety of temperatures and conditions. I wonder if it would be possible that I could develop such a bond of affection with a form not so like my own."

165

"I'm sure I don't know," said Jason. "I know now that we are so primitive here."

"But that isn't so bad," she told him. "The thrill of discovery and adventure is with us all, on its various levels. The possibility of evil is everywhere, in some places such as this more pronounced than in others. But without the existence of evil, there would not be that supreme opportunity to choose. The Divine Center, the One God, wants to be the choice, and that is the choice we must make to remain ascendant."

"I want to climb Long's Peak with you."

"You are sure of that?"

"I yearn deeply for this kind of accomplishment, to demonstrate this kind of courage."

She stared at him for a few seconds, as if fathoming his depths.

"Then you shall go," she said. "It will be our last day together, a great adventure, and I would not want to deprive you of it."

"There is no way I can go on with you, join Mega and all of you?"

She faced him, looked into his eyes under the moonlight, there under the millions of stars: "You would do so, wouldn't you. Go with me into the great unknown, leave everything here behind. Listen. Listen to me, Jason. In our minds and, as you would say, in our hearts, we will always be together. That is a promise."

"Then I will remember? It won't be erased?"

"Today," she said, "you passed an important test. You now have an assignment in the mission, and it is only the beginning of an exciting and eternal adventure of discovery if you maintain your faith."

On this joyous evening, as they embraced and kissed under the vast creation, he suspected nothing of the conflicts that would rock their lives the following day.

NINE: *Oaks, Acorns, Infusions*

The camp stirred to life the next morning, its occupants' heads muddled and bodies still tired. Chuck complained of a headache and searched futilely for aspirins, Sandra was taciturn and grumpy. Kevin wordlessly went about building fire, and Jason helped him by gathering sticks. Susan fished out some of the food they had brought and endeavored to slice some apples and oranges.

Jason felt better than them, he knew, as he and Roci pulled their articles together for the trek downward. For every emotional high that they could induce, he thought, there is a price to be exacted for it later, a hangover, a downside. Must be a lesson there about artificiality, he thought, but he was not inclined to get into any philosophy today. He felt his mind needed a rest.

Then he noticed that Susan had cut herself, was standing there, face scrunched, holding her finger, blood streaming down it and onto the ground. Kevin quit the fire to go to her. She was crying.

"Holy shit!," said Chuck. "What happened?"

"Oh…so dumb. Cut my finger with the damned knife. No big deal."

"Oh, baby, here, let me look at it," said Kevin sympathetically. Roci stepped forward."

"I think I've got something in the pack," said Sandra, "a band-aid, I know, maybe some iodine."

"Foolish," said Susan. "How did I do that?" She and Kevin were examining the small gash.

"Well," said Kevin. "We're all gonna be kinda dulled out today, not really with it. That's just the way it is."

Roci had already strapped on her vest and now pulled something from one of the slitted pockets — a vial which she opened. It contained a syrupy substance that she rubbed on Susan's wound, then she wrapped it with the band-aid offered by Chuck.

"Damn! I don't know where my mind is," said Susan.

"I got a headache like you wouldn't believe," said Chuck.

"It's especially a good time for us to love one another," said Roci, "and to be there to support each another." She embraced both Susan and Kevin and kissed both of them on the cheek.

Again, Jason's friends didn't know what to make of her open affection, but he was sure they liked it. Who wouldn't? Roci embraced Chuck then and kissed him, and then Sandra. "Love each other especially today, brothers and sisters, and try hard to love and nurture each other always," she said matter-of-factly."

To Jason and to most other humans, it probably sounded melodramatic, over-the-top. But Jason knew she meant every syllable of it.

They may not have understood but they all, including Jason, were moved. Jason came forward and clutched the hands of his friends. They all embraced and it cheered everyone's mood. The rest of the morning chores seemed lighter, and the mood seemed bright enough through their mental dullness as they trekked back toward Loch Vail.

A positive energy had been unleashed by her presence. Jason realized that the simple love formula seemed frustratingly beyond human reach, inexplicably. The love power had always been there, throughout religion, throughout history, throughout practical experience, but now was still beyond their reach because of some curse that belabored them all. Whether of Lucifer or Satan or Anvil or some other evil presence he didn't know, that enmity was still here with them.

Unconditional love was both the answer and the ultimate secret. It was well-recorded, well-hidden, well-disguised, well-confused, well-framed in the realization of their own continuing fallibility. They would fail Roci's example promptly and ultimately, maybe dismiss it as a cliché, as a piece of naiveté, as an impossible unreality. It depressed him to realize that. This was an oblique fault line running through their mortal existence here. They could achieve only within their ability, share only in a limited, superficial way and no more, never reach the pinnacle in this world and can only hope to do so in the next. Luckily, there is a "next." That was the ultimate peace of it. There is an ascension plan for mortals, despite Lucifer's protestations. There will be another chance.

They walked downward. Jason pondered through his troubled mind about the danger of the climb, worrying that he could do it, without jeopardizing them both. What would they tell his friends? They hadn't made up a story.

Then it struck him that he would be left alone — on the top! Could he survive that? Could he get down? Surely by the easiest route. And then he would be alone again to his miserable life.

He remembered her charge — to love one another. He would have his friends, could make more friends, could try to love and nurture them, and others too, if he only could in all his frailties and confusions and ignorance and in the face of their individual and collective resistance. She would still be his inspiration but she would no longer be here to help him be strong, to be his ecstatic intimacy.

He resolved to be strong of will and purpose and goodness in the face of this impending loss. Of all the words in his language that he had to keep foremost, there was the one — love. Maintain a loving disposition each day. He knew that so very plainly, whether it was derived or implanted or inspired to him.

In reality, it was some of all these methodologies. That's what he had to remember; there were many different kinds of energy, communications tools, realities that he just couldn't fathom right now, and it didn't matter at all.

He knew he would be fully conscious of choices and their importance now, the record he was building in the material experience that would represent him at the gates to the beyond. And his record would always be weighted based on the particular place that he and his people occupied in time and space, the stage of ignorance, the state of evolution. This was indeed his own time and space, and he knew he needed to accept it as it was, and above all, accept mortal life as a divine gift to fully appreciate, the opportunity to do the will of the creator and take a place in the ascension plan toward ultimate spiritual perfection.

Loch Vail was soon within clear sight, the gentle expanse of blue water and the three tents they had left. As they drew closer, they saw people there, finally discerning two men in the brown uniform of park rangers.

"What the hell do they want?" asked Kevin with a worried look.

"I wonder if we're not supposed to camp here," said Sandra.

"I can't see that we hurt anything," said Chuck, who seemed very perturbed.

"I know we weren't supposed to have a fire up here," said Jason. "There's a rule against that."

They were soon walking back into the campsite, confronting the two men who stood waiting. One of them was paunchy, his gut hanging over his belt, face ruddy, with a big nose filled with pockmarks. The other was slender, neater, with a small clipped black mustache and a cold, slightly crossed look in his eyes.

"Good morning," said Kevin cheerily, the others mumbling it too.

"Mornin'," said the big guy. "These tents here belong to you people?"

"Yessir," said Kevin. "It's all right to camp up here, isn't it officer?" Kevin was the leader as usual.

"No. As a matter of fact it isn't. You should've been told that when you got your back country permit. The camping area is about five hundred yards over in that direction. They's signs. This here fire ya'll built isn't allowed either. You people do have a backcountry permit, don't you?"

"Well, no sir. We didn't realize we were supposed to have a permit or we sure would've gotten one."

"It's a little late now, don't you think?" said the big one. "We're going to have to give you a citation for that, and for the fire. This is not a campground. We've got plenty of other places to camp in the park. Ya'll been up to the falls?"

"Yessir. We camped up there last night, just in our sleeping bags."

The big man just shook his head. "I reckon you're the people we got the complaints about then. A couple and their little boy came back saying there was some people up there laying out naked on the rocks, and acting pretty peculiar. Ya'll know anything about that?"

"No sir. Well...we might have been getting a little sunshine. We sure didn't think there was anybody around."

"This is a public park, people. We can't have families coming up here and finding naked people layin' around. We've got to have some standards of decency up here just like they do wherever you're from."

"Well, we sure did make an effort to get away from everybody," said Jason. "We were just looking for a very secluded spot to get some sunshine. We didn't see anybody around anywhere."

"Well, my God, son, that's still the main trail up there. Wouldn't you think somebody might come along? Ya'll could at least keep your clothes on," said the big man.

"Any of you people lose this?" asked the thin one. He was holding up a roach clip, an ornate metal one, bought at a head shop, decorated with colorful beads. Several of them denied it, with heads shaking and furrowed brows.

"Well, it was laying right over there by that illegal fire ya'll built. I figure one of you lost it there."

"What is it?" asked Chuck. Jason knew that it belonged to Chuck.

"Well, I think you know what it is. Looks like sumpin' you'd use to smoke marijuana to me. Don't it to you?"

"Well, it doesn't belong to us," Chuck lied.

"Them people up at the falls said it looked like ya'll were smokin' the stuff to them," said the big man.

"No sir," said Kevin. "We might have been smoking cigarettes. We got a couple of smokers in the group."

"We was smoking cigarettes, officers, but that's all," said Chuck. "I've never seen that thing before."

"Well, it's mighty funny it was laying right here in your campsite. Ain't that a funny coincidence?"

No one answered.

"We got a pickup truck down there a piece, on the utility road. I think maybe ya'll better pack up this gear here and come on back down to headquarters with us and we'll try to get to the bottom of this," said the big one. "And for right now, I think ya'll all better get out some kind of identification. The thin one already had a note pad out and fished a pen out of his shirt pocket.

"I can't go down with you officers," said Roci. "I have to meet someone up here later today. And I didn't bring any identification." The rest of them were shocked at her forthrightness. The officers looked at her, first with surprise, then with humor.

"I don't think you understand, little lady," said the big one. "We didn't ask you if you wanted to come. You're going to have to come on down and help us get this thing straightened out. As far as we're concerned, you're just as guilty as the rest of these people."

"As far as I'm concerned, we're not guilty of anything of consequence," she said without hesitation. "We apologize for not knowing or following the camping rules, but we didn't harm anything in any way. This is a beautiful place and we would surely treat it with reverence."

"Reverence ain't got nothing to do with it. When you break the rules, little lady, you've got to pay the price. And runnin' around naked and doing drugs in the park is a lot more than just a simple thing. I think you better be calming down your attitude about what you gonna do and ain't gonna do."

"There's nothing wrong with exposing our bodies to a little sunlight," said Roci. "It's good for them. And this herb you're talking about is relatively harmless. I think you ought to give some more consideration to your stupid laws if you think these things are serious."

"It don't make no difference what I think. We're just here to enforce the law and if you think showin' off naked in front of a young couple and their child and smoking drugs isn't serious, I think you better kinda reconsider your position. Now I'm not going to argue with you about it any more, little lady."

"I think you better quit calling me little lady before I show you that I'm not."

"Whoa now!" said Kevin. "Let's be cool."

"You gonna get yourself handcuffed, woman, if you don't close your mouth right now," said the fat man, pointing a finger in her face. She reached out quickly and grabbed the finger. He jerked at it but couldn't pull away. She held it tight. His eyes bulged. He tried to speak.

"I…I…ah!…ah!" The fat man's face turned redder. He seemed petrified, legs began to tremble, then shake, as if being electrocuted. Roci held fast, looked hard, coldly, into his eyes. A wetness poured through the man's pants legs. The other officer stared in surprise as they all did. The fat man sank to his knees, urine now dripping onto his shoes.

"Hold on now!" hollered the thin officer. "What the hell's going on?" He had one finger pointed rigidly at her, the only hand on his holster.

Roci turned the finger loose and the fat one, eyes dazed, fell over on his face. The thin one was unstrapping his handgun by then, tried to pull it out, but she was too fast.

With lightning speed, she delivered a hard fist to his jaw with one hand, slapping the revolver from his hand with the other. He fell to the ground and the gun clattered on the rock beside him. Without thinking, Jason reached quickly and picked it up.

"Oh my God!" moaned Chuck. "Oh my God!" Kevin and the others were dumbfounded. It had happened so fast.

The thin one, dazed, tried to get up. Jason pointed the gun at his head and commanded: "Don't move an inch."

The fat one was struggling to get up too. Roci delivered a hard foot to his crotch and with a resounding grunt he crumpled again to his knees.

Chuck and Sandra were both shrinking away, frightened. Susan clutched at Kevin and they stared in amazement, not knowing what to do.

Neither did Jason, but he stood there with the revolver pressed on the ranger. "Get down! Flat on your stomach!" he commanded. The thin one did so. The fat one lay on his side, face red and contorted, both hands cupping his crotch, his face swelled into a puffy red grip.

"Nice work," Roci said to him. "I think you people had better get some rope and gags and blindfolds and we'll tie these guys up."

"Oh no! Hell no!" said Chuck. "We ain't gettin' involved in this. We got nothin' to do with this."

"Strike your tents and get the hell out then," said Jason. "There's no way to turn back now, so get the hell out. We'll take care of it." He didn't know what he was doing, but he was right. There was no turning back. He knew they had to tie down the rangers and escape as soon as possible, before the day's hikers began arriving.

Even Kevin was speechless. While Jason and Roci trussed up the rangers, covered their eyes and mouths with tight bandannas, the rest of the group feverishly began getting their tents down and packing gear. Finally, Jason and Roci dragged the two bound-up rangers out of the campsite and behind a large boulder. Then they were all confronting one another.

"Roci! I can't believe you did that," said Kevin. "How the hell are we going to get out of this?"

"If we get caught," moaned Chuck, "they're gonna put us all in prison You know that, don't you?"

"We should've gone on down with them," said Susan. "We could have talked our way out of it."

"I doubt that," said Jason. "But they don't know who you are. You'll be a long way from here before they're able to do anything."

"They know what we look like," said Sandra.

"You look like a lot of other humans," said Roci. "Jason and I will take care of everything. You should get on the trail and don't look back until you're home. Don't worry about it."

"She's right. That's all we can do now," said Kevin, "cut a trail and keep going until we're home."

Roci pulled two rolls of bills from her vest, handed one to Kevin and another to Sandra. "Take this money. I have plenty of it. It's for the trouble I've caused you, and as a gift of friendship. Use it wisely and remember to love one another."

Kevin unfolded it. It was hundred dollar bills. I don't understand. Why are you —?"

"It's a gift for you. I just told you. You're all going home. Jason and I are going in another direction."

"Where? You'd better get a long way from here too," said Chuck.

"Yeah," said Sandra. "You better be gone fast."

"We will," said Roci. "Sorry about the inconvenience. Sometimes I just don't have much patience with primitives. I have an appointment to keep tonight and I just didn't have the time to waste going down and arguing with people who substitute rules and regulations for intelligence."

"I guess we were breaking the law," said Susan.

"We knew that. I just didn't think they'd be up here enforcing it," said Kevin.

Roci was holding up ignition keys. "I think the rangers' truck is probably in that direction," she pointed. "I saw a part of the utility road. You can get down faster that way. But don't leave your fingerprints anywhere on the truck, or anything inside, and throw the keys away when you get down. Make it as tough for them as you can."

Kevin took them, stared at her. "I've never met anyone like you," he said.

"There isn't anyone like me," she replied.

When they had said final goodbyes, Roci led Jason back to the rangers, who were sitting up by then, still blindfolded, gagged and struggling with their ropes. She pulled a small vial and syringe from her all-purpose vest. While Jason watched, she filled it with a brown substance and injected each of them behind the ear, motioning for Jason to be quiet as she worked. The two officers relaxed and fell over limp.

173

When they were out of hearing distance, he asked her if they were harmed. "No," she replied. "They'll sleep a while, and their minds will be hazy about everything that happened. It'll be several days before they're able to remember much of it at all, and then it will be confused."

They struck the tent, gathered on their warmest clothes and the packs and made ready to climb Long's Peak.

"You're sure you still want to go?" she asked him.

"More than ever," he said. She noticed the two revolvers he had laid on the ground, picked them up and flung them into the lake. "You should outlaw these things," she said certainly. "Let's go." They began the trek upward.

Her pace was demanding, but she willingly stopped for Jason to rest and he had to do so frequently. Not only was the trail steep but his lungs had not fully adjusted to the lower oxygen level of the high country.

They stopped in a huge boulder field, the massive behemoth of Long's Peak looming up hard in front of them, larger than Jason had ever seen it. She gave him a small red pill from her vest. He took it with a swig of water.

She determined they would stash the packs there, keeping one sleeping bag and a few essentials for their night on the top. She warned him to remember the place since he would be returning alone, but by a safer route that she outlined for him, one hand on his shoulder, her finger pointing out the way for Jason from this distant vantage point so that he could, hopefully, remember and follow it.

It was hard for him to imagine that she would be ascending from the peak, that he would come down alone. It was hard, too, to realize that he would finally be climbing the legendary mountain, and not by the easiest route. She had outlined for him a route that would require a partial scaling of the dangerous north face.

They planned their ascent, their strategy from there, her pointing to a long vertical crack in the wall that she asserted would be the best way to go. Jason could make out what appeared to be some tough going just above it, wishing he could see more plainly just how many hand and footholds would be there. Above these seemingly precarious places was a steep snowfield which would carry them all the way to the top.

It was all clear and visible in the sunshine of this pleasant morning, but Jason knew the weather could change quickly up there, and there were clouds here and there that could turn into thunderstorms very quickly.

They had a single rope and she checked it thoroughly for frays. It appeared sound. After hiding the packs under an outcrop of rock, they were off. But soon they had to rest again, Jason gasping a little for breath. The pill was beginning to take effect, though, increasing his oxygen assimilation.

It was getting colder, the wind swirling around them, whistling against the rock. They had left the tree line far below and their landscape was now rock and tundra and patches of snow.

They rested again at the base of the crack. Jason looked up to see that it disappeared out of sight up the side. His hands were cold but he had to have the sensitivity of his fingertips to feel the rock; he had to be almost as one with the rock, he knew, stretching his body in the right way to embrace the fingerholds, the toeholds, foot by foot by foot, with patience, with calm dedication and concentration.

Roci seemed relaxed; he knew that he must appear nervous to her since he was. He was, in fact, fighting the inner pangs of fear in his heart, but was determined to go on. Somehow, it was an important challenge to him; he had to do it, not understanding exactly why.

"Do you think you can do it?" she asked him.

"I don't know," he replied honestly. "I'm trying to concentrate with all my heart and mind on technique, to do everything right, step by step. I wish I had some real climbing boots. I wish I had more knowledge, more strength, more confidence."

"That's usual in many important endeavors, isn't it?"

"I suppose so. But this one is damned important. I can't make a mistake here. I feel like…I have to be better than I really am. And…I'm just not ready to die or hurt you with some fuck-up. Pretty damned sobering."

"Maybe this is the way you grow, but only if it's important to you to grow in this way. Certainly, it's good to face fear and beat it."

"Maybe it's foolish for me to be doing this. Maybe my talents, my future, my destiny is elsewhere. You said it yourself, and maybe I should have listened. Rock-climbing is not any of these things to me. I don't really know why I'm doing it any more. What's important is writing, expressing myself. If I fall off some mountain, I sure won't be able to do that."

"Well," she said. "Climbing this rock may not be important in a practical sense, but maybe it's an exciting one-time adventure against fear. The peak may be symbolic. You often yearn for achievement to feed your egos, and so you strive for some things whether they're really important or not. This challenge appears romantic to you, maybe something you could boast about, something that would earn you respect and recognition from others. And maybe if that's all it is, maybe it isn't something you want to do. Maybe it isn't worth the risk. Maybe you should stop here. We can say our goodbyes."

Jason thought about her words before speaking. "Maybe there's truth in that. But…I do believe there would be an inner satisfaction from the achievement, and from the experience. I like to beat fear. Maybe I could write about it. Maybe I will learn something really profound. And maybe I want to be with you every possible minute and see you finally ascend into the clouds, or wherever you're going. So…there's a lot of definite maybes for you anyway."

She laughed. "And often you do things and then, later, figure out the reason why anyway. Let's just do it!"

Jason felt too sickly to respond with any wit. He gripped his lips and said nothing, felt his heart thumping.

She led the way and they started the ascent up the crack, an ancient rupture in the gigantic rock wall that now, ages after some cataclysmic event, they were utilizing to try for some dubious achievement that he didn't fully understand but was determined to pursue.

It was human-like, he guessed, and it was like her too, her people, and maybe like all of the created mortal and perhaps spirit beings of the universe. Adventure for experiential learning, growth toward perfection, overcoming fear in faith to produce love.

All of the answers, he knew, would one day open up before him for his understanding if he kept the faith, just as the endless vista of the blue sky was opening up and enlarging before him as they climbed slowly, surely up the line.

Their progress was slow and methodical. He strained and sweated as they moved upward, her in the lead with the sleeping bag on her back, with some food wrapped inside. They sure-handed the critical crack one sure grip after another, carefully picking out hand and footholds, working the two in cohesion.

He slipped once and his stomach dropped sickeningly before he grabbed for control again, spreadeagled, face flush against the cold rock, his heart thumping loudly. He was sweating in the cold air.

Finally they reached the ledge. He looked down to see the vast expanse their climb had opened below them. It had required more than an hour and he was tired. She seemed not to be.

He looked up and saw that his vision was blind over the slanting rock wall above them, and that there were precious few hand or footholds to use. There was a yawning nothingness below them. It would be a long, swooning drop through the icy air down to a violent bone-shattering and sudden death below. "My God," he muttered to himself. "My God."

"Think positive!" she said, standing next to him on the narrow ledge.

"It's important that you think positive. think confidently, think that you will do it, do it successfully. Visualize it."

Jason was a bit shaken.

"Are you listening?" she asked him, eyes hard upon him.

"Yes."

"Look in my eyes."

He did so.

"We will climb to the top. Visualize the top. See us doing it. We will do it."

Her eyes instilled some strength back into his waning body, his doubting mind. She clutched his body to her, her warm lips touching his cheek. She was much warmer than him, her warm breath upon him, kissing him, hardly, passionately, then pulling away. "Power up!" she commanded.

The wind was howling louder up here. She took his hands in hers, warming their shivering coldness inside her vest. He was trembling from fear or cold or both but she gave him renewed strength.

In a few moments, she was ready again. "I am going up free-hand," she said. "I'm taking the rope and will throw it down, but you must help me. You must stand strong here and help me over the ledge, and you can do it. You can do it!"

He stood firmly, grasping his hands hard into the two deepest cracks he could find, wedging one foot into a crevice to give added support. She lofted her body onto his back, her hard boots hurting his shoulders as he braced himself, gritted his teeth, sagged slightly but held firm under her weight. He felt her bend her knees and thrust herself upward. The weight lifted. He looked up to see her boots disappear above him.

He took deep breaths, working to regain his strength and maintain his composure. His forehead fell against the rough, cold rock as he sucked for more oxygen. He closed his eyes and said a silent prayer for her safety. PleaseGodPleasepleasepleaseplease.

Then he felt a coldness pelt against his cheek, opened his eyes to see that the sun was now shaded. The wind had picked up velocity, whirring loudly as it poured around the rock. Dark clouds loomed overhead and the cold pelting was hail. Hail! Pieces of ice. No...no! The sun was hidden now, and flecks of ice were flying out of the clouds, a summer hailstorm. No...no...no...no...

He looked up in vain, could see nothing and couldn't lean out further from the ledge. The white pellets clattered against the rock and bounced awry, pattering against his jacket, lodging in his hair. A large one thumped his forehead. "Damn!"

He heard nothing but the clattering and the wind. Maybe they would be stranded here to suffer and shiver on the ledge if it didn't let up.

Then the rope came flying down the side, flopping against the rock beside him. He stared at it, wide-eyed. She was up there and safe, and it was his turn to go. He glanced downward for a second. Stay positive! He grabbed the rope, gripped it tightly and pulled to test it.

"Come on up!" she called. Without thinking, he sturdied his muscles, tied the rope tightly around his waist and started climbing.

Over the ledge he scrambled, one knee banging painfully on the rock. He climbed over it, puffing every foot, pausing to see her up ahead, hanging onto yet another ledge, even smaller, the rope tied down, taut, helping to pull him up.

He soon reached her, tired again, out-of-breath, but higher of spirits.

"Nice work," she said calmly.

"Thanks," he replied. "What's next?"

He looked up to see for himself, another precarious distance to cover from their crowded ledge, fifty feet or more of rock that would require more daring, more courage, more skill. But he was determined to make it now, and believed that he could. His confidence was on the upbeat.

At the same time, he had the fleeting thought again that it was all foolish. He was risking death and didn't understand why. There seemed little point in it. The sense of achievement wouldn't be something to brag about now, as he had envisioned it would be when climbing this peak was an abstract idea, the whim of a dreamer, a tool to earn praise. He didn't care about feeding his ego any more.

But here he was today — well up the side of this precarious wall. Too late to re-think. He was determined to do it. Not quitting seemed more important than anything else at this point. And maybe his ego still needed food now and then, if it was healthy food.

The hailstorm had stopped as suddenly as it had begun but the clouds still massed overhead, blocking the sun.

"It's your turn to lead," she said.

He just stared at her.

"You want to do it?" she asked.

"I'll try," he said, scanning the rock for holds. He looked back at her. "I don't need a boost," he said, lifting his foot to the first hold. "Maybe you could brace my back a little. Okay? All right. I'm going up." He lofted himself upward, the rope around his waist and hers. He climbed, one hand, one toehold after another, steadily upward, and she followed.

He centered his mind on the rock, on his determination, all concentration on the hold, then the next one, then the next, upward and upward, patiently, surely, firmly, no gambles, testing it first, taking it, then lifting and taking another, no hesitation, all the while seeing himself making each successful linkage.

In a few minutes, he reached a new ledge, secured the rope and helped her come up beside him."

On this ledge, he realized something new. As he was climbing, he was growing too, in character, in strength, and in other ways that he would have to think about later, when he was back on the ground with the rest of his kind. And he knew there would certainly be many occasions to think about it and wonder about it. He believed strongly that he was going to make it and have this as a life experience forever more. That was surely worth a lot. Being brave and courageous, facing danger and challenge and winning was surely worthwhile no matter the endeavor, not to advertise to someone else but to feel and know inside.

They reached the snowfield. Jason felt good to have his feet sink deeply into the pure white, to lead the way as they crunched through it, step by deep step up toward the peak. It loomed in the shining of the sun just up ahead and he felt exhilarated, plunging one wet leg after another, step by step toward the top until finally he had to stop, panting in the thin air, and rest, just one more time, before reaching the apex.

He struggled to catch his labored breath and she came up alongside him. He looked up at the massive rocky peak, washed in sunshine then at the broad expanse of Colorado's mountain ranges surrounding them.

"Hard...to breathe...up here," he panted at her.

"Listen," she said. "I hear something."

They were within a couple hundred yards of the top from here, his leg muscles weary and rigored. He stood gasping and trembling cold in the deep snow.

He heard the noise now, turned to look in that northward direction and see an Air Force fighter jet coming down hard and very fast, not too far overhead.

The jet was at them suddenly, zipped past with a streaking roar, quivering the air.

Just ahead of them, a crack opened in the snow and split ever wider. The whole surface began to slide under their feet, cracking again, then again, slipping, sliding. The icy sheet of snow was all collapsing underneath them. Jason struggled to keep his balance as a flurry of snow above and ahead of them began to roll and tumble down, smashing against him heavily.

He fell to his knees, grasping desperately through the wet whiteness for something to hold onto, in vain. It was all silently rolling down upon them, he sliding with it. He saw her struggling for footing too. A white puffy mass enveloped and buried him, and carried him downward. More weight covered his head and he began rolling, sputtering to breathe, sliding helplessly in the silent roar, hands clutching vainly for a hold, eyes searching for her to no avail.

The precipice! He screamed to himself. It's right down there. He slid downward, helplessly clawing through the shroud of white.

Enveloped and buried in snow, he tried to holler, but it was muffled in the darkening mass of white, whooshing and rumbling softly. The precipice loomed just below them now. They were going off the side of the mountain.

David took the binoculars from his eyes but still stared upward to Long's Peak. There appeared to be an avalanche underway near the top, near where the sensors determined Blest to be. They had already lost three explorers, having heard the news yesterday that Eastone 23 had died trying to save a wounded child in the streets of Beirut.

He walked back to the campground tent as Cezanne was emerging from it, dressed in blue jeans and a plaid shirt.

"Do I look like a camper?" she asked. In truth, she looked like a fashion model, on a remote shoot for outdoor clothing.

"Very...earthly," David replied. "There has just been an avalanche near the top of Long's. Do you know that word — avalanche?"

"A lot of snow falling, all at once."

"Right. Blest may be there. She's somewhere in the area. I'm going to the pay phone and call a monitoring station. Maybe we could do a quick tracing."

"Is she still with the native?"

"Yes. He's still persistent. They would say, 'hanging in there.' I don't know why."

"I assume she's still preparing him for his mission. Jariel and Valgotha are making ready his environment now, as I understand it."

"Have you received a new monitor on Steve and the earth woman?"

"Everything is on schedule."

David faced the mountain again. "I hope everything is all right up there. Three dead and one wounded is not the safety record I had hoped to achieve."

"It's a very volatile place, David," said Cezanne. "It could have been much worse."

"Well...it isn't over," said David with a heavy frown.

Jason clung desperately to the jagged outcrop, his forearm painfully pressed over the granite, hurting like hell, the veins of his arm bulged, his back and shoulders aching against some terrible weight pulling him down.

The rope pulled hard against his waist, burning his skin even through the shirts and jacket. He tried to see downward and could not, dared not move, only hang on, his hanging feet desperately fumbling for a hold that could ease the pressure off his arms. One boot toe found a tiny niche and pressed into it, just a tiny modicum of relief. Fear gripped him; how long could he hang here? There was no strength to do any more.

It had to be Roci, hanging free below him, her weight threatening to pull them both down to death. He couldn't hold on here much longer.

"Roci! Roci!" he rasped hoarsely, loudly. There was no answer. He strained to look down again, still couldn't see. Maybe she was unconscious, hurt badly, no way to tell, only to cling to that lip of rock with everything he had until the last gasp of energy was gone and they would both go down.

His grip slipped. The last ebb of strength seemed to be leaving him and he began mumbling the Lord's Prayer. There seemed nothing else to do. He gritted his teeth and struggled to pull up against the heavy weight, gasping in pain and weakness and failure. It was no use. He had to resolve himself to death.

"Roci...Roci...Roci..." His wail grew increasingly desperate. He fought back tears.

No reply. He felt he had only minutes left. They would be dead — both of them.

For a moment, he realized that he might be able to undo the rope, let her fall. Then he might have the strength to pull himself up. That was possible. That could save his life. Save his life!

No! He resolved not to do it. He couldn't kill her. He was ready to go too. He decided to just hang on and pray, and wait these final minutes...seconds...

The acorn! He thought of it suddenly — the magic acorn. The energy food! It was in his shirt pocket if he could only reach it. He pulled one arm off the cold rock tentatively. Could he hang on with one while he fished out the acorn? Could it even help? Seemed a foolish notion, really, but then a silent voice inside him said: Yes. Yes. Yes. Yes.

Jason struggled to wrap his right forearm harder over the jagged rock, trying to ignore the increasing pain, the fierce aching all over his body. With his free hand, he fumbled at the pocket. Don't drop it! The silent voice called: Don't drop it! Don't drop it!

He managed to pull out the canister and with a firm fingernail flip open the top. Up he turned it. The acorn and mescaline capsule both fell into his mouth. He dropped the cannister, it flying away, and spat out the capsule carefully, biting hard then into the acorn, chewing on the hard surface. Was he supposed to eat it all, or only the kernel? His mouth bulged. He chewed and chewed, breaking the hull, tucking it to the side of his mouth, tasting the bitterness, chewing hard and fast into the kernel, chewing and chewing and finally swallowing, dry-mouthed, almost gagging.

It was foolish, but he thought of Popeye, bursting open that can of spinach, gulping it down. He couldn't laugh. He had to live. He had to save Roci somehow. He clung hard to the rock with both hands, waiting, hoping, praying.

In a moment he felt it — a surge of power, then another, vibrating his muscles. Energy was swelling into his body. His mind raced; his arm strengthened. He felt strong enough to hold on longer, but how long he didn't know. He had to have a plan.

181

It came to him.

There, to his side some five or six critical yards away and just below him was another outcrop. He might be able to struggle over in that direction, despite the heavy weight that now seemed bearable. He might be able to wedge the rope over that outcrop. If he could make his way over far enough, then, even if he slipped and fell, the rope might then catch on the outcropping and hold them both up. He could visualize them hanging together there, like the collapsed hands of some melted Salvador Dali clock, both sagging on six.

Suddenly, he feared again that she was hurt, her head crushed like her co-pilot's had been.

Jason hung there, gathering his composure and will. He felt he had the strength now to hang on here indefinitely, might even be able to climb up and carry her weight. He tested that theory, but her weight was still too heavy. He had best come up with some solution fast because his strength might ebb again.

Again he reasoned it out. Even if he fell before succeeding, if the rope fell over that outcrop, or another he saw further down, it might just catch and hang them up there. He had a strong will now; he believed he could do it. He visualized it.

He unlocked his arm from its painful pressure and began to try, moving to his left, one hand after another, strong of body, strong of will, strong of determination, another handhold then another, grasping desperately for a foothold, yearning for blessed relief from the powerful pull of her weight. His arm muscles bulged — but held! He pulled his tautly stretched legs with him.

Below, the rope pushed against the outcrop and nestled itself neatly into a crevice. Jason strained his eyes downward to see it, could feel it too. How strong is it?

The next handhold was precariously far away because of the oppressive weight. All of both weights would be on the one right arm, while his left hand tried to reach it. His toes continued to find small nicks and niches below but he couldn't see if there were others down there he could reach if he pushed away.

A silent voice said: Go for it!

Jason pushed off his precarious toehold boldly and pushed himself with all his might toward the handhold just ahead, teeth gritted in grim determination, clothes scratching hard against the ragged rock.

Jason's hand grabbed the hold firmly and he pulled his leg over, toes scrambling to find some kind of surface. Yes! A toehold! It held!

He stretched boldly and reached yet another handhold, felt a bead of sweat roll down his forehead into his eye, burning it. He stretched his foot again, testing another foothold, felt some loose rock crumbling away under it, but it held, though precariously. He gave it more weight, wondered if he dared rely on it, eyeing his next handhold. Was he far enough across for the rope to catch and hold them? Would the outcroppings below give way? He had to try. He reached again.

But the foothold crashed away this time, both his feet falling free, hands tearing against the ragged rock, slipping fingernails ripping. He was skidding, sliding down, then completely losing his hold, falling free, plunging —

Then the rope tore against his stomach and ripped upward under his arms, racking his ribs with pain, sucking his breath away, jerking him to a painful stop. He could feel his racked, hurting body swinging free, throat gasping for breath, the rope pushed up under his armpits, holding them against the rock as he hung helplessly, spinning around, his head banging against the side — ouch! — finally crashing against her.

He regained his senses to see that he was hanging there beside Roci, her head bruised and bleeding, limp and unconscious from a hard blow. He grasped at her in vain once, twice, as they swung crazily about each other, before clutching her jacket and pulling her to him.

They clung there together, crippled pendulum, still alive, locked in embrace. He found a handhold on the wall, then a foothold and steadied their swinging.

"Roci! Roci! Please! Are you all right?"

She gripped her eyes, trying to come out of it, still in a stupor. She blinked, in a daze, recovering her senses.

Then he heard her inside his head, her thoughts. Or maybe they were Mega's. They said to him to open the vest she wore, another powerful suggestion that he hastened to obey. He scrambled to get to the pockets. This one, this pocket, said the silent voice.

He pulled a small flat can out of it, some kind of sprayer on top. Use it, use it, said the quiet suggestion. He aimed it at the wound on her head and pushed. It emitted a hard, clear spray all over her head, the wound. Yes. Yes. Yes. Something had guided him, spoken to him, commanded him.

In a few seconds, she was awakening recovered from the blow, holding onto him tightly as he stared at her. She looked into his eyes with amazement. "You...saved my life, Earth man," she mumbled. "How...could I leave you?"

He couldn't speak, only clung to her body as tight as he could, losing his precarious foothold. They hung there together by the rope, their bodies and minds embraced together, it seemed almost as one. They swung gently, listening to the cold air begin to swirl noisily around the granite face.

183

Then she laughed loudly over his shoulder as they swung there, back and forth, a triumphant and soaring laugh that echoed off the mountain and down over the countryside. She was laughing as they swung helplessly.

He laughed too, a thundering noise, releasing all the tension from their near disaster, unleashing the sound of victory over the grasping emptiness of death. The echo roared out their life affirmation, reverberating over the cold, hard rocks, up and down the massive earthly citadel they had challenged and struggled against and survived.

They were strong together and soon, united, reached the peak.

The vista at sunset was magnificent before them. Though his body was racked with soreness, and the bruises and cuts of their perilous ascent, Jason felt at calm peace there with her as night fell.

The icy coldness swept down upon them in the darkness but he knew the warmth of her special body and their togetherness in the sleeping bag would carry them through the night.

They lay together in their cocoon. They slipped his hardness inside her and, fully clothed, they lay almost still as he surged closer and closer to a final climax that reached its own peak and seemed everlasting in its length and its ecstatic joy. And they still lay together, enjoined, as they talked one last time.

"Do you have anyone when you go back, Jason? Is there no woman you could join like this?"

"No," he said. "Of course not. You said...that you couldn't leave me now."

"No," said Roci. "I asked the question. There is a big difference. Our people are preparing a place for you. You have only to return to your home and follow the path they have laid out. It will be fruitful. If you want to fulfill the mission we envision to be the best for you, then you only must follow our lead. Do you want to?"

"I do. I haven't been fulfilled before. I believe in your wisdom and insight if I can only remember and understand it. I'm anxious to learn more — and do more."

"It may be lonely work for a while. It will be a mission specifically for you."

"I'll accept that."

"Are there no others depending on you, your family?"

"My parents are dead," he said. "I would hope to communicate with my other family by phone or by letter. That's all. I even lost my dog last year."

"You had a dog?"

"A beautiful dog, a golden retriever. Got out of my fenced yard in Dallas and got hit by a car. Rushed him to the vet but they couldn't save him. I haven't wanted a dog since. It's too hard in the city, keeping a dog fenced-in. Isn't even fair to the dog, I think. A dog like Goldie ought to be in the country, where she could run free."

"It's great to be free," she said. They fell asleep together for the last time.

Jason was awakened by a nudge, then another as he collected his senses. He strained to look up into the darkness and saw a shadowy figure surrounded by the thousands of stars in the bright night sky. He tried in vain to make it out. It had to be Mega.

"Perhaps you'd like to join me for a nightcap," said the melodious, radio-sounding, baritone voice. "We have a few other things we should discuss before we leave your colorful domain."

Jason looked over at Roci. She had turned over and appeared to be asleep.

"She's tired," said Mega. "You guys have had a busy day. Let's let her sleep."

Jason looked perplexed.

"Come on," said Mega. "Get unzipped. You're going to get that tux all wrinkled."

Jason looked down into the sleeping bag and saw that he was fully dressed, in formal dinner wear. He unzipped the bag partly, enough to lift himself out and stand resplendent there on the rocky surface of Long's Peak. He could see that his shirt was ruffled, pale blue with shiny studs.

He looked down at Roci, in still repose, and zipped the bag back as if to keep her warm. He followed Mega over the hard rock surface, looking down to admire shiny black shoes, then upward to see that a full moon and a sea of stars was lighting their way.

There was no cold wind up here; it was remarkably quiet and calm, unreal. He still couldn't make out Mega's features very well in the darkness.

They reached a small round table and two chairs which he could barely see. Then a match rasped and burst into a crisp flame. Mega lighted two candles on the table, which was covered with a red and white checkered tablecloth. In the candlelight he saw that Mega was also dressed in a black tuxedo with a blue shirt and white cummerbund, his white hair and beard trimmed and combed neatly. He was the picture of elegance.

"I like to get dressed up now and then," said Mega. "I'm sure we will avoid the storms and the mudslides this evening, and perhaps will not have an intrusion by any of the denizens below."

"I'd hate to have to fit Anvil for a tux," Jason deadpanned.

"He might be more likely on the cover of 'Field and Stream,' said Mega, "or perhaps 'Rolling Stone.' Please sit down." He motioned for Jason to sit on one of the small round wooden chairs with interlaced cane bottoms. He did so.

To Jason's surprise, a handsome young waiter in a white dinner jacket and blue bowtie appeared from out of the darkness, handing each of them a large fancy menu. "The Omega" was sculpted in large cursive letters on the front.

"Hello, Alessandro," said Mega pleasantly, as if they were old friends. The waiter, sporting a ridiculously pencil thin mustache and slicked-back black hair, smiled reservedly and nodded.

"We're just here for a nightcap," said Mega, "Just bring some coffee from your fresh-roasted beans, please, and large snifters of cognac." The waiter collected the menus, nodded pleasantly and was gone.

"We'll all be leaving in the next day or two," said Mega, "without making any significant changes here on your little planet, except that you, my friend, are being allowed to remember us sufficiently well to carry out a mission. It will not seem unusual to you; you will take it all in stride, remarkably enough. You are something of an experiment, too, I must tell you, so I hope that you are successful."

"Sounds like I'm pretty special. I'm honored."

"Just fortunate enough to be on the right planet at the right time. You saved the life of one of our beloved," said Mega. "You engaged in sexual liaison with her and have greatly influenced her mind. Yes, I would say you're special.

"Fortunate," mused Jason. "Yes. I wonder why. Why me?

"The universe of universe is full of accidents," said Mega, "and also full of spiritual, celestially inspired leadings. The trick is to know which is which. I must tell you, though that there are a number of others here who will be carrying out unconscious missions, large and small, but they will know little about their inspirations."

Mega paused to see if it was all sinking in. "Your friend, Ellen, is one. They have been influenced in more subtle ways. We have endeavored to bring their best qualities to the surface, give them more hope and purpose, higher ideals, expanded energies. I trust you will be secretive about your work since you know a good deal more than they should know."

"You can implant all of those things?"

"They are already there," said Mega. "They only have to be, as you say, developed, or cultivated. When high ideals are represented, everything works fine. Each of you has a fragment of God inside, you see, the urge toward perfection, the idea of becoming God-like, living the pure life. In some, of course, it is more developed than others, depending on a great many things. But that is what makes each of you, and each of us, sons and daughters of God. We truly are. Each of us are unique expressions."

"Yes," said Jason. "I believe that. But we have so many weaknesses."

"The influences of animal ancestry and the sin of rebellion and default, as you have learned during this adventure," said Mega. "But you are not expected to live beyond your capabilities. You have only to believe in the One God, choose to do, as you would likely say, your Heavenly Father's will. That can be achieved by anyone who listens to the voice inside, whether you call it your guardian angel, your conscience, your thought adjuster, whatever. God, the Divine Center, the First Source, whatever you say, has given you this inner guidance to influence you in the direction of purity and perfection. You won't achieve it in this mortal life, but you eventually can. This is just the first step — for both of us. We're mortals too. We've just learned a lot more. The Pleiades is a highly developed system."

"Well, I feel strongly inspired to be part of this. Just point me in the right direction."

Alessandro returned, neatly laid down a silver setting of coffee and cognac, with cream and sugar on the side, then swiftly departed.

"How about more wisdom before you go?" asked Jason. "Anything. Anything I can use, anything we can use."

"I just gave you all that you really need to know," said Mega, lifting the snifter. "To mankind," he said, clinking his glass to Jason's. They sipped together. It was strong — warming inside.

"There's so much suffering, Mega. Horrible sickness, starvation, war, self-serving greed, the preaching of false prophets. It's everywhere...everywhere."

"It's all your own doing, believe me. There's no one to blame but yourselves. You'll just have to evolve, although you should know that the immediate years ahead will be filled with much change and transformation on your planet, and there are new spiritual personalities here who are helping as they can, and more coming to this amazing planet all the time."

"Religious truth has always been twisted and distorted," Jason complained. "How will we know what to believe? What about all this hellfire and damnation stuff? What about all these denominations of religion fighting among themselves?"

"Don't let organized religions, all of them very imperfect, get between you and the One God, your Heavenly Father. There is no intermediary between you and your ultimate creator, save the one you know as Jesus, the creator and ruler of this particular universe. Look at the example he gave you. And there is no such place as Hell. Just as your mortal father on earth would not have doomed you to such suffering, neither would your Heavenly Father do such a thing? Hell is your creation. A control mechanism. For the most part, so is punishment. You should think much more seriously about rehabilitations here. That is what is needed."

"Think positively, think constructively, think of God as a compassionate and loving father who wants you to succeed and only allows your personality to dematerialize if you choose to turn against the divine plan for paradise ascension, Mega preached on. "You will get every opportunity to continue your journey if you put forth an effort. That's what we are supposed to do — try to find God and align with the Divine Will — and we're amply rewarded with exciting adventures of learning and growth."

"That's very comforting to know," said Jason. "And I really have a million other questions. I'm hungry for the truth, the truth about everything, the history of the universe, the history of our earth, where we go after mortal death, many things."

"All those answers are out there. They will be delivered to you very soon by a friend."

"A friend? I can have those answers?"

"Keep an open ear, an open mind and an open heart, Jason. You can listen with them all." He downed the remainder of his brandy. "I have to go, many things to do before we're ready to leave. Stay here and finish your brandy and coffee, and when you are ready to return to sleep, just snap your fingers and you will. It will be your decision this time."

Mega arose and stepped away from the table. He reached out to take Jason's hand.

Jason stood up, filled with a confidence and exuberance he had never felt before. He took Mega's large, mature hand. They gripped solidly. Mega smiled at him benevolently.

"I love you, fellow mortal Jason," he said.

"I love you, Mega," he replied, tears welling up in his eyes.

Mega turned and walked swiftly into the darkness, vaporizing into nothingness, leaving Jason to stare after him into the night. He finally sat back down, alone now, imbued and enthralled with both wonder and wisdom, an ignorant primitive perhaps but with great hope and an imaginary snifter of brandy and a cup of fresh, still steaming imaginary coffee there in his dream world.

It all seemed so real and he knew that it was. There are separate realities, of course. He and his people would probably have to understand a lot more about them before they could regain dominion over this troubled planet. Or maybe that was the problem — too much dominion.

But finding the answers to all these myriad of fascinating questions are what the generations in time and space are for, he realized, more strongly than ever before. And people still wonder about life's purpose. And wonder if there's life on other planets. And wonder if there's a God. Abysmally lagging in our collective comprehension of reality.

He felt life now as an exhilarating opportunity to lead the way out of such ignorance, beyond such simple questions. He could now see the collective billions of personalities of time and space, each unique, each a blend of evolutionary origin, a physical body evolved for our use, and a divine spiritual spark inside. From this fusion, we seek higher fusion of our personalities with the indwelling spirit, to be born again finally within the aura of the Universal Father's magnificent world of the spirit.

That's what all these time and space classrooms of material experience, these laboratories of experiential living, are all about, it came to Jason, and each of us is an expression of the First Source and Center — with an opportunity to ascend to spiritual perfection. "Be ye perfect," was a very real imperative.

This life in mortal flesh was only a small part, a beginning, but a pivotal one. He reasoned that, on an ascension from our lowly state toward perfection, there would be things that could be learned in this physical form, in this challenging world, by actual experience, that couldn't be learned any other way. As we say…you just had to be there to understand it.

That's what Jesus did too, experienced mortal life as we do, in amazing empathy, showed us how to live and serve nobly, how to die nobly, becoming perfectly attuned with the indwelling spirit of his Heavenly Father inside, even as we still should strive to do.

His life example discredited the ideas of Lucifer forever, effectively ended the rebellion, affirmed the great potential of humans and justified the Father's ascension plan. He whipped Lucifer, and Caligastia, the dark prince, and Satan and the others who rebelled, and he did it, amazingly enough, as a flesh and blood mortal.

With Jesus' triumphant seventh incarnation, from birth as a helpless child of an oppressed people through an incredible life and noble death that affirmed his right to rule the local universe, to stand at the right hand of God, with demonstrated ability to live just as the various creatures and personalities of his own creation, the ideas of Lucifer were discredited. It came to Jason that he and his ilk were never taken seriously again, were incarcerated awaiting adjudication.

Jason shook his head slightly, sipping the coffee. Where are these thoughts coming from? Is it knowledge or what?

Life is not a curse of original sin, it came to him. It is an original experience, both for our emerging personalities and for our indwelling spirit, this fragment of God, this tiny unique light of the great light inside us. Amazingly, Jason knew, God experiences life with us in this way, so surely must love us, must have faith in us, must even, to a degree, trust us. Can this be true?

Enraptured by thoughts and ideas, Jason sat there for a while, how long he didn't know, until both the brandy and coffee were gone.

His mind seemed to have become an open channel to some new perspectives to consider, some new insights, and a strong conviction to really do something about them. Just how he didn't know. He wondered if it would be left to him, his own devices. Would there be a linkage of mind after they had gone?

The words came into his mind in Mega's mature and expressive voice:

"The Stillness each day. Just you and God. Ask. Listen. Feel. Learn. Know. Give. Serve Truth, Beauty and Goodness with Love. Love is all you need."

Jason sat there in the pure dark silence alone, on that small outcropping of flat rock high up among the jagged snowcapped peaks of the Rockies. The candle on the table burned steadily in the calm air.

All above him was a sea of stars, twinkling a million times at him in the richness of the forever darkness that surrounded their creation. A gentle breeze had picked up now, the rustling seemed to speak to him, not in words but in floating, wafting, rushing spirit sounds and feelings, all dancing up here high in the night with him. He never wanted this moment to end.

But from this momentary brush with spiritual ecstasy, his mind came down to reality once again. He sat there with a benevolent and peaceful smile, armed with spirit, a purpose to feel and reflect love around him — whatever the challenges that lay ahead. This life was his only mortal chance. There is life on the other side, he knew it now, but this was his human adventure, the one he needed to make count — with the kind of learning and growing experiences that will give us a good record when we report in — after graduation. First step was to get in touch with God and establish a relationship, and that's easy. He's inside each of us.

So…bring on the world!

Jason stared at his fingers for a moment, then snapped them.

Again, he was in the sleeping bag, wide awake. And quickly he noticed that he was alone. He scrambled furiously about in the bag. She was gone. Gone! He unzipped it and kicked free, grabbing desperately for his boots, looking all around in the darkness, reminding himself of that first night down at the Texas campsite. It was cold now; this was real!

"Roci! Roci!" There was no answer.

Off he went, stumbling over the rocks, trying to accustom his eyes to the night, seeing a bright light somewhere over a rocky plateau. He made his way in that direction, hurriedly, climbing over the cold rock to see an amazing sight.

There, hanging at a precipice was a shiny silver cylinder, brightly lit from within. In the circular window stood Roci. She stood calmly there inside the round carrier, her hands upon the window in the door, looking at him in kindness, love. Oh no, Jason moaned silently.

He reached up his arm to her unconsciously. Her two open hands pressed tightly to the window as the cylinder began to rise. Her eyes reached out and touched him with a powerful compassion that he could feel in a shiver running up his spine.

Jason raised both open hands upward as the carrier moved steadily up into the sky. A silent voice inside him told him they would meet again. I love you, loveyou, loveyou, loveyou, loveyou, he thought desperately. And the words reflected right back to him…loveyouloveyouloveyou…

He watched the cylinder become ever-smaller, until it became just a tiny light, like the stars, and finally disappeared altogether into the night.

He wiped a tear away and sighed.

The vastness above him seemed to go on forever.

But now he saw it in a whole new light.

It was his neighborhood.

TEN: *To Struggle in Love*

The sunrise was glorious atop Long's Peak. Jason watched it from the edge of the east face, having slept not at all since Blest's departure, but he was neither sleepy nor tired. She was Blest now; she was not Roci any more.

He sat there in thoughtful reflection until the sunshine was bright upon him. He felt good — grizzled and soiled and sore, but good.

When he had filled himself with all the good vibrations he could, he began making the descent, by a safer route that would still carry him reasonably near the packs. There had been enough challenges already; he didn't feel the need to challenge himself further.

He realized that he would have to carry both packs from the boulder field, which was a long distance from Loch Vail and especially from the campground trailhead. He studied the map and planned a new, slightly longer route, away from the loch, in case rangers were still in the vicinity searching for their protagonists. He knew he would have to keep a wary eye out for brown uniforms.

When he finally reached the place where they had stashed the packs, he found that hers was missing. Pinned to his was a note:

"We have retrieved Blest's pack. See you at the campground, David and Cezanne." Ummm, Jason wondered. They could just as well have carried his down.

He ate the crumbly remains of some bread and a crushed clot of raisins, and a granola bar, washing it all down with tepid canteen water. He made his way on.

At Timberline Falls, the waters glistened as they poured over the side, swirling in the wind, forming a rainbow. Silvery droplets soared, disappearing in the noontide sun. He was anxious to call his friends, make sure they were okay.

From there, he moved along an alternate route to a place called Millford Pond. There he saw a man in bermuda shorts and black nylon socks, carrying a tiny Japanese camera, a budget type. He photographed his wife, a portly woman in pink polyester and their young, freckle-faced daughter, with the pond as a backdrop. He knew he was getting close to civilization again.

When he reached the Long's Peak campground at mid-afternoon, there was no sign of his friends as expected. His new van sat there as he had left it. He looked down the narrow paved campground road and saw a statuesque woman with long black hair, motioning to him with an open hand, holding a coffee mug. He walked down the road to face her.

She smiled at him knowingly. "You look a little beat, neighbor. You want some coffee?" She handed him a steaming mug.

Jason turned to see a handsome male sitting at the picnic table, also with coffee. The pot sat on the grill, over a wood fire.

The man had a clean-cut face, blonde hair and a friendly smile. "Hope you'll join us so we can get acquainted" he said.

"Sure. Thanks a lot. I could use some coffee." Jason knew who they were. He took the mug and walked over.

"I'm David," said the man, offering his hand to shake. It was firm.

"Jason," he said, "but I'll bet you already knew that."

David only laughed. Jason removed the pack from his sore shoulders and dropped it on the ground.

"This is Cezanne," said David, introducing him to his beautiful companion. She carried a silver tray now, filled with fancy pastries, which she placed on the picnic table before them.

"I'm pleased to know you both," said Jason. He noticed their white van with the familiar blue circle and dove. The campsite was clean otherwise; they appeared ready to leave.

"Your friends didn't stay long. They seemed anxious to get home," said David.

"Didn't even want to…chat," said Cezanne, with a sly smile.

"They were in a hurry," said Jason. "They're good people when you get to know them. We got into a little trouble. I'll bet you know about that too."

"I'll…bet," said David, thoughtfully.

Jason sat down tiredly at the picnic table and she joined them. He took a long, deep breath and flexed his tired shoulders.

Without a word, Cezanne reached out a large green acorn to him. "For energy. Just the kernel this time," she said with a wry smile. "You won't have to rush this one."

"Thanks." He took it gratefully.

"We'll be leaving in a few minutes," said David. "We have much to do. Finish your…repast and then go over to campsite seven. It is four sites down the road from yours. A friend will be waiting for you there."

Jason was trying in vain to get into the acorn. "Here," said Cezanne, "let me show you." She took it, popped it open with the heel on her hand and pulled the full kernel from it expertly.

"Thanks again," said Jason wearily.

"Don't mention it," she said. "What are friends for?"

"We'll leave you in peace and purpose," said David. "It's been a very fine adventure for us, and we hope for you."

"That's what it is then. That's what it really is," said Jason, framing it as both a realization and a question. "An adventure."

"We all have our adventures," said Cezanne, "intentional or otherwise, and depending on where we are in the evolution."

"And...who's at campsite seven?"

David smiled in good-humored confidence: "Someone to help with your destiny and their own, for this time and space and place." He winked at Jason slyly.

Cezanne smiled at him, and reached with long slender fingers and polished nails to touch his cheek kindly: "Stay close with your friends, Jason. They will need you from time to time. They will have their projects too, though unknowing of it." She looked directly into his eyes when she spoke to him, and Jason was convinced that he would be pleased to do anything she would ask, and would remember this request vividly.

"And am I part of the team now?"

"Yes," said David, "and you and Blest are also, as you might say, the 'talk of the ship.'"

Elsewhere at this time:

Park Ranger Roy Murphy was trudging down a residential sidewalk in Estes Park, Colorado. He had always had a steady mind, strictly focused on the business-side, and he had been a good ranger for nearly five years. He was a neat and methodical young man who always kept his close-cropped hair and his small mustache neatly trimmed and his uniform cleaned and pressed.

The events of yesterday had grieved him greatly, first being so utterly embarrassed at having himself and John Healy trussed up, blindfolded and gagged, and found by a group of Boy Scouts, then remembering hardly anything about what had happened to them. It was all very strange.

John sat at his kitchen table nearby as Roy neared his house. He didn't remember anything either. In between trying to be sensible back at headquarters and trying to make up a story, each of them and collectively, in order to appear rational, it had been quite an ordeal.

194

Roy knew one thing for sure; someone had sure busted him in the jaw. It was swollen and it was hard to chew. Neither of their revolvers had been found.

John, meantime, sat swirling in his cigarette smoke, a ranger for nearly twenty years who had never, ever peed in his pants. The humility, combined with the discomfort, and the smell of it in the hot sun was nearly unbearable. His soreness was in his balls. He knew that someone had delivered a hard blow there, and he was still swollen and walking with a limp.

Inexplicably, and to his embarrassment, he had become a little wild-eyed during the interrogation. For some reason, he had grabbed another officer's weapon from his holster and waved it about the room to demonstrate something that might have or could have happened. Two of them grabbed him and wrestled it away from him, and he then wondered why they did it. He later guessed he may have been acting a little irrational, but he really didn't know. A mass of confusion had gripped them both, and neither could adequately explain it. He later recalled waving the pistol…and wondering why. It was all too much.

They finally agreed that they had been jumped from behind by a bunch of hippies.

That Tuesday afternoon, John sat at his kitchen table drinking coffee, still taxing his mind in vain, sitting and puffing on a cigarette and facing an ashtray filled with butts.

Roy came up to the back screen door and knocked.

"Come on in, Roy. You feelin' any better?"

He swung open the door and stepped in. "Not too much. I still can't remember shit about what happened. You?"

"Still beats the hell out of me. I do think it was a bunch of hippies, though, and they must have give us some kind of dope to make us forget. They ain't called you about them blood tests, have they?"

"Nope. Ain't heard a word. I know one thing. I sure as hell got a sore jaw."

"They gonna find some kinda drugs in them blood tests. They bound to. Somethin' that took our minds away, and I don't know what the hell that could be."

"I tell you one thing," said Roy. "If I ever get a bead on them mother fuckers, they gonna pay through the ass."

"Had to be a bunch a' lowlifes. Had to be."

"I kinda remember somethin', just a little bit. It kinda comes and goes in my mind. I feel like it's gonna come back to me good some time," said Roy. "When I do remember, I'm just hopin' we can get a bulletin out on them long-haired bastards."

"Was they long-haired?"

"Well...I don't know if they was long-haired. Seems like I remember that. I remember that's what we told 'em at headquarters anyway, for some reason. It damned sure wadn't them Boy Scouts."

"Probably was a bunch of dopeheads. They'll pay for it in the end. Even if we don't get 'em, they'll o.d. on it one of these days. You mess with that dope long enough it'll do you in," said John with absolute certainty.

"Was they doin' dope? You remember that?"

"Well, I don't rightly remember that neither for sure," said John. "But there again, I remember that's what we told 'em at headquarters. I'd bet my badge on it. Didn't we?"

"I'd like to kick their ass up one side a' that mountain and down the other," said Roy angrily. "I got to go down to the hardware store right now. Long as we're off for the day, I got to do a little work at the house."

"What's the problem? You want some coffee?"

"No, thanks. I got a leakin' pipe under the sink. I might oughta borrow your pipe wrench. Ain't you got a pipe wrench?"

"I got one, but I'll be damned if I know where it is."

Later, John called the park headquarters. No one suspicious had been found but there had been some more fallen rocks down on the Fall Creek Road. And they had found some unknown substance in the blood sample, didn't know what. They were running some more tests. He told them he was feeling better.

Meanwhile, Kevin was squinting at some grotesque imagery in acrylic, anguished eyes and fingers and limbs and hard-edged reds and browns.

"What you call this one?" he asked Chuck, "paranoia?"

"Something like that," said Chuck, with a twisted grin, "just what I was thinking about at the time."

"Were you doing drugs?"

"Like about always," Chuck confirmed. "Speeding, I recall, and of course a little weed and beer."

"Those pills ain't too good for you if you do too much," said Kevin.

"I know," said Chuck, as if confirming it, "but what the hell. You know what they say, life's a bitch and then you die."

"Sometimes faster than you want. You just got to stay on top of it. You got to handle it or it'll handle you," Kevin confirmed.

"It's easy to overdo," said Chuck. "Makes you feel too damn good."

They heard Susan and Sandra coming down the stairs.

"You oughta try to sell some of these," said Kevin, eyeing the array of paintings and neon sculptures in Chuck's junky studio.

"People are buying landscapes. They aren't buying this stuff. It depresses them. Hell, it depresses me."

196

"You can't tell. I've seen some really far-out stuff in places you wouldn't believe," said Kevin. Chuck seemed unconvinced about Kevin's status in the art scene.

"Roci seemed real interested in my stuff. I was looking forward to showing them to her," said Chuck. Susan and Sandra walked in to join them.

"Man, wasn't that the damnedest adventure you've ever experienced," said Kevin. "I got to get hold of Jason as soon as he gets back. There's a lot I don't understand about that woman."

"She sure laid some nice money on us. She's got to be wealthy, or her family is," said Sandra.

"She's more than I can figure out," said Chuck, "and seems like none of us ever really found out much about her."

"Soon as we get back, I'm gonna be calling Jason," said Kevin.

"She's a pretty amazing woman," said Susan. "She had a real...aura about her, something hard to understand, like she's in some other dimension or something."

They hugged and said their goodbyes in front of Chuck and Sandra's apartment house. Kevin was soon driving them home, and Susan pulled the note from her purse and read it again:

Susan,

I have chosen you to be a messenger of love, as I am. This may sound strange to you and you may think me to be a peculiar person, but I assure you that I am filled with compassion and caring although the beta vibrations I feel here can be disconcerting to me and cause me to act in certain unusual ways. I will soon return to the tranquillity of my native environment.

My short time with you was very rewarding, especially your sharing of thoughts with me on Sunday. If you explore the ideals you expressed to me, you will contribute much toward making life good for you and your loved ones. Your basic goodness is very rich and only needs to be developed as you mature.

I won't see you again, but I leave confident that your love will continue to shine ever-brighter and illuminate the paths of those around you.

In Eternal Friendship,
Roci

197

Susan thought again that it would be her private note for a while, maybe forever. She soon lay dreamily in the back of the van as Kevin drove them home. Unknown to her, he also had found a note in his pack. As he drove, he pulled it from his shirt pocket and looked at it again.

> *Kevin,*
>
> *Though I won't see you again, I want you to know how much I admire your strength of will and leadership qualities. I urge you to use these qualities as a love messenger. This is how I use mine; I know that it is the best way. Give Susan your special love. She's deserving of it, needs it and will make you happy.*
>
> *Your Friend Forever,*
> *Roci*

Kevin folded the note neatly and slipped it into a compartment of his wallet, leaning on the steering wheel and gazing steadily at the broad sunlit highway in front of him. He felt strong, confident, very good.

But Chuck was restless and nervous. If only he could decide what to do. The second beer wasn't as good as the first, his cigarette just tasted like ashes, and his body was empty, yearning to feel good. He leaned into the refrigerator to pull out his pill bottle, far to the back. He had put it there soon after they had returned.

He found the rolled-up note inside, written in an attractive cursive style and Roci's name on the bottom:

> *Chuck,*
>
> *I know that you could be ultimately happy as an artist, but if you don't develop a stronger self-reliance, you will be shackled to a drug habit that will cruelly dominate your life. Drugs may serve as windows and provide you with views that otherwise wouldn't have been possible for you. These are their legitimate function. But you alone can open the door and go outside...or inside. Do more than look through the window, my friend. Control your life through balance, don't let the means become the end, don't enslave your body and mind to self-gratifying habit.*
> *Power and peace both flow in and out of you and Sandra. Believe that they are there. Bring them into your everyday*

198

for you are potentially a fine creation. Your creator does not desire you to be weak, but rather to fulfill your talents, in your work and in your artistry. Both are worthwhile; you can give both to your people in a loving, caring way. Do it and take joy in it. Consider the Denver Art Academy to help you along.

In Loving Friendship,
Roci

P.S. You may not believe that I could barely write and spell in English until a few days ago. We are capable of learning things quickly and well, when we concentrate.

He read it again and again. She was incredible and he just didn't understand. Why did she care? What was her motive? Was it just 'loving friendship' or more? He walked about restlessly while he thought about it, holding the pill bottle in his fist. Finally, he walked back to the refrigerator and put it back, placing it in the far back of the bottom shelf. He hoped it would stay there, but he doubted that it would.

He would try.

He walked about a little more, staring out the window at the sunshine, thinking about the door she said that he alone could open. He went to the front door and opened it, looking outside at the parking lot, the lines of cars in the sunshine. He guessed he would have a cup of Sandra's herb tea and a joint. That's all he needed, he figured. That's all he needed.

He put on the water and walked into the den, slumping into his favorite rocker. He unfolded the note again, waiting for the water to boil.

Upstairs, Sandra lay naked on the bed, feeling clean and rested after her warm shower. She was tired. They had spent a lot of time recounting their adventure the night before, drinking and smoking with Kevin and Susan. It felt good to be alone with herself in the quiet apartment. She figured Chuck must be reading or painting.

She wondered why she couldn't feel more relaxed, like this, around people more of the time, rather than feeling peculiar about some apprehension or other, fearful of some judgment no one had the right to make, insecure about her ability to talk to people, to express herself, less inclined to be pessimistic and judgmental herself. All that shit! She was too tired to think about it. Soon, she dozed into a light sleep.

The voice came to her softly, calling her name in gentle askance, time and again, until she was nudged to a new kind of consciousness and was receptive to hear. "You must develop these things together," said the loving voice, "your mind and body and spirit altogether, working as one, flowing as one, seeing as one, doing as one."

The voice was Roci's but she wasn't here. The room was empty except for herself, sleeping here, and she saw herself lying on the bed, naked and free, as she floated above it and looked down benevolently. It was only her body there, and she knew it to be temporal. "The strength comes from being together," said the voice, "from being altogether. And when you feel good about yourself, you will feel good about others and will give to others and will feel even better about yourself, and want to give more...more..."

Her body lay there before her and she loved it.

In a few moments, the sun shifted and poured through the window, upon her face. She awakened, refreshed, and recalled a wondrous dream. She sat up and yawned, pulled on her housecoat and walked downstairs.

"Hi," said Chuck. "Did you get a nice rest?"

"Very nice, thanks. Are you working?"

"I'm getting ready to," he said. "I'm gonna get out and offer some of these for sale too. I'm tired of looking at them. You want some hot tea?"

"That's exactly what you need to do, sweetheart."

"It'll be like part of me going if I ever sell one."

"It'll be like getting rid of some of the past," said Sandra. "I think we need to get rid of some of it."

"Maybe it's like I've been...like hoarding up the past. Maybe I need to do a little housecleaning," Chuck offered. "Get on with my life, get into the present, get into the future. The longer all this stuff lies around here, it's like the longer I'm gonna be chained to the past. Does that makes sense?"

"Yeah," she said. "Makes all the sense in the world. We both need to be making more progress, get a more positive attitude about things."

Chuck stared at the array of paintings another minute. "You know, I think I'll be doing some different things with my new stuff. I just, you know, feel differently, so I'm bound to express myself differently. Don't you think?"

"Of course you will. It comes from inside you. Whatever's inside is bound to come out if you're an artist."

"Well, that's got to be true for anybody," said Chuck.

"Sure. I guess so." She walked over to him silently and took him in her arms. He caressed her hair and she laid her head on his shoulder. The warm sunshine filled the room.

Jason didn't finish the coffee back at the campground. When David and Cezanne pulled away in the white van, he carried his pack and locked it inside his own van and made his way to campsite seven as they had directed, carrying the coffee mug. He couldn't wait.

There was a blue dome tent but no vehicle there. As he made his way closer, the flap moved and out climbed Ellen Mackey, standing there facing him with her big hips, bulging breasts and mangled locks of sandy hair.

"There's my bro," she grinned at him. "It's about time you got here." They moved together and he embraced her with all his might, burying his face in her hair, loving her dearly.

Her story was an amazing and circuitous concoction that he and only he knew as a web of extraterrestrial lies, a creative series of fabrications that had put them together by this purposeful route. How cool Steve is, she said. Yes, cool.

She told him about it in short order, soon after he had concocted a lie about trading for a new van. He would not tell her about the extraterrestrials. No. And not even Roci, or the climb. It would raise too many questions.

Ellen's story showed their mastery at magical deception and manipulation.

She had first told Steve about the gathering up here, the mescaline trip. He persuaded her to drive up to Colorado with him to meet the group, which he did effortlessly, without ever getting tired, in a car they rented at the airport. She left her house in the care of her mother, who had made a miraculous recovery and now seemed as spry as a teenager. Strange, but wonderful.

Ellen knew that the group was at the Long's Peak Campground and they arrived late Monday, meeting David and Cezanne there as new acquaintances. They found that, by coincidence, the couple had met Jason's four friends earlier in the day on their return from an overnight hike to the loch. They had decided to leave early, not stay until Wednesday as planned.

The quartet had departed, but Jason was still up in the mountains and would be returning Tuesday. It was all an interwoven deception, and there was more.

Steve had subsequently checked with his home on the phone down at the bathhouse. His mother in California had suddenly fallen ill and he had to go there immediately. He left Ellen with David and Cezanne to wait on Jason's return from the mountain and left to catch a flight.

Jason almost wanted to ask her how she had believed all of this, but he already knew. They made it easy. And that wasn't all.

Steve had a wealthy family, Ellen reported. Jason just nodded. He had told her of a building his family owned in Chicago, one he needed to clean up and renovate and devote to some commercial use. There was an apartment upstairs, furnished, and he asked if she would enjoy a trip there to look it over for him, visit with the real estate people taking care of it, and give him some advice about what to do with it, maybe put it to some use herself if she was interested in moving to the city. He would tend his mother's needs in California, call her, and return to meet her there later. He supposedly had another home in Chicago.

Jason just nodded periodically at the wondrous web of deceit. Steve had given her nearly a thousand dollars for the trip to Chicago, told her to take a flight out of Denver whenever she chose. David and Cezanne had said their goodbyes to go home only an hour or so before Jason had arrived, although Jason knew they had simply moved clandestinely to the nearby campsite to wait on Jason.

"My, what a story," said Jason. "Looks like this could change your life around. Do you think you'd like to move to Chicago? It'd be a big change from south Texas."

"I don't know," she said. "I've been restless for some kind of change. I'd kind of like to get in the middle of something, make some kind of positive contribution, help people, do some good. We've talked about that. You know I studied social work in college for a while. Does any of this make sense to you?"

"Sure, it does. You need to decide where you'll be happy, what you'll be happy doing. A person needs to feel fulfilled in life."

"Well, I figured, why not check it out? What can I lose? Thanks to Steve, I've got the money to make the trip. And we'll just see what happens with us two."

Jason had begun building a campfire, on his knees breaking up kindling and firing the tiny blaze, thinking that Steve must be somewhere in outer space by now.

Ellen looked into the distance, dreamily. "You know, the truth of the matter is…I really do have a strong urgency to carry through with this, and it's a peaceful feeling, a kind of loving feeling. It's something that just seems right for me to do. I can't explain it. We'll see."

Jason could only agree, lost in his own thoughts there, stoking up the fire. His mind's commitment was growing stronger too; some kind of focusing was going on within him.

Soon they had a roaring fire, and a happy evening of talking, laughing and reminiscing.

They slept together in the domed tent, made love passionately, as old friends, as lustful searchers of ecstasy, as spirit children coalescing.

Jason had a vivid dream. He saw himself naked out in a primeval wilderness. The day was bright with sunshine, warming a dense undergrowth of tropical plants, ferns, cicads, vines and small trees, springing up all around him. The scene was rich with foliage and blooms, like a jungle in the making, bees buzzing and birds singing, families of monkeys scurrying past, a toucan on a nearby branch, preening its rainbow feathers, the smell of deep, wet green.

He saw the ruin of the giant tree looming up in front of him, a dark crater torn out of its trunk, dead relic and monarch of the vast valley, split apart as he remembered it, and now also charred and blackened by fire.

The tree was gradually deteriorating, recycling, green vines running up its side, and lush vibrant botanical life all around.

Some of its large dead limbs had fallen to the ground where they were being covered over by the advancing jungle. One day the tree would be no more, leaving not a trace, but somehow part of the whole again. The lightning that ripped through it, he believed, was from the night of the storm, when he came face-to-face with Anvil — and recognized that he was Everyman. And so was he.

Jason stood facing the rotting giant and wondering at the things he still didn't understand, maybe was not intended to understand yet. He heard his own voice speaking behind him: "I'm glad you came back."

He turned to face himself, his own countenance, heavy of beard and hair, grimy with dirt, clad in furry skin and carrying a spear. His own eyes pierced his own; his own body there before him, but harder and baked reddish brown by the fiery, ancient sun, rippling with muscles, carrying a quiver of arrows and a bow over his shoulder and wearing heavy fur boots. A jagged scar crossed his ancient cheek.

Jason couldn't help admiring his own strong and savage countenance as being — heroic! What was intelligence and culture in the face of material survival? This was strength of the animal evolution kind, still admirable, even to partly civilized man.

Then he looked at his own body for the first time, naked and white, unexposed to the realities of time-space wildernesses, rather a personality of the modern day, searching backward into time here through some kind of mind connection.

He thought of the Pleiadians. These highly advanced, benevolent mortal personalities had tried to settle here, to colonize, and had fallen backwards through the fabric of time He remembered the sequence of mindvisits preceding them. The...serpents, dinosaurs, reptiles, whatever they were, that drove them out of the garden.

"Did you people...lead to me?" Jason asked his own primitive self before him. "Are you the beginnings of us, today?"

This image of primitive savagery belied his countenance by speaking softly, precisely: "We are all a part of one another. There is a Oneness which we all must discover," he said in near melodious tones. "It is not confined to planets or even systems."

Jason could feel the vibrational tones of his speech quiver inside him. "We seem so alike," he said.

"There is a universal pattern," he was told, "but there are many variations, even here on this small planet. The Oneness will be long in achieving. So much the better; the more to incorporate learning and growing experiences of many kinds."

"But we need teachers," Jason protested. "We can't teach ourselves. We need leaders, like Mega, to show us the way."

"Go into the Stillness each day for celestial guidance directly from the First Source," said his primitive counterpart. "Remember, we are only material personalities as you are. We have learned to trust the Divine Plan, as you can."

"But it all got mixed up with the Lucifer Rebellion against God, you said. What happened? How did it turn out? How are we supposed to deal with the consequences?"

"As you have been told, struggle to gain balance, to learn and grow, but struggle in love —not fear. The struggle itself is necessary because you grow best through adversity. All of the evolutionary worlds learn this over time. Time, you know, is a tool.

"But you look exactly like me, more than like a pattern. Who are you? Do you have a name?

"The face we wear is not important. We're all expressions of the One," said his likeness, "only separated by time and space and each one's uniqueness. You do understand that you're not finite material as you appear with your material eyes, don't you? You haven't lost this thread in the tapestry of truth. The light of spiritual love lives inside you. Identify with this spirit. That's what matters. And that's who you'll become in the evolution. When your material life is lost in the adventure, it doesn't matter in the eternal plan of reality. The time and space worlds are full of adversity. Without adversity, there can be no triumph," he said confidently, "and there is always the opportunity to go on in the ascension plan if you can choose to do so on the record you have already made."

"But, look at what happened to you people. You were cursed here. It wasn't fair."

"No," his likeness told him. "Life is always a blessing."

"How can it be a blessing?," Jason asked earnestly. "You lost it all; you tried to come here, colonize, build a beautiful garden, and the elements would have none of it. The serpents, those giants, they beat you, didn't they? And the volcanoes. And the harshness of the land. And you were just trying to help."

"Things of great value must be strived for," said his Everyman self. "Without failures, there would be no successes, and none of the attendant learning that accompanies both success and failure. Mortals die in order to graduate. Sometimes evil takes a hold, challenges us to defeat it, and to learn even more in achieving the victory. The rebellion, of course, was crushed, but in the One God's wisdom, it was allowed to play out as a highly intellectual debate in the heavens, for many thousands of years. In fact, it goes on still. And so evil still maintains it has honor, and its messengers even tell you this today. But because of the learning and growing inherent in this audacity against ultimate truth, beauty and goodness, the value of the Lucifer rebellion in this sector has wrought far more good than bad over the ages. The millions of personalities who have watched the rebellion play out throughout the local universe have all learned much from the experience."

"How can I understand all this?" Jason sighed, and from someone who looks like me, but in primitive garb. This all warps the ages, it doesn't make any sense right now. I can't put it all together."

"Of course," said the Everyman projection. "It will require using the time tool, and others as well. In the daily Stillness, you will be able to tap readily into areas of the Universal Mind which will guide you well."

Suddenly, the figure before Jason melted into another countenance.

"Mega!"

Jason faced his familiar mentor and friend now, radiant in his long white robe with the blue emblem, his cascading white hair flowing freely down his back.

"We're all part of the same. That is the point," said Mega. "You, me, Roci, Ellen. In time, you will understand this Oneness of all creation through the Great Source, the Universal Father. Until then, this is your time and space adventure as mortals, each of you with emerging, expanding, growing individual personalities, for the time being housed in a material body. At some point in time, we may be together again, for a new mission, a new adventure, when we meet each other again in the spiritual world, for I address you as my spiritual essence to your spiritual essence, the spirit within you and I that will survive when our material bodies die, when your share of the Universal Mind is reintegrated into the whole, and your spirit and personality ascend up to the next level."

"You are fully losing me with all of this," said Jason.

"As promised, it will clarify incrementally for you as you begin to do the writing. You have merely to reach for it, for we have implanted you with the circuitry and the potential. But in the meantime, I am here primarily to clear up some of our missing pieces before we depart."

"Please continue," said Jason in resignation.

"First, we don't have time to follow the rest of the colony's history on this visit," said Mega. "We'll have to follow the thread in our library. Perhaps another ship will visit soon."

"Well, then, you don't know if the colonists survived or not? Or the couple, Adam and Dawn. But how can you just leave it like that? How? There's a history gap here I'd think you would want to fill in yourselves."

"We need to be in orbit around Jezhume very soon." said Mega.

"It's no more important than that — to know? I want to know myself, Jason protested.

"You know that your civilization had its beginnings at some point, and continues on. It's not so important knowing all the details as in recognizing your purpose right now, who you are and what you're doing here."

"But we learn this by exploring roots," Jason protested, "by studying origins. Don't we?"

"The meanings of life aren't uncovered in archaeological sites or academic journals," said Mega. "They are found in inspired realizations in the present moment, tapping into Universal Mind energy. Your mission should be to make your world better by instilling love in every passing moment. This activates powerful spiritual energies.

"When you live life in this way, life becomes blessed," said Mega. "You may not know how or why the blessings of insight and peace come upon you, and you may say it is mysterious how good life becomes with no apparent reason. But know that love given is love received, and can only be received through giving. This is the secret that is God, the ultimate principle that frees the universe and all in it to rise toward perfection.

"The more love you can exude, the greater your reciprocal blessing. There are so many things for which to express genuine love — for God, for the garden created here for you, for the unique personality you are, for all brothers and sisters who are here with you, even those lost and frustrated and fearful, for the time-space adventure opportunity, for the path that we can walk to perfection, for all of the vast resources that are put to use bringing mortals like us to perfection through an ascension plan, for the intricacy of the creation that keeps all of us busy trying to understand — scientists, philosophers, theologians, engineers, writers — all of us enthralled in the great adventure-gift of time-space that the Great Source has graciously put before us.

"And God has graciously agreed to live this life with you, as an indwelling spirit that will guide you truly. God is an inner compass, a pilot for your living vessel. You are experiencing together, creating together, progressing together, and you'll eventually attune to that indwelling spirit, fuse with its eternal reality, creating a whole new being. When you cross the passageway of death, you'll awaken and truly know that you are a worthy child of the Father, of the universe, and can work positively toward this fusion.

"So, while you're here, make a record that you will be proud of when you stand in front of the Ancients of Days. You will want to continue your ascension, and if your motives and intentions be good you will continue on. As will we, dear Jason, as will we. We are mortals and we're all in this together. Do you finally understand?"

"Well…" There was so much that Jason didn't know how to say, how to ask.

"No rush," said Mega calmly. "Remember, use time and space as tools."

"Who was to blame for the beasts? Surely not the celestials."

"Lucifer and Caligastia. They couldn't tolerate the loyalty of our colony, and so they devised a genetical nightmare, re-introducing the plasm of these long hence departed monsters, and fomenting the hatchings in large lakes surrounding the garden. They sought to throw blame on the Ancients of Days and lure the Pleiadians to their cause."

"And so Anvil was betrayed by the rebels themselves," said Jason.

"Causes that call for liberation rarely do," said Mega.

"So the Planetary Adam and Eve, the assigned superhumans, came thousands of years later," Jason reasoned. "And what happened to them?"

"Tempted by Satan, who was still being allowed to roam about and express his ideas, and lured them into default of their mission. They violated the plan. They were impatient too, like Lucifer. It is another story. It is a continuing story."

Well, if each planet has a Material Son and Daughter, what about yours?"

"We still have ours. They're distinguished citizens, responsible for all the beautiful landscaping and animal life all over our world. They encourage our explorations, with the understanding that we don't tamper with evolution too much. As you have seen, this Urantian colony was one of our least successful sojourns, thanks to Lucifer's outburst of arrogant pride and self-love."

"This is all very amazing," said Jason. "Am I going to remember all of this. Can all this be put to good use?"

"Well, what do you think, Jason? Life on your planet is your own quest, whatever your historical misfortunes. We're not really part of it. We're only visitors. We're just able to tap into energies, do mind projections, timedrops, and a lot of other things you haven't managed yet. We've told you that we're not allowed to do very much to interfere with evolution, nor would we want to. But, I think there is good news coming. I hear through the circuits that the Lucifer Rebellion is finally going to be adjudicated. That will open the way for the celestial administration to restore the circuits and send you some help.

"More people than not are saying we'll be destroyed. Too much evil here, and environmental pollution, and nuclear bombs," said Jason.

"No," said Mega. "Not the Father's style. Building, rehabilitating, co-creating, all the things that emanate from love. That's God's style. So that's likely your future. It may look bleak for you now, but as you can see it's been bleaker.

"The immediate years ahead for you will likely be a time of great and positive change," said Mega, "a disintegration of old and false concepts of narrow self-interest, an integration of true spiritual love values into all facets and institutions of your lives, a growing individual and collective higher consciousness, a burgeoning awareness of universal truths, brought on with the help of incremental openings of spiritual energies that will help you humans regenerate your planet. I think you can succeed this time. I think you're ready to eventually achieve dominion in a whole new enlightened way."

"Thanks for the vote of confidence," said Jason. He looked away at the huge shell that remained of the ancient oak, slowly being covered over by the living vines of advancing time. "I hope that your colonists are, somehow, in my ancestry. I like them. They struggled here."

"You struggle still," said Mega, "but do so in love, remember, not fear. That's the key."

ELEVEN: Separate Ways

Jason's new van glided easily toward the Denver airport. He listened to Ellen talk about her infatuation with Steve, that he would call her in a few days, wondering if they would burst her bubble, disappoint her. He decided that it would be very unlike them to hurt her, so they would likely let her down easily if they could.

He wondered what was in Chicago for her; he wondered what was waiting for him for they had not really advised him specifically.

He knew that he and Ellen would still have each other, as friends and maybe even sometimes as more. He would hear from her about the building, her future in Chicago. He was curious about all of it, but not nearly as curious as he was about his own mission, what he had committed himself to do.

"It's been quite a week, hasn't it Jason?" she said, beaming with more than her usual cheerful exuberance.

"It has at that," said Jason. "A little time off from work can do wonders. I feel like making a fresh start."

"Are you going back to the tile company?"

"Yeah, to give them my notice. I don't know what I'm going to do but I don't want to advertise floor tiles any more. I feel inspired to contribute something of value. If I don't have the talents to do that, I need to get some new talents. There must be something else out there that's more worthwhile, more worth doing, that helps people. We'll be in touch."

"Yeah, and that sounds like my attitude exactly. Seems like I've got a new spark inside."

They wheeled onto the airport exit and unloaded her bags at the curb. She grasped his hand and they looked into each other's eyes.

"You know I love you, don't you Jason? I'm not going to call you promo man any more. You're much bigger than that."

"Thank you, my beautiful friend. I've always loved you, Ellen, and I love you now more than ever."

"I...wonder why we never did get together ourselves, you and I, you know, seriously. Why was there always somebody in between?" she asked.

"I didn't want to think about it because of Stuart," he said. "And now there's Steve. But...who knows? Sometimes life can take some surprising turns, can't it?"

"I'll say," she said, grinning broadly, grasping his hand harder.

He saw something special in her eyes, and hoped that she saw some of it in his. "I'll come see you, beautiful person," he said, "and I hope you'll come see me."

"You can count on it," she said.

He watched as the large silver plane carried its fated pocket of humanity up into the sky, including a woman he was seeing in a new light. Maybe he would be seeing everything in a new light. And maybe she was doing that too, still influenced in some hypnotic way. He knew it would take a few days to settle out.

Ellen slept late in the Ambassador Hotel, had breakfast in the dining room, and walked for a while in the bustling Chicago streets. The grinding noises of the traffic, the clicks of many heels on the concrete, bodies moving in every direction around her gave it all an air of mystery and challenge. It was an exciting place, full of good and evil, loves and fears, in a deathless grip against one another.

The city bus that carried her to the south side was half-filled with odd-houred working people, men and women in misshapen bodies, with miseducated minds, in boring repetition and struggle, moving across the jungle of pavement to another scheduled place. Some of the women, white and black and Hispanic, clutched purses and wadded-up brown bags, tiny possessions of the day, foraging for necessities and niceties with their measured money.

The bus door rattled shut noisily and the guttural exhaust spewed another blue puff of poison into the bright, hot day. She watched it pull away, forcing itself into the labored traffic. Horns were blowing somewhere, a siren was signaling serious injury or death. To the denizens it seemed not to matter.

Ellen stared up at the sturdy old brick building, three stories high, vacant, with flaked white paint on the window frames and a large "For Sale by Owner" sign on the front with a phone number.

The crusty age of the neighborhood showed in the cracked and dirty streets, litter, and decaying brick buildings, several of them vacant. A family drug store, enshrouded with crowded advertisements, occupied the corner. There was a hardware store, and a grocery that advertised pork loin, neckbones and red potatoes on scrawled white butcher paper.

She saw a fat Chicano woman herding along three children, an aging black man tottering on a cane, boys on bicycles, a kid on a tricycle behind a gray wire fence, women waiting on the bus, a sinister teenager with torn-out t-shirt sleeves in a noisy black car, red flames painted on the side and its rear end elevated to jaunty vulgarity. Apartment buildings and houses on all sides housed families of old and young, in colors of black and white and brown.

Ellen opened a strong door lock with one of the keys Steve had given her and walked inside. The light switch revealed a large bare room, a small yellow pile of newspapers strewn in one corner and the dust of many days settled gently upon all of the scene. The back room was opened with another key, to reveal all of the equipment Steve had mentioned, a printing press, platemaker and graphics camera, as well as other printing paraphernalia, all covered with protective plastic shrouds. It was a former neighborhood newspaper and print shop, done in by the ravages of change.

On the second floor she found empty file cabinets and a desk, steel storage racks that were empty except for the trash left behind and a blanket of dust. On the third, also firmly locked, the living quarters were modest but comfortable, typical bargain chairs, couch and tables, two dimly lit bedrooms with squeaking mattresses and worn carpets. The bathroom had a soiled shower stall and mildewed curtain and the back bedroom opened onto a small balcony that overlooked a small fenced back yard.

A small oak tree stood firmly in the middle of it, a rusty swing hanging from a lower limb. Two bare clotheslines were dotted with wooden pins. The board fence separated the property from the parking lot of a modest apartment building. She could see two small children on the other side, trying to manipulate a hula hoop.

She strolled through the rooms for a while, hearing the muffled sounds of the surrounding neighborhood. Some kids were hollering, a car horn sounded, another siren wailed mournfully in the distance, signaling more misfortune.

The first floor windows opened onto the neighborhood, which seemed in steady decline, partly from age, also from restlessness, also from poverty, eroding into careless disrepair and hopelessness, unrealized dreams and compromised satisfactions, older people settling in to live out their lives, younger ones scheming daily to overcome their inequalities and find something better.

She turned as the front door creaked. There was a wide crack, and it creaked again, pushed open by tiny fingers to reveal the wide eyes of a small black girl, about five or six. The child stared in curiosity, wonder, into the bare and open room, clad in a clean pink dress and sandals, her frizzed bouquet of hair decorated with a white bow. Her bright eyes captured Ellen's with their innocence, open and asking in.

"Angela. You come back heah, young 'un." An elderly black woman stooped to the doorway to pick up the wayward child, her straight, gray hair tied into a bun in the old way, walking on plain black shoes and wearing an old-style flowery dress over her dumpy body. She strained to lift the child.

Ellen walked toward the door. "Hello, I'm Ellen. She's a beautiful child."

"Thank 'ye ma'am," said the woman humbly. "I'm sorry. She jus' thank she can go anywhurs."

"That's all right. She can come see me anytime." Ellen chucked the child's chin. She grinned mightily and hid her face into the black woman's shoulder. "I might just adopt you for a special friend, sweetie pie," said Ellen.

The black woman laughed a jolly laugh. "You done bought this place, ma'am?"

"I sure have."

"Lawdy mussy, you gonna run them big printin' presses agin?"

"Well, I don't know about that. I'm just gonna check everything out and see what we could do here."

"Well, law-w-w-dy," said the black woman, revealing a gold tooth.

"I'm Ellen Mackey." She held out her hand. The black woman slipped the small child back to the floor and offered a limp hand, still shy, unused to introductions.

"My name Marie," she said softly.

"Do you live close by?"

"Yes'm. 'Bout three blocks down Vance." She raised her wrinkled arm to the right.

"Do you like the neighborhood?"

"Oh, yes ma'am. It changed a lot but they still lots of nice folks live here."

"Well, you don't have to call me ma'am," said Ellen. "We're probably going to be neighbors."

"Sho nuff? They ain't many people moves heah no mo'. They's too busy movin' out."

"Are you from Chicago?" Ellen asked.

"No'm. From Missippi. I come up heah to live with my boy and his wife 'las yeah, but they done separated. This heah's they baby." She looked down at the child, who clung to her leg and eyed Ellen mournfully. "She done gone home to Tennessee to huh mama, and James ain't got no way to look afta. He got to work, ova 't 'th Holsum Bakery."

"Where are you going, right now?"

Marie looked puzzled. "Well, Mista Rayford, my neighbor, he gonna pick me up on this connuh heah dreckly. He say a lady live ovuh neah da' Smith Park maybe need somebody to do some cleanin' and ironin' and I goin' to see 'bout 'dat. He say she don' mind, maybe, if Angela come along."

"How would you like to work for me?"

"I don' know. What could I do?"

"A lot of things. I might even need a secretary."

"Oh, no ma'am. I can' do no typin' or nothin'."

"There are a lot of things you can do. You're perfect. You're just who I need."

She shook her gray head doubtfully. "You ought just hire Mr. Rayford, my neighbor. He usta work heah runnin' that big press."

"Why did he leave?"

"They close the place down. Said they couldn't make no money doin' printin' no mo'. They say he too old anyway."

"You think he's too old?"

Marie shrugged. "They say…Me too, they say. But you know I feels good in mah heart. The Lawd keep blessin' me with anothuh day."

"Are you healthy, Marie?" Ellen was walking about again, looking over the bare room.

"Yes'm. I kinda is. I got lotsa stamina, you know."

"That's what we're going to need, Marie, and some enthusiasm. Do you believe in this neighborhood and the people in it?" Ellen pulled the drawcord for the front blinds, which were battered and bent. Sun streamed in.

"Yes'm. I like this neighborhood. I believe people heah, you know, they just wanna chance."

"We've got to get these blinds out of here. I think we need some nice curtains," said Ellen.

"Yes'm. I made curtains befo'."

"Good!" Ellen swirled over to open a closet door, revealing open, dusty shelves. "This place is perfect too. It's just going to take a lot of work."

"Yes'm. What kind of business we gonna be in?"

Ellen looked out into the bright day, finger on her lips thoughtfully. "Souls, I think…kind of like a soul mission in a way, a place for people to come and do things, arts and crafts, things to make a little money, little cottage businesses all joined together. Maybe we could form a co-op. We might even have a soup kitchen here, get food from the backs of supermarkets, it's available. We'll put together all kinds of projects, give people a place to come, a place to be together, do things to help out, be useful."

She walked to the other window and pulled up the other blinds, letting the sunlight pour in, watching millions of dust particles float weightlessly through the bright rays of the sun.

"We'll just build it as we go," said Ellen positively. "Everyone will have ideas. It'll be exciting. Mr. Rayford can help, and Angela might even help too. She can keep us cheered up."

Marie seemed a little dazed by it all.

"I know it sounds a little uncertain," said Ellen, reaching to grasp Marie's hand. "But people can live happily with some uncertainty if they have hope and vocations. There's the thrill of it, the challenge, the continuing questions to answer, working out possibilities and realities together. I know people often don't think they can do that, but they can."

"Yes'm, I reckon."

Ellen reached down to pick up Angela, beautiful, dark child, helpless in the arms of a changing day, a lovely bauble to be molded into an oracle, to carry forever the impressions of those who chose to impress upon her.

She hugged the child and kissed her, and looked into her innocent and gentle eyes. "You're beautiful," she told her.

"Ain' she a purty thing?" said Marie, her gold tooth shining.

Their ship was planning its departure out of the system. Blest, tending to parting details, was seeing things in a new light too.

The visitors had stored great amounts of information into their live oak, and would be delving into it and sorting it in different ways in the immediate time ahead, until they reached the system from where they would explore Jezhume.

The oak had grown very fast and was a magnificent spectacle that they all admired. It reminded them too that there were environmental limits to what could be effectively absorbed, a liaison with nature and nature's way that had to be respected. They would plant the tree on one of Saturn's hidden moons before leaving the system. It would be there for the research of others who would come to the system and want information about its only inhabited world and its unknowing denizens. It would be an educational prelude to any future visits, a signpost out of sight and unknown to Earth's subjects that would guide future researchers or any of the excursions of various kinds that came into the vicinity.

The museum underneath the dome would feature the many artifacts they had collected on their visit and now had stored in the lower part of the ship. It was a remarkable collection of both natural and manmade objects, representing the arts, music, religion, industry, government and the whole spectrum of history of this evolving world.

One day, the Earthlings would actually discover this hidden treasure themselves, just in back of Saturn. But that would be a while into the future.

In the rich moon soil of Edentia, the oak would grow ever-larger, and since it would be connected to the universe circuits they could periodically send it information updates that they would glean from the planet's television and radio broadcasts, and computer communications. It would be a wonderful and replete museum of Urantian (Earth) history, and so close at hand to the actual place.

Another acorn would be implanted aboard the ship and stimulated to produce another tree for the Jezhume adventure. It should begin sprouting soon.

For Blest, the turmoil of thoughts in her head was not something she had expected would happen. She was having trouble getting free from her Earth mind.

When Mega came to visit her, she was sitting cross-legged, meditating and praying. Two large candles, widely separated, gave the room a faint and flickering light. She didn't want him to look deeply into her eyes.

He joined her on the rug, facing her quietly and soon knowing that his mind could not penetrate hers effectively. She had pulled away. He spoke to her in English, for he knew that was where her mind resided still, and this was, in fact, the root of her problem.

"High logic dictates that we break from the Earth mode tomorrow," said Mega. "I trust you are prepared to do that."

"I supposed I must do it," she said sadly.

"I don't understand why you would hesitate," he said. "You know that these lingering thoughtwaves would do nothing but confuse the next mission, and all those thereafter. Earth is only one world of thousands. Mission Control knows it is best to make a clean break and start fresh."

"I know what Control...pure logic dictates," she said. "I suppose I am being influenced by emotions. I almost want to stay here. It is such an exciting place. But I know the consequences. I know that I might never be able to return home."

"You will feel better about it when we assume the new language. This should be tomorrow sometime."

"Is there any way I could stay here, or return soon?"

Mega looked at her with earnest concern. "I believe this would be a completely unprecedented request, so I have no way of knowing. If you sincerely wish it, we could input into Mission Control. We could get an answer. But I don't understand why. There is adventure elsewhere, everywhere."

"I could work with the people here. They need so much help. They have been isolated from the system for so long. I would like to work with children."

"There are other worlds still isolated by the rebellion," said Mega. "We will visit many others, many high adventures that you will miss. They need your qualities no less than this one. You are a fine young explorer, with great potential for service and leadership. I hate to see you give it all up to stay on this troubled place."

Blest just sat quietly between the candles.

"I have made a start on this one. And...Jason is here. We have had a...sharing that others have not experienced. Perhaps it was bold and unprecedented, but it happened."

"I think I understand," said Mega. "You are pregnant?"

She sat there in the candleglow, afraid to answer, not knowing what to say, finally nodding that she was.

Mega was now sure the case was without precedent. It seemed a situation which only Control should decide upon.

"Is High Logic always highest?" he asked philosophically, "and what happens when emotions become involved? We have succeeded over time in separating these two conflicting factors, bringing them into harmonic interaction. Or so we thought. Now, on your brief sojourn here, you have joined them again. To be fully honest, I don't know what is best out here in this wild frontier."

"Should not the decision really be mine, Mega? Wouldn't Control agree with that? This is a very personal matter."

"We seemed beyond these questions, my beloved sister," said Mega, "and now I see that we are not beyond them at all. Through your living with them, even for a short while, we must regress and deal with them once again. You said an oath as an explorer. You have one of the finest life plans in all the Pleiades."

"Will Mission Control let me decide? Will I be allowed to stay?" Her questions came at him out of the darkness as affirmation that she wanted to stay behind. For once, Mega had no answers.

"Should we not be the masters of our own fates?" she asked. "Even if we don't have the superior intellect that we have imbued within our finest creation, our symbol of God, our eternal Mission Control, should we not be allowed to decide some things for ourselves, make our own decisions and make our own mistakes if it happens that way? Isn't it our own lives after all? Aren't we individuals and are we not individuals in the final judgment? Isn't this what these elaborate adventures are staged to do, give us these kinds of decision-making experiences? Do we have the gift of free will or do we not?"

"Maybe," said Mega, "we should have called you Eve. She had many questions as well."

He got up and moved to the portal, in great thought, looking back from the threshold to see her still sitting quietly, unmoving, between the candles. They both appeared frail, flickering, but the flames burned on. She looked up at him, troubled.

"I will not default," she said, getting up smoothly and walking forward to Mega. She wore a long, simple, flowing white gown. "But it may be that Mission Control believes I should be there, helping the Urantians. There is such a co-creative connection that I feel about it. I will request it. Perhaps it will be granted. Perhaps I will rejoin the Earth man."

"If you do," said Mega, showing deep concern. He looked into her soft green eyes, which melted into his. His look turned softer as well. "I wish you Godspeed," he said.

She kissed him lightly on the lips, then pulled gently away again.

Mega smiled wryly. "Well, whatever the outcome, they have some good stories back at the academy."

She couldn't help laughing.

Jason was on the road again, making his way toward Pagosa Springs in southern Colorado, the hand drawn map laid out beside him in the seat, the deed to his new home under it.

He had found these in his Dallas apartment, along with a roll of bills, receipts showing that his lease had been paid up and that the moving company had been contracted and paid to pack and move him next week. A note stated succinctly: "Welcome to PeaceQuest. Your new home and mission are awaiting your arrival." It wasn't signed.

He followed the directions easily. Just outside of the town, he turned onto a gravel road and made his way for a mile or more to a scenic overlook. It was late afternoon and the sky was darkening, the sun sinking heavily in the western sky.

A modest cabin waited for him at the end of the road. He got out of the van tiredly, stretched and made his way to the front door. He liked it. It was a picturesque and peaceful setting. He could hear a stream rippling down the tree-lined hill, straining his eyes in the gathering night to see the white curl of the water rushing by below.

The front door was locked. Jason thought about it a moment. He had been given no key. He reached up over the door sill and pulled one down, as if he had known it was there.

Inside, the furnishings were simple but clean. There was a word processor over by the window that faced the wooden deck and the overlook, illuminated in a puddle of light from a floor lamp. A laserprinter and a stack of paper sat beside it. The paper was clean, white and bare. He knew it was his job to fill it up.

The refrigerator and freezer were stocked with food and drink. The fluffy bed looked inviting, covers turned down on one corner for him.

Outside on the deck, he heard the crickets singing. The moon and stars came up brightly before him. He wondered where Blest was, and Mega and the rest of them, and realized he might never know anything more, left to wonder with the rest of his kind, but at least with a glorious affirmation in his mind. There would be no need confiding in anyone; no one would believe it.

Maybe he would write about it. They could all accept it if it were called fiction. He also knew that people accepted various fictions as truth every day, and also accepted great truths dramatized in fiction. Tell a story, said a voice inside.

He sat down on a small cane-bottomed chair, noticed that it and the other one and the small table strongly resembled the ones where he and Mega had their last visit atop Long's.

How very undeserving he felt of his good fortune, the money, his new freedom, all the more reason to work hard with a powerful dedication to fulfill their trust, to earn his standing, to put aside his shallow life in return for a quest of spiritual significance.

Some small noise caused him to turn his head to the edge of the deck and see the dog. It was golden brown, a gangly young animal, too old to be a puppy but not grown, awkward, with big paws and curious nose, sniffing here and there and then looking up at him with an innocent question in its eyes.

Jason whistled softly, got up quietly and moved toward him, opening the sliding door to the deck, stepping outside and reaching out an open palm. The dog shied away, staring at him with a look of doubt and worry. He only smiled and left his hand proffered.

He could see that the dog had a collar so probably belonged to a neighbor. It sniffed the boards of the deck in front of him, head down, eyes turned up, then stretched a long neck to his fingers, wet black nose searching for a friendly scent, flinching only slightly when Jason reached to touch his head, pat him, and rub him gently.

"Yeah," said Jason softly. "You're a good boy, aren't you."

The dog's tail began wagging and he seemed to relax. He stroked the dog's head and scratched behind his ears. When he stopped, the dog waggled a warm tongue and nuzzled his hand for more.

Jason's mood brightened. He reminded himself to fill his life with moments with love.

He might go back inside in a little while and sit in front of his new computer. Maybe he wouldn't write a word tonight, just get used to the idea, get some thoughts organized in his head, some deep feelings in his heart of what he could and should say, think about the craft of writing itself, a message stronger and more meaningful for his fellow creatures than just imploring them to buy a household product or some objective discourse on what somebody said for shallow public consumption at a chamber of commerce banquet or a city council meeting.

He really didn't know if he had wisdom to impart, but whatever he had he wanted to give. It might be a lonely business here in the cabin, but he knew greater deeds had been done by lonelier men. And their minds probably hadn't been inspired to the extent his had in the past week.

But...he really couldn't say about that. He had just as soon keep his newly expanded mind opened to all possibilities.

He turned over the round silver tag on the dog's collar.

"Goldie II," it read.

EPILOGUE: Flowers and Seeds

The man and woman who went northward to pursue agriculture never rejoined Anvil's band. They foraged for food, planted seeds and built a rock sanctuary that protected them from the savage storms and upheavals of the young planet and the animals that remained ever desperate to survive.

Harsh winter winds beat down upon them. They huddled together for warmth and safety from the wilderness. They fortified themselves from the creatures of the night and their love grew ever stronger in their solitude and sharing.

On the night that she gave birth, their cave echoed with the screams of her pain. But he was able to comfort and help her to bring forth a new life, damaged and bleeding though it was. Both mother and child survived, and the child began to grow.

In the southwest, the earth did indeed rupture as the man had told Anvil it would. The volcano exploded and the mountainside did fall down upon Anvil and the marooned colonists, burying several of their number. In a desperate race, Anvil led the survivors away from the wave of scorching lava that poured down the mountainside, carrying a small boy on his shoulders.

The twenty-seven who survived this catastrophe continued to dwindle in number, from the onslaughts of the beasts and another volcanic eruption that spread even more fire and desolation across the land, turning the high plains into a flaming inferno, sending stampedes of wildlife and lumbering reptiles fleeing across the landscape in clouds of dust and smoke.

Torn from one encampment and then another, Anvil, increasingly embittered by their fate, loyally led the small band in their labors to survive. They brought their enslaved beasts of burden, the apes, with them, at first tied securely and held in fear, then later as sharing allies, partners in the game of survival. An affinity and affection was struck between them in their common plight.

Anvil would never tell the colonists that in the dark days of facing the devils that had been unleashed upon them, he had taken it upon himself to align the band with the rebellious forces of Lucifer. He had been personally bitter at the Ancients of Days, his mind poisoned. Caligastia had accused them of every evil — lying! Anvil had believed him, the celestial prince's brilliance and bearing simply holding sway over the soldier's limited mortal mind. It had been like a hypnotic entrancement.

Gradually now, Anvil's clouded mind was becoming clearer. In fitful sleeps and nightly contemplations, he was beginning to grasp that the truest guidance comes from within the heart, and that the seeking brings forth the power to resist all evil — though not error, which is a mortal learning and growing experience. Even the error of rebelling against God's plan. This might even be commonplace.

Whatever the case, whatever the truth, Anvil knew that survival was his immediate and all-encompassing mission, and that surely would be the case for some time in these time and space worlds. In the end, no mortals would survive death, but in the celestial plan it didn't matter. They had to survive not death but life, this mortal life, by the way they lived it. Death would be a passageway to ascension or dissolution depending on one's own soul worthiness.

Intermittently, Anvil felt this in his heart. He was encouraged by his faith for he intended to give all that he had to the service of his siblings — love them and fight for them.

He wondered if it were always the case that God's imperfect mortals would be forgiven their errors, their succumbing to evil influences, if they did not openly and knowingly embrace sin and iniquity.

He believed this sometimes. At other times, he simply hoped it was true.

Anvil came to expect no rescue from any source, for in their wanderings they could not likely be found. All instruments had been destroyed. He kept the others hoping for a time with lies, but soon despaired of pretending.

They were all facing death at some point anyway, and they would each answer then to the Ancients of Days, the One God's tribunal, there in the true world of spirit, beyond this veil of material mortality. The Ancients waited for each mortal to enter from the passageway of death, to stand before them. He would have to deal with his record then, and sometimes, in the night, he practiced what he would say.

But now, in this savage time, Anvil, hairy arm of the beast greatly helping his survival, sought merely to lead the band to the most modest goals in all of evolution — food and shelter, survival for another day. To survive here, they would have to regress into the cold savagery that his people had moved beyond centuries earlier, so ironic.

From the south, dark masses of locusts came to blacken the sky, compounding their miseries. Their roar was maddening, their ravenous mouths stripping large areas of the earth from its life-giving sustenance.

A mysterious fever brought a slow and suffering death to several of their number, including his beloved Tara. He sat holding her hand, watching her finally slip away in the darkness of the night.

The last of the women died while they foraged for the eggs of birds on the plain, overrun and attacked, screaming in vain, by a marauding lioness. Anvil and the few men arrived too late, only to find the remains of her bloodied body under the powerful claws of the beast.

Anvil, his red beard flowing long and bushy, his sun-ravaged face wrought with hatred, joined his beastly arm with his other, firing a sure arrow that pounded into the heart of the predator. The lioness flailed helplessly for a moment and fell dead. So long ago, it seemed, he had killed another lion.

The men decapitated and skinned the beast, tearing away and eating their choice of the flesh and leaving the rest to the other predators, joining the endless and remorseless circle of life which constantly preyed upon other life not of its kind.

The dark clouds that rolled through their sky heralded another storm. They used their crude tools to dig a shallow grave for the woman. They covered it with rocks and embedded into them the dead branch of an oak tree.

They stood in reverent memory once again for one of their kind, but there was no one to speak this time. There seemed nothing to say any more, no message of hope upon which to cling. They had fallen too far. Anvil's face was a mask of cold and cruel endurance to which the others felt they could no longer look, even though he was their leader.

He turned them from the grave and they loaded their several apes with the bulky, bloody fur of the lion and their meager provisions.

As they prepared to leave and find new shelter, Anvil ripped up a handful of tiny flowers, fondled and smelled them briefly and placed them on the burial rocks with grimy, callused hands. His tangled, dirty masses of hair and beard, his dark and scarred body clad in the stinking skin, gave him the sinister appearance of the man animal he had become. But he wiped a tear from his hairy cheek before he turned resolutely, to strap on his bow and trudge forward again.

He struggled for faith. If they could survive, then perhaps a rescue ship would finally come and they could regain dominion, achieve the eminence that fate would again be beholden to them, their kind, that paradise lost would be regained. But forgetting all else, he had to survive and fulfill the leadership role thrust upon him and taken desperately to heart as a reason to live, which now had become Anvil's driving motivation.

But his hopes for any kind of mortal peace, in this life, were small. They were trapped in a spiraling whirlpool, backwards into de-evolution, as helpless as their ancient ancestors, settling toward the bottom of the mammal-to-human ladder, for all their tools of civilization were gone. It was all back to basics.

More tears flowed down Anvil's grimy face as he walked forward and took his place at the head of the band.

But then this unique expression of the One God disdained further crying and turned with gritted jaw to his tasks. He constantly reminded himself that he still was imbued with the indwelling spirit of God. And another day of life.

They had gone when the storm reached the valley, first with heavy drops of rain that pelted the hard, hot rocks of the grave, then with a relentless wind that gradually built in force and swept most of the flowers to the ground where they were pounded and splattered by the deluge.

The rains soaked the parched earth and the creatures drank and lived. The torn flowers died where they lay but the plant began to grow more flowers and the seeds on the ground spread to grow even more.

Update on the Planetary Rebellion, Urantia Paper #67, published in 1955

IMMEDIATE RESULTS OF REBELLION

Great confusion reigned in Dalamatia and thereabout for almost fifty years after the instigation of rebellion. The complete and radical reorganization of the whole world was attempted; revolution displaced evolution as the policy of cultural advancement and racial improvement. Among the superior and partially trained sojourners in and near Dalamatia there appeared a sudden advancement in cultural status, but when these new and radical methods were attempted on the outlying peoples, indescribable confusion and racial pandemonium was the immediate result. Liberty was quickly translated into license by the half-evolved primitive men of those days.

Very soon after the rebellion the entire staff of sedition were engaged in energetic defense of the city against the hordes of semisavages who besieged its walls as a result of the doctrines of liberty which had been prematurely taught them. And years before the beautiful headquarters went down beneath the southern waves, the misled and mistaught tribes of the Dalamatia hinterland had already swept down in semisavage assault on the splendid city, driving the secession staff and their associates northward.

The Caligastia scheme for the immediate reconstruction of human society in accordance with his ideas of individual freedom and group liberties, proved a swift and more or less complete failure. Society quickly sank back to its old biologic level, and the forward struggle began all over, starting not very far in advance of where it was at the beginning of the Caligastia regime, this upheaval having left the world in confusion worse confounded.

AUTHOR'S ENDNOTES

Our planet of Earth is known as "Urantia" in the Urantia Papers, a huge collection of celestial transmissions published by The Urantia Foundation of Chicago. In splendidly-wrought prose, they discuss our superuniverse, local universe and planetary history, and conclude with a full and dynamic history of Jesus and his mission. The papers were transmitted in the early part of the century, eventually published in 1955, and are now available in book form in some 2,100 pages from the Foundation. More than 25,000 copies have been sold worldwide in various translations. In recent years, the copyright of the basic text was not successfully renewed and the papers are in the public domain and available at various sources, including the Urantia Fellowship.

It is my personal belief that these papers are indeed celestial revelation, an opinion I affirmed to myself only after years of study. Their authenticity or lack thereof can only be decided by each reader, however, and I commend them to you for your evaluation. As Jesus said, by their fruits you shall know them.

I believe there are as many paths to God as there are souls to walk them, and individuals should accept those sources that ring true for their stage of spiritual development, whether fundamental or radically different from the mainstream. Spiritual truths for the individual can be found in many sources, perhaps in the next person you meet. The Urantia perspective is one of many, and as I personally explore many of them, I find remarkable compatabilities, and a central mother stream of truth that is bountiful enough for all tributaries when hearts are pure in the searching.

The Urantia papers provide the characters and events of the Lucifer Rebellion which we describe in these pages. To these purported real events, I have added fictional characters and episodes for the process of storytelling. For the real truth about our planetary history, without our superimposed characters from the Pleiades, we recommend to you the pure Urantia revelation. You can also read the perspectives of the visiting Pleiadians in several spiritually-inspiring books which chronicle the mission of these visiting celestials.

The full description of the Lucifer Rebellion in the Urantia Papers is touched upon in the Christian religion as the "war in the heavens." The Archangel "Michael" who fights the dragon in the Book of Revelations is identified in the Urantia Papers as a Creator Son of God, who created our planet and many others in his local universe of Nebadon, and who incarnated on our world in flesh and blood as Jesus to present a greatly expanded spiritual message — the loving and compassionate father nature of God; the forgiving, serving brotherhood of all humankind, Gentile and

Jew, all races, all religions, all creeds; and the reality of eternal life on a 'Be Ye Perfect' ascension path.

By whatever terminologies and perspectives, may your own individual spiritual searches be exciting and fruitful. For Light. For Truth. For Wisdom. For Spirit. For Inspiration. For Salvation. For Love. For Service. For Adventure. For God — a personal relationship developed from within in the daily Stillness.

Jim Cleveland
www.lightandlife.com

RELATED SOURCES:

The Light and Life Journal and Light and Life Online Express newspaper are available in current issues and complete libraries at www.lightandlife.com, along with Teaching Mission transmissions, and other explorations of the spiritual universe in books, art and music. The original Urantia Book text of 1995 is available for free download.

The Teaching Mission Archives, hundreds of pages of celestial transmissions from the TeaM Stillness groups around the U.S. through the 1990s and into the new century, may be accessed directly at www.tmarchives.com

The Stillness Foundation is dedicated to the daily practice of Stillness, in which meditation joins worship, prayer, forgiveness and love. The organization offers educational programs and publications. Contact Michael Painter at mikepain@aol.com.

The Center for Christ Consciousness, evolving from the Stillness Foundation, provides worship and Christ centering programs from its California headquarters. Contact Donna D'Ingillo at donnadingillo@juno.com and visit www.ctrforchristcon.org.

The Urantia Foundation at www.urantia.org has published The Urantia Book since 1955, and held the copyright until the text was moved into the public domain. The organization is translating the work into languages throughout the world.

The Urantia Book Fellowship also publishes the Urantia papers via its Uversa Press, and provides socializing and educational opportunities worldwide. Visit their extensive website at www.ubfellowship.org.

TR/News Network. For a paper newsletter featuring recent celestial transmissions and news of humans working with supernals, contact Allene Vick at allenetnn@sprintmail.com.

The Church Within is dedicated to developing our personal relationships with God, our Universal Father. Pastors offer weekly services and other features at www.churchwithin.org.

Urantia Book related publications, including books and "The Circular" newsletter, are available from Square Circles Publishing Company at www.squarecircles.com.

"The Center Within," a book of teachings from celestial teacher Will, and other related mind-body-spirit books are available from Origin Press at www.originpress.com.

Teaching Mission transmissions from teachers Olfana, Tarkas and others are available from the Half Moon Bay, CA group at www.hmbtm.com.

The Jesusonian Foundation provides a wealth of information about the Urantia papers at it extensive website at www.truthbook.org.

About the Author:

JIM CLEVELAND has had a long career in journalism, public relations, publications and marketing. He has a B.S. in journalism from the University of Southern Mississippi and an M.A. from the University of Mississippi, along with years of theological and spiritual studies. He is owner and manager of lightandlife.com and its related periodicals, a charter director of The Stillness Foundation, and active with Urantia Book, Teaching Mission and *A Course in Miracles* organizations.

Printed in the United States
31464LVS00005B/73-75

9 781410 733986